The Witchfinder's Sister

ABOUT THE AUTHOR

Beth Underdown lectures in Creative Writing at the University of Manchester. Her first novel, *The Witchfinder's Sister*, is based on the life of the 1640s witchfinder Matthew Hopkins. Beth came across a brief mention of the self-styled 'Witchfinder General' while reading a book about midwifery, igniting an interest that turned into an all-consuming hunt for the truth about this infamous killer.

The Witchfinder's Sister

BETH UNDERDOWN

VIKING
an imprint of
PENGUIN BOOKS

VIKING

UK | USA | Canada | Ireland | Australia
India | New Zealand | South Africa

Viking is part of the Penguin Random House group of companies
whose addresses can be found at global.penguinrandomhouse.com.

First published 2017
004

Copyright © Beth Underdown, 2017

The moral right of the author has been asserted

Map created by Jeff Edwards

Set in 12.84/15.81 pt Dante MT Std
Typeset by Jouve (UK), Milton Keynes
Printed in Great Britain by Clays Ltd, St Ives plc

A CIP catalogue record for this book is available from the British Library

TRADE PAPERBACK ISBN: 978–0–241–97804–7

www.greenpenguin.co.uk

MIX
Paper from
responsible sources
FSC® C018179

Penguin Random House is committed to a
sustainable future for our business, our readers
and our planet. This book is made from Forest
Stewardship Council® certified paper.

For Kath Boardman

Thou shalt not suffer a witch to live.

Exodus 22:18

And a man's foes shall be they of his own household.

Matthew 10:36

1645, and the Civil War in England has begun its fourth year.

It is a war about God, and how best we should worship Him. It is a war about who should govern, and why; whether the Parliament should rule, or whether the ousted King.

It is a war of thoughts, of words printed or hurled in anger: but this is also a war of guns. Last year, at Marston Moor, more than four thousand men were killed.

Before this, women have seldom been hanged for witchcraft – one or two, every five years, or ten. Eight were sentenced in Pendle, thirty years ago, when the land still knew peace.

But now this country is falling apart at the seams. Now, all England is looking the other way: so there is nothing to stop Matthew Hopkins stepping forward. Starting to make his list of names.

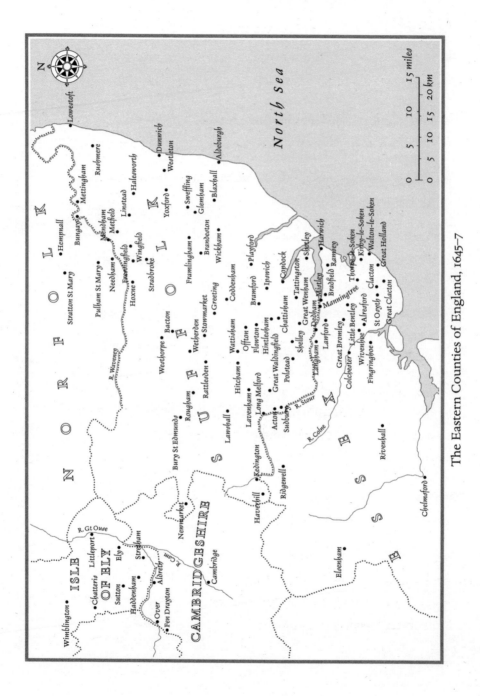

The Eastern Counties of England, 1645–7

Mary Starling of Langham, for murder and the keeping of imps

Elizabeth Clarke of Manningtree, for the killing of Richard Edwards's son

Widow. Poor and lame of one leg

Elizabeth Gooding of Manningtree, for the killing of Robert Taylor's horse

Widow

Sarah Hatyn of Ramsey, for the killing on diverse occasions of the wife, children and servant of Francis Stock, constable of Ramsey

One son of her own

Mary Johnson of Great Clacton, for the killing of the child of Daniel Otley and the child of George Durrant of Fingringhoe

Widow

Rebecca Jones of St Osyth, for the killing of Thomas Bumstead and his wife

Widow, having one son

Nan Leech of Manningtree, for the killing of a woman who would not give to her a bonnet made of linen

Widow, mother of Helen Leech

Helen Leech of Manningtree, for sending an imp against the Parsley child

Widow

Margaret Moone of Thorpe-le-Soken, for the killing of the wife and child of Henry Cornwall and for causing Phillip Daniel's horse to break its neck while pulling a cart downhill

Amended: This one not hung but did collapse and die on her way to the scaffold

I

I

The fifth day of Christmas, this year of our Lord 1645

Once, I scarcely believed in the devil. I scorned the kind of folk who earnestly think he can put on physical form, like a coat, whether that form be like a cat or a dog or some warped combining of the two; those who have it that the devil can enter a person in such a manner that he can be deftly taken out again, like a stone from a plum. I scorned those who believe such things. I lived in London once: I can remember how to sneer.

But I am not in London any more. Nine months ago I had cause to come back to my own strange corner of Essex; and since I did, things have happened that make it harder to say what I do and do not believe.

My coming home at the end of March, those first few days are still sharp in my mind. Each day, each of those first hours, is preserved like an etching, separate and clear. But the later days, those later weeks as matters progressed, they are already starting to become somewhat bleached, somewhat blurred, like faces seen from a cart as it gathers up downhill speed.

Now it is Christmastide: I know it is, for I have been notching a floorboard each day, as prisoners do in tales. I have kept my count faithfully, showed myself methodical

3

for once, like my brother. While I have been counting, the weather has changed and changed again: the pricking heat of late summer, and then the autumn chill. Today I can see my breath, and as I finish each line I have to break off from writing to curl my cold fingers into the neck of my gown. Soon I will have to lay aside my pen, and walk up and down to keep warm.

This chamber measures six of my paces along, though I must change direction slightly at one end to avoid my small bed and the things next to it – my chamber pot, a pitcher for water and a flimsy bowl for washing. Up and down I pace, back and forth in front of the chamber's sturdy door. I try to avoid the sight of the keyhole, to resist the urge to stop and look through it. I never see anything, only the patch of wall across the passage as some slow movement of air dries my eye, but I cannot stop myself looking. I cannot shake the feeling, when I put my eye to the gap, that what I will see is another eye, looking back.

So, you see, I am glad to have the distraction of writing. I need distraction, not least from my stomach, for this now is my third day without food. Though perhaps it is apt that I should be hungry: since the King fled his palace, Christmas is a time for fasting, rather than feasting. But I am resolved to mark the season in the old way, by making a Christmas gift, and my gift will be to myself. It will be the chance to tell the truth. I will set it down now, while my memory holds. There is nothing to prevent me, for though I am imprisoned, I am not forbidden writing materials: ink, and pens, and paper have been brought to me without complaint. I fear it means they do not intend to let me go.

But I will not think of that. I will not flinch. I will set it down, the full history of my brother, what he has done. I will lay it out in black and white, and my tale will contain more truth than the great dead histories on my father's bookshelves. For they say what happened, but not what it was like. They say what happened, but they do not say why.

In these middle days of Christmas, when I was a child, everything would stop. The whole world would grow still. You would venture out for an hour to take the air, and coming in again you would stamp your feet, knock yourself free of snow. Then later, because it was a holiday, someone would tell a story: some tale, invented wholly or in part, but always full of dread and death and strangeness. This tale of mine, for certain it contains its share of those things, but though I wish to God it was invented, my tale is true.

For nine months ago, my brother Matthew set himself to killing women. He took women from houses never quiet from the sound of waves, from inland places by damp tidal creeks where the salt on the wind is a reminder of their men – husbands, sons – who never came back from the sea or the war; who didn't want to come back, or could not. Matthew took those women and he killed them, but without once breaking the law. He took women who did not want their own children, women who wanted other people's, and, at least at first, there was hardly a murmur to prevent him. For a woman is brought up to believe that children are her life's work – to make them and feed them and kiss their hurts. But what happens if you cannot have children? If you have too many? If you have them, and they cannot protect you? If you have them, and they die? If you weep for your loss too much, or not enough – that is when folk begin to wonder if it is your fault, your misfortune. They begin to wonder how you can have offended God, and their wonderings turn ripe for a man like my brother to exploit.

I will write the whole sad business down, for no one living knows as much of Matthew's reasons as I. Though they do not excuse him, Matthew has his reasons, and they are there for the finding, in his past; in our past. You might wonder why I did not prevent him from what he embarked upon. Well, I will set that down, too. These last months, I have learned that the acknowledged history that belongs to the daylight, that is not the only history. Turn over the stone and you will find another history, wriggling to escape.

2

The twentieth day of March, year of our Lord 1645

Once I had finished talking down the price of the journey home, it struck me how I had never thought to see Manningtree again. Or not in such circumstances. I think I had expected to go back to visit Mother, with my husband and my several children. But not to go back like this: empty-handed and alone.

I did not bargain too hard with the carter: it had taken me all morning to find someone carrying cloth and wine all the way to Colchester, with a break in the journey at a reputable inn. I was glad for a moment when he nodded, and let me climb up among the bales of cloth, but all I felt was numbness as we left the walls of London behind. Numbness, and weariness. It seemed beyond me to find the correct words and the correct way to speak them, to do all the small pieces of work of arranging my cap and standing up straight and offering a sad smile as I would need to do to meet my brother again.

The dark days of the new year had taken first Mother and then my husband, Joseph, into death, and I had not been sleeping, and nor had I yet cried. I lay in the cart, hardly seeing the houses and fields as they went by until, lulled by the cart's rocking, I had to dismiss the strange fancy that I was a girl again, going home to nothing more demanding than a scolding and a hot meal. As if my marriage had been some holiday lark that I was sorry for now: some jest, which had got slightly out of hand. I forced myself to sit up straight; reminded myself that I was coming back to a brother I had not seen in five long years, who, when last we spoke, had called me a word I had never thought to hear him say.

Matthew knew I was coming home, though I had not told him why. I had not had the strength to tell him that my husband was dead. After Joseph's burial I had started a letter to Matthew, beginning with a greeting; I had counted on my fingers, and written down a date in March. But then I had paused. We had always sworn when we were little, Matthew and I, that when we were grown up and living apart, we would write every week. But as matters had turned out, I had heard nothing from him in all those five years. The pen dried in my hand, and when I sent him the note it contained only my formal good wishes, and the date I would return.

Cramped in the cart, I tried to comfort myself by taking out the one letter my brother had ever written me: at the turn of the year, a most civil letter, to tell me that Mother was dead. He had written, *The minister will want to bury her as soon as this cold eases.* He had written, *You would be welcome with me at the Thorn.* The words after that were darker, as if he had sat thinking for long enough to need to dip his pen again, before adding, *Your husband will be welcome, too.* The letter had arrived only days after Joseph's death. Though it was indeed a civil letter, I could not help noticing that my brother still would not make Joseph any greeting, or even write his name.

As the cart came down into Chelmsford a pair of vaga-bonds were sitting on the wall outside the gate, shouting, 'Parliament or King?' at anyone passing. Soon we pulled up, and as I climbed painfully down, I heard the carter give a subdued greeting, and turned to see five or six men idling outside the inn. They looked hard, sharp-eyed, equipped for cold and for disaster alike, as if those twin things had grown ordinary – as indeed they have. For this now is the fourth year there has been trouble in England.

It is the common kind of war, about who should govern and how; but it is worse than any war that came before it. For since this war, there are villages missing half their men, gone pressed or – almost worse – gone willingly. This war, it is being fought not only with swords, or even with the guns they have now. This is also a war of thoughts, of words printed or hurled in anger between father and son, between brothers. Arguments that start about King Charles's Cath-olic wife and finish with whether there should be bishops or no. This war will not end, and it has divided families, and it has taught a generation of women to endure the lurches of fighting and waiting as they do the weather.

That night at the Chelmsford inn, I had the money for only a shared bed, and by the time I had eaten and got myself upstairs the other woman was already under the covers, lying very still, embracing her bundled possessions. I took her to be asleep, until I saw that her eyes were open, and she was watching me. I greeted her, and asked her where she was bound.

'London,' she said.

'Do you have kin there?'

'No.' She shifted beneath the blankets.

9

She did not seem to wish to share more, so I fell to getting my things stowed for the night. But while I was undressing, her stomach growled, breaking the quiet. I thought to ignore it, not wanting to shame her, but as I was about to get in beside her, the growling came again.

'Would you take some bread?' I said. I found what I had bought for the next day's journey, broke off part of it and held it out. She looked at me, mistrustful, but then she pushed herself up in the bed, the blanket bunched over her legs, and reached out to take the food. She did not thank me.

'It's either eat or sleep safely,' she said, when she had swallowed her first bite. 'Can't do both.'

I let her eat in peace as I closed my bag and laid it away. When I lifted my side of the covers she was chewing her last mouthful, and when at last I had settled myself, she turned her head on the pillow and said, 'I can tell fortunes, you know.'

I shook my head, thinking she was offering it as some foolish payment for the bread. But she said, 'Indeed, you should believe me. I learned it off my grandmother, and though I can see but little, what I do see, it always comes true.' She spoke softly. 'I will tell yours, mistress, for three-pence.' Her voice was warmer, more confiding than before.

I knew she had taken me for someone who could soon be parted from what belonged to her. But then I thought of the noise the woman's stomach had made. I did not have much, but if I judged right, she had next to nothing. I was on my way home, to safety. God knew where she was on her way to. And, in truth, I was curious. Though it was a small risk, it was still a risk, offering such a thing to a stranger.

'Very well,' I said awkwardly, and she took my hand. Surprised at her sudden grip, I pulled back, but she kept hold of it, and spread it flat.

'It is a foreign way of doing it,' she said, settling herself. 'Very ancient, though.'

She said that first I must tell her my name; when I spoke one, she shook her head. 'No, your true name,' she repeated. I told it to her, but I did not like it, her having hold of me like that. Her own hands were cold and not clean. Yet I did not pull away again; for a moment later she began to speak.

'You are troubled, Alice,' she said. 'You are mourning your husband.'

So much I could have guessed myself, about a woman travelling alone in a black dress. But then she peered more closely. 'But there will be a man soon to keep you finer than your husband did. Tall, dark,' she said. I felt a fool, and almost shook my hand out of her grip, but then she added, 'Five children you'll have had, by the time you're done.' She looked up to see if I was pleased.

'Go on,' I said. I did not feel pleased, but I was listening now.

She rubbed with her thumb at my palm, as though she were trying to clean a smear from it. 'You'll make a journey this summer, June, July, and then August you will be confined.' My heart quickened. She was right. That would be my time. She was seeing the darkness of the birthing chamber.

'What about September?' I could not stop myself asking her. 'Will I have a child in my arms?'

She pressed the fleshy part of my thumb, and blinked. Suddenly she seemed uncertain. 'I cannot see,' she said. She studied my hand a moment longer, and then she sat up. 'I cannot tell you,' she said. Her face was closed. She bit her lip, then murmured something about how it often came and then went again. But she seemed troubled after that. For an hour or more, she kept me awake, turning over and over in the dark.

3

I felt uneasy, the next morning, as I climbed back up into the cart. It did not help that as we moved off one of the horses startled and the cart jerked forward, throwing me hard against its wooden side. Shaking, I braced myself more firmly between the bales of cloth, the better to protect my belly and what it contained.

Through the morning the way grew more familiar, but the familiarity was comfortless: each church or gate I recognized only sharpened the memory of myself as a hopeful bride, going the other way.

It was March, remember, and rain had followed the winter's hard freeze, which of late had come back again. The road was mud under thin ice, bad for the horses. At Colchester I had to wait two hours in the rain to change to another cart, this one carrying grain, and from it I gazed out over fields where anything that could feel the cold was dead, or looked it. The grass in the verge, the willow and hazel in the hedge, all were sodden brown and silent. Great oaks waited, their branches black with wet, but only the ivy and mistletoe that twined them seemed awake. A holly standing by the wayside hurt my eyes with unaccustomed green.

Manningtree is on the Essex side, where the Stour divides that county from Suffolk, then spreads itself to the sea. You smell the place before you reach it: rank tidal mud, and people, the muck that comes with people. It is a scant seven miles from Wenham, where Matthew and I were born, but it feels leagues distant. Where Wenham is only a church, a vicarage, some scattered farms, Manningtree is a town. It has a square and a market to occupy it; it has docks, from which sailors come and go, speaking their own saltier version of English. There are hovels and low dwellings out along the road before the town proper, and there were more of these than I remembered, the day I came back. Folk stooped out of them to regard the cart as we went by, their stares hungry, and the carter clicked his tongue that the horses should quicken their pace.

When we reached the docks, he did not move to help me down: I was grubby from the road, and not yet showing. I shifted for myself and paid him carefully, counting the coins into his hand, with one more for him to leave my box where I could send someone to collect it. As the cart moved off behind the warehouses, I put away my empty purse. My tongue felt dry. I stayed a minute, across the road from the Thorn, and tried to be calm, brushing myself down, picking off the lint that had coated my dress. Underfoot the paving was slick with wet, and the docks quiet. I pulled my cloak tighter and paused.

When Matthew had written to me of Mother's death, he had told me that he had taken the lease on the Thorn, and was living there for a time. I had wondered what my brother could want with an inn, but now I saw the place through his eyes: the small windows and the riveted door, the great height of the gate that led into the stableyard. How it would be warm inside; how you could defend it, with four men, or five.

It was a solid building, just as I remembered; a staid and

respectable building, though a decade past its glory. The sign wanted retouching, where the dark tree and the letters were flaking into the air. I had thought it might be easier, reacquainting ourselves somewhere less familiar than the house we had lived in with Mother. Now, though, something about the place felt wrong. Yet it might have been only the quiet that discomforted me, for while the inn was well lit, it had what seemed a purposeful quiet, like a child's when you have told it to fasten its lips.

I was aware of my dirty face and neck, as if the yellow light in the Thorn's windows could reach across the road to expose them. I stood still a minute, and spoke severely to myself. He's your little brother. You got married, it's not a crime: and what if you did dismay him? It has been years. Looking at the lit windows of the public room, I thought, Well, I can at least avoid greeting him in front of strangers.

I crossed the road, and went through the yard at the side of the inn. A man leaned in the stable entry and stared at me, but offered no greeting. I walked straight past him, avoiding his gaze, and knocked at the back door. The light inside made a bright straight gap underneath. I felt sick and jolted; all I wanted was to rest, but I prepared a smile. I heard no feet approaching, so I knocked again, and had scarce lowered my arm when the door was yanked open.

It was a servant, plain-faced. She was broad, and when she placed her hand on the doorframe I saw that her nails were bitten down to nothing. She had dark brows, and she looked at me from under them. I watched her take me in: my dress, my lack of baggage, the state of my gloveless hands before I could draw them out of sight. Her mouth tightened.

'We've no jobs,' she said.

'I'm looking for Master Hopkins.'

'He's out.' The woman made to shut the door, but I placed my foot discreetly in its path.

'I am his sister,' I said. I looked the woman in the eye. 'You may show me a room, if you please, and send a boy for my box over the road.' I took in her hard eyes, the cap crammed on her head. I knew she would think politeness weak. 'I'll have hot water in half an hour,' I said, and stepped forward. 'Did you not expect me?'

Grudging, she stood back to let me pass. I did not know what it meant, that Matthew was not there; I had braced myself to face him. The servant was making a business of fastening the latch behind us, mumbling something about expecting me at the *front* door, which I permitted myself not to hear.

I glanced about me. To my right was what I guessed, from the steam and heat, to be the kitchens; then two more doors before the stairs turned up left into darkness, away from the uncertain rush light. I could hear no voices within, until the woman finished with the door, and called out, not taking her eyes from me. I wondered what portion she had heard of the gossip that must have got about when I had gone away.

'You are not much like your brother, mistress,' she said, 'he being so dark.'

I smiled, the even smile with which Father had always met any rudeness. 'People remark upon it,' I said.

A girl came out from the kitchen, wiping her hands, which were plump like a child's and red from hot water. Her name was Grace, she told me, climbing ahead up the stairs. I took them slowly, found myself swaying, suddenly, with tiredness. She showed me the upper floor, leading me along the passage; these were for guests, this the room the servants shared, that way the attic. At last she led me back towards the stairs, and into another chamber, but not before she had pointed to the door beside my own and said, 'That one is the master's.'

The room Grace showed me had a bed with blue hangings, a chest, a cupboard and a chair. A fire was laid ready in the cold grate. Grace went downstairs to fetch a taper, and I sat on the bed, just as I was. I felt unsteady, from facing the woman below, from the ordeals of the journey, and from the meeting with my brother, for which I had readied myself but been spared. I could hear no voices, only a distant clanking that might have been from the kitchen, and the wind, sighing in the chimney.

I dug with my fingers into the soft blue quilt. How long had I been wanting a quilt like that, a quilt to lie under, and not think, a bed with the right balance of firmness and give?

Money had been spent, I saw, on the heavy fabric of the bed drapes, which hung straight down to brush the floor; the glazing in the windows, unfoxed and clear; the quantity of logs on the fire, and the gleam of the pitcher and bowl on the corner washing stand. Everything had been thought of; the room contained all that a guest could need. But nothing in the room was familiar – there was nothing from Mother's house that I could recognize, and that was a relief, too.

It was odd to think that all this was my brother's; if he allowed me to stay, it would be mine. You must understand that, after my years in London, it felt appealing, the possibility of comfort, and someone to provide it. The mere thought of not needing to worry about eating, about rent.

I barely heard the sound of feet on the stairs, and then Grace was back in the room. She knelt to touch her taper to the kindling, and began to add small coals with her fingers. The rustlings and scrapings she made were comforting. Then there was noise on the stairs, and a little lad dragged my box into the room. After he had laid it down he stared a moment, so that Grace had cause to give him a look, ask him if there were anything else. When he had gone, she shut the door behind him and came nearer. 'Shall I, mistress?' she said, pointing to my boots.

I thanked her, and she knelt to pick at the lacings, which were swollen with wet. I saw she had pretty hair, the light red that was almost gold. I guessed, from the simple way she took each boot into her lap, that she seldom helped ladies. That the last time she had done this task it had been for someone old, or else for a little brother or sister, some child too young to learn their knots. It touched me, the rough way about her.

'I'm afraid the room will take some warming through, mistress,' Grace said. Though her accent made me smile, her deference perturbed me. I was not used to servants any more; we had never had more than a scullery maid since moving to Manningtree after Father's death, and I had done most of the work of the house. In London, the training turned useful, for once I married Joseph, I had not been able to afford a servant. So it felt peculiar, sitting still to let Grace unlace my boots. Despite my weariness, a portion of my mind was occupied in how I could prevent her from looking through my box, seeing the state of my clothes.

I wondered if she knew who I was, like the one downstairs. Whether she knew that I was a minister's daughter who had married a servant's son. I swallowed, and tried to think that it did not matter now. That the gossip would be stale, though in truth I knew that the child I was carrying would refresh it. I was not yet used to the thought of the child, growing in the dark: it had been only a few weeks that I had been certain.

I watched Grace, as she worked at my laces. Thick with weariness, I could think of nothing to ask her, but I felt the need to say something; to make an ally, after the coldness of the woman downstairs. The first knot finally gave to Grace's picking, and I felt the right boot loosen. I said, 'My husband's mother told us in her letter how at Christmas the river froze.'

Grace nodded, tugging at the boot. 'Not here, but as far down as Flatford. And it didn't thaw for a good fortnight. Not until the frost broke in January.' She looked at me, but then dipped her head, as though she would bite her tongue.

I knew how Matthew had been forced to wait for that same frost's breaking to be able to bury Mother: she must have lain at least a week before the ground had softened itself to receive her. Now Grace was thinking she had misspoken, had grieved me.

I cleared my throat, casting for another subject. 'And do you know when my brother is coming home?'

'He said tomorrow night, mistress. He's only gone to Ipswich. But he does come back early, in the night sometimes. Mary Phillips, who let you in, she says he does it to catch us idling,' she finished, her little face solemn.

I smiled. 'Does she?' I said.

Grace stood up, the paired boots in her hand. 'Mary says therefore we should never be idle,' she added, and then she turned to settling the fire.

It was too strange to think of my brother managing servants, managing women servants; this peculiar small girl. What could she be? Seventeen? I wondered what her history was.

Adding the larger coals, Grace seemed to grow less wary. She talked about my brother's trips to see the man who weighed the grain onto his boats; how he did all manner of writing and reading, but only for folk of the good sort, and she named some, names I knew as the men who ran the town. She said how they came to the Thorn to wait on him while he scribed for them. Her voice turned so reverent when she spoke of Matthew's reading and writing that I interrupted her. 'You make it sound as though folk have set up worshipping my brother, Grace, since I have been away. The men you mention, they can read and write well enough themselves.'

She stood up, dusting her hands. 'Mary says the master has greater learning than any round here. She says he has as much knowledge of religion as the minister and of the Bible also. He has a book as well that has the names of all the witches written down in it. Mary says.'

Seeing my face, she faltered. I was thinking that the older servant had been amusing herself at the girl's expense. In the silence, a log moved as it burned.

'Indeed,' I said lightly. 'I wonder where he acquired it?' I smiled, and cleared my throat, tried to make my voice brisk. 'I should get washed,' I said, and began to shed layers of clothing – cloak, and a shawl underneath, onto the bed. Grace stepped nearer to pick them up, and then she halted.

'He has talked of you more often, mistress. The master. Since your mother died,' she said.

'Has he?' I wondered if it showed, how hungry I was to hear of his goodwill.

Dropping her eyes, she carefully folded my damp and dirty cloak. 'It seems fitting,' she said, 'that there should be a woman in the house again. For men do not manage well, do they? Alone.'

It almost made me smile again, to hear that pronouncement from her, at her young age. I made my voice jesting: 'Well, but he has Mary Phillips,' I said. 'He has you.'

Before Grace turned away for the door, I caught her blush. As I continued undressing myself, I thought, surely she cannot be soft for him – for my brother, who had always looked at a girl as at some strange item brought in by the tide. Like poor Thomas Witham's daughter. But then I wondered if I had been mistaken, for a minute later, when Grace came back in with a bath sheet, she was more formal with me again, her face betraying no sign of the colour it had shown before.

When she had gone, I slipped off my gown, longing for the steaming water. As I laid it aside, I saw a dark mark on my belly. At first I thought it was dirt, but when I licked my thumb and rubbed it lightly, it hurt, and I remembered how I had fallen in the cart. It was a bruise. As I stepped into the bath I tried not to think that it boded badly. For certain, it would not help to worry.

Later, as I rubbed my hair dry, I noticed there was no mirror in the room. But, of course, there would not be:

Matthew had always disliked them, and had even learned to shave himself with only his dark reflection swimming in a bowl of water. I knew then that I was even more afraid to see him than I had been before my arrival, and not only because of our bad parting. Growing up, I had ceased to notice how he looked different from other people. I was afraid that, with our long separation, I would notice his scars afresh, and that he would see it in my face, and be angry, and ashamed.

After the lights were put out I lay dry-eyed, staring at the ceiling. I could not help but listen for the hoofs that might mean my brother; could not help but wonder whether Grace was in her own bed, somewhere nearby, her ears trained towards the same sound. I fell asleep thinking how peculiar it was, to hear my brother called 'master'.

4

When Matthew was an infant he was burned in the kitchen fire. He must have gone in hands and head first, for even once it had healed all it ever would the scars still extended up the delicate flesh of his left forearm to his neck, and from his neck the red puckered rawness crept up about his chin to touch the left side of his face.

Being less than two years older than him, I do not remember the burns when they were fresh. Though I do remember, as a girl standing thoughtful by the kitchen hearth, watching the blaze, wondering whether there was a moment when the warmth, the licking, felt almost pleasant, before the pain. But my brother could not enlighten me: he had no memory either of what had passed, the day he was burned. Yet I often suspected that his flesh remembered, for he would flinch almost before touching anything hot, and when we all sat together in the evening he always kept well back from the fire, in the colder and darker portions of the room.

My brother had other peculiarities, apart from his scars. His heart, for instance, did never beat steadily as yours or mine, but with an odd beat that was heavier, like a limp. The physician put it down to a shock received so early in life: the shock of the fire, he meant. Matthew would let me lay my head on his chest, when we were little, to hear the strange ticking. That wounded beat marked him from the beginning, for he was not able to run as fast as the other children.

Matthew had dreams that made him shout out, and he was sensitive to all smells, could not go near the privy without retching. Mother indulged him, let him use his chamber pot day as well as night, until Father stopped her. After that my brother had to govern himself and go outside, but I still knew Matthew to hold it in for hours together, when we went with Father on some rare visit to another house, rather than relieve himself where it might not be clean.

His strangenesses made other children laugh and stare. But if his scars were bad, I hardly saw them, and I never made fun of him, or pitied him either: that would have been like making fun of my own right hand, or pitying my left. It is no more than the truth to say that I was my brother's only friend.

Yet still I was aware that Matthew was different, especially when I had cause to see him through the eyes of any new person, such as that acquaintance from Father's Cambridge days who came to dine, the one indelicate enough to ask about the burns. I was perhaps eight, and Matthew six – those ages when childless men think you scarce understand four words strung together. The man was on his way south, to take up his ministry somewhere, and Father had invited him to dine with us in the vicarage at Wenham.

They talked for a while about a vicious mousing cat from their old college, before the man said, 'What happened to your boy, Hopkins?'

Father put down his napkin. 'He got into the fire,' he said. 'When he was still away with his wet nurse. The woman and her servant between them were supposed to have an eye on him, but they were not watching. If you want the truth, I have never trusted a servant since.'

Mother cleared her throat. 'But, husband,' she said, 'do you remember also that Matthew, he was always a great crawler?' She smiled at the visitor, but as she did her voice trembled. 'Believe me, sir, at that age, show him some book-shelves, and he would climb them. Show him something bright, and he would try to touch it.' I looked at Mother: I had never heard her say so much in company.

'Hm,' said the man, chewing. 'And this your only boy, is it?'

'No, I have three older. And Alice here, my daughter. All from my late wife.'

'The Lord rest her soul,' the man replied.

Mother had stopped eating. I still remember my confusion at hearing her speak thus of Matthew. For he always kept his hands to himself, never fidgeted as I did. I had never seen him climb anything in his life.

If he had done, I would have known of it, for we were always together. Our physician once gave us something to rub into his scarred skin, that it might not itch or peel, and it was only me he would suffer to do it; that is the kind of thing folk want to hear about, when they find out who I am. They take it as a measure of how close we were.

We used to say, the two of us, that, though he was so dark and I was fair, inside we were just alike. We grew together, twined like young trees, our plight the same; for from very early on, Matthew and I knew that we were spare children. Father had his heirs, three strong ones, already out in the world; what remained were Matthew with his strange-nesses, and myself, the only girl.

25

For certain, Father encouraged Matthew in his collecting of birds' eggs, old coins. He showed him how to tell if a penny was bad, or if it was from King Henry's time. But also Father watched Matthew, as though he were a puzzle he might solve. That struck me, even from a young age, for little else seemed to perplex Father. When my elder brothers visited he was easy and jesting, and as a minister he was warm and firm, beloved of his congregation.

Mother, though, was not so well liked. Her afflictions had not taken on their later proportion, but still she did not do the sick-visiting and lending and handing out of preserves that was expected of a minister's wife. Father had met her when he was seeking someone to see after my three elder brothers and myself, just weaned. In town searching for a nurse, he had looked in on his friend Thomas Witham of Manningtree, in whose house Mother was staying. He had gone in search of a nurse, and he came away with a wife who in truth needed nursing herself.

Father always insisted that hers was only an imbalance of the humours, curable with tinctures and purges. But she did not get better; rather, she got worse. By the time I was old enough to know something was amiss, she had a hundred strange habits that dominated all her hours between waking and sleeping. She was changing her linen twice a day, and she would put it on damp if the servant or I failed to get it dry in time.

She clung overmuch to Matthew, fretted about his dress and diet, and even as he grew older held him to her longer than most mothers would when he said goodnight. She was not the same with me, but I thought it was simply because Matthew was her true child. I do not remember being jealous: I took it as natural, with him being her own, that she would prefer him. And Father took more than enough trouble over me, teaching me equally with Matthew, even the Latin and history that are not thought needful for girls. We would read together in the afternoons, and when Father got ill, he would often ask me to sing for him instead.

His death, when it came, was not sudden. Father had the same bad lungs as his father before him, and he declined first, the flesh stripped from him. I hoped he would get better. I hoped and hoped, until the morning I went in to him and he did not look like himself. His face was all sunk in. That morning he looked like something that belonged under the ground, and it was the worst pain I had known.

Grief did not quieten the world's demands, and I was thankful to be kept busy. There were claims to sort out, Mother being Father's second wife, and Matthew lent a hand. The vicarage was wanted for the next man; I under-took the cleaning out and packing. Mother did not weep much. Rather, she wandered about the house – picking things up, putting them down. She was quiet, stunned.

Father's burial was perhaps only the third or fourth time I had seen my elder brothers. When we were little, my aunt had brought them at Christmas or at Easter, bigger boys from Cambridge. They felt more like my half-relatives than Matthew did, however closely I resembled them. But when they came for the burial they were polite to Mother and to Matthew, took my hands warmly. They all of them seemed to be trying to grow beards. The two younger were taking their inheritance and going to Father's friends in America; James, the eldest, said that as soon as he had taken his master's degree he would be following them, in fulfilment of Father's wishes.

With my brothers gone, I knew our aunt's large house in Cambridge would have many empty rooms. As folk ate and drank after the burial, I tried to linger near Mother and my aunt to hear whether they were speaking of us going to her household. I knew Matthew was already excited at the thought of being near the colleges, and that he hoped Mother might be brought to find him a tutor, now that such things would fall to her to decide. I hoped it, too: that some good thing for my brother might come out of the calamity of Father's death. For though Father had delayed in sending him away to school, Matthew had long made it plain that he wished to follow him and my three elder brothers into the ministry. Matthew was still but fifteen, and it would not have been too late for him to be sent away to a tutor.

But Mother spoke with my aunt very little that afternoon, and when they did speak it was only to comment on the turnout, or the state of the roads. When it was over, and those in attendance had been fed and watered and had gone, I helped Mother to fold the tablecloths away. I was amazed that she had lasted the day without a headache, but she seemed calm enough. We were folding in the dark, nearly, for we were running short of candles; so it was that I could not see the look on her face when she said, 'I have heard of a house in Manningtree.' And then, 'Take this.' She held out the squared corners of a cloth to me, and obediently I pinched them together.

I said, 'We thought –' I stopped. 'I thought we would go to Cambridge.'

But Mother's voice was brisk, as she finished folding the cloth. 'Cambridge is expensive, Alice. You know that.' And then she said defiantly, 'And it will do me good to be near Bridget again.'

'Who is Bridget?'

'She was my servant, before I married your father,' Mother replied. 'She came with me from London. She came here, though she left – she left when you were a baby. Do you not remember her?' She stacked the folded cloths together. 'I suppose you would not. She looked after you. But she moved, just after Matthew was born, back to Manningtree and took in a little boy, I think, and lives there still. That is why she came to my mind.'

When Mother said this, I remember thinking, servants have never had names before. Servants, in our parents' stories, had always been 'that ungainly girl' or 'that girl with the red hair, the one from Colchester'. Mother had most usually recalled them only when she came across a bad piece of mending, or a burn mark on the table, and had occasion to remember the culprit. And beneath each instance of dismissiveness, each complaint, was the unspoken name of the wet nurse who had let Matthew crawl too near the fire, who, though I could not have known it then, would one day cross into our lives again.

But that day, that funeral day, I remember only my surprise, and Mother's worried look as she handed me the folded stack of linen. 'You'll tell your brother?' she said. She was aware, I think, that it would be a blow.

Matthew took the news quietly enough. No Cambridge after all: instead, only Manningtree, its little docks, its bustle not of scholars but of farmers and small merchants.

I remember Matthew on our last day in Wenham, how he went out into the garden while Mother and I did the packing. He said he wanted to leave things in good order: stayed out past dark, pulling weeds viciously from the vegetable beds, and burning them in a heap. I watched him for a while out of the kitchen window, kicking loose pieces of brush into the fire, not even moving out of the way of the upward billowing sparks.

My brother buried his resentment that day. But resentment buried is not gone. It is like burying a seed: for a season it may stay hidden in the dark, but in the end, it will always grow. I did not see it, though we were still close, even at that age. I think now that to be close to someone can be to underestimate them. Grow too close, and you do not see what they are capable of; or you do not see it in time.

Here listed the old ways of finding them out, so far as I can discover. See fuller notes on each method elsewhere.

1. The tradition of the witches not weeping.

2. The witches making ill-favoured faces and mumbling.

3. To burn the thing bewitched, & c.

4. The burning of the thatch of the witch's house, & c.

5. The heating of the horseshoe, & c.

6. The scalding water, & c.

7. The sticking of knives across, & c.

8. The putting of such and such things under the threshold, and in the bedstraw, & c.

9. The sieve and the shears, & c.

10. The casting the witch into the water with thumbs and toes tied across, & c.

11. The tying of knots, & c.

5

When I woke, my first morning at the Thorn, it took me a moment to come to where I was. The inn was quiet. I changed my shift and found a cap and apron in my box, fresh but creased. There was dirt in the fine cracks of my palms. I would need to soak my hands later: like Mother, Matthew had always been particular about such things.

My only black dress had been taken out for brushing: it would have to be the brown. Brown was easier, anyway, on my pale winter nubbin of a face, my cracked lips, my red hands. I walked about the chamber plenty, in getting myself ready; then I waited for some minutes, but Grace did not come.

The stairs and passage were quiet. I knocked on the door beside my own, but there was no sound within: Matthew was not back, then. I stuck my head into the kitchen, and saw only a scullery maid. I asked her for something hot to drink. I knew it was time to go to Bridget.

I felt shaky, skittish, as I took the familiar field path along the edge of the woods. The wind was cold and dry from the east, and from the heath you could see the small grey shapes of waiting ships out in the channel. The walk to Bridget's house took longer than I remembered, for there were fences on the common land where there had been no fences before.

The strangeness of the fields made me think of the first time I had walked them, the day after we moved to Manningtree. Mother had prevailed upon us to take a basket of something to her old servant Bridget's house; we took apples, I think, from the orchard at Wenham, though it was not the season, and the small yellow fruits were soft from their long winter storage. I remember knocking, the way the suspicion had dispersed from Bridget's face as I said our names: like watching the sun come out. Her house was larger than I expected, for one who had once been a servant: two hearths, hives, chickens, and plenty of space for growing things.

Bridget fed us that day on cheese and radishes, and she answered my questions about her books – she had Mother to thank, she told us, for being able to read – and likewise about the various places she had lived throughout the Tendring Hundred since leaving our parents' service, and about how she made money now with her bees, and by the dosing of horses and pigs.

Most folk, receiving scant answer from my brother, would begin after a time to talk only to me, but Bridget talked to both of us. She met Matthew's eyes, and told him that he had been that tiny when she left, and what hair he had been possessed of, even at that tender age. She had included him in each of her stories, and not only did she keep from staring at his scars, but she never even glanced at them. Even that first day I was drawn to Bridget: though it was impossible, it was as if I remembered her face.

The next day, she returned the visit, and this time, as Matthew let her in, I saw she had a boy with her. We all sat in the front parlour, which was still full of crates, Bridget in what I would come to know as her one good dress; she made sure to ask Mother about her health, before introducing her Joseph, who I knew must be the boy she had taken in, awkward in his Sunday clothes.

While Bridget talked with Mother of the journey from Wenham, what things had been broken in the course of the unloading, I stole looks at Joseph. I had not met many boys with whom I had not grown up, and as Bridget and Mother talked about nothing very much, I noticed him: his thin, boyish height, his strong hands, his yellow hair, which wanted cutting. And though I did not catch him doing it, I knew he was glancing back at me.

At length, Mother finished lamenting how the fire did smoke, and smiled at Joseph, and said, 'You are a tall lad, Joseph. What age are you?'

Here was an excuse to look at him properly: at once I noticed his gentle eyes, as he replied, 'Mistress Hopkins, I believe I am nineteen.'

Matthew said, 'Cannot you remember?'

Joseph paused, looked at Bridget: his face turned a faint pink, and he did not seem to know what to say.

It was left to Bridget to explain that his precise age was not certain, for he had not come to her as a baby, but as a child five years old, or seven: the son of a woman who had died in Colchester gaol and a man who had gone away to sea.

As Bridget spoke, Matthew sat kicking his heels on the rung of his chair, and I did not look at him. I had not imagined a tale so bad, when Mother had spoken of Bridget taking in a child. I knew that my brother would be shocked that Bridget was so plain about Joseph's low birth.

As Mother said how fortunate Joseph had been, Bridget replied, 'But your boy here. What would he be now? Fifteen? And so handsome. I think he has just his father's forehead.'

Mother smiled, made some uncertain agreement. What with the scars, it was not common for folk to call my brother handsome. An awkward silence fell, and again I studied the floor. I was grateful when Joseph cleared his throat, shifted in his chair, and told Mother that he knew some lads who would be glad to come and sweep the chimneys. As Mother thanked him, I looked up in relief, and at last I caught him resting his gentle eyes on me.

I do not know what Matthew saw or knew, but when he wished our guests good day it was stiffly, and only once they were at a safe distance from the front door did I see him grow calm.

'Did you not like them?' I said.

He turned to me. 'You saw the state of her fingernails?'

I let it go, on that occasion. I thought he was still sore about Cambridge; I thought that Father's caution about servants had found its mark in Matthew, that he had perhaps picked it up like an affectation, a thing of no consequence.

But it soon became clear that Mother trusted Bridget, and I grew close with her, also. I was not well placed to make friends among the other girls in Manningtree – at nearly seventeen I had arrived somewhat late for it, and Mother did not go visiting much. But I found my refuge in Bridget's house. She had a whole shelf of books, and unlike Father's, Bridget's books were not only about God. I remember looking along their spines, turning to her, saying, 'You have three books on the keeping of hounds.' I turned back to the titles. 'Two on the proper arrangement of troops in battle.'

Bridget stopped stirring what she was stirring, wiped her hands, and placed them on her hips. 'I do,' she said. 'Though if women would write more books, I live in hope that they'll find some other topics.'

But while my liking for Bridget grew, while I found more and more reasons to look in on her – and, of course, on Joseph, too – Matthew's first dislike persisted. Bridget became brittle about him in return, saying plainly once that he was spoiled. When she said it, I knew that it was true, that part of why Matthew disliked her was because she did not put down her sewing whenever he began to speak, as Mother did. But Matthew's disapproval did not prevent me seeking to become Bridget's kin.

I believe I thought that in marrying Joseph I would be getting a new mother. But as soon as he told her of our plans, she changed with me, withdrew, and I turned sulky: told myself she was jealous, that she was like those mothers who want to keep their sons always babies. Her affection for Joseph remained undiminished, and once we were married and moved to London, she wrote to him most weeks – she greeted both of us at the start of each letter, but I knew they were written for him. When he died, I read and reread the thick pile of her letters he kept on our bedchamber sill, pored afresh over their detailed complaints and small news.

Bridget's letters were like a pattern for the life that I had failed to make for Joseph in London; a life with gossip, little disputes, neighbours' births and their marriages. The thought tasted bitter: even among so many people, I had not made enough friends. For where we took our rooms, there were only the Dutch women who would watch me pass with their amused dark eyes, and the French ones who would clatter by me, laughing together, the tips of their noses red with cold. In our part of London each kept with their own kind, except there were none of my kind, or else I did not find them, and Joseph and I were alone, with Bridget's letters the only link to our old life in Manningtree.

Her letters kept arriving after Joseph was dead, after a fortnight and after three weeks, the second hoping, more pointedly than the first, that he was in good health. I did not know what else to do but read them, then let them lie unanswered, sitting at the kitchen table in order to have something solid to lean on, eating what my landlady brought me, trying not to think.

Though I had failed to tell Matthew of my husband's death in my letter to him, I made myself do it when I wrote to Bridget, finishing the note quickly so that I would not have to think long on what the words meant. Now, on my first day back in Manningtree, as I walked towards her house, I was glad that I had told her. That I would not have to see her first shock and pain.

The path led downhill in sight of the church from the top of the heath to Bridget's place, but when I reached the cottage, from the gate I could see the thick, dead grass all around and the damp rising up the brickwork. An aging cow lay against the wall, chewing. I knew that something was wrong for certain when I saw Bridget's little patch, likewise choked with grass, and beyond it the old wooden hives, one blown or kicked over, the other upended and filled with dung. It was impossible that Bridget could have let it get to this.

Then a dog came from around the side and towards me, barking and crouching low to the ground. Keeping my eyes on it I called out: a woman, not Bridget, replied from the back of the cottage, and the dog disappeared. I gathered my courage and followed it. The woman was standing on the back step, wringing out clothes for a child, little shirts and breeches. She had dark hair, and I noticed the thickness of her arms. The dog stood at her feet. Close up, I saw it was half blind, with one milky eye.

'I'm looking for Bridget,' I said.

'Aye. Moved on.' She was Irish. I smiled, but I could feel the dog watching me.

'Do you know where to?'

'Friend of hers, is it?' The woman shaded her eyes.

'Family,' I said. 'I'm her son's wife.'

She nodded. 'She's in one of them cottages now, on the road up from the dairy. Decent woman, she is. We're still burning the wood she left us.' She pulled a damp hand across her nose. 'Never spoke of a son.'

The back of the cottage was like the front, scrubby wildness now running down to the stream and what was left of the hen coop, which had been stripped for usable wood. Mint still grew by the door, a dead winter thicket at the woman's feet. I had stood just there and watched Joseph build that hen coop. Seen him measuring the pieces of it with his forearm and his hand span. I had held Joseph at bay, all the road from London to Manningtree, all the way from the Thorn to that doorstep, but now he was coming back to me, whether I willed it or no. I touched the wall, to steady myself.

I saw the Irish woman was waiting, and I tried to judge

what might win her, what she would best understand. 'We went to London, for work,' I said. 'But he got himself killed.'

She did not trouble to ask how, but made a sort of noise in her throat, not without sympathy.

'Well, I thank you,' I said. And then, 'It's good ground this, at the front especially. You won't find stones. You can get carrots to come up with no work at all. They'll grow like weeds,' I finished quickly: her face had changed, and I thought she was losing patience. But when I fell quiet, she was regarding me, the damp clothes over her arm.

'Will you wait?' she said then, and disappeared inside. The dog lay down, and I waited, thinking she would offer me something to eat, wondering how to refuse.

But the woman came back without the washing, and held out to me some folded paper. As her rough hand grazed mine, I felt my face tremble. It was my letter: the one from me to Bridget, in which I had told her that Joseph was dead. And another, a little older; the direction written in Joseph's hand. I thought, She does not know. How can she not know?

'Your pardon,' the woman said. 'But while you're going, would you mind? They gave these to my husband. That was their mistake. I only found them last week, I was going to step over with them –'

I thanked her, said I would pass on her regards, and I would see them into Bridget's hands. The dog tailed me back round the side of the house, making low sounds in its throat, and came as far as the gate before it turned back again. I did not stop till I was out of sight, clutching Joseph's letter, and my own.

As I followed the directions the woman had given, I tried to think what words I could use, how to make Bridget sit down for me to say them. I had not spoken of Joseph since his death, did not know whether I could speak of him now without crying out or falling down. Before I was ready, my feet brought me to where the cottages were and I halted, realizing as I looked down the row that I did not even know which one was hers.

They were much poorer than her old house. You could see from the chimneys that there would be only one hearth apiece; the windows were unglazed and the roofs needed work doing. There was a child playing in the dirt of the road, but when I beckoned, it ran away indoors. I stood for a moment, at a loss. Then I saw the bench outside the house at the end. I began to walk towards it, and when I reached it, I touched the pool of wax on the seat.

We had spilled that the night we had agreed to marry. We had been sitting outside Bridget's back door, her old back door. Joseph had brought out the stub of a candle. True, I had prompted him a little, but that was forgotten as soon as I felt his lips' softness, the heat of falling wax on my fingertips where he had knocked the candle in its dish, the sudden hardness and shrinking as the wax cooled where it fell on my fingers and on the bench between us.

Soon, Joseph had gone in, to give Bridget the news. I was raw that night, for I had just fought with Matthew, and I wanted and expected to overhear an exclamation of joy, of surprise. But, though I could not catch what she said, when Bridget's voice came it sounded doubtful.

I wrote to my brother in Ipswich, telling him the date of the wedding, but I received no reply. Mother, for her part, did not object. She scarcely said anything at all. I remember she frowned, and asked, 'Do you think he can take care of you?'

'We can take care of each other,' I replied. And I confess it, I did feel some relief in that moment, at the thought that my youth might now be more than caring for her. After a minute I added, 'I love him,' and she said only, 'Well, then.' Wearily, regretfully, as if over a pail of milk that was already spilled.

Father's executor, Thomas Witham, gave up my portion gladly enough. But though he was minister at the main Manningtree church, he was reluctant to marry us without Matthew's blessing, so I went to the other church, up on the heath, and the minister there who did not know us. I was careful to look coy, and let my hand creep to my stomach, when he asked what the hurry was. I am ashamed to own to that, now, though God knows how I was paid out for it in the end.

Pulling my eyes from the bench, I raised one hand to knock at Bridget's doorframe, the unopened letters tucked tight in my sleeve. The knock sounded faint, and far away. I still did not know what I would say; I felt as though I was drowning in the past. Inside, I heard Bridget moving about, saying, 'God rot this door.' Then it jerked open, and she saw me. She reached out her arms. 'Get yourself inside!' she said. 'You'll be perished.'

She looked the same, but she felt lighter, smaller, and I embraced her carefully. When she let me go I stepped in at her urging, and I saw her glance up and down the street before she shut the door. She began to talk straight away as she tidied, fumbling in her pockets, whisking things out of sight. She retreated to the far corner of the room, where a few pans hung from hooks on the wall, and began to move things about, chattering.

I saw she was bent now, and went more slowly. I recognized her hearth brush and the bucket for taking out ashes; many of her possessions were the same, though there seemed to be fewer. On the table there was a round of coarse cheat bread a quarter gone, and the ordinariness of it made my throat catch with what I had to say.

'Sit by the fire,' Bridget insisted. 'But tell me, where is Joe? Is he coming on with the baggage? I don't know. If you'd said you were coming, I'd have got something better for dinner.' She was smiling, had lifted a jug of something to pour, but when I remained standing and silent, the table between us, she put the jug down. I felt queasiness wash over me, worse than it had been in recent mornings.

'Will you sit down?' I said.

But she did not move. She put her hands in her apron pocket, and stood waiting. For a moment I was certain that if I tried to open my mouth, I would be sick. But at my silence, Bridget's face changed.

'What?' she said, at last.

'I did write, but it went to your old place.' I put my letter on the table, and we both looked at it. It seemed crumpled and small.

I said it quickly, about him being dead.

I did not meet her eyes. After a moment she picked up the jug again, and poured from it into a pan. She gathered two cups, set the pan over the fire and sat down in one of the chairs; slowly, I took the other.

'It was in December,' I said, but she raised her hand to silence me. I had forgotten how her face was never still; how openly pain moved over it. I bit my lip, surprised that I felt almost angry. That I wanted her to tell me how my loss was greater. I fought the feeling down.

The wine steaming, Bridget picked up a cloth, neatly lifted the pan from the fire, and divided the wine equally between the cups. She handed me one, and only then did she look at me. 'How, then?'

'They were testing some new guns,' I said, but Bridget shifted in her chair, and then the tears came. I had never seen her cry before. For a time, neither of us spoke. Bridget sniffed, not delicately, and picked up her cup. I watched her drain it, the steady movement of the skin folds at her throat. When she had done, she shook her head bleakly. 'My own baby boy,' she said. She touched the letter, but did not move to open it. I looked down at my hands.

'I did try to make him keep clear of it,' I said. 'Do not think I did not try.'

We fell quiet. When I looked up, she was regarding me. 'You're fatter in the face,' she said. I nodded, and her eyes started to soften, but then she swallowed, and said, 'Well. I can always take it, if you want. When it comes.'

I was amazed. 'You think I'd part from it?'

'I only meant, you'll marry again, won't you?' She spread her hands, spoke more gently. 'Not every man would want another's infant in his household.'

'Bridget. I'd never let this child go.' I paused. 'We lost four.'

'You what?' She stopped still at that, covered her mouth a moment. 'He never said.'

She reached for my hand, but I pulled it away from her, trying to push back the thought of my last child, how I had lost it at three months in the privy; of the one before that, on the kitchen floor. Bridget had never been a proper mid-wife, but for small coins she would do simple physic, help with birthing for folk too poor to pay a surgeon; also, with bringing unwanted babies away. Clutching my cup of wine, I was trying to push back the memory of a day not long after we first came to Manningtree, when at my knock she had opened her front door slightly, and through the gap said, 'What?' She had let the door fall wider when she saw who it was. There was blood all down her apron, and one hand slick, the rust of it bedded in her nails. 'You can't come in just now,' she had said, 'I have company.' The look on her face was impatient, matter-of-fact, as if I had surprised her in an act no more harrowing than the plucking and jointing of a bird.

I bit my lip, and said to myself that none of what had happened to me, none of it was her doing. She was watching me; frowning. I cleared my throat. 'You moved,' I began, and tried a smile.

'In the autumn. Your brother's friend Grimston put the rent up on the old house,' she replied, her voice dry.

'You should have told us. We could have helped,' I said. And then, 'But what do you mean, his friend?'

'Matthew has found his way into favour with the great men hereabouts.'

'Grace said something about him scribing for people,' I said. 'It surprised me, for before, he was never –' I stopped, for I could see she knew what I meant. He was never one for making friends.

'I've heard the same,' she said. I could see her discomfort. She had unsealed my letter, and glanced at it; now she shut her eyes, and laid it aside. When she opened them, she said, 'There was a reason I didn't tell you, Alice, when I moved.

I'm not a fool. There was more in Joseph's letters than he wrote. I know you were in trouble.'

'I took in washing,' I said. It was true: to tide us over, I had started to take sheets from our landlady. She being a midwife herself, there was always plenty. She favoured me, and paid more than she had to, but even so, there had been no room for mistakes in my house-keeping. Spoiled milk had mattered. A dropped egg. My labours were never enough to keep away the cramping fear of relentless thrift; so when Joseph had found work through a man at his church who was a gunsmith, God forgive me, I had been glad.

We lapsed into quiet. Bridget and I had talked so easily together, once: but now every possible subject was loaded with sadness. But I thought, At least I can try to help her from thinking about Joseph.

'I was sorry not to come back and see Mother buried,' I said.

'I do not think she had much pain, at the end.'

'Were you with her?'

'I saw her the day before,' she said. 'Your brother pre-ferred her not to have visitors, but as chance would have it I went over that day. Grace let me in. Your mother was fret-ful, I'll not deny. But not in too much pain.' She folded her hands. 'Will you stay here?'

'With Matthew.'

She nodded. 'You'll need some new gowns, with who's visiting at the Thorn these days,' she said. I saw that she did not mean to be abrupt: it was only that she was speaking to me as she would another woman. As though I was not a child any more.

She looked at me, and her voice turned troubled. 'Alice, there's been talk,' she said. 'In town.'

She had left the wine-pan near the heat, and just then I caught the fumes, of hedges and old cellars. 'What do you mean?'

Bridget shook her head. 'Richard Edwards has decided that someone looked funny at his youngest, and the child died after.' I recognized Richard Edwards's name. He had the most land in Manningtree, next to Sir Harbottle Grimston. 'And there have been other infants –' She broke off, lowered her voice despite the thick walls. 'Certain women are stirrers, on top of being bone idle. But men have been crediting it who are learned enough to know better.'

'What do you mean? Are they saying someone is to blame?' I remembered what Grace had told me the night before, about the book with the names in it.

'You'd know Bess Clarke?'

Elizabeth Clarke. Bess. For certain I remembered her. She had one leg that buckled under her so she used a rough crutch, which made sores in her armpit, which in turn stank.

Bridget spread her hands. 'Elizabeth Clarke is a sharp-tongued woman, she keeps a dirty house. But what would she want with killing a child?'

'Richard Edwards's child? They accuse Bess? But how –'

'Then there's Ned Parsley's baby –'

'What about it?' I asked, fearful suddenly.

She sat down again, and passed a hand over her face. 'Christ,' she said, and I did not admonish her. 'I'm telling you this because I know your brother won't. They're saying it was done with witchcraft.'

I bit my lip. 'Surely Matthew could not give currency to such foolishness.'

Bridget stood up slowly. 'It is not only Bess Clarke. There are others. For every sudden death, every accident – Prudence Hart fell down and lost her child, and was took numb all down one side, and they've decided that's someone's fault. Robert Taylor's out for blood, too, something about a dead horse. I've heard others accused besides Bess Clarke.'

She was shaken, that was clear enough. I waited, but then she said, 'No, what I think is, I will not say who. It is women jawing that help damn them, along with meddling men who think they know the law.' She turned away to take the pan back to the sink. 'Matthew's been scribing for them,' she said. 'You ask him *what* he's been scribing.'

I drank the last of my wine: I felt aggrieved that she would not confide in me. Despite what Grace had said, I did not believe that Matthew could be involved in such proceedings. I felt the dregs of the wine fur my mouth. 'I must go,' I said. 'I will ask him about it, of course I will. But I am certain it is not what you think. I am sure it will be nothing.' I stood up, and she moved ahead of me to unlatch the door.

As I shrugged on my cloak, I felt Joseph's letter in my sleeve, and the thought of him slid across me, his cheerfulness, his cold-weather cough. But I could not bring myself to give it to her, to part with it yet.

'Take care of yourself, then,' Bridget said, standing by to let me out. In the daylight, her eyes were red, and she clutched her elbows against the cold. I put a hand on her shoulder, and before I could move she had folded me into her arms again. I felt tears start in my eyes. For a long minute, she did not let me go. When she did, she smiled a tight, brave smile as I stepped away.

I had assured her that I would come again soon, had already turned, when she blurted, 'There was a boy tampering with my thatch. Last Friday night. He ran off before I could raise a light.' She stepped forward. 'Do you think that will be nothing, too?'

Her face looked brittle, all bone, and she seemed suddenly on the verge of tears. I thought of how any noise after dark would seem, if the town was on edge as she had described. I put my hand on her arm, and softened my voice. 'Just boys,' I said.

I felt in my bones as if hours had passed as I walked back to the Thorn. I have told her, I thought, I have done my duty. But that did not comfort me. I tried to put away the guilt of Joseph's letter in my sleeve. At the top of the heath, I stopped for breath. The tide was coming in, the river flowing imperceptibly backwards.

I tried to be sensible about the witch nonsense. Things were happening in the town. That was clear enough. Some personal grudges, no doubt. Folk often resorted to talk of witchcraft when other charges were hard to prove. Women were taken up for it, one or two, every five years, or ten; it was done to teach them a lesson, but these days they only passed a month or two waiting in gaol before being acquitted when it came to trial. They were sometimes drunken women, or women who had inconvenient babies, or who bawled insults in the street. But there had been no spates of witch-hanging for many years. Such things were a matter for Scotland, France, wild places across the sea or north of the border.

Even if Bridget is not wrong, I thought, all that will happen is Elizabeth Clarke will be taken away and given a slap on the wrist. And if Matthew does have some part in it, then it will be as a record-keeper alone. I tried to smother the picture of Bridget at the door, how frail she had looked, hugging her elbows.

Grace greeted me, as I came in the door at the Thorn, and followed me up the stairs. 'Have you been visiting, mistress?' She took my shawl from me and folded it over her arm. 'I didn't know where you were.'

'I've been to see my late husband's mother,' I said.

Grace ducked her head, but she did not move away. 'The master is due back this evening,' she said.

'Yes, I remember,' I said. I wished to sit down. I felt cold and empty. 'Listen, Grace, will you bring me up something to eat? Something hot?'

'If he asks where you've been today, I shall just tell him you've been visiting,' said Grace, and then, without looking at me, she turned, and went away downstairs.

Later that afternoon, as I was combing my hair, using the faint reflection in the window, I thought of Grace's odd behaviour. Matthew had never liked Bridget, but why should Grace think he would trouble over me paying her a visit?

I pulled a clump of hair out of my comb, enjoying its cleanness. I rubbed it into a ball, and threw it on the fire, where it fizzled and smoked to nothing. And that was when it came back, the knowledge that belonged with Bridget's parting words. The boy tampering with her thatch: that old method of finding out a witch. That you could take a piece of a witch's thatch, burn it, and bring her running.

Superstitions like that one were common among village folk. Father used to frown over those among his congregation who would indulge them, probably the more because he knew that Mother believed such things, too, as readily and fearfully as she believed the gospel. She had got worse with it after we moved to Manningtree; it grew trying when she would not stir out of doors because the woman over the road had hung a certain blue petticoat to dry again from an upper window. Or when I did persuade her to take the air, and she would grow agitated if we saw a magpie, and would not come in until she had seen another, even if it took an hour of cold waiting.

Matthew did not witness much of her sickness, having gone to Ipswich by then to learn his trade in a grain-merchant's house, but that last Christmas before my marriage, when he was at home, Mother had taken a particularly bad turn. She had gone to bed early, and Matthew and I had stayed up, talking quietly for a time; but we had been reading in silence more than an hour when I heard movement in the room above. I looked at Matthew, got ready to mark my place, but before I could move there were feet on the stairs, and then Mother was in the room.

'Will you be quiet?' she said loudly. Her hair was round her ears.

'Mother,' I said, but she seemed not to hear me.

'Will you just please be quiet?' She was talking too loudly, almost shouting. Her eyes were strange: I wondered if she could be dreaming, walking and speaking in her sleep.

'Mother!' Matthew said, louder. 'What is it?'

'You two. Talking and talking. How can I sleep when you're talking so loud?' she said.

Matthew had gone to her, but he turned to me then, stricken. I laid my book aside, went nearer, and then I saw what he saw: that she had plugged her ears with wadded cloth, as she often did to ensure a good night's rest.

I took her arm, put my own around her shoulders. Swiftly and gently I pulled out the plugs of cloth, and threw the pieces on the fire. 'Come, Mother,' I said. 'I'll sit with you while you go to sleep. Then you won't be troubled by us talking at all.'

Things had been different from that day. Soon after, Matthew took over the household accounts. He found Mother a new physician, with a new regime of purging and bleeding to balance her humours, and he would not listen when I asked him what we would do if it did not work, if what was wrong with her could not be cured in that way. It was then that he began to come back from Ipswich more often and unannounced. It was then that I had decided to fall in love.

My hair brushed smooth, I threw the final clump on the fire, and watched it disappear, thinking. If Mother had always been impressionable, then Bridget had always been steady, and it gave me pause that a piece of nonsense, like that about the thatch, could have frightened her. I could not know that it was more than nonsense. That it was a beginning. I see now how Bridget was right to tell me no names. Names were how it had begun. One woman accuses another in a fit of grief or rage. And once you have said a name, there is no unsaying.

6

I was still holding the comb, still standing in the window, when I heard the horses come round into the yard. Moving back from the glass, I saw my brother's greyhound nosing the ground by the stables, where a groom held the head of a bay horse. Matthew was wearing a hat, but I knew him by his manner of dismounting, the lurch that made the horse skip sideways before it settled again. I smoothed my skirt, wishing afresh that I had a mirror to check myself in. When I had last seen my brother I had been untidily dressed, my face red, my hair falling out of its pins; I would sooner not remind him of that day.

As I stepped further back from the window, Matthew's voice came below. Then a tread I knew on the stair, but at the top, my brother halted. I thought he would pass on into his own room, for a change of linen or to wash the smell of horse-leather from his hands, but there he still paused, on the other side of the door. So I breathed out, and opened it.

He had a beard, slightly redder in hue than the rest of his hair, as Father's had been. It did not quite cover the scars, where they spread over his neck and cheek – they could still be seen, the small patches of pink web, pulling minutely against each other. But the beard rendered them less stark. There was grey now, incredibly, at his temples. Suddenly I saw why perhaps he might have caught Grace's fancy. His breeches, his coat, were of fine black wool, and his broad collar very clean, despite his journey. His boots were of the tall riding style he had always worn, not for vanity but to keep his legs from chafing, yet they fitted him now; suited him, even. He clutched a large, stiff hat, the kind that keeps the rain off, but his free hand as he held it out was steady: likewise his gaze. He had become a man, my brother, and I had missed the moment of it.

'Alice,' he said. My name in his mouth sounded awkward after all this time; his holding out his hand to me seemed oddly formal, and it felt cold as I took it. I noticed how smooth it was in my own, and I could not stop myself turning it over and touching the palm.

'Your skin!' I exclaimed. The scarring was so much improved. Matthew drew the hand out of my grasp, and gave a quick smile. 'Forgive me,' I said, but he shook his head.

'I have a different physician, now, the same one Grimston uses. He gave me something different to apply. The left is still bad, though.' He seemed unsure whether to embrace me, so I saved him by stepping away. He said, 'It is good to see you looking so well.'

We gazed at each other again, and in meeting his eyes I felt washed with relief. For all his faults, I had missed him. He gestured with his hat back down the stairs. 'I gather I must beg pardon for my housekeeper.'

I smiled. 'Nonsense. Why would she know my face?' I meant it lightly, but we both looked away.

'Indeed. It has been some time,' Matthew said. In the quiet, our last meeting grew large between us. 'How was your journey?'

I thought back to the woman at the inn, how she had failed to see me holding my child. I tried to smile. 'Cold,' I said.

'Well.' He shifted a little, and his boots squeaked on the boards. 'Will you come down and dine with me? It's early, I know.' His greyhound was standing beside him.

'Of course,' I said. I murmured to the dog and put out my hand, but it backed away: it had forgotten my scent.

Matthew stepped towards his chamber. 'First I must –'

'I'll give you a few minutes,' I said.

I closed my door, and heard him shout down the stairs for hot water. I sat by the hearth. My hair was neat and tucked away, and I could not think how to fill the minutes, so I sat, pressing the teeth of the comb lightly into my palm. A comb, I thought. If you came across it and did not know its purpose, it looks like a thing for hurting.

At length, I heard Matthew go down, and a moment later I followed him. Smoothing my hand over my bodice, tight-laced to hide the small roundness there, I thought, It will be better to tell him straight away.

At the bottom of the stairs, Mary Phillips gestured to the last door in the passage, and as I went into the large chamber, Matthew stood up to greet me.

There was a table with twelve wooden chairs, but also two softer ones drawn up close to a good fire, and it was to one of these that Matthew pointed me as he settled in the other. This room was smaller than the public room at the front of the inn; still, it was clear that this was where Matthew did his entertaining. The rich plainness of my chamber was repeated throughout the Thorn, and this room was governed by the same solid panelling, which still smelt fresh, like sawdust. On the table were good candles, waiting in their brackets to be lit; the kind that when we were children would have been brought out only for guests.

'Well,' Matthew said, but then Grace came in. I smiled at her, but as she set her tray down, she did not meet my eyes. Drawing a small side table nearer, she put a jug and two cups on it, as well as a platter of cut bread and cheese, glancing large-eyed at Matthew as she placed each item to be certain he did not disapprove. I wondered again whether she had a liking for him, or whether it was just diligence, fear even. I studied my brother's face as she poured the ale, but he was calm under her scrutiny.

When she had wiped the mouth of the jug, I thanked her, but she did not go until Matthew nodded. As the door closed behind her, he cleared his throat. He had crossed his legs at the ankle, and he was joggling one foot, which was ever a habit of his.

'You have come alone,' he said.

I had almost forgotten that he did not know about Joseph. It was strange to be aware that, until I spoke out, for Matthew, my husband was still alive.

'Joseph,' I said. 'Joseph, just after Christmas – he died.' At the edge of my sight I saw Matthew's eyes shoot to my face, but I did not meet them, in case they showed something other than sorrow. He put down the piece of bread he had chosen.

At length, he said, 'How did he – I mean, how?'

'A fellow from his church set up gunsmithing.'

Matthew frowned, waiting, but I knew he would have noticed the slip – *his* church. I pressed my lips together.

'There are plenty of contracts to fill, with how things

have been,' I said. 'They were taking folk on, at a piece rate. You remember Joseph helped the smith in Manningtree for a time? He knew about metal. They thought he would have a feel for it. Apparently.' I swallowed, looked down. I did not want to describe it. 'He was testing one of the new guns, and it blew itself apart,' I went on quickly. 'His face, they said, and part of his chest.'

Matthew did not shake his head, or call on God, as my landlady had done. He was silent for so long that I looked up.

'They said it was no man's fault. So that's something,' I said, but I could not keep the tightness from my voice, for suddenly I knew that I was furious with Joseph, after all those weeks of feeling numb. I was furious with him for leaving me, and at how ridiculous the tale sounded, how clumsy, a man blown up with a gun that he himself had made. I thought that in his silence Matthew must be con- cealing gladness, or at least derision.

But my brother surprised me, for his eyes were sad; he brought out his handkerchief, tucked it into my hand. I held it up to my face. It smelt of rosemary, and of the smoke and soap and ink that could come only from a man's pocket. It smelt of Father, and that made me weep. After a while my breaths began to slow.

Matthew was watching me, leaning back in his chair. 'I am so sorry, Alice,' he said.

'But you didn't like him,' I said, into the handkerchief.

My brother leaned forward and touched the back of my hand. 'Alice. Look, it's done, now.' He paused. 'It's past. But listen. Mary Phillips told me you came here with only one box.' He dropped his voice. 'If there are debts, you should tell me now. We can settle them.'

I felt my face crumple again at the mention of money, the dull and crippling worry that had weighed on me for months. But I shook my head, tried to smile. 'There are no debts, brother. Our landlady was kind, and – I brought in a little money myself, so.'

'Oh?'

I saw that I could not speak of the scrubbing I had done. If I ever knew fifteen tricks for getting blood out of a sheet, I must forget them, now. 'I was a midwife,' I said. 'The woman who let us our rooms took a liking to me, trained me to it.' It surprised me, how easily the lie came to my tongue.

'I see,' he said, raising his eyebrows in approval. He cleared his throat, and pushed the plate of bread towards me. 'Now, please. Eat something,' he said.

While I ate, I asked him about his business. He had been another two years in Ipswich, after I had gone to London, learning his trade in the merchant's household. When he felt he had got what there was to know, including something of conveyancing as well as of trade, he had come home to set up on his own and, as he said, to be nearer to Mother. He was earning still on his interest in the mill at Flatford, and a tenancy or two that he had inherited from Father. He had taken on the Thorn to provide him with better stabling and some modest income. As he talked, I could see him growing open and easy.

'And do you hear often from our brothers?' I said. James had died, not long after Father, but Thomas and John were both in America still. They would be prosperous men, having divided James's part of Father's wealth between them.

'I write often to them,' Matthew replied. 'Most recently

about the last piece of Wenham land. I thought it right to ask them if they might wish to buy me out, before I sell it.' I knew the piece he meant, with the apple trees, beside the church. It surprised me that he could speak of disposing of Father's orchard so composedly. He must have seen my face. 'It saddens me, of course, to do it. But I have made certain improvements here.' He wiped his mouth on his napkin. 'And then I have plans for work on our mother's house. I wish it all cleared out and cleaned, painted. Everything from my old chamber thrown away, and the front bedroom needs a new bed.' He stopped, and pushed his plate away. I knew at once why the new bed must be needed. Mother's had not been a pleasant end, then.

I knew already that it would not have been her unsettled mind that had taken her, but her other illness, which had to do with her monthly terms. She never spoke of it, but I dealt with her napkins, and I had to burn them as often as wash them. It was not only the quantity of blood in them that was troubling, but the thin high scarlet of it, more like the blood that would flow if someone opened your vein.

I swallowed. 'I am sorry I did not come back,' I said. 'When she died.'

'I did not expect you to.' He looked up. 'What I mean is, it is a long way.' Though he swiftly averted them, I had seen his eyes were full.

We were quiet a minute. Then he said, 'She was gentled by it, you know. Her illness. There was nothing of sharpness by the end, nothing of discontent.' He looked down, an admission that what sharpness, what discontent there had been was most often saved for me.

She was always more tractable on Matthew's visits; she

would quietly drink for him any powders the physician prescribed. After purging, she would be calmer, and calmer still after she had been bled, and that made Matthew glad. But it made me guilty, knowing that her calm would never be more than temporary; knowing, though Matthew would not admit it, that it was not only her body that was unwell but her mind.

Watching me bite my lip, Matthew shuffled in his chair. 'Did she ever write to you? Or send you anything?'

I smiled sadly. 'A note or two in the first years.'

'Her fingers, I suppose,' he said vaguely, examining his own large knuckles.

Mother's joints, by the time of my marriage, had been too bad for much writing. She could just about sew still, having devised her own crabbed way of holding a needle, but a pen was almost beyond her.

Mary Phillips came in, then, with a pair of apples, and set them down by Matthew. I topped up our cups, reaching for something else to speak of. 'You said there is work wants doing at our old house?' I said. He nodded. 'So you mean to live there again?'

'Of course,' he said, choosing an apple. 'And you with me, Alice. It would be a weight off my mind, if you would oversee what is to be done. That is, if you wanted something, sister. To occupy your time.' He was watching my face, to see if I was pleased, and I could not help but smile.

'I did not know if you would ask me to stay,' I said.

'I feared you wouldn't want to.'

We sat in silence for a minute, Matthew concentrating on the peeling of his apple. I knew that it was dangerous to give in to my relief, but it was such a simple luxury, after all that time, to sit in silence. I see now how that winter had left an empty space at the middle of me, which was was the size and shape of a man.

And yet, our last meeting had not simply disappeared for not speaking of it; and neither had the secret in my belly. I had not forgotten what Bridget had said, about the fine new friends my brother had made among the men of the town; about the piece of witch nonsense. I knew I would have to tread carefully with him: though as a child Matthew had been as superstitious as Mother, I knew he would not wish to think of himself thus.

I had not forgotten, either, Grace's awkwardness over my visit to Bridget. So as I took a piece of the peeled apple, I sat back and lightly said, 'Bridget told me she got over to see Mother the day before she died.' I felt Matthew look at me. Then I added, 'I was there, this afternoon. I was pleased to hear her say so. Mother must have been comforted by it.'

A moment passed, Matthew flicking his knife out of the slit in its wooden handle and then in again; out, then in. 'I did not think you would have been to see her yet,' he said.

'I had to tell her about Joseph,' I said, and when he did not reply at once, I added, 'She's moved – did you know? She said that it was because Sir Harbottle raised her rent. She called him your friend. If it is true that you have his ear, then it's a shame you could not speak to him about it.'

Matthew cleared his throat, and when he spoke, his voice was brisk. 'Did she mention the will?'

'What?'

'Did Bridget mention Mother's will?'

'No. What do you mean?'

'Ah.' He put the knife down, blade out. 'I had intended to

write to you about it. But then you said you were coming, and so – What it is, Mother amended things, the day she died. She had me call in Richard Edwards to witness it,' he said. 'Her ring, her Bible, things of that nature, she has left to Bridget.'

I looked at my hands. Why had Bridget not said anything?

'I'm not sure how to put it,' Matthew went on carefully. 'Well, if you remember, it is a gold ring. I heard from Grimston that Bridget couldn't keep up with the rent. I thought she might try to sell it.' He spoke as if it was a purely legal matter.

'I see,' I said. I had to swallow, hard, for I felt a tightness in my throat. That Mother should have done this, in anger at my abandoning her. For though she had been difficult with me, I had spent near every waking moment with her during my time in Manningtree. And she would often say that when she died, her good gold ring would come to me, though whenever she spoke in that manner I would always take her hand, and tell her to hush.

I did not care about the ring itself, but what it meant – her leaving it to someone else. That was a blow; and a blow, too, that Bridget would conceal it from me.

Matthew stood up. I thought I had made him awkward, for though he had earlier given me his handkerchief, in the past he had never liked a crying woman, and I knew my eyes were full. But as he moved from his chair his dog set up whining, pacing back and forth towards the door. Rather than look at me, Matthew stooped to sweep the crumbs carefully from the side table into a cupped palm, and cast them into the fire. Then, as though it was an afterthought, he said, 'Our mother did leave you her clothes.'

'I see,' I said. A tear escaped down my face.

Matthew turned away to the hearth, the door opened, and Grace came in with a tray.

'Forgive me, master,' she said. The dog made a sound, and began to nose around Grace's feet. Perhaps it was the sight of my red eyes, but loading the tray she fumbled the plates and dropped a crust, which fell to the floor. Bending to fetch it, she knocked the table.

'For God's sake, Grace, careful,' Matthew said, and the dog, going for the crust, got under his feet. He seized it quick, gripping the loose flesh behind the ears hard enough that the dog's eyes stood out white from its pulled skin; then he half threw the animal towards the door. '*Out,*' he shouted, and it yelped and retreated, disappearing ahead of Grace as she crept out with her loaded tray.

I tried not to meet Matthew's eyes, tried not to breathe. The thought came to me that from now on every morsel in my mouth, every stitch on my back, would come from him.

Matthew stood quite silent, and then, 'Forgive me,' he said, in an ordinary voice. 'I was going to speak of the will another day.' He turned towards the fire and stood there for a moment, looking into the flames. 'I have papers to get on with,' he said.

I got up, hastily dabbing at my eyes. 'I could go and sit by the kitchen hearth, if I'd disturb you in here,' I said. I wanted to be near someone. Even Mary Phillips's hard face would have been a comfort.

But Matthew replied, 'Why not go to your chamber, Alice?' He crouched to put another log on the fire. 'I'm sure you need to rest.'

Climbing the stairs, I put out my hand to the rail, and

noticed it shaking. In my chamber, my own fire had burned low. I thought of Father, how often he would tell Mother to rest. Tell her she was tired, as though she were a child. But she would always agree: 'I am tired, James,' she would say, and pass a hand over her eyes. I shut my chamber door behind me, and leaned against it, thinking over what had passed.

It was mention of Bridget, I thought, that had made Matthew angry. He had changed when I had spoken of her new house. That was when he had grown brisk and talked about the will. But it was strange. Though he had never loved Bridget, it was my marriage to Joseph that had truly displeased him. Yet tonight, he had tolerated talk of Joseph as sweetly as anything. But when I had spoken of Bridget?

I thought of the look in Matthew's eyes, as he had restrainedly swept up the crumbs from the table. It had not been one of dislike. It had been one of hate, concealed under only the thinnest of veils.

Here a minister speaks of the best method of watching; see further notes on the same, in the Tendring file.

Having taken the suspected witch, she is placed in the middle of a room upon a stool, or table, cross-legged, or in some other uneasy posture, to which if she submits not, she is then bound with cords, there is she watched and kept without meat or sleep for the space of 24 hours. For within that time they shall see her imp come and suck; a little hole is likewise made in the door for the imp to come in at: and lest it might come in some less discernible shape, they that watch are taught to be ever and anon sweeping the room, and if they see any spiders or flies, to kill them. And if they cannot kill them, then they may be sure they are her imps.

7

I made sure to be up early the next morning, ready for church. Washing my hands, I thought of the woman from the inn at Chelmsford, who had looked at my palm and then turned so pale. The memory did nothing to help me feel calm, but as I scrubbed my face and neck, I was already making my excuses for Matthew: surely he had been tired, frayed. Perhaps it was the fifth time the dog had acted up that day. Perhaps Grace was habitually clumsy, and deserved some admonishment.

I dressed with care, noticing how difficult it was becoming to lace myself tightly. Brushing my hair, I tried not to brood on Mother's will, on the mute way she had found to punish me for my neglect. As my night's sleep had drained me of alarm over Matthew, what had filled me in its place was aggrievedness, that Bridget should have inherited what ought to have been mine, and not had even the good grace to tell me so to my face.

I thought of how she had hurried to tidy things away when I came to her house the day before. What if it had been Mother's Bible she had whisked from the table? What if she had been working Mother's gold ring off her finger and into her pocket, out of sight? The thought, once planted, was hard to dismiss. Then there was the knowledge that she had been to see Mother the day before she died: the day before she amended her will. But though I was hurting,

I was certain that it would be explained, just as I was certain that my brother could not be involved in anything unpleasant.

When Matthew came down, he greeted me cheerfully without quite looking me in the eye. He had a brown leather case with him, which seemed more fitted for business than for worship. As we stepped out into the passage, he said he hoped that I was well rested, and I replied that I was. Grace brought me my hood, then stood back to let us out of the front door.

There was a hill to climb up the lane to the church. It was not the one we had attended when we were young, the newer one nearer the docks in Manningtree; this was the other church, the one I had been married in. From Bridget's letters, I knew that there was a different minister now. The day was fine, almost warm, with small high clouds; in the sunlight, I found my eye could pretend it saw a first show of green in the fields and hedges.

As we walked, Matthew did not speak of the night before. Rather, he said, 'I should think that many folk will remember you.' Then he glanced at the houses we were passing, and began to tell me who had been born in them since I had been gone, and who had died. We passed a short row of cottages, and Matthew said, 'I did the papers for Sir Harbottle Grimston, when he bought these last year. These are his tenants now.'

Thinking to speak while I had my courage, I said, 'Brother, I hear that you have been helping him – Grimston. Scribing, for certain proceedings that are to be taken in the town.'

We had reached the church gate. Matthew stopped. 'He

is my client, Alice. I cannot discuss his business in the street.'
His voice was gentle, no more than reproving. He held open
the gate for me, then squeezed my arm and tucked it into
his own as we set off up the path. 'Come and meet everyone
again,' he said, and then we were at the church door, and he
was returning the greeting of Richard Edwards, who had
hailed him, and I saw Matthew grasp his hand, his smile
never faltering.

Once we were inside the church, more people wished
Matthew good day. He introduced me to several, and I did
remember them, after Matthew reminded me of their names.
Those who had been parents when I left were some of them
now grandparents; most of the girls of my own age keeping
eagle eyes on their own little children. Likewise most, I
could tell, remembered me. Some took my hands, and told
me how good it was to see me looking so well and how
much they had loved Mother, but none asked after Joseph. I
do not think they had forgotten I had been married; I think
they were too polite to mention it, and though they must
have suspected that my mourning was for my husband as
well as for Mother, it was easier to give their condolences
only for her. I saw it might have had a certain weight, their
tact, their politeness, which since my marriage to Joseph
my brother would have had to withstand.

I waited behind Matthew while he talked, glancing around
for Bridget. I could not see her, but as we at last filed into a
pew near the front, I noticed the new minister making his
way forward to the pulpit. In my experience of those who had
come to dine with us in the vicarage at Wenham, there were
two kinds of men who were ministers: those, like my father,
who looked as though after preaching their sermon they

might find it agreeable to spend an hour digging over their vegetable gardens – solid men, with outdoor complexions – and then the thin, earnest kind, who looked as though they most often did forget to eat. This new minister, I noticed, was thin, but more as though whatever he ate he would burn up too quickly. He was young, with the kind of curly brown hair that will never look tidy, however closely it is cropped.

I turned away from him, as the rustle of the congregation sitting down faded. I looked around again for Bridget, among the servants and labourers gathered at the back, but she was still not there.

The new minister preached simply but well. I found I could follow what he said without watching his lips, so I used the time to look about me. The church had changed since Dowsing had visited. While I had been in London, Bridget had written to us of him, William Dowsing: a little, wiry man, who held a piece of paper from the Earl of Manchester and had travelled the length of the county breaking church statues, beating the Latin prayers off bells, and getting paid to do so. I knew there was hardly a church round about that had escaped his loving attention.

There was a plain light, now, there in the church, with the coloured glazing gone. The hands had been knocked off the praying saints that stood guard over each pillar, making the figures appear more, not less, beseeching; surely not what the great man had intended. As I listened to the sermon, the saints met my eyes piteously, holding out their martyred stumps. I tried to remember the warm day I had been married there, when the building had felt blessedly cool, smelling gently of stone. Now, even with the bodies packed into it, the place was chill.

68

My mind went back to the day in London when I had given in, and gone to Joseph's so-called church. I did it to try to bring him back to me, to mend the distance our losses had made, but before we were even inside I knew that I should not have come there. The place was too near the shambles, and you could smell the beasts and the mixture of blood and shit that is like no other smell. I thought that Joseph could not have had the right street, but then he stepped up to a door and tapped on it. When it opened I saw a crowd of faces turned towards us, whitened by the daylight. On the threshold, I hesitated.

'Shut the door,' someone said.

The room was a poor ground-floor workshop, the tools and tables pushed aside, and tallow candles for light. Someone was speaking, his text taken from Romans, and the fellow blundered his way through it. I was struck by his rough voice, his certain manner, how quick he was and how sure to expound the meaning of what trained minds have fretted over for generations. But his voice, though rough, had a depth and a note and an urgency that was compelling and bound his congregation together in their rapt attention. He was a gunmaker, Joseph admitted to me later, and among the crowd were leather-sellers and cow-keepers and journeymen, apprentices from the surrounding district.

As I listened to the man preach, I thought how his star must be rising, with the times disordered, the sky so red with war. Today a poor workshop, but tomorrow where might he not go? A man who has taught himself to read. Who, though his voice is rough, when he speaks somebody listens; and more like him, in a hundred cellars across London.

In a pause between speakers, Joseph steered me to the

side of the room, where there was a large tub, of the kind great laundries use. I thought it was empty, until a drip from the ceiling landed in the water below. Joseph saw me looking. 'That is where folk are baptized,' he said. 'They must crouch, and put their heads under.' He saw my face. 'They are full-clothed, when it happens,' he said, but I dare say I did not seem comforted. Indeed I brooded on it, as we walked home: you could be arrested, hauled before a magistrate, for dipping folk. God knew I was no Papist, but it seemed my husband had gone the other way, had fallen in with those who do not care about the law or the old ways of doing things, those who think they can make the Bible mean whatever they say it means.

It was a month or so later that Joseph came home wet through from his collar to his hose. He was elated, and though the weather was cold it was all I could do to make him sit near the fire. His smooth head with his hair plastered down looked as round as a child's when I put a blanket about him; even in the act of wrapping him warmly, I could feel my husband slipping away from me. Later, as I lay next to him in bed, he felt entirely cold, like corpse-flesh.

†

After the service I stood waiting, hands folded, for Matthew to finish speaking with his friends. I was aware of the minister shaking someone's hand near the front of the church, before he made his way up the aisle towards the doors. I expected him to pass me by, but instead he stopped and smiled. He had nice hands; no wedding ring. 'A new face,' he said.

'Sir, I am Master Hopkins's sister.' He waited. 'Alice. My husband lately died. We lived in London, sir.'

He bowed slightly. 'Yes,' he said. His eyes rested on my black dress, before raising themselves to my face again. 'What did you think of the sermon? If you've been living in London, you must be used to subtler preaching than mine.'

'I liked the simplicity of it, sir,' I said. I caught his merry look, felt myself reddening. 'That is – I knew what it was that you meant. Believe me, that is an advance on many of your London preachers.' I met his eyes again; my face felt hot.

He nodded, and smiled. 'Well salvaged, mistress,' he said. He glanced at the door, where several faces were turned towards us: they were waiting on him, to make their farewells. 'Well,' he said, gesturing towards them, 'I ought to –'

I stepped aside. 'Of course.'

As he moved away, Matthew took my arm. 'Alice. You remember Master Edwards's sister?'

There was a woman beside him, slight with brown hair, the look of a small hedge bird, a single wary eye between leaves. 'Indeed,' I said. As Matthew turned away, the woman offered her hand. I tried to dredge up what I knew of her: five years older than I, or ten. She lived with her brother, Richard, and his wife – Ruth, that was her name.

'I'm sorry about your husband,' she said. 'The Lord rest his soul,' she added, with a pious look.

'I thank you,' I replied. 'Amen.' The hum of sober conversation was rising up around us, each murmured exchange confusing the others. I was no longer used to crowds. Close by us, I was distracted by a pair of women, who were trying to decide whether the winter's last frost had come down.

'You don't have children?' Ruth Edwards said.

I smiled, shaking my head. 'No.'

'Well, I suppose that will make it easier.' She must have seen my expression. 'To start again,' she added. I could have been mistaken, but I thought she then flicked her eyes to the church door, where the minister stood. I felt myself colouring again, not knowing how to answer. I could not tell whether she had meant it unkindly, but as I tried to think whether I had stood or laughed in a way that was improper, I heard one of the women beside us say, 'For certain, Rebecca West is accused for a witch as well.'

In shock I turned full towards the women, catching their attention as I did so. I did not know either of them. One frowned, for it was clear I had been listening. She touched her friend's arm, and together they turned away.

'Ruth,' someone else said then, 'we're going,' and I turned back to Ruth Edwards. She was staring at me, and her face was thoughtful.

But suddenly Matthew was there and I had to take my leave of four people or five, then stand still and avoid the minister's eye while Matthew shook his hand at the door, all the time thinking, *Rebecca West*. Remembering Bridget saying how others had been accused. Rebecca West was a name I had once thought never to hear again, and it turned me cold to hear it so soon after I had been thinking of Joseph. It turned me cold, to hear it spoken of in the same breath as witchcraft.

And yet it made a grim sense, I thought, as I walked behind Matthew out of the church. For Rebecca West's mother, Anne, had been accused of it once before, I remembered, in one of those infrequent suits so clearly a product of small local dispute that the judge would throw them out almost before he had drawn breath. For unlike Bess Clarke, Anne West had clean fingernails, and most of her own teeth, and she had never been a burden on the parish. She was not from Manningtree, but had moved there from further south, three years after us; a widow, and before that a sailor's wife.

Instead of going to church, Anne West would wait at the lych gate afterwards, selling an infusion that the women found good for their cramps, the ointment they liked for their babies' scalps. Doubtless it was no harm, a bit of grease and scent. She could easily have gone around the houses with the stuff, passed the jars close-handed in warm kitchens, as most women would. But she liked to taunt the Lawford minister, John Edes, a red-faced man even without provocation. When his pigs got rotten mouths, he had found it easy to know who to blame; but Anne West had eventually been acquitted, and that had been the end of it. I had never spoken two words to Anne West, could hardly remember her face. But of her daughter Rebecca's face, I could still picture every detail.

'Come and see our mother's grave,' my brother said, interrupting my thoughts, and he led me around the side of the church. The grave was at the southern end, in the dry shadow of a large yew. It was dim, under the tree; above, the sky was lowering, and suddenly it felt as if it would rain. No stone had gone up yet, but Matthew described the one he had sketched out for the mason. I hardly heard him.

I had thought coming back would be simple, but I saw now that it was not; that I had walked back into a thicket of something. Suddenly I felt the low simmer of threat. And though it was not aimed at me, still it made me want to hold my breath, say nothing. I knew I must try to force myself to be easy with Matthew. To be direct.

I heard him say something about the sermon, about how the minister had got to the point quicker than Father.

'For our father did have a tendency to hesitate, do you not think?' Matthew said. He stooped to pull a dandelion from the grave, working to bring up the whole of the root, and after a moment it came, white as a tooth. The question caught my attention; once, Matthew would have spoken nothing of Father but praise.

I said, 'I heard in there . . .' He did not look up at me, but cast one weed away before he began to work on another. 'I heard some women in there, talking about Rebecca West. That she is accused of witchcraft, like Bess Clarke.'

He set to work upon another weed, and the bitter scent of it rose up. 'You have to get these out this time of year,' he said. And then, 'You heard right.' He cleared his throat, and his reasonable, gentle tone did not alter. 'It is an unfortunate thing. For is not your mother-in-law friendly with Anne West? She is accused again, also. And did not the daughter live with Bridget, at one time?'

I said, 'Bridget took her in as a servant.'

I did not wish to make him angry by saying that everyone knew Anne West's arrest had been a farce. That the only reason she had even stayed in prison until her trial was for refusing to pay her bail; that had been when Bridget had taken in Rebecca, for a bit of help around the house in return for her bed and meals. I tried to sort out my feelings: I wanted to ask why Rebecca West was accused, but at the same time I did not want to know. It was not as though I liked her.

But then Matthew said, 'It might be better if you did not visit Bridget for a while. Until this business is clear.' His voice was harder. He was crouching still, over the grave, and I could see he was pulling up clumps of soil now, along with the weeds, that the dirt was thick under his fingernails.

'I don't see how this business comes near Bridget,' I said, stung. But then, watching his scrabbling hand, I said, 'Let me do that another time. Come out of the rain.' For it was just then starting, great fat drops falling into the grass around us.

Without looking at me, Matthew got up, and we both hurried towards the lych gate, and were just under the shelter when the rain began in earnest. The rest of the congregation had gone. A minute passed, two, as we watched the ground darken spot by spot, and then the spots joining and spreading. What I could see of his face by glancing sideways was stern, and I thought he was going to reprove me for what I had said, for being difficult.

But then, 'How was it, to your knowledge,' he said, 'that I was burned?'

I was bewildered. What had this to do with anything? 'You crawled too near the fire, brother,' I said. 'Your wet nurse was not watching, or her servant wasn't, and –' I broke off.

'Yes,' he said softly, then continued, more determined. 'You know I was two years in Ipswich, after you left.' I nodded. 'And you know that as well as having a hand in the grain-merchant's business, I was secretary to a lawyer there.' He looked to check I was listening. 'Once, when a will was being contested, we were obliged to bring in the witnesses.'

'Yes?' I said.

He had turned away again. 'One of the witnesses was my wet nurse.'

Silence, apart from the rain on the lych-gate roof. 'You're certain?'

'There are not many in Ipswich engaged in that occupation. She recognized my name, too. Her husband had died and she had remarried a brewer, taken to helping him in his business, demand for her old service seeming to have declined soon after I left her house. Though she did not seem to know why.' He paused. 'She said how my face had healed nicely, and that it had been a sad thing for a child to be left so disfigured. It surprised me that she would mention it. But she seemed a kind woman, so I said that she should not feel any blame, that my parents had always said I was an unruly infant and a great crawler. She was confused, when I spoke of blame, said she would never have described me as unruly. Said I came to her a week old, and stayed near two years, and never crawled an inch, under her roof, nor walked either.' He looked at me, as he finished.

'What? No, but –'

'When I explained to her the tale we were told, she was livid. She insisted I had come to her a week old. *And already marked.*'

'That cannot be.'

'Nevertheless.' He peered out at the rain. 'I thought her honest.'

'But this was – three years ago, more. Did you ask Mother about it?'

His face closed, set. 'I would not have so distressed her.'

'The woman must have made some mistake,' I said. 'Our parents, they always said your accident happened at the wet nurse's house. Why would they have said so, were it not true?'

Matthew turned to me again. 'Think when Bridget left Wenham.'

Then I saw what he meant: Bridget had left our parents' service soon after Matthew's birth. And if his accident had occurred not in the wet nurse's house but under our own roof, the roof that Bridget had shared, before she left so suddenly . . .

I put a hand on the gate to steady myself. The rain was loud on the shelter now so that I had to raise my voice to say, 'No, brother. You must have it wrong. Have you asked Bridget about it? You'll soon see how you are mistaken. Let me ask her,' I said, but then he clapped his hand over mine, where it rested on the gate.

'Don't you dare,' he said. 'You keep clear of her.' He was hurting me, but as I tried to pull my hand back I met his eyes: then I was still. 'Don't you dare speak of this,' he said again. 'To anyone.' His hand was wet, and unpleasantly soft, where the scars were.

Perhaps he was waiting for me to agree to keep silent, but I said nothing, for I was suddenly taken back to that day before my marriage, the last time we had met, and as on that day I flinched away from his gaze. A moment later, he wrenched open the gate, and walked away into the rain, while I stayed under the lych gate, watching water streaming down the road after him, clenching and unclenching the hand he had crushed.

†

I walked back to the Thorn. Matthew was not there: he must have gone to the Edwardses' house, or somewhere else. Asking a scullery maid to bring me something warming to drink, I went to my chamber, and looked out upon my small view; my brother's stableyard, and the backs of the warehouses beyond. By leaning I could see a narrow strip of the estuary, and Brantham on the far shore. I heard someone below asking about a room, and Mary Phillips saying we were full: that puzzled me, for I knew all the rooms were empty. I would have liked there to be guests in, for the Thorn was too quiet. Down in the yard I saw a stablehand leading a pair of horses out to water them; one was the mare I had ridden sometimes, before my marriage. As if he felt himself watched, the man glanced up at my window, and I ducked away from the glass, but looking inward at my dim chamber I found no better comfort.

I did not know what to make of what I had been told. Matthew did not ever lie: even as a child, he had always been bluntly truthful. He had hardly seemed to grasp the purpose of falsehood; one more thing that had not helped his popularity with the village boys.

In my mind, I walked it through. If Matthew had been burned not as a crawling infant but as one just born, days old and incapable – at just the time that Bridget had left our family's service. Father had been suspicious, always, of servants, and had often expressed that suspicion. As for Bridget, her name had never been spoken in our household until after Father's death. But then we had moved to Manningtree, and she had made herself comfortable in our lives as if she had always been there. She had benefited from Mother's will.

It made no sense. Why would Mother have protected Bridget, why would she have left her anything at all, if it was she who had been the cause of harm to Matthew?

Leaning on the sill, weary and confused, I heard a knock on the door and, thinking it was the scullery maid, I shouted to her without ceremony to come in. But it was Mary Phillips who entered, holding a cup of wine. She held it out to me, and I took it; I thanked her, but she did not turn away.

'I have seen no guests here, yet,' I said, my voice friendly, but Mary did not smile.

'The master does not wish me to take any, while he is residing here. He prefers it quiet.'

'I see,' I said, and then, when she still did not go, I said, 'Is there anything else, Mary?'

'You were at church this morning, mistress.'

'Yes.'

'Did you see Mistress Edwards there?'

'I did.'

'Do you not think she looks well?'

I paused. 'Very well,' I said, at last. Mary nodded, satisfied, only taking her eyes from me as she turned away down the stairs. I wondered if I had been too harsh in my first impression of her: whether in fact she was simply different. But she had reminded me of Ruth Edwards, and there was another thing to worry about: how barbed Mistress Edwards had been at church that day. I had few enough friends as it was.

I stayed in my chamber for the rest of the afternoon, and into the evening. At last, after I was in bed, I heard Matthew come in, and Grace bring hot water up to him; heard her set the heavy pitcher down halfway before she hefted it again to go on up the stairs. I heard her knock, and Matthew murmur his thanks. I tried to dismiss my worry, but could not prevent myself running through it again and again, coming up against the same barrier: if the negligence was Bridget's, why would our parents lie? But Matthew suspected her. That was clear. I could not avoid the certainty that, if the wet nurse had spoken the truth and he had got into the fire at a few days old, it could hardly have been an accident.

I thought of going to see Bridget. But Matthew had been so insistent that I should not speak to her of it. I wondered what precisely he thought had happened. For it pained me, in truth, to think anything other than good of Bridget. She, after all, was half the kin I had left. At last, I got out of bed and crouched to find the small pale square of Joseph's letter to her, where I had hidden it in the shoes at the bottom of my box.

It was months since I had seen my husband's handwriting. To look on the lines of direction on the letter's front took me back to London, and I remembered our arrival there, a pair of frightened children. How at first we thought we could get by on bits and pieces, but we knew no one to give us the necessary trust and tips and favours; then the war, and folk had scarce enough vigour to take care of their own. My portion was soon spent, and we changed our rooms for cheaper ones, and still Joseph found no work, and I began then to hear the whisper in my head, the whisper that grew louder day by day: that we had made a mistake in going there. A mistake, perhaps, in marrying.

I started to mention to Joseph, how you could not get ling now for under two shillings, so yet again I had got a mix of fish heads to see what I could do about a soup. I pointed out their dull, clouded eyes where they waited in the pail. I told him there would be more meatless days, if he did not get work, because rent and coal, they cost what they cost. Saying these things, I would chop at the onions more roughly, but I would not lay the knife down, even when I could hardly see for tears.

Then I began to miscarry, once and then again and again, and my husband started to go out more in the afternoons. He always left me a note, for what time to expect him home, but he never wrote where he was going. Sometimes he would come back smelling of smoke, and I would suppose he had been to an alehouse. Other times he would come back not smelling of smoke, and I thought he must be seeing some woman; one more sweet-tempered than me. Now, I almost wish it had been a woman. A woman was the worst I could imagine then. Of course I know now he did not go to women but to preachers. To hear them speak, in cellars and back rooms. I think their words gave him some certainty, in this world that has turned so uncertain.

But for a long time I was sure it was women he was seeing, since although he had always been careful, hesitant in putting his hands on me, once we began to lose the children he hardly touched me at all: by the time he died, we were lying together once a month, or less. I did not have the words to tell him that I wanted him, whether children came of it or not. I might have wondered then whether he even desired me at all, except that he still held me close at night, in his sleep.

To sit with his letter to Bridget in my hands was to think of the days when I would find a scrap of paper to tell me he would be back at eight, the small sinking at reading such a message with all the day still left before me. But when I broke open the letter and began to read, it was as if Joseph was in the room with me: his dead voice speaking.

He greeted his mother, told her he had found employment, at a gunsmith's. *Only piece-work*, he wrote, *but it pays well. Soon they will start me doing the workings for the flintlocks, and then I will earn still more.* My breath caught as he spoke of his work, the ordinary pieces of metal and wood that he had smoothed and fitted together. That had seemed so harmless.

I skimmed over his next words, but then my eye caught on my own name. *I am glad I have found work, for Alice has shown herself so strong and capable. I think I have been near useless to her, since we came here. I think I have not done my duty in providing for her, though she has had such sorrows to bear, and I know I have fallen short in other ways. So you may see how I am the more glad now that I can finally do this one thing for her, of bringing this money home.*

I had to break off reading to wipe my face; I could not bear it, that Joseph should ever have thought himself useless in my eyes. They came back to me, all the mornings he was up while it was still dark, our last winter together, and how each day he would kiss me and whisper to me to keep safe before he went out to his work.

I made myself finish the letter, to the end where my husband sent Bridget his best love. It made me think of Bridget's letters to him, their rambling openness. There must be some reasonable explanation for Matthew's accusations, I thought. There must. For Bridget had always been one to face a mistake, not to run from it. And surely she could never have harmed a child. Why would she? She loved children: she had taken Joseph in from the street, and her love for him had shown in every word of her letters.

Lying awake, I thought, I will go and see her: never mind what Matthew said. I determined that I would work for them to be reconciled – they would need to be reconciled, when the child came. Though my resolve did not feel as firm as I tried to pretend. As I finally fell asleep, I thought, 'strong and capable'. It was like reading a stranger described.

8

The Monday morning I woke late. I had passed a fitful night, reaching out in my sleep for Joseph, probing with my cold feet between the sheets to seek the warm nook of his knee, as had been my habit when he was alive.

Grace brought water up, and told me Matthew had gone out, likely for the whole day. I thought about going to Bridget's, to ask her about Mother's will, and what Matthew had told me of meeting his wet nurse. But my resolve to do so had cooled. Perhaps it would be better to win Matthew over, I thought; get his permission to speak to Bridget about it. I could ask him, and go the next day. Instead, why should not Grace and I go to Mother's house, and make a start on what was to be done there? All I needed was the key.

A few minutes later I went downstairs and stood in the kitchen entry, watching Mary Phillips's back as she dealt with some salt cod. She had been soaking it, and now she held a bit out to one of the kitchen girls for her to taste whether it was ready: as the girl noticed me, I knocked on the door post, and said where I was going.

Mary had a civil enough face as she extracted the front-door key to Mother's house from the large bunch at her waist. She had already turned back to her fish when she said politely, 'Shall I tell the master where you'll be, mistress?'

I stopped. 'Of course tell him.'

'And shall I tell him anything else?'

She spoke so quietly, and I thought I had not caught her words – I stepped back towards her. 'What was that, Mary?' I said, but as I spoke, she turned with the bowl of salt-fish water in her hands, turned round too fast or made it look as if she had, and the soiled water spilled all down me, and the bowl fell to the floor, and shattered.

'Oh, mistress!' she said. I felt the coldness soak through to my skin. The gown would clearly need washing, but still Mary stooped to brush at it, knocking shreds of fish to the floor: I was aware of the tight roundness of my belly, scared she would feel it.

'Don't,' I said, stepping back, and as soon as I saw her face I knew that she had already guessed about the baby: that was what she had meant, about telling my brother anything else. My breath halted. How could she know?

I had to wait, soaking, while one of the scullery maids rinsed a cloth to get the worst of the mess off, and then I went back upstairs to change. In my chamber, I sat down. I had been sickly, the previous morning: it would be like Mary, I thought, to be inspecting the contents of chamber pots.

Though Matthew would not be pleased, I knew I would have to tell him soon about the child: even supposing Mary had not done it already, I could not keep lacing so tight. But I had schooled myself by then, through each long, painful time that had gone before, to keep from thinking of the baby as a true living child: not until it breathed outside me. With how unsettled matters had been since my return, I was reluctant to tell my brother this piece of news, which might soon change everything so completely.

I was reluctant to tell him that the first child in his house would not be his, but mine. That he might have to pay out himself for the upbringing of my Joseph's daughter or son. And I did not want my brother to see how my stay in his household might last the rest of my life; for it was unlikely that any new man would be keen to marry me, if it meant taking in another's child, too. I did not wish to think of any of it, for I also knew that if I did carry this baby, and it did live, then I would never be able to go back to London. I would be dependent, wholly, on my brother's goodwill, however things turned out in Manningtree.

I would wait, I decided. Though Mary seemed unkind, I thought that it could not especially profit her to tell Matthew of my condition. And any day, I thought, I might feel the child quicken. If that happened, I would tell him.

†

Troubled thoughts spoiled my pleasure in walking into town with Grace, though the day was crisp and the wind from the sea. As we drew near the square a late-rising weaver was fastening back his shutters to let the bright day in; a blacksmith waited for his forge fire to get going, leaning in the sun. A woman came out to her doorway to shake a mat, and smiled at me as she folded it in two and turned back inside. Business was going on as usual. It did not seem like a town crippled by suspicion; it seemed just as it had when I was young, if a little plainer, a little smaller, after London. Yet of the six or seven men working on the roof of the assembly rooms, repairing winter-blown slates, three were in their forties, or older, the others not sixteen. War had not left Manningtree entirely untouched.

Grace was wondering aloud what would be done about the Whitsun fair this year: Christmas had been but solemnly kept, she said, what with the cold and in obedience to the Parliament-men, but there had been nothing said so far about not feasting a little on Whitsun. 'I went my first year or two, when I came into your mother's service,' she said, 'and what they do with the ox is they put two kinds of pudding inside it, and then they roast it whole like that.' She sighed. 'I can't wait till Lent is done with,' she said, and I smiled. She had shown no sign of awkwardness after my brother's performance the other night, how he had scolded her. But perhaps she came from a household in which shouting and banging things about were simply what a man did.

Suddenly I wondered whether I should have asked Matthew's permission to come out. But no, I thought. Even when Mother's health had declined and Matthew had begun to make the decisions for our household, I had always been able to come and go freely in the daily running of it – he could hardly have prevented me, without paying someone to do the work I did. In any case, he had asked me to attend to the sorting and the renovations in our old home. So I was only doing his bidding.

It was strange to turn into South Street and see the closed shutters at Mother's house. The building was as I remembered: the tall brick face with its five windows giving out into the street, and the short stretch of gravel between the front door and the road. Grace was quiet as she held open the gate for me. Some maintenance had been kept up: though there were weeds in the gravel, the raised beds at the front, which once held strawberry plants, had been dug up and raked over. The side gate that led round to the stable had been rehung. All at once I did not feel so much fondness for the house as melancholy. What did it mean, I thought, that the wrought-iron boot-scraper by the door could outlast my husband? Aware of Grace's eyes on me, I governed myself to be steady. I fitted the key into the front door and turned it.

I let Grace go in before me. Tactfully, she excused herself and went off down to the kitchen, but I stood for a moment. In the passage were Mother's soft indoor shoes, left unregarded where she must last have slipped them off, before she ceased to be able to climb the stairs.

I climbed them myself, trailing a hand up along the wall. I went into the guest room; it still contained the same bed, with a pallet-bed tucked underneath, the whole draped in sheets against the dust. I checked the chest at the foot of the bed: linen, and under that a few men's shirts and collars, cleaned recently, by the smell. Matthew must stay here, then, I thought. I wondered whether it was for some purpose, say when he was late at a dinner in town, or whether it was for sentiment that he came.

I went along to Mother's room next, thinking to check her clothes were shut away against moths. When I opened the door, the air was very still. The bed was spread with a red counterpane; briskly, I flipped it back. Matthew was right: the mattress had been scrubbed and aired by someone, but even though the careful application of cold water had soaked most of the red out, still the yellow trace of the bloodstains remained, blossoming across the surface. It would need to be burned. The bed hangings, too, were faded and worn. For the first time, I thought of what it must be like to wake day after day and stare at that same drab canopy.

I crossed to the cupboard and opened it, and the smell

that came out was Mother. I stood, gazing at her clothes, her other things. It is peculiar to feel you are prying somewhere you should not, but to know that the only person who could catch you is dead. On the top shelf of the cupboard sat her sewing box, and my throat caught as I thought of how many times when Mother grew distant and fretful I had snarled my sewing on purpose, to give her something to untangle, something to chide me for: something to take her out of her thoughts. I looked at her clothes, where they were laid away on the lower shelves. They had a dampish smell, from her habit of putting on her clean shifts when they were not quite dry. But there was another smell over the damp, like old herbs, pleasant.

I began to look through the clothes, rummaging, trying to fight the feeling of furtiveness it gave me to do so. The gowns seemed like bodies, sleeves like arms. Shawls and cloaks. Everything had been hastily stowed, and some of the pockets were turned out: one of Mother's nurses, perhaps, searching for stray coins. At length I reached the nightgowns. All had once been white, but some now were grey with washing. Others had specific stains that had refused to fade, stains like those on the mattress, which despite Grace's undoubted efforts were still the pale, delicate yellow of butter when it melts in the pan. I was surprised to feel tears start in my eyes. These things would be good only for rags.

I felt again the sting of having been left such scraps of worthlessness, but at the same time I knew that they were all I deserved. For I felt keenly, standing there, that I had abandoned Mother. Each piece of briskness I had shown her came back to me; each wistful thought of my true mother, and all the times when, as a young, restless girl, I had secretly wished that she was still alive and in Mother's place. I shut the cupboard door: I would come another time to pack the clothes away.

As I left the room, I found I was holding Mother's warmest shawl, the red one she had worn every day. I tucked it under my arm as I shut the door behind me, and went to my own old chamber, thinking to look in there. But when I tested the door, it would not shift. Next I tried the door to Matthew's old chamber, and tried it again, using my shoulder. But it would not move. I thought of the size of the bunch of keys at Mary Phillips's belt. I placed a hand on the upper panel of Matthew's door, and then I bent to put my eye to the keyhole. I could see only the dim, draped shapes of furniture. I thought of a tale told to me once by our servant Sarah at Wenham – Sarah who had half brought me up. It was a tale in which a curious child's eye was met with a darning needle. I blinked as I went back down the stairs, and stopped in the parlour to lay down Mother's shawl and collect myself before I went into the kitchen.

Hearing me, Grace turned, holding a large, fine, glazed bowl. 'Look, mistress! I had forgotten this.'

'Some of the doors upstairs are locked.'

Grace put down the bowl. 'Yes, mistress. Your own old chamber and the master's. They were storerooms in truth, by the time your mother died, and they were always kept locked. Did Mary Phillips not give you the keys?'

I pulled out a chair from the kitchen table. 'She must have forgotten,' I said. 'In any case, let us work in here for today, and in the parlour. We can look at the bedchambers another time.'

We began with checking and packaging the dry goods

that had been left behind – oats, flour – to send back to the Thorn. As we worked, I let Grace ask questions about my life in London: I took care that what I said should match anything I had already told my brother, but still I found that I grew merry, as we worked and talked. When she asked about my midwifing, I wondered whether Matthew had mentioned it to her, or whether Mary Phillips had overheard something and passed it on. But I was ready with my answers to Grace, having spent some time recalling what my landlady had told me of her profession. I made my life in London sound charmed and easy, exciting even.

We had moved into the parlour, and Grace was helping me lift the drapes from the chairs so that I could feel each for dampness, when she paused. 'Mary said – she told me that you have lost your husband,' she said.

I straightened. 'That's right.'

'I wish – I wish you had said, mistress.'

'I suppose that God –' I began, thinking to say, 'I suppose that God will take back whom He loves.' But I halted, wishing to meet Grace's kindness with some greater honesty than that. 'I suppose it is a thing that happens,' I said. Though I had not thought it would happen to me.

I could push it aside no longer. It was melancholy to be back in the house where I had cherished my first secret liking for Joseph: where he had arrived in my life, disguised as a piece of good fortune.

I forced a smile, and turned myself to folding one of the drapes. 'You ought to marry, Grace,' I said.

Shaking out a cushion, she avoided my gaze. 'Mistress, I am happy where I am.'

That made me wonder again, about her liking Matthew.

91

Still, I felt sorry for her. Draped over the back of one of the other seats where I had placed it, I saw Mother's shawl. I took it up, ran the fabric through my hands then bundled it, and held it out to Grace. 'Here.'

'Surely not, mistress,' she said, reaching out for the shawl, stroking the material herself, admiring.

'My brother will not like to see you in it,' I said, 'but you can wear it when you leave us. When you marry,' I repeated, 'or go into service in some other house.'

Grace held the shawl doubtfully, but she did not give it back. I wanted to ask her, now that we had built up a confidence, what precisely she had meant when she said my brother had a book with witches' names in. What she had heard, and from whom. But something held me back. We went on working, and I felt the day slipping away too fast. The truth was that I did not want to go back to the Thorn: to Matthew, to Mary Phillips, and to everything else I did not understand. I had thought that a few hours away from there would leave me knowing what I should do. But I did not know. I felt even less certain than before.

†

We worked until five or so, when the light was declining; then we covered the piles we had made in the parlour with dust-sheets, and stood looking at what we had accomplished. Then I said, 'Why don't we stay?'

'Beg pardon, mistress?'

'We could stay the night.' I saw her face turn wary. 'It is what I often did in London, with long birthings. Why walk back to the Thorn only to come again in the morning?' The bed and pallet in the guest room, I thought, would serve. It might even be pleasant, to hear breathing in the night again that was not my own.

'Will it be all right?' Grace said, uncertain.

'Of course,' I said. 'I will answer for you to Mary.'

So Grace lit a fire, then went to the Bell to get us some cold pies and have a boy sent over to let them know at the Thorn that we would not be back. I went upstairs to make the beds, and when Grace returned, we uncovered the two chairs nearest the hearth and sat with our plates, the rest of the furniture crouched around us as darkness came down.

'I know nothing of you, Grace,' I said. 'Your family, where are they from?'

She finished her mouthful. 'My people are from Cambridge,' she said. 'Though my mother and father, they are both dead.'

'You have no kin here?' I said.

'Mary Parsley, she is my second cousin,' she said.

'Ned Parsley's wife?'

Grace nodded. Had not Bridget said something about Ned Parsley, about his child dying?

'Grace,' I said. 'I have been thinking on what you said, the night I came here: about my brother having a book of witches' names.' She put down her pie crust. 'Can you tell me, to your knowledge, of what Elizabeth Clarke is accused?'

'I believe that the Rivets did refuse her some alms,' Grace replied. 'And then, soon after, Goodwife Rivet was taken in a fit.'

'I see,' I said, though I did not, and Grace seemed disinclined to say more. I could tell she thought it odd, us staying there at Mother's house, and I was beginning to worry that it was odd, that I had made the wrong decision.

While Grace took our dishes through, I picked up a book of sermons. When she had finished in the kitchen, Grace came back to settle in her chair, and soon began to doze. Trying to read, I could not prevent my mind flitting between how agitated Matthew had been after church and, at the same time, how ridiculous it was that he should suspect Bridget of having any hand in harming him. I could not settle to the sermons: the language of them seemed in some strange cadence, which had me thinking of the sing-song way we had been made to learn our catechism when we were small. I laid the book aside.

Cold, I edged my chair closer to the fire. Sitting there made me think of when the chimney-sweepers had come, those friends of Joseph's, and knocked a thing down that had smashed in the grate. It was one of those bottles, witch bottles some called them, which folk put in their chimneys to catch anything that might try to come down: come down in some altered shape, wanting to get into the house. In sweeping up the fragments, I had swept up also a ball of hair, foul with soot. Matthew had been out of the house on some errand; Mother got herself worked up about the thing having been displaced, and made me put just the same contents – the hair, the rusty bent pins – into a different bottle. Sealing it up with ordinary wax, I had felt uneasy, thinking that Father, surely, would never have approved such a proceeding. But Mother had made me get the sweeping men to stow the bottle again, in the same niche inside the chimney: it was up there now, not three feet above where I was sitting.

I wondered if it truly afforded any protection, as the superstition holds it does. I remembered once when Bridget had spoken of how, when I was tiny, she would trim my fingernails with her teeth, casting the clippings straight onto the blaze that no one might get hold of them and use them to do me harm. I remember she caught my look, as she said this, then added that it was the usual practice of most mothers and nurses, and rather careful than ungodly.

Listening to Grace breathe, I stretched myself. I had hoped that Matthew and Bridget would have reconciled, in the years I had been away, but instead my coming back to Manningtree had been like entering a room where two people are sitting; they may have fallen quiet, but you know that in your absence something has been done, something said. I wished Father was there to counsel me, and not only about Matthew and Bridget, but about other things. What a person should believe, and not believe.

In the distance, Lawford church clock struck ten. I got up to stand over the fire, held out my arms to it; with my foot, I nudged Grace. 'Go to bed.' My voice brought her awake, and she clutched the arms of the chair.

She rubbed her face. 'Are you coming, mistress?'

'In a while. You might bring me a blanket, before you go.'

She brought one, and then went up, yawning. It was pleasant to hear her moving about overhead as she settled herself, but the comfort soon died away. Hunched in my chair, listening to Grace's snores carry down the stairs, I tried to read again, to distract myself, a household book of Mother's: how to preserve green walnuts, make a poultice for a hot wound.

†

I woke with the book in my lap, and a hammering at the front door as if someone was trying to break it down. The fire was almost out, and I heard Joseph calling my name: *Alice, Alice!* It sounded as if he was crying. I scrambled to my feet, but then the cold brought me round and I stopped, because of course it could not be Joseph. I stood still, rooted by the certainty that it had been Joseph's voice I had heard, and if it was not him then it was something else, using his voice. Then it came louder – 'Alice!' – and I heard the panic in it and I thought: Matthew.

I felt along the hall. Even fumbling with the door I was doubtful, but then I got it open and my brother was there, solid and panting.

'Alice, thank you – where's your light?' He was trembling, clinging to the door and in the way of me getting it shut. I felt his dog slip past me into the house.

'I'll get one, just come in,' I said. His breathing was so fast in the dark I laid a hand on his chest to calm him, or to convince myself that he was truly living and himself. The air was cold. 'Matthew. Matthew,' I said, 'what are you doing here? What is it?'

'I thought – there was a – God!' His voice cracked. 'There was something there, just there.' He was holding the doorframe for support, and pointing into the dark. All I could make out were the empty strawberry beds, the gravel and the quiet road beyond.

'Matthew, take a breath. You're all right. Now, what, out here?' Once I was sure he was not hurt I had almost teased him for making such a racket, but I saw now that his fear was real.

He was at my shoulder, almost hiding behind me. I turned to see his eyes searching the raised bed just beside the front door. 'Just there.' He pointed, whispering. 'It was

96

sitting in the strawberry bed. I didn't see it till I was close, and then I cried out. I dropped my keys. I think it ran –'

'Well, a fox, then?' I said.

'Hush! No. I don't know. It was like one, of that size, but it was black, I don't know –' He let go of my arm, but then he swayed, and took hold of it again.

'Perhaps it was a loose dog,' I said quietly.

He was starting to get his breath. 'It wasn't a dog.'

'What are you doing here?' I said to him. 'Where have you been?' I heard a noise from behind us and saw Grace already on the stairs, tucking herself in with one hand and holding up a lamp. 'Matthew, why don't you come in now?' I tried to guide his elbow. 'You should have something to drink.'

He resisted. 'Alice. I think it was sent. I think it was sent to wait for me.'

'Come now, brother –'

'My keys,' he said.

I lowered my voice. 'Brother. Why don't you come in? I'll go and check outside – you warm yourself.' I gestured to Grace. 'Give me that light. Take the master into the parlour and get some wine for him, something strong if it can be found. And then you go and look him out a spare shirt. There are some upstairs.' Matthew did not look as if he wanted to let go of my arm. I prised at his cold fingers. 'I won't be a minute, brother,' I said. I felt myself pretending to be brave, though I didn't know whether for him or for Grace, who was waiting, looking fearful and cold.

He looked as if he would speak, but he allowed Grace to take his arm. When she had led him into the parlour I stepped outside, and shut the front door behind me. It was a moonless night, and I could hardly see black shapes from darker black, though I could make out a small light on the river or beyond it, and nearer at hand the thickness of the hedges. The wind from earlier had dropped. I could see nothing shining in the gravel. I felt my breath catch in my throat, and told myself it was only the deep cold and still-ness, which do always make a feeling of waiting. I had been going to walk out as far as the gate, but suddenly I did not dare: quickly I turned back inside, feeling almost foolish at my relief when the door opened to my touch. I bolted it firmly behind me.

I found my brother by the parlour fire. Grace had left him a shirt to warm, but he was shaking too much to unfasten the one he was wearing.

'Matthew.' I put his hands away from their fumbling. 'Just let me do it,' I said, and to my surprise, he let his arms drop and stood still, patient as a child.

'Alice –' he said. Grace dropped something in the kitchen and we both twitched. 'Did you see anything?'

I shook my head. Close up, his face was covered with standing sweat, like a horse gets, ridden hard in the cold.

'My keys?'

'I could not see them. I'll look in the morning. I'll find them then. But listen, brother. Where have you been?'

'I've been at Bess Clarke's.' He closed his eyes. 'Thank God you were here. I went to Richard Edwards's house after. He asked me to tell him when we were stopping for the night. I thought to walk back to the Thorn, but then I did not like to – and I remembered Mary said you were here. But – it must have followed me.' He closed his eyes.

'What were you doing at Bess Clarke's at this hour?' I

said. I wanted to say, 'Stopping what for the night?' but I did not dare.

He opened his eyes. 'The worst thing is, it made no sound. Not even breathing. You couldn't even see any eyes . . .' His breath began to come faster.

I had got his shirt undone. 'Brother. Let us speak of it tomorrow, then, eh? Let it be in the daylight.' I signed for him to lift his arms; it made me think of the times I had helped him when we were children, and in his sleep he wet himself. When we were between servants, or the ones we had were deep sleepers, and Matthew's dreaming cries woke Father, who would come to our chamber and frown over what Matthew had done, speak plainly to him about how his dreams were not real. I used to keep spare linen in our chamber, and I would always have to help Matthew with it, for his fingers were sometimes too cold to unknot the ties at the throat of his nightshift by the time Father went away.

I went to hang Matthew's damp shirt by the hearth, then turned to him with the fresh one. My brother's body was not like Joseph's. It was pale even in the firelight, almost hairless. The marks on his neck and forearms were pink still, a yellow-pink, not silvered, for they had never seen air or sun. I stepped to him with the dry shirt and pushed it over his head, feeling that I should not have looked. I heard Grace come in with the wine before I had got it done up properly; Matthew stared over my shoulder as I finished the last knot.

'Forgive me,' Grace said, behind me, and I turned, took the cups from her.

'Brother, sit down and drink that,' I said. Then, 'Grace.

You may find us two more blankets, and then you may go back to bed.'

She looked awkward, her eyes directed around my knees. 'Yes, mistress,' she said.

When I had Matthew settled in his chair, a blanket tucked around his lap, and another around his shoulders, I sat and drank my cup of wine. He placed his on the arm of his chair and let his head drop backwards, resting his skull on the chair's hard back. I dug underneath myself, and passed him a small cushion.

I thought, This can only help my cause tomorrow. He'll feel foolish, not only about this business but about carrying on in such a fashion over Bridget. He'll come with me to her house, and we'll talk it through. Nip it all in the bud, and I can tell him about the child, too.

Then I remembered. 'Oh. Where is your dog?' I said. 'I'll get her some water, before we put out the light.'

Matthew frowned. 'I left her at home. She was limping this morning. A splinter in her pad, perhaps.' His hand moved on the arm of the chair as he looked at me. 'What is it? Why?'

I had gone cold for I had felt something, I was certain. When I had opened the front door for Matthew, it had pushed past my legs. It was hard to keep my eyes from leaping to the corners of the room and the shadows there, but I governed myself, thinking, I am imagining things, I am tired. I must not alarm him. 'Nothing,' I said, but when he leaned over to put out the light, I touched his arm. 'Why don't we leave it?' I said.

I drew my chair up close to Matthew's, trying not to look into the shadows, to dismiss what I thought I had felt.

Trying not to think of what I might have let into the house, besides my brother.

To help my courage, I began to hum, and as I did I let Matthew drop his head bit by bit onto my shoulder, to hear the music coming through the bone. As he slackened into sleep, I left off my humming, for I could feel the tremble and catch in my voice. I told myself it was only that I had got cold outside. But I was astonished that I did not wake my brother, with the way the very core of me was shaking.

9

I have told you how the boys in Wenham did disdain my brother Matthew when we were little children, for his scars, for his fastidiousness, because he could not run for long. What I have not told you is that when I was twelve years old, all that changed: something happened, which won him their respect.

It was an afternoon when I had been sitting with Mother, as Father had begun to ask me to do; he had sent Matthew out, to get some fresh air and stretch his legs. It was cold, and February, and it was dark before he was missed. Father looked and shouted around the church first before rousing a couple of the stouter men who lived near us, who each roused a couple more. All of them brought out their dogs, and their sons ran along too, more gawping than helping as the fathers thrashed and yelled in the woods, while I stayed at the house, and tried to keep Mother calm.

When he heard Father calling the first time, Matthew had shouted from the bottom of the fresh-dug grave, but the earth had swallowed the sound. It was someone's dog that found him in the end, when they went over the churchyard again and the animal panted and strained towards the great hole with the mounded earth beside. When the searchers all peered over the edge with lights, there was Matthew, blinking up at them, smear-faced but calm. Ropes were brought and they got him out – no small task, as he had turned his ankle – and for the rest of that week I made him sit by the fire. There had been a quantity of water in the hole, and there was the suspicion of a cough, but it surprised me that, though his ankle pained him, he did not seem distressed.

The next week, the village lads were eager to crowd around him, to hear what it had been like. With each of their retellings it was not the dog but a different one among them who had found him. Were you not frightened, they asked Matthew, when you fell in the grave? 'But it wasn't a grave,' I heard my brother reply. 'It was only a hole.'

I knew then that Matthew had finally taken to heart Father's words, on the nights when he dreamed and cried out and Father came in to explain patiently how this thing he was afraid of, this horror, it was just a shadow on the wall, or the sound of a tree branch tapping on the window. I saw Matthew's pride in being able to amaze the Wenham boys simply by shrugging, and calling the grave a mere hole in the ground. But those boys had not seen what I had seen, his many nights of waking and weeping. They did not see how it was the thinnest of tricks: if a thing frightens you, to call it something else. They did not see that to classify a thing away from fearfulness rather shows fear, than any lack of it.

†

I cannot now think of the grave day without thinking, therefore, of the notes my brother must have taken, soon after that night of Bess Clarke's watching. After he had come running to Mother's house, after his brief loss of courage there in the dark. The notes have stuck in my memory, since the day I finally seized my chance to read them, for their cold calmness. How Matthew described Bess Clarke in the briefest terms: old, widow, lame of one leg. How he did not call her by her name, but rather only 'the accused'.

He noted at first that they had walked her a little, up and down the small parlour. Then they placed her on a stool, the accused, legs drawn up painfully so that she might be watched in case any of her imps came near her skirts to be fed. They alternated the sitting with the walking, not for any ease or comfort but in whatever manner would most weary her. Neither sleep nor food was permitted, while they waited for her supposed imps to come.

My brother noted the smell in the accused's house; how he pressed his kerchief to his nose the whole time. After the walking, they had kept her sitting for three hours, and then some of the women had taken her to use the chamber pot, but when they brought her back she had seemed in pain. She had begun then to laugh a horrible bold laugh and my brother had known from the suddenness of the change that the devil had come upon her.

Between the laughing she would call out, 'Holt, Ho-olt', like that, as you would call to a toddling child. But nothing came, nothing. Then she called out again, in a strange dry voice, 'Jermarah!' And a thing bolted down the stairs, through the room and out into the kitchen. Some there thought it was a stag, but Matthew noted that it was certainly a greyhound, but of great size. Yet when someone went in with a light, there was nothing in the kitchen to be seen.

It was decided then that the women should go home, so one of the other men took them. When they had gone, Bess Clarke brought out something from under her wraps. 'This here is Elimauzer,' she said. 'He was out on an errand for me when you came before.'

But one of the men said, 'Come, madam, enough of this silliness. That is a rabbit.'

At which she smiled. 'It may look like one,' she said, 'but if I gave the word he would squeeze himself down your throat and lay a feast of toads in your belly.'

When ten o'clock passed, Matthew noted that the accused became sleepy, so she was walked again, up and down, up and down, between two of the other men. They began to ask her more questions: you could ask her any question then and she would answer. One of them said, 'How long have you been lying with the devil?' And she said, 'Oh, six years, seven. When he comes he will not wait. He presses my hand and says, "Bess, I must lie with you."' She said, 'I killed Richard Edwards's pigs. The devil pestered me into it.' She said, 'He wouldn't leave me alone.'

But Matthew noted that the accused would not admit any of the murders they put to her. Two more women from Lawford, a clothier's child: she did deny them all. Denied them, and said she did not know what had done for them, but Anne West, that one, she would know. Then one of the men said, 'What about my brother, when his ship broke up, and only a mile off Harwich? Was that Anne West, too?'

And she said, 'It was, it was her.'

I still think now of Bess Clarke's addled face, her small intelligence. She would have been broken with tiredness, that night; shitting herself with fear. She would have been trying to work out what they wanted, those men, what would make them go away. To work out the mix of truth and show that would leave her alive and them satisfied. A name would have suggested itself, one which was a fit. One with whom she had few dealings; not an enemy, but not a friend either.

I wonder now if she was angry at being brought to the end of her courage. Perhaps she simply did not like Matthew's face. For as the men were making ready to leave, she called out, 'Master Hopkins – do not fear. I have asked one of my children to see you safely home.'

When I came across my brother's notes of that night, and saw his bland formality as he spoke of Bess Clarke, I knew it at once for fear. That night on the doorstep, unmade by panic, that was the true feeling that hid beneath his calm procedure, his chilling attention to detail. He suppressed it most perfectly, but still it was there: a child's fear. For I am certain that, despite his proficiency, my brother still believes in the devil as a present fact, as you or I might believe in the moon in the sky.

When Matthew was seven, I remember, he came indoors from a dimming November day and said he had spoken with the devil. Father, humouring him for once, asked, 'What did the devil say?'

And Matthew answered, 'He asked where we keep the axe for the logs. He asked if there is a screen on the kitchen fire.'

Father looked at Mother. 'You mustn't be fibbing like that,' Father said. Mother had hidden her mouth behind her hand. 'Talk about something else,' Father said, 'or don't talk at all.'

Later, in the chamber we still shared, I hissed across from under my covers to ask how he had known it was the devil. Did it have horns?

'He had no smell,' Matthew replied, quite plainly and with no trace of deceit. 'He was like a man, but he smelt of nothing.'

10

When I woke in my chair, the one beside me was already empty, set back in its proper place, the blankets folded and draped over the arm. My limbs felt squashed and sore and grubby, and the grate was cold. I was chilled right through, my own blanket having slipped to the floor. All the corners of the parlour that had lain in shadow were full of plain daylight, and straight away I felt ashamed of myself, of the nonsense I had imagined, as I tried to neaten my clothes.

I found Matthew in the kitchen, and Grace serving him what I had not eaten of our poor supper. She clattered the dishes, her arms red with cold below her rolled-up sleeves, and avoided my eye. Matthew looked impatient.

'Good morning, brother,' I said. 'I hope you slept.'

He cleared his throat. 'It hardly matters. I am accustomed to very little.'

I smiled. 'I think we were jumping at shadows, brother.'

'I am sorry if you did suffer any alarm,' he said, but he would not meet my eyes.

Grace stood waiting with my beer. I took the cup from her, but she did not move. I said, 'Thank you, Grace,' and then she went out of the room. 'What passed at Bess Clarke's house?' I said, making my voice firm.

'It's not a business fit for your ears, sister.'

Lightly, then, I said, 'Well. Perhaps we can speak later.

For certain we had better get back, once I have drunk this.'

'You go,' he said. 'I must see Grimston. His agent is ill. I have said I will help him with the quarter rents.'

'Now, brother,' I said, 'listen. You had a fright last night. You had a shock, undoubtedly. But I beg you, think of it. What in truth did happen? What did you actually see?' I went on, carefully: 'Be certain that Grimston and the others are not fixing on Bess Clarke, that you are not fixing on her, simply because she lives alone, or uses ill speech, or happens to need more charity than she is offered. It would not become you to have a hand in bullying old women, however bad they may be as tenants.'

I moved closer, to pick off the bits of lint from his coat where it had been cast over a chair through the night. But Matthew stepped away from me, and brushed himself down unsteadily. Brought up short by his coldness, I saw how pale, how sweaty he still was.

'I am surprised that you would ask me about this,' he said. 'You must know it is none of your business.' He hesitated, but then he went on: 'It was convenient to me that you were here, on this occasion, Alice. I cannot deny that last night I was tired, and I was glad to find you here.' He held my eyes for a long moment, and then he said, 'But you know I cannot approve of you ranging about, not coming home at night.'

I blushed. 'I wasn't ranging about,' I said.

He turned away, gathering his papers, patting his pockets. I was at a loss.

'Well. I'll go out for your keys,' I said.

He thanked me, his voice absent; the way you thank a servant.

I unlatched the front door, and on the threshold I stood still, breathing the crisp air. I thought, He is only ashamed. Not for what he thinks he has seen, but for showing his fear to me, to Grace. That is all it is. I ought to be ashamed, too.

The morning was fine, with a soft frost. Each dead leaf on the hedge, each blade of grass, was made bright by it. A boy passed the front gate, leading a mule, and took off his hat to me. Uneasy, I scuffed out over the gravel, casting my eyes about. Beside the gatepost, my brother's keys lay neatly between the silvered leaves of a dandelion, almost as if they had been carefully tucked there. They were so cold that I held them between finger and thumb, as I turned back to the house, hoping they might soften his mood.

It was only then that I noticed the old strawberry beds beside the front door: where the frozen soil was all pressed down, packed tight, as if something large and warm had lain there, crouched in the dark, waiting. I stopped, unable to credit what I saw. But then I heard a noise inside the house, Matthew shouting up for Grace to come down, and without stopping to think I walked very fast through the side gate to the yard to find a rake. By the time Matthew came out, everything was as it should have been, the rake leaning against the wall. As he stopped on the steps, I could not tell whether he glanced at the strawberry bed.

'Found them,' I said.

Matthew was putting on his gloves. 'Straight back to the Thorn, when you've locked up here,' he said blandly.

The keys when I passed them to him were warm from my grip, though my hand itself was frozen. I tried to clutch some warmth back into it, as I watched him walk away.

I made Grace sit in the parlour while I searched the house.

I could not know what she had overheard of my talk with Matthew, but she seemed uneasy; no doubt she had gathered enough. I was fearful as I searched, half angrily, determined to prove that there was nothing there at all. I looked carefully around the kitchen, under the table, the space beneath the stairs. I searched the guest chamber, the bed tucked neat away; on the landing I tried again each of the locked doors, and even listened at them, but I could hear no movement through the wood.

In truth, I do not know what I could sensibly have been looking for: perhaps my brother's dog, secreted somewhere to be collected later. But Matthew had not left my sight the night before, and the thought of him arranging it all to frighten me made little sense; he had not known where I would be. I tried to govern myself to be calm. Matthew would be with Grimston that day, and I was already out of the Thorn. I made up my mind. I came back downstairs, and sent Grace home, telling her I had some further errands in town. She looked weary and perturbed, and it did not take much encouragement to make her gather her things and leave.

As I locked the door, hearing her crunch away over the gravel, I turned to the strawberry bed again: it looked back at me, smooth, giving nothing away. I almost wished that I had not raked over those marks, for now would have been my chance to examine them more closely, whether they contained anything that could have been the print of a boot. I tried to dismiss the feeling of whatever had brushed against my legs: tried to think that it could have been Matthew's hand, or his coat, or nothing at all.

I nearly turned away from Bridget's front door, when I had knocked on the post the third time and still she didn't come. I was loath to call out or hammer louder on the wood, not wishing to draw the notice of her neighbours. But when I tried the door, it opened.

Inside, the room was dim, the shutters still closed, and it took me a moment to see the humped shape in the chair by the hearth. Bridget got up, dragging on her shawl. 'Alice.'

On the table lay the same round of bread, half gone now and slowly drying in the air, my letter beside it. The same few bits of washing hung from the line rigged up over the fire. The fire itself was mostly ash. She had neglected to change her linen.

Suddenly I was not sure how to begin. 'I missed you in church on Sunday.' She did not answer. 'I'll speak to the minister. You won't get fined, I'm sure you will not. Not for just once.'

She looked at me. 'So now you have seen him, what do you think?' I thought she meant the minister, until she said, 'Matthew.'

I licked my lips, and put down my bag. 'He met a woman in Ipswich said she was his wet nurse. And she told him that he came to her a few days old, and already burned, already marked. He reminded me of how you left our mother's service not long after he was born.' Her eyes had not left my face, and I said, 'Bridget, you need to tell me the truth, now. If there was an accident, you must tell me. You must tell me what you know.'

I expected anger from her, but she only turned away, back to the fire. She sat down in her chair heavily. 'I am sorry he has found out. It does explain some things.' She shook her head. 'She was a good woman, that wet nurse. It was a shame, how her reputation suffered.'

I stayed standing. 'She spoke the truth, then?'

'Alice, there was no accident.' She nodded at the chair across from her. 'Your brother was burned the day he was born.' Shakily, I let myself down into the seat. Suddenly I thought I knew what it was she had to tell me.

'Your mother's labour started well enough, in the morning,' Bridget said. 'I had made her up a bed in the kitchen, for it got warmer in there, you could build up the fire larger. I judged she would have a baby before it was dark again, so your father went off for the doctor, for she would not have a midwife, none being to her liking. Then two o'clock passed, and three, and she was tiring. Your father was not back. The country was deep in snow.' She stopped, looked at me. 'You know as well as I that your mother was not right in her mind. Well, I never saw her as she was that day. I remember her pleading for a minister, pleading for your father to take out what was inhabiting her: I tried to keep her calm, told her that a minister would be neither use nor ornament, but if she would only do what I told her she would come through it. Then, your father still gone, the pains quickened, and Matthew was born.' She hesitated, choosing her words. 'He did not cry on the instant, I think he had been somewhat squashed, and his not crying, I think it troubled your mother. She said, "Why won't it cry?" And I said, "Look, it's a boy." I remember she said, "It's not a good baby, is it?" and she was asking had it all its fingers. And I said, "Hush, he's a perfect baby," and then he set up with a bit of crying, and that seemed to quiet her.'

Bridget shook her head. 'I sometimes think, if there had been someone else there, a midwife . . . if it had not snowed . . . In any case, I sat with her for some minutes, after he was out and the cord cut and the afterbirth come away. She seemed clearer in her mind than she had been as she laboured, but she would not lie quiet on the bed. She would be up and walking. At length, I persuaded her to sit in the rocking chair by the hearth. It was drawn up close to the blaze. I had put all the mess on the fire, and the baby was feeding a little, so I thought it would be all right to go out to the privy, I had not been since the morning – God forgive me, I was gone three minutes at the most. And when I came back –' She stopped.

'What?'

Bridget spoke her next words quietly. 'I came in from the yard, and I saw she was not supporting the child up to the breast, but holding him in her lap, staring at him. Like something unpleasant on a tray.' She gestured. 'She had her feet up on the hearthstone, like this. And then she looked up at me, she looked me clear in the eye, and then she just stood up. And he fell.' She joined her hands. 'He fell limp, as a child that age will, and of course did not fall full into the fire but struck the grate – his face struck the grate and his hands were in the fire. It cannot have been for more than a moment or two, but I could scarce believe – And then I was pushing your mother away, and I snatched him out. He was wailing by then, and the sound of that seemed to bring her back, and I had knocked her down when I pushed her.' She glanced away. 'But it was that moment your father came in the door. He had ridden ahead of the doctor. He stood in the kitchen doorway and stared at us, your mother weeping on the floor, myself crouching by the hearth. And he took Matthew from me, and I still think now that if I had been able to get some snow on those burns, they might have done better. The doctor was an hour behind. Your father pushed me out of the room. I heard voices raised, your mother weeping, making no sense. I hammered at the door, asked if he would not let me help her, help the baby. But no one answered. When he came out a few minutes later, I had to watch him throwing my things out into the snow around the back doorstep. And so I went.' There was a silence.

'But why – but why did she not tell him the truth?'

'She did, I think, later. But I was gone by then, settled in Manningtree.'

'But then Father – how did they lie about it, for all this time?'

'For shame, Alice. What mother wants her children to know that her mind is so poorly? What parents would wish to explain that? I think they wanted to distance that sad event from your mother entirely. And I loved her enough not to gainsay it, not even when I heard how they blamed the wet nurse. I think perhaps your mother insisted on that, so evil rumours would not follow me. Though I feel sorry for her – the wet nurse, how she suffered.' She fixed her eyes on me. 'After Matthew met her, did he never speak to your mother of it?'

'He said not. So you must tell him the truth of it, now. We must.'

There was the smallest pause. 'But would he believe it?' Bridget said. 'Folk look for someone to blame, and Matthew is no different. Perhaps it is better, if he blames me. He loved your mother well.' She looked distant. 'All those years he had the physician coming, when there was nothing he could do for her, poor lady. I do not think we can change your brother's mind now, about the nature of her illness. Though I am certain that it is no shame, but a sickness like any other sent from God. Only that you cannot put a poultice on a mind. You cannot so easily draw the poison out.' She shook her head. 'No. Even if he could be made to believe it, it would break him, send him worse. I don't mind if he hates me. It is enough that I made my peace with your mother. We were friends again, by the end.'

As she spoke, my mind was working, trying to understand. Now, carefully, I said, 'So I hear.'

Bridget frowned. 'He told you about the will.'

'Why didn't you?'

'I knew how it would hurt you. She left you her gowns?'

I nodded.

'But she left you nothing else?'

I was surprised that she would push, when she knew that the little Mother owned of value had gone to her. 'No, Bridget, nothing else,' I said, sharply.

She frowned, and reached into her pocket, brought out the gold ring, and placed it on the table with a click. 'She left me this, with her Bible,' she said.

'Matthew thought you might have sold it.'

'I don't want it,' she said, and pushed it across the table to me.

But I pushed it back. 'No, Bridget. She meant it for you,

clearly.' It made all the more sense, now, how Mother had seemed bound to Bridget; that she might have been grateful enough to leave her something of worth when she died.

Bridget studied her hands. 'You must believe me, I did not wish for this. When your mother took me in, I had nothing. She was so merry and content when I first knew her . . . She was the first soul I ever loved. I have tried always to do right by her family.'

'Then respect her wishes now. It seems clear enough she was displeased with me.'

She looked up at me. 'I do not think it was that. The day before she died, she spoke of you. She prayed for your coming.'

I bit my lip. 'That is not why I am here, Bridget. I did not come for the ring. I came to learn what is in my brother's heart.' I stood up, and paced to the table. After a moment, I said, 'You were right about Bess Clarke. My brother was at her house last night. And I heard the Wests named, at church.' I watched her face.

She was quiet, and then she said, 'Not just Anne West?'

'Rebecca, too.' It felt peculiar to say her name, after all this long time.

Bridget's face was fearful. She had always been as fond of Rebecca as I disliked her. 'I didn't know. Since you came I've not been out.'

'No,' I said, trying not to look at the uncovered bread on the table.

'So, then, who else?' said Bridget. I looked at her. 'I hoped they would leave off at Bess Clarke. But if he's named the Wests, it won't stop there.'

'I don't know, Bridget. The Wests are not well liked.

Other times, it's been one woman or two, then matters die down. Perhaps this time, it will be three.'

'Grimston sent four to Colchester seven years ago.'

'And they were all acquitted.'

She shook her head. 'Things have changed since then, God knows. You weren't here when there were riots, when they sacked the Countess Rivers's house, the priory at St Osyth.'

I sat down again. 'I remember. You wrote to Joseph of it.'

'But you didn't see it. Bands of the young men going from village to village, smashing things, setting fires wherever Catholics were whispered to live. And then there was Dowsing, smashing things with a bit of paper to sanction it, smashing things on commission.'

I frowned. 'You think this is about piety? Bess Clarke might say the old prayers. But Anne West is no Papist.'

Bridget dropped her head. 'I don't know. If it is about piety, it's as much about what there is to go around. For men like Edwards, like Cutler –' She broke off, thinking, and then went on more firmly, 'Listen, men like that, as much as they are Bible men they are rich men. They have good businesses, they have warm households and families. They try to make themselves perfect before their God.' She stopped again, struggling to say what she meant. 'Right, but think of a misfortune. Say – say a child dies. Now, a poor man of small learning, when his child dies, he is like enough to stack up the death with all his other misfortunes, and throw up his hands. But a rich man, the misfortunes that befall him are dwarfed by the ones he fears. He feels guilty at having so much, yet defiant. A certain kind of poor woman, she is at once a reproach to his good fortune and a threat. Even if he does not know it, such a man lives in expectation of a levelling, and rather than wait for one, he strikes first.'

I was quiet for a moment. 'You have given it some thought,' I said.

Her face was grim. 'It gets you thinking, when folk start stealing your thatch.'

When I was young, we had spoken often, but Bridget had never talked to me like that. As an adult, confiding her fears. I leaned forward. 'But what you describe, it seems so – thought out.'

'Don't misunderstand me. Edwards, Grimston and the rest, I doubt they consider it thus. They know only that they are angry. Afraid.' She bit her lip. 'Matthew is angry and afraid. But you know him best. He'll listen to you.' She leaned back. 'Your brother's never taken to me. But it isn't me on my way to Colchester gaol. Leave all the rest of it aside. Let us not risk vexing him, with talk of his birth. But you must bring him to his senses about this sad business in Manningtree.'

Suddenly she seemed weary. I had been going to talk to her further, about the marks in the strawberry bed, but I put away the thought. Though she was feigning bravery, she looked frail. She did not need frightening. 'I am sure all will be well,' I said. I got up, and put on my shawl. 'So, promise me you will eat something?' I pointed. 'Not that bread? You've lost weight, Bridget. You must eat.'

We went to the door. 'It is hard to make myself cook, just for one,' she said.

I made my way back over the heath. My hands were numb: I had not even noticed the cold at Bridget's. I wondered whether she had been saving fuel, or whether she was too taken up with grief to mend the fire.

I wondered, too, whether anyone would have noticed me gone, whether Matthew would be back. Perhaps, it being Lady Day, he would have stayed for a glass of something. Grimston must be in high spirits after the sight of his long line of tenants waiting to pay their rent and make their mark in the rolls. I hoped he had detained my brother, and I could slip back in at the Thorn unnoticed.

If Bridget were telling the truth, it made sense of how Mother had always behaved with Matthew, how she could scarcely bear for him to be far from her; how she was too careful with him – and too rough with me, as a consequence. It was hard to imagine Father lying, but perhaps to spare Mother shame he would have done so. But that Matthew hated Bridget now and suspected her of having had a hand in his accident was clear enough. I felt scared for her: I knew that Matthew would rather believe anything than that Mother's problems had had their origin in her mind. It cut too near for him to his own childhood strangenesses; the superstitions and fears that I had thought, till the night before, he had left behind.

When I came to the Thorn, it was as I hoped, and taking off my cloak, I was able to get inside unobserved. There were no servants in the kitchen, only Matthew's dog. Standing quite still, I watched it limp over to its water bowl. There was a good fire in the room, but I felt no warmth from it. Instead I felt again what I had felt the night before: the solid push of something against my skirts as I had held open the door for Matthew; the thing I knew I had felt and, try as I might, I could not dismiss.

The testimony of Prudence Hart, wife of Thomas Hart of Lawford, given against the Wests before Sir Harbottle Grimston in April, this year of our Lord 1645.

This informant saith, that about eight week since, being at her parish church, on the Sabbath day, and being about twenty weeks gone with child, and to her thinking, very well and healthful, upon the sudden she was taken with great pains, and miscarried before she could be got home; and this examinant saith, that about two months since, being in her bed, in the night, something fell down upon her right side, but being dark, she cannot tell in what shape it was: And that presently she was taken lame on that side, with extraordinary pains and burning, but recovered again within a few days after: And this informant further saith, that she verily believeth, that Rebecca West, and Anne West her mother, were the cause of her pains.

12

Iscarcely saw my brother over the next days. Each morning I rose and washed, though I waited an hour at times for Grace to bring me hot water. With how Matthew was occupied, I took to breaking my fast in my chamber, to keep clear of the folk he was inviting each day now into the downstairs parlour. Grace did not say, at first, who they were or why they came, and I did not press her, for I did not wish to bring trouble on her from my brother. I knew I should be trying to speak to him, but he scarce stood still, and it had shaken me, the business that night at Mother's house.

And there was another reason I let matters drift. That was the week when I first felt the child inside me flutter. I was standing over a basin washing my hair, when I felt it. I stood up straight, thinking I had imagined it; kept still, water streaming over my shoulders. I did not believe it until I felt it flutter once more, then lurch into life. Joy made me cover my mouth with my hand. At once I felt different: afraid. It seemed doubly important, after that, to retain my brother's favour.

So for a while I kept to my chamber at the Thorn, or walked out gently along the river path towards the town. But one day, coming in from my walk, the passage being oddly quiet, I lingered near the parlour door, and heard Prudence Hart's voice, saying Rebecca West's name. How she could not get a husband herself but must lure the husbands of her betters. How she was a harlot, and everyone knew it, and though she had a pure face, for certain she had a rotten heart.

After that I began to seek chances to listen, lingering whenever Mary and Grace were occupied in the kitchen. One day soon after Prudence's visit, Ned Parsley and his wife came; Grace's cousins, of whose baby Bridget had spoken. I heard them in the passage, listened to Ned refusing any refreshment. I heard the door to the parlour open and close, and waited a few moments before I crept down the stairs, put my ear near the wood, and stilled my breath.

I heard Ned Parsley say their child had been doing well, a good pair of lungs on her, until one Friday when she set up crying in the middle of her usual nap and, his wife having her hands full, Ned had gone in to pick up the child, only to see a great dark bee fly out of the cradle. He had yelled for help, he said, and tried to kill the thing with a bottle, but it wouldn't die, and soon got away under the door, the same way it must have got in. He said it was like a bee, but not like any bee he had ever seen. I heard Matthew ask what happened next, and Ned's wife answered, said her child's little face had swelled up, and her throat. She had swelled right up and kept swelling, and her breathing got tight, and then – There was a pause, a sigh. I heard Mistress Parsley say how she nearly died herself after the baby went, her milk having turned bad. Then Matthew was asking serious questions: dates, times.

My heart sank. It was beginning properly, then, the testimony being collected, the tales gathering force, gaining credence. I felt the pressure of knowing that Bridget would be hearing them, too, would be wondering why I did not act. I feared she would come to the Thorn, though I could not put a name to what I feared would happen if she did. I thought of writing to my aunt in Cambridge for advice, but she was old, and we had not seen her since Father died. My elder brothers, they were across the sea. I thought of writing to my old landlady in London, but immediately I felt foolish, for we were not kin: what did she owe me? And, in any case, what could I say? Surely it would do no harm, I thought, to watch and wait a little. The women would be shamed, but they would never be convicted. That would not happen – not in these days.

†

Two Sundays passed, two Sundays, and Bridget did not show herself at church. I spent the services huddled into myself, keeping my eyes lowered from the minister's, but I could not avoid him entirely. The second Sunday was Easter, and that day he stopped me, and asked after Bridget. I said I did not know where she was; he said he would like not to fine her, and when I only nodded, he asked me more quietly if there was any matter I might wish to speak of. But I murmured that there was nothing; and I only permitted myself to look up at him when he had already turned away.

That week, Helen Leech was taken. It was Grace who told me the tale. The Parsleys had helped Helen Leech with money since her husband died, but then a few months earlier with their own baby on the way they had asked her to settle the debt. When they asked her, she had used certain words against them, high words that no one had given much thought to, until the baby died. When the men came for her, Helen Leech had ready what she owed Ned Parsley, counted out precisely in her hand, but when she held it out to him, Grace said Ned would not touch the money: he told her to keep it for the hangman.

It was her own mother, Nan, who had accused her, Grace told me. Nan had admitted on her own account to being at a meeting at Bess Clarke's house, and to wishing Richard Edwards's boy dead, making him shake though he was not cold, and his eyes to roll back in his head. And, Grace told me, Nan Leech had not stopped there, but added that her daughter, Helen, had wished ill on the Parsleys.

'Surely not,' I said to Grace. 'Why would she say such a thing of her own daughter?'

'I cannot tell you, mistress,' Grace said. 'Though the talk is that the two of them have not spoken in a good three years.'

I thought about Mother in the days that followed. How far from perfectly I had cared for her, and about the sad, worn clothes, which I could not bear to go back for, that were all she had left me. Yet she had apparently been asking for me in the days before she died. I thought how distressed she must have been by the sad knowledge she had carried so long. I wondered whether perhaps all she had wanted at the end was my listening ear, to put her secret into it before she died. Whether she had looked for me every day, but I had never come.

I hoped that after Helen Leech there might be an end to the accusations. I overheard one of the stablehands saying she had admitted at last to working the death of the Parsleys' daughter, but that she had accused no others, so I hoped there might be the last of it. But though she had named no one else, she had spoken of keeping an imp, a thing like a small ratting dog, and someone noticed that it was like the kind kept by Elizabeth Gooding, the shoe-maker's widow. Elizabeth Gooding doted on her little dog, and indeed was reading aloud to it when the men let themselves into her cottage. She was reading from the Proverbs, and she had such a strong, clear voice that, without meaning to, they let her get to the end of a verse, after which she marked her place, and looked at them.

Elizabeth Gooding was the oldest woman accused yet. I heard how when they sent her to Colchester they did not spare her, but took her without any proper garments, in an open cart, though the day was wet. In the gaol at Colchester, I heard, they moved the men to the smaller cell, and gave over the larger one for the women, which, though it was more generously proportioned, was open to the sky.

I could hardly believe they had truly taken Elizabeth Gooding, whose husband had only lately died, the gentle old man who had once made our everyday boots. When Grace told me of it, I only gave a nod, and waited until she had left the chamber before I allowed my face to fall open in dismay. I liked Elizabeth Gooding. Every person in the town was obliged to her for some kindness or other. If she were named, then who was safe?

And there was another reason her taking troubled me, though I tried to put it from my mind. Elizabeth Gooding had been more than an acquaintance of Bridget's: undoubtedly, she had been a friend. The witch business was coming nearer to Bridget, but it had not touched her. Not yet.

13

I think of those taken that mild fortnight in April. Though I could never forget their names, I write them down: Elizabeth Clarke, Nan Leech, Helen Leech, Elizabeth Gooding, Anne West, Rebecca West.

I should have seen that the detailed testimony being collected, the urgent bustle at the Thorn, meant real danger; that it was not just Matthew, his methodical way. It was not just my brother, proceeding with more thoroughness than the great men of the town had expected or asked for. But I did not see the danger. I still thought it would turn out like such cases had before – a brief outpouring of spite, two or three months in prison for the accused, then at trial, an acquittal.

Yet I rack myself, here in the dark where there is time to think, over whether I did not have a more selfish reason for not speaking out; a reason that had nothing to do with concern for my unborn child. I rack myself over whether I did not also keep my silence because in some fashion I was glad they had named Rebecca West.

Anne West's daughter was the youngest to be taken from Manningtree. She was fair as her mother was dark, obliging as her mother was secretive. No one remembered her father, but he must have been a pretty fellow, for Rebecca had pale wide eyes, and clear skin, and though six years younger than me, she was forward for her age so that even when she first came to the town men were watching her up the street. Bridget used to give her small coins to do errands, and when Rebecca came, Bridget would joke with her about marrying Joseph. She used to tug her golden braids: say, 'Think of it! Grandchildren with that hair!' At first the girl would laugh along with her, but soon she began to redden, and Joseph to look away.

As she got older, Rebecca West blossomed. She would dawdle past Bridget's house with her basket full from illegal gleaning on Richard Edwards's fields, having risked a reprimand and a bit of rough treatment for the best share of the spoils. She would linger near the lean-to where Joseph kept his tools. And if I had disliked her before, I liked Rebecca still less once Bridget took her in, while her mother was in gaol awaiting her trial over John Edes's pigs. I did not like the way Rebecca strove to be quicker than me in fetching things for Joseph, how she watched him eat as if the food were as nourishing to her as dining herself.

But she had been an obliging child for certain, and she remained obliging, Rebecca West, after she was not a child any longer, and that was how she came to be accused over Prudence Hart, who lived down the road from the Wests' cottage at Lawford. Prudence Hart, who had never been much liked but whom everyone pitied: all those stillbirths, all those girls, and Thomas's wandering hands. Then, this last February, the pain in the middle of the sermon that had made her run out into the street, and fall. The beginning of the sixth month: not usually a treacherous time. No one would touch the mess she left, not even Thomas Hart, who stalked home after his wife, treading her blood up the lane. The mess stayed there in the road outside the Wests' house till dark, but in the morning it was gone. Of course a fox must have had it, but girls began to whisper that Rebecca West had taken the unfinished child and eaten it; she was known to be obliging Thomas Hart, and so for certain she must wish Prudence away.

The rumours spread, and Rebecca was taken off to Colchester gaol, and I have racked myself over whether I did not feel a small kind of triumph when I heard of it. Whether I did not feel that she had got what was in some way coming to her.

14

But though I found myself able for a time not to think of Rebecca West, the news of Elizabeth Gooding's arrest would not leave my mind, and the memory of the first time my brother and I had gone to be measured for boots and she had given us a cake of sugar to share; how she had taken such pleasure in watching us divide it, though we were far too old for such treats. A simple memory: but the guilt it stirred set me trying in earnest to find a way to talk to Matthew.

Though as children we had always spoken of our small daily worries and concerns, after Father's death, after we moved to Manningtree and Matthew's life departed from what he had thought it would be, he and I had slowly stopped talking. When I tried to speak to him about Mother, whether bleeding or purging was the proper thing for her, I too easily let him dismiss it. As I had let him dismiss it that time Thomas Witham's daughter had conceived a foolish liking for him, having decided his scars were romantic. She had come to see me one day only to entreat Matthew to walk home with her. She had not come again, and although he stood near her at church, she never said a word to him. And I had allowed Matthew to claim that it was fine, to say it was nothing.

So I had no pattern, no tested template now for speaking to my brother of things he did not wish to speak of, yet it was weighing on me, what was happening in the town, what Bridget had told me of his birth. So it was a clumsy beginning I made one day when he hesitated beside me on the yard steps. I had found some empty jars in one of the unlocked rooms, good jars but full of dead moths and flies, and though I had no use for them I had set about cleaning them, trying to do something ordinary that I might not have to hide in my chamber. But the baby was heavy inside me that day, so I was moving slowly.

I had filled a pitcher with hot water and carried the jars out to the steps, so Matthew coming in had to pause with his hat in his hands while I moved them out of his way, and that was when I took my chance to speak. I tipped out the dust from one of the jars. I will speak plainly, I thought. I wiped my hands on my apron, and said, 'Surely not Elizabeth Gooding.'

He studied the band of his hat. 'I agree, it is surprising. It is regrettable.' He took a breath. 'But, you see, I cannot exempt her. Having been accused, she will be examined, and if she is clear she will be let go.'

I forced myself not to back down. 'I was thinking . . .' I said. 'Might she not be unwell?' He looked at me. 'Might she not be unwell in the manner that our mother was unwell?'

'I don't know what you mean.'

I folded my hands. 'What you told me of your wet nurse – how you came to her, already – already as you are now. I do not believe our father would have been untruthful only to protect Bridget. And so,' I met his eyes, 'do you see? You can free yourself of any suspicion for her. Perhaps an accident happened, with Bridget or with Mother, for you know she was uneasy in her mind –'

'You've been to see her, haven't you? Bridget? What lie did she tell you?' He half turned away, agitated. 'How can you doubt it, after she fixed our mother to change her will? And now she tries to slur our mother's memory, tries to imply that she was otherwise than she should have been. I think that Bridget was jealous. She wanted a husband, she wanted a child. What did she do when she came here? Found some urchin, and took him in.'

'What are you saying, Matthew? She took Joseph in for kindness.'

He shook his head slowly. 'Not only did she play our mother. She's always played you, Alice. Like a flute. Do you not see how she led you into your foolish marriage?'

'But she suspected nothing of that before we told her,' I said. I could feel matters getting away from me and tried to speak more gently. 'Matthew, I thought you reconciled. I cannot undo my marriage now.'

He dropped his voice to a whisper. 'How could I be reconciled to that shameful piece of folly?'

I swallowed. 'Our mother did not forbid it,' I said.

'You shouldn't have needed forbidding,' he said, his voice rising as he forgot himself, and I became aware of one of the stablemen, who had been leaning against the wall, disappearing into the stable. 'I wonder at times, Alice, if our father did not make a mistake in the licence he gave you. Running about the countryside, thinking yourself greatly learned. Perhaps he thought for a child it was no harm, but God strike me if it did not turn you into a –' He stopped himself. I flinched, certain the servants must be listening. But he had not finished. 'Well, you will obey me now. You will do your duty. You will not go any more to Bridget's house. You will do what I have asked you to, at Mother's, which should be enough to occupy you.'

As he spoke, I saw a live moth creep out from where it had slept in the jar, its grey wings dusty. Quickly Matthew put out his foot and crushed it. He stepped into the entry and wiped his feet on the mat. Then he turned back.

'Do you know what happened to my wet nurse?' he said. His face was calm and even. 'She died. Not two weeks after she spoke to me, standing there in perfect health. She was found cold in her bed, and those who washed the body never could determine the cause.' He looked at me. 'What I think is, she crossed Bridget, and that was the cause.'

I said nothing in reply. The stableman was back, and a scullery maid peeped out from the entry, and I did not want to say in front of them that what he spoke was foolishness. I thought he would go, then, but instead he stood watching as I hefted the pitcher and poured my hot water over the jars. I could hardly believe how he had gone so quickly from cold to hot to cold again. My heart beat hard, and I could feel the baby tapping inside me in response. Matthew stayed regarding me for one long moment, and then another; by the time the steam had blown away, he had gone.

I put the jars to dry, and going in, I almost knocked into Grace. From her eyes, I knew she had heard what had passed in the yard.

'My brother is out of temper,' I said to her, trying to produce a smile. 'I cannot think why, for all his business goes smooth before him, and my mother-in-law is nothing but a harmless old woman. But there! They have never seen eye to eye. There is nothing to account for it.'

But Grace did not look soothed by my words. 'Mistress,' she said, 'I –'

But Mary Phillips appeared then in the kitchen entry. She told Grace to stop detaining me, and to get back to her work. Shaky, I climbed the stairs to my chamber.

I pitied Matthew. I knew I had scarcely scratched the surface of the horror he must feel, if in some fashion he was aware that it was Mother who had harmed him, and on purpose. But along with the pity, doubt was creeping in. I wondered, not for the first time, whether Mother's weakness of mind could have passed to him in the blood. Whether he was himself quite well. And with the pity, with the doubt, came the fear. It shook me that, in front of everyone, he should have raised his voice to me in that way.

What was worse was that the thing of which he had accused Bridget was hard to dismiss, though on the steps I had wanted to refute it. I thought of how many times I had seen her with babies, the children of the women round about, who would be passed to her for inspection. I thought of how swiftly she had offered to take my own, when it came. I tried to dismiss a shiver of doubt – to put from my mind the many years Bridget had spent childless. For I knew the strength of that pain. I tried not to think of a wrong and fruitless wanting, long and carefully concealed.

15

The next day I took Grace with me into town. Since I had come back to Manningtree, especially after what Bridget had said, I had been aware of how few gowns I had and how sorely they were worn. But I had been reluctant to go to John Rivet, the draper, for Grace had told me that he and his sister had been among the first spreading rumours about Bess Clarke. That was not the only reason that I was reluctant to be measured for new things: the truth was, I knew my waist was thickening. But I had been mistaken for a servant by more than one of my brother's visitors to the Thorn, and Matthew himself dressed so carefully. He had mentioned more than once since my return how he had credit with every tradesman in Manningtree, and that I should order whatever I needed.

So, after our scene on the steps, I thought it best to make a show of obedience, and so I made sure to stop Matthew as he came out of the parlour that morning, and tell him where I was going. He nodded. He did not move away, but his face made me think he would speak.

'Forgive me for saying what I did,' he said, at last. 'My temper is not what it ought to be – I have been much engaged. I beg you, sister. Consider it unsaid.'

I said, 'Of course,' watching his eyes for any insincerity. I could see none there, but as I waited for Grace to be ready to go, it struck me that, although he had asked for forgiveness, for me to consider it all unsaid, he had not told me he had not meant them, the words he had spoken. About the freedom Father had given me, and what it had turned me into.

Mary Phillips had asked Grace to bring some few things back to the Thorn, so we stopped first at the victualler's, and the butcher's, who had once again put out his sign, and was selling good spring lamb, Lent being done with. Watching Grace pay, counting out the coins from the leather purse Mary Phillips had handed her, I was suddenly aware that I had no money of my own.

When the tailor's shop door closed behind us, Rivet's wife put down a piece of close-work, rose and shouted up the stairs. I smiled at her, for I remembered her as a gentle, harried person, the opposite of her husband. Before I could ask whether she was yet well recovered from her illness, she had taken up her work again, and Rivet came in, occupying at once all the space between floor and ceiling. He was not only a tall man but fleshy also, and he always made you want to take a step back, that you might not have to see too close the nut-brown teeth he showed each time he smiled.

'Is that Matthew Hopkins's sister? I am at your service, mistress,' he said. Clasping his hands, he asked after my brother's health.

'I need two mourning gowns,' I told him. 'And gloves, two pairs.'

Rivet smiled, and his wife again put down her sewing and stepped towards me with a length of measuring cord. I bundled my cloak to Grace.

'We heard your brother's seeing about these witches,' Rivet said, after a minute. He said 'witches' not fearfully, but like you might say 'rats' or 'beetles'.

I glanced at Grace. 'My brother has many kinds of business,' I replied. 'I can scarce keep up with it all.'

Rivet leaned on the counter. 'Never mind Bess Clarke. Rebecca West, it's her that frightens me,' he said. 'That one's no better than she should be. They do say that Thomas Hart was bringing her a half-dozen eggs a week for her services.' He dropped his voice. 'Folk say it's never the ones you'd think – but in my experience, it's always the ones you would think.'

As Rivet continued in this vein, I spoke quietly to his wife, asking her to put a bit of room in when she made up the gowns. Her eyes shot to my face, as she caught my meaning; fortunately, Grace did not see.

'I heard he has a warrant, your brother, for all of Essex,' Rivet was saying. 'That'll make him a nice sum.'

'I have heard nothing about it,' I said. I ought to have known Rivet would be peddling inflated rumours, for what could Matthew want with a warrant? Though he was scribing for Grimston, he was not high-placed enough to be considered to serve as constable.

Rivet's wife crouched to open a drawer, making more noise than she might have done, and began to bring out pairs of gloves, black ones and grey. Then she stood, dusting her hands, and I was saved from replying to her husband by the need to make my choice. Looking at the gloves I pointed to, Rivet excused himself and went into the back to find his credit book.

†

After the tailor's, Grace and I went on to Mother's house: we had agreed not to spend long, but only to finish packing up the kitchen items, the flour and preserves we had judged should come back to the Thorn, and arrange for a boy from the Bell to bring them.

There was a moment of awkwardness as I let Grace into the passage ahead of me and, through the open parlour door, we were met with the two chairs, still drawn up in the pose in which Matthew and I had left them. But then I went ahead of Grace to the kitchen: I did not intend to waste this time alone with her. I had been thinking of the accusations Matthew had levelled against Bridget, one being that Mother had changed her will under Bridget's influence. And it had struck me that, as to what had or had not happened the day before Mother's death, Grace might be the one to know.

When we had the kitchen crate half packed, I said, 'It must have been hard, with my mother as she was. When you first came into our service.'

She leaned back on her hands. 'I liked the mistress,' she replied. 'She was kind to me. There are worse houses.' She saw I was listening. 'I have heard of houses where maids are pinched or starved for nothing. Where the master . . .' She met my eyes, to check I knew what she meant.

I nodded. 'But I have been thinking – you know my mother did amend her will, the day she died?'

'I remember it.'

'Was she – lucid, when she did it? For I know she had good days and bad.'

'The master must have judged her to be.' She dusted her hands, and stood up, and we took the chairs at the kitchen table. 'Her health was breaking, poor lady,' Grace said. 'She had pains in her womb. She would fret herself over little things. But if you want my opinion, the day she died, she was in her wits.' She cleared her throat. 'I would have said she was more restless the night before, after your mother-in-law came to see her.' She avoided my eyes.

'What do you mean? She was distressed?'

'No, it was more – she seemed excited. She would not settle. She sat up late doing needlework, nothing fancy either, but mending one of her gowns, though she was that ill, and not like to be out of bed to wear it again.'

'I see,' I said. Though it did not seem so out of the ordinary: Mother had always taken up her sewing when she wanted soothing. Her clothes were always stuck full of pins, where she would insert them, then forget them.

Slowly, Grace said, 'The master was angry with me, for letting your mother-in-law in. He did not like it, but he forgave me my mistake.' She looked at me with meaning. I saw she was speaking of Matthew, how he had admonished me in the yard. She was trying to comfort me.

'He had told you not to admit Bridget, then?'

'Not as such.' She was frowning to remember. 'He said nothing about her in particular, mistress – but he had told me not to let anyone in. We had sent the nurse away, for she was no good. I was trying to clean the mistress's sores, but they were worse than I had realized, and she wouldn't keep still, and then I heard the knocking below.'

'And you showed Bridget up?'

Grace nodded. 'She helped me change her bedlinen, and stayed a while after. I went up after half an hour, and heard them parting.'

'And my mother was excited?'

'I heard your mother-in-law saying, "I don't want it." And the mistress saying, "You must, you must." I heard her saying, "I can't keep it where I am going."'

'And you think they were speaking of the will? Of my mother's ring, perhaps?'

'I thought so. But then your mother was so restless, and – I only remembered it, after. After she had died. I tried to speak to you of it the other day, mistress – for I told the master of it, and I think now I should not have done.'

'Told him of what?'

'What brought it back to me was, the master asked me, after she had died, whether I had heard or seen anything unusual in the mistress before her death.' She looked at me. 'And I did. I did see something. It was not – I do not know that it had anything to do with your mother-in-law. It was earlier on that day, the day before your mother died. It was in the morning.'

'Yes?'

'I went to wake her, and I saw something in the bed.'

'What do you mean? Saw what?' I thought of the accusations that had been troubling the town. 'A creature?' I said.

'No, not a creature.' She looked strangely at me. 'I don't know what it was. It was this big.' She showed me the size, with finger and thumb against her flattened hand. 'I had not seen it before. I think perhaps she had been holding it while she slept. It was made of – if I did not know better, I would have said it was made of hair, coarse dark hair woven into a shape like a child's shape, crude. But not like a little girl's doll. It didn't look – it didn't look nice. It didn't look *good*.' She paused. 'I searched for it – the item – after the mistress died. Once I remembered it, I searched for it everywhere. So as to dispose of it.' She met my eyes. 'So that the master would not find it, and be puzzled or otherwise distressed. But I could not find it. I scoured her chamber, and I could not find it. So it gives me to think, whether your mother-in-law took it away.'

I swallowed. 'And you told my brother this.'

A quick nod. 'He questioned me deeply about it. He even bade me draw it on paper. I believe he did hunt for it also, for a day or two after.' I remembered Mother's gowns, how the pockets had been turned out. She leaned forward. 'Mistress, I did not speak of it before, for I have heard nothing about it since. I do not know that it was anything to do with Bridget. But I think the master decided it was, as I was speaking the very words. I see how he has taken against her.' She spread her hands. 'I don't know, mistress. I can't know. But with all the talk in the town now . . .'

I tried to calm Grace, and reassure her that she had done only what she thought best. We finished packing, and set off back to the Thorn in silence. Grace's words spoke themselves over again in my mind: an item, about this big, like a child woven out of coarse black hair. I did not know what good such a thing could signify. Or what Matthew might have made of it. It worried me that he had not spoken of it.

Grace was silent for most of the walk. But when we were nearly back, she said, 'Do you think it is true, about the master having a warrant for all of Essex?'

I wanted to soothe her. 'John Rivet talks renowned nonsense,' I said. But it could be true, I thought. Grimston, as a justice of the peace, he could have given Matthew a warrant to act on his behalf in finding out supposed witches. Though even he could not have written one for the whole of Essex. In any case, I could not think why Matthew would be driven to search beyond Manningtree: Bridget was here, already within his reach, and so were the fine new friends he might impress with his diligence.

Grace must have heard the doubt in my voice. For she said, 'Sir Harbottle will know. They are coming tomorrow night to dine.'

†

If I had thought that talking to Grace would render matters clearer I was wrong, for it had done the reverse. I spent that night in my chamber, thinking about the item she had described, and what it could mean. There would be no virtue in trying to speak to Matthew of it, but now it felt more urgent than ever to know what was in his mind: in his heart. And since talking to my brother had only made him angry, I was forced to turn to other means.

When we were little, Father had encouraged us to keep daily books, though it had taken us a long time to grasp that they were meant to be private, for our own confessions to God. I was eleven or twelve before we each left off writing messages for the other to find, among the accounts of the wrongs and shortcomings our little lives contained. Even when I was older – fifteen, seventeen – I had often written some difficulty in my daily book as if I were writing it to Matthew, it being easier to say what I meant in that way, than to write as if to no one. I had left off keeping my daily book with my marriage; but my brother, I suspected, would have continued faithfully with his. He had always used to write in it before bed, as regularly as washing his face.

Recalling this, I saw that my long days of hesitation had not been wasted. The routine of the Thorn had seeped into me in those days I had spent huddled in my chamber, alive to sounds from other parts of the house. I had noticed my own room was dealt with by one or other of the scullery maids, but my brother's chamber Mary Phillips did herself, going in each afternoon for the chamber pot and the ashes, and to lay that evening's fire. His room was most often kept locked, but Mary Phillips did not lock the door when she took his chamber pot. I had heard her, each day, knocking the ashes into the pot, then going away downstairs. Soon, she would come back to replace the pot, and only then would she lock up. Most of the time she was quick – a minute, perhaps two. But more than once I had heard one of the girls ask her something as she went out at the yard door or came back in, and in those cases Matthew's door would stand unlocked for five minutes or six.

The next day, the day Grimston and the other men were coming to dine, was a Saturday. Grace came in to me in the morning, to bring me my bread and beer, and asked whether I was warm enough. I assured her I was comfortable, and then she said, 'Mistress, this evening, the master said to let you know, I will bring you a tray in your chamber. There will be no other ladies at the dinner, and so . . .'

'Thank you, Grace. I shall not mind that – but this afternoon –' I knew that to ask it of her was to take a chance. But the opportunity would not happen without help, and suddenly, since what she had told me the day before, matters had gained an urgency. 'When Mary comes down with my brother's chamber pot,' I said, 'perhaps you might choose that moment to ask her for something.' I kept my voice low. 'Detain her. Grace, believe me, just as for good reasons you told me yesterday what you did, I wish for only good reasons to have five minutes alone in my brother's room.' I sat back, searched her face. 'I mean only good by this. For his own sake, I need to know what he is planning to do. Do you believe me?'

She seemed uncertain, but she agreed to do as I asked. Perhaps she felt bound, having confided so much to me the day before, or perhaps she, too, was beginning to fear how things were turning. Some few hours later, I heard Mary Phillips come up, unlock my brother's chamber and clatter about for a short while. Then, when I heard her clumping down the stairs, I let myself out of my chamber, and slipped along the passage to my brother's door.

The room was laid out as though a mirror had been held to my own, with the swept grate on the right hand, the high bed on the left as I shut the door to an inch open, then stood still and listened. I looked about me, for any familiar possessions, but there was nothing. It was a man's temporary room, furnished singularly bare. I opened the chest at the foot of the bed: shirts in stacks, white on white. The best quality, you could tell without even feeling them. I shut the chest again. No Bible on the little stand by the bed, but there were a few spills, perhaps used for marking pages. The only cluttered place was the desk.

I crossed the room and began to search, trying to replace each item as I moved it, looking for his daily book, or any personal scrap of my brother's. My hands sweated, and I felt sure that I must be leaving prints, so I wiped the cover of each book on my sleeve as I replaced it. Accounts, a book of sermons: I picked that one up by its spine and shook, but nothing fell out. Receipts, lists. I opened the drawers of the desk. A reminder of the last year's production of the mill at Flatford, and a witnessed statement detailing my brother's interest in the same. One large sheet that I unfolded proved to be Mother's will. I could not prevent myself reading it: it was not long. Near the end, I read, *To my faithful servant Bridget, my Bible and my gold ring. For my late husband's daughter Alice, I do most particularly will her all my clothing.* I fought down my anger and hurt, folded it and placed it back where I had found it.

But as I put it back, I saw another sheet underneath: neat, official writing, and a seal. A warrant. So Rivet had been right. The warrant was long and the phrasing tortuous, in what I took to be Grimston's hand. Though it did not cover all of Essex, it did cover the Tendring Hundred, the part of the county in Grimston's charge from Colchester to Harwich to Wivenhoe, half a day's riding from end to end. I glanced down the warrant quickly, then made myself lay it aside. I did not have much longer.

But in a minute or two more, I had searched through every paper on Matthew's desk, and I still could not find his daily book. I thought of the brown leather case he carried always with him. Perhaps he kept it in there. But what need to be so careful? He never had been before.

I stood back, and glanced at the bookshelf above the desk. Biblical commentaries, and then a small volume, *A Guide to Grand Jury Men*, no doubt some dry legal text. Then another whole row, all bound alike in dark brown leather.

As I gazed at them I remembered: it had been Matthew's habit as a child to keep his daily books on the shelf, with his other volumes. The row of books had looked so dull, had been in such plain view that I had not noticed them.

Then I heard Mary Phillips's voice in the passage below and, panicked, I grabbed the book at the end of the row, and slipped out onto the landing. I heard her heavy tread start up the stairs as I crept along to my chamber, and closed my door only as she reached the turn: I heard her halt before she carried on up the second flight, though I did not know whether it was from suspicion or only to catch her breath.

It took me a while to breathe freely myself. I put the book under my pillow, while I waited to hear Mary finish in Matthew's chamber and go back downstairs. The baby was moving, and I felt alarmed: I had not intended to take anything from the room. Though I could hardly undo it now. I had heard her turn the key again in the lock.

I took out the book from under my pillow. I felt oddly reluctant to open it, where my brother's thoughts resided. But I thought of Elizabeth Gooding, and of Bridget, and I steeled myself.

It took me a moment to see the words, to decipher the handwriting I had not seen for so long, then the date of the entry on the open page. This daily book was not Matthew's, but Father's, and the words on the page written soon before his death.

I could not help but read them. I turned the pages guiltily at first, but soon I grew absorbed. Though it seemed my father's thoughts were wandering, in those last days, it touched my heart to read his lyrical praise of Cambridge, his memories from his time as a student there. Of the garden kept in readiness for only the dean to walk in, and to be seen by lesser souls at a distance from behind a rope. Of cloisters, books and lamps in the short winter days, of learning for its own sake.

But as I turned the pages, moving closer to the date of Father's death, the writing grew fragmented, and it changed. Regret seeped in. *I wish I had been able to resist the snares the devil has laid for me*, he wrote. *I wish I had been able to see through the fair guises of those who are false and riddled with sin. But it is too late now for me to amend where I have fallen short.* I looked up from the page. I had never seen my father uncertain, never seen him cast down. I could not imagine what falling short he could have been speaking of: I thought of the daily small disputes he had resolved as minister at Wenham, the steady leadership he had provided, his patience with Mother and with Matthew. I read on, through his worries about Mother's health, half expecting to find some reference to Matthew's birth, but I did not, nor any more mention of the regrets he had spoken of; but then I turned back, leafing swiftly. That was when I saw it. There were pages missing, many of them. I had scarcely noticed it at first, but pressing the book apart in one place, and then another place further on, and then yet another, I saw what had been done. The pages had not been torn out, but cut precisely, and close to the spine.

I hid the book in my box, beneath my summer nightgown. I almost wished I had not opened it. That was the first time, there in my chamber, that I was frightened of Matthew, with a cold fear. For there was some deep matter, I saw, some deep thing that I was not yet at the heart of.

Something had prompted him to so precisely and profoundly alter the record. I felt more vulnerable, more lost than ever. I think now of how as a child I had always wanted to read the books that Father said were too hard for me, not realizing yet that understanding a book is not the same as being able to spell out all the words.

16

That evening, I heard Sir Harbottle Grimston shout a greeting to my brother as his coach pulled into the yard. Despite my awareness of the daily book hidden in my box, despite my fear, as I listened to the backslapping coming up from below, my stomach growled. Grace had told me that there would be four kinds of meat. There would be spring greens and the kind of mushroom with the savoury taste that is almost like flesh. I had been smelling the result of the kitchen's efforts all afternoon, but Grace had not yet brought up my tray.

Grimston must have been the last to arrive, for it soon fell quiet downstairs. I went back to thinking over what I had read in Father's daily book; thinking, too, how I might return it before it was missed. I could not avoid the thought that on the missing pages there might be some version of what had happened the day Matthew was born: but if it was there, it could not be the whole and true version. For Matthew's face had softened when he had spoken of Mother, the night I had come to the Thorn, it was Bridget he seemed to hate. I brooded on what the missing pages contained, and why they had been cut out.

Before long there was a knock at my chamber door, and I said, 'Come in.' I checked my shoulders were covered, eager for my supper. It was Grace, tired and hot, but she was holding no tray, and when she saw me in my shift, she said,

'Oh – I beg your pardon, mistress. It's the master. He asks if you will join them for dinner.'

'But you said this morning that I should leave it to him.'

She shut the door behind her and came nearer. 'Mistress, it was not the master as such, but Sir Harbottle. He did ask me if you had already supped, and it came to me that I had forgot you, and I said so before the company. Then one of them made a jest about the master's ill manners, and all were calling for you to come down. They were banging on the table.' She lowered her voice. 'Sir Harbottle, in particular, is somewhat ahead of himself.'

For a moment I thought about pleading illness, but then I stood up and folded my blanket. 'Very well, Grace. Tell my brother I shall be down.'

I took out the better of my gowns, the black one I had arrived in, and looked it over. It was a pity my new ones were not ready. At least, I thought, it would be candlelight. I put it on, struggling to lace it tight enough. I pinched my cheeks, though not too much. Then I followed the sound of laughter down the stairs.

On the threshold I hesitated, so none saw me at first. Sir Harbottle Grimston was seated nearest, his chair pushed back that he might rest his hands on his belly. Matthew sat to his right. There also was Richard Edwards, with his smooth head of golden hair, and Robert Taylor, the victualler. Two others, whom I did not know, completed the group, but how they were seated told me enough: Grimston at the head of the table, Taylor at the far end, the others in between. The room, which in daylight had felt large and sparse, seemed more welcoming filled with solid men and candles burning.

I could tell that Grimston, at the least, had been drinking before he arrived. 'She's a good cook, then, is she, this Grace?' he was saying. 'Now she would be the one with the . . .' He made signs over his chest, like cabbages, and I caught my brother's stricken look.

The dark-haired man across from Matthew snorted into his glass. 'Well, sir, you were saying you need a pastry girl. Perhaps Hopkins can tell you if she has cold hands.'

'Stearne!' Richard Edwards shook his golden head, but he was laughing.

It was Matthew who spotted me, and stood up. He seemed so far from pleased to see me that it made me wish to behave perfectly; I resolved to keep my manners perfect, to listen to their talk, and learn what I could. I would find out more here than I would sitting in my chamber. 'Sister,' Matthew said, and the others stood too, except Grimston, who kept his seat.

'Is this she?' he said, straining to turn. I had seen him going by in his carriage before, but he had never had cause to speak a word to me. 'Mistress Alice, forgive our loudness. Now, is not this table in need of a sweet face? Come and sit here, by me. Move up, Stearne.'

The man called Stearne and the one beside him rose and began moving their plates, cups and knives to the left. As they shifted Grimston introduced me to them: John Stearne and John Cutler. Men of business, Grimston said. I recalled Cutler's name: I had heard from Grace how his boy had been carried off by a fever, not long before Edwards's baby son had died. While the men took my hand in turn, Matthew was signing to Mary Phillips where to place the fresh dishes she was carrying in.

I had often dined at a table full of men, taking over for

Mother when her spirits were low and Father was giving a dinner for some friend or other. But this felt different. Seeing my brother, my cheeks burned that he might have guessed I had been in his chamber, noticed the missing book. But there was no sign of it. His nod as I sat down was civil enough.

'There now,' said Grimston. 'You sit here. Don't mind the crumbs that foul creature Stearne has left on the cloth, you just sit there where I can look at you. God Himself must know why this rogue would keep you ferreted away upstairs.'

I glanced at Matthew. 'Perhaps my brother does not trust you, sir. Among the women of his house.' Grimston roared at that.

The one called John Stearne reached across to help me to the wine, telling me how he was in the midst of buying a property a few doors down. Though his voice was friendly, he had a forbidding brow, and large, blunt hands. I had to place my own over the mouth of the glass to keep it to half full. As the stir of my arrival passed, the men returned to their own talk. I took a helping of fish in butter sauce and looked around the table.

Grimston had grown redder, more hard-worn since I had seen him last. As well as serving justice, I knew that he had been sheriff in those years, and Edwards was doing a long turn as constable for the Tendring Hundred. They had been in those posts at the time of the riots. It had been a bad business: Bridget had written to Joseph of how the rioters had broken apart a house in St Osyth and Sir John Lucas's house, near Colchester. Though Sir John was known to be a Papist he was a kind man, and had always been tolerated before, but Bridget said that the rioters would have broken him, too, if Grimston had not ridden out with the trained bands and put them down. Some of those gentlemen with Catholic forebears left our part of Essex after that; others let their houses sit empty and went to where the King was, which might have made the godly men glad, except that it left fewer to manage the land and law-keeping.

Grimston, Edwards and the rest, they were the ones who had endured, and in the time I had been gone it seemed they had grown all the more tight together, perhaps for the knowledge of how many rougher folk they had between them to contain; like trees, knitting themselves into a hedge.

I sat quiet, and listened to their conversation. After a time, Grimston put down his glass. 'It beggars me,' he said, 'how I spent six months, six months entire, at Harwich, on the sea defences there. Six months checking builders' drawings, checking batches of stone, as if I know a damned thing about stone. It was the Spanish then, when we all thought the Armada might be back. We never thought to look within for any threat.'

Taylor nodded; it made his small beard twitch. 'But the King did allow vipers into his household,' he said. 'Laud, those Papists around the Queen.' He smiled as he wiped his mouth, but Richard Edwards did not smile, nor any of the others. The memory of Archbishop Laud was not cherished by them – he had been beheaded that January, for his love of music and other Catholic practices; beheaded, in truth, as a warning to the King, during the same freeze that had left Joseph dead and Mother lying unburied. But though those godly men disliked Laud, even they did not like such earnest talk against the King himself.

I said, 'I have a memory that Archbishop Laud did once come to Manningtree. Before we lived here. But some of you, masters, must remember his coming. Did he not give us some communion plate?'

John Cutler shifted in his chair. 'Aye, that stuff. It fetched enough to put plain glazing in the church windows, against Dowsing last year.' He raised his glass, and Edwards laughed.

'I remember Laud's coming,' Taylor said. 'His pomp and pride, his wheedling. No one who thinks on sin could forget that day.' He did not see John Cutler glance at Richard Edwards and lift his eyes to Heaven, or Richard Edwards smile behind his hand.

Mary Phillips came in, to clear what was finished with, and Edwards coughed a little. 'We have not yet thanked you, Hopkins, for your efforts these last weeks.'

'Aye,' said Grimston, tapping his glass for Mary to fill.

My brother smiled, inclined his head. 'Stearne has done as much as I,' he said.

Swallowing his mouthful, Stearne glanced sideways at Robert Taylor. 'Though Bess Clarke did give us trouble,' he said. 'Did you hear? She would not admit to Taylor's horse.'

My brother shook his head. 'Nor did she admit any murder. Though she told us much else, sirs, and, as you know, I was able to discover from her, after long watching, the names of those who did mischief to these two gentlemen's sons.'

He spoke matter-of-factly and, loading a morsel of bread with sauce, he missed their faces falling, Edwards bringing his napkin to his lips and Cutler pushing his glass away, as if his son was standing again at his shoulder, a lively boy and tall for his age, but silent now, leaning on his father's chair; in Edwards's lap a little bundle, stilled from the fits that had taken him. Matthew did not see those first-born sons, but went on calmly with his wine and his fish, exempt from the shudder that had passed around the table, the touching of wood.

I think now that is why they trusted him, with this their most delicate business: his ability to talk of witchcraft, and still to finish his dinner. He had all their trappings, but he was not like those men, my brother. They were afraid, but they feared not so much the devil in himself, but rather – it was as Bridget had said – the ill will that might reach out from his servants to hurt their wealth and families. They believed in witchcraft, and yet they didn't; it was one of several convenient labels to put upon their fear. But Matthew believed in it wholly, and they saw that clarity in my brother, that certainty. They chose him for it, yet it made them uneasy. As Matthew went on eating, I saw Stearne and Edwards look at each other.

'Gentlemen,' Stearne said, 'this is heavy talk. We have not met since Hopkins was promised to Richard Edwards's lovely sister, and with Mistress Alice captive here, we can find out all his secrets and whisper them to his bride. Then she will know what a poor bargain her brother has struck for her.'

Cutler grinned; Edwards planted his elbow on the table and laughed. Stearne had clearly sought only to lighten the mood, but from the corner of my eye I had seen Matthew's gaze move straight to my face. I tried to fix my smile.

Promised to Ruth Edwards? I thought of him introducing me to her at church. His face had been calm and there had been nothing in his voice – but in hers? I thought of when she had been rude to me about the minister, then of Mary Phillips asking whether I had met her that day, whether I had thought she looked well.

'To begin with,' Stearne said to me, 'you can tell us in which of Sir Harbottle's orchards your brother did go scrumping.'

'Sir!' I smiled, recovering myself. 'A shocking suggestion.'

Edwards was smiling, too. 'Your brother. What a child he was! I remember once he asked my father what he did earn in a year. Came out with it, just like that. "You need not be exact," he said. "It is a round figure I am interested in."'

Laughing, Grimston belched. Robert Taylor was laughing, too. Grimston said, 'But has not asking your questions served you well, Hopkins? I never knew a more rigorous man for business. If everyone at this table had made of their inheritance what you have made of yours, they'd all be as rich as me.' Sir Harbottle, laughing at his own joke, thumped himself on the chest, and turned to listen to Stearne and Cutler, who were talking of the war again.

'And have you heard in Somerset, those club men they have now?' Stearne was saying. 'Neither for one side nor the other, they say, but they protect each other's houses, and the womenfolk, when the armies are near.'

'When the King's army is near, you mean,' said Cutler. 'For our soldiers are better governed. Everyone speaks of their discipline.'

'And yet Waller is resigning, for he cannot hold them steady.' John Stearne picked up the bottle, to offer round again. There followed a little more talk of who would command, and I could see my brother calming himself.

But then John Cutler turned to me. 'Mistress Hopkins,' he said. 'What would you say, then, is the mood in London at present? All this talk one hears, of public meetings – but perhaps they are more peaceful than they sound?'

Grimston snorted. 'What would she know of public meetings? A little girl keeping indoors with her needle-work –' The men laughed. Grimston turned away, and I could not help it: I answered John Cutler, and as I did so, I raised my voice.

'The mood is uneasy, sir,' I said. 'There are many abandoning their parishes. Meeting in new congregations, under those who say they are Bible men. But if they can read the gospels, then it is because they have taught themselves.' I faltered, aware of eyes on me: Grimston's, Matthew's. 'They are wild men, mostly, and poor,' I continued. 'I have heard them say that they will not forgive the generations of slights they have been offered.'

Grimston made a dismissive sign. 'It is no slight to be born into a lowly state,' he said. 'That is the world, how God has ordered it.'

Robert Taylor frowned. 'I must confess, it is hard to think when you would have had occasion to hear such talk, Mistress Hopkins.'

Matthew cleared his throat. 'My sister did have reason to walk abroad in the city. She was a midwife.'

'Ah,' Taylor said.

Richard Edwards turned to Matthew. 'My wife spoke of learning that trade, but in the end I did not permit her. Out on the roads all hours, you know –'

'For good cause, sir,' I said. There was silence for a moment, at my cutting across him; I dared not look at my brother.

'But it is a respectable trade, surely, in a married woman,' John Stearne said, his easy tone strained. 'For instance, Mistress Hopkins, I'm sure your husband saw you between houses at night?'

I looked at the men around the table, their flushed drunk faces. Suddenly I wanted to make them see what it had been like in London, for me, for my landlady, for women like her. I wanted to show them some scrap of the truth. 'Most midwives I knew, sir, had no husband to see after their safety.'

Robert Taylor made a noise. 'But what could an unmarried woman want with such a trade?' he said.

'They were not unmarried, sir. But since Marston Moor last year, I knew many midwives who were made widows.'

Richard Edwards looked confused. 'But that fight went for us – scarce any of our side perished there –'

'You are right, sir,' I replied. There was a moment, as they digested what I meant.

Robert Taylor pursed his lips. 'Your sister favours the King, then, Hopkins. She names Papists among her friends, it seems.'

'London is like that, Taylor,' John Stearne said, uncertain. 'You do not choose who you live cheek by jowl with.'

'Thank God,' I added quietly. I could not look straight at Matthew, but from the side of my eye I could see that he had gone very still. Yet I turned back to Robert Taylor. 'I am no Papist, sir. But those friends I made, I was proud to know them. And, believe me, not one of them chose which side in this war it pleased her husband to prefer. Not one of us chose that there should be a war at all.'

I sounded very calm, but in my lap I could feel my hands shaking. The men were all averting their faces; uncomfortable, they were turning to my brother.

Robert Taylor looked just as helpless. For a moment, he looked as though he would answer me, but then he put down his glass. 'I thought we were come to talk of the witch business,' he said. 'I am anxious that we should be thorough, sirs, and certain that *all* the guilty have been named.'

Matthew looked at him. 'Be assured, it still holds my fullest attention,' he said.

Taylor picked up his glass again. 'I should hope it does. For while it no doubt resides in families – a taint in the blood, if you will, and I am certain you do right to look into daughters, mothers, and so on – I do wonder if we should think also of neighbours. Familiar friends. For I dined once on the road with a surgeon who served the lunatics at Bedlam, and it was his opinion that madness could be passed on not only through kinship but also by frequent companionship. If madness can be passed on, could not weakness? Could not vice? And you know these women, they are always in and out of each other's houses . . .'

As Taylor rattled on, I felt my face redden, and saw Richard Edwards's head turn to Matthew. Edwards, the only one among the guests who had conversed with Mother. Who knew something of her trouble.

My brother wouldn't meet his eye. He simply said to me, 'You must be tired, sister.' He spoke up to the company. 'We should have a care for my sister's health.'

I put down my napkin, and stood up. 'Indeed. Gentlemen, you must excuse me. I am for my bed.'

They got up with me, and said pleasantries as I backed out of the door. With it shut behind me, the passage was dark: Mary and Grace must have been having their own dinner. It was cool there, and I lingered, my hand on the doorframe, my face hot from wine and shame.

On the other side of the wood I heard the low hum of conversation start up again, and I was about to move away when one or two of the voices grew louder as more than one man began speaking at once. I heard Matthew say, 'confession', and then, 'proper method of interrogation'. I heard someone mention St Osyth, and Great Bentley; I heard John Stearne say, 'Six or seven in Great Holland alone.'

It was clear that they intended my brother's business to expand through the Tendring Hundred; it struck me that what was in train was a process, organized and methodical, not merely a piece of random spite. And more: though he had described it as Grimston's business, it was my brother's voice I heard most frequently, coming through the shut door. It was clear that Matthew was not at the edge of the matter: he was at its centre. As I listened, I could hear my own heart thumping, as in the parlour the men who ran Manningtree discussed their next steps. A heavy tread from down the passage drove me away up the dark stairs; Mary Phillips, come to see if anything was wanted.

In my chamber later, the shouted farewells of the men broke the evening's stillness. Lying in bed, I listened to them, and I wonder now where in truth the real power rested that night: whether in the hands of men like Grimston, men like Edwards. Whether it slept with the King at Oxford in an ordinary bed, dormant, like a taint in the blood. Whether it rested on the waiting benches of the Commons, or whether it went home with their plain occupants, like a shilling in each of their pockets.

I think the truth is that, rather than resting in any one or several places, all real power had gone loose by that night through the realm; and the land might have belonged to any man. Any man with the will to impose on others his own strange mission. Any man with the will to say, 'This is what we shall do.'

17

I walked quietly beside Matthew to church the next day, and though he spoke little, I felt as though he was watching me more carefully than usual. I wondered whether he was angry at how I had spoken out the night before. I wondered about Father's daily book, whether Matthew had noticed it gone, but he said nothing to make me think he had. Still, I was relieved to get to church that we might leave off our stilted conversation, and that I might rest myself, for the baby weighed on me.

But the brief solace I felt as I sat down in the pew was soon dispelled, when I overheard the talk of those behind us. One man telling his neighbour he had heard that Elizabeth Gooding had killed five head of someone's cattle; the neighbour replying that it was a shame someone so rotten could appear so good. Hearing that made me listen to the talk of those in front of us and to either side; I heard Bess Clarke mentioned, and the Leeches. When the minister stepped up to the pulpit, everyone broke off their talk and settled fervently to prayer, but in the gaps between prayers, the name I heard whispered around me was that of Rebecca West. *Rebecca Wessst*, echoing, hissing through the church.

The spring I was twenty-one, Rebecca West was fifteen, but she looked older. Her mother Anne was in the gaol, awaiting her trial. Bridget had moved Rebecca into the little alcove bed behind the kitchen hearth, and that spring, in between cooking and washing, the girl began her campaign of looking through her hair at Joseph, of touching his hand under pretence of taking his empty dish.

Once, I had come to see Joseph, late – Matthew was in Ipswich, and by then Mother went early to her bed. Joseph slept downstairs, and I could tap at his window; we had never done more than kiss, and every time I felt the thrill of being out alone in the twilight to see him. I came into Bridget's back garden, checking behind me to be sure I was not seen, and then, as I rounded the wall, I saw him standing by the bench, peering up at the sky. I was about to whisper, when the dark shape of him moved, divided from itself: it was not one figure, I saw, but two. In the moonlight I caught the flash of Rebecca's pale hair, her face as she murmured something, then hurried away up the steps, shutting the door softly behind her.

I should have asked him then whether he was fond of her. But I did not: I let it fester. Even when I had a ring on my finger and we were miles away from Manningtree, I still could not dismiss the sight of that single dark shape in the yard. I could not quash the thought that if there had been any money between them she would have been his choice. And as our marriage wore on, wore down, in the manner I have described, as I lost one child and then another, somehow as the years went by Rebecca West did not disappear. She lay under every disagreement: the choice my husband had not made, the phantom wife he had not taken. She lay between us, I felt, even in our bed. So it was mired in the worst mixed feelings that I heard her name whispered in Manningtree church that day.

†

After the prayers, you could feel folk waiting to discover what sermon the new minister would preach: half expecting, perhaps, something from Exodus; something with warnings, something with punishments. But instead, the minister took Job as his text, from the fourth chapter: how They that plough iniquity, and sow wickedness, do reap the same. I was heartened by his brave choice, and waited for him to speak out more explicitly against the fever of accusation that had gripped the town. But he said nothing overt, spoke only in a careful, general way, and I found myself disappointed.

After the sermon, I stood by while Matthew conversed with Richard Edwards a little. I was at a loss for what to do – for how to speak to my brother, having failed so badly the last time. I was glad, for once, that Bridget was absent from church: it felt suddenly delicate, what I had to accomplish. Before long, Ruth Edwards drifted over to me, and I prepared a smile. 'I hear I am to congratulate you,' I said.

'The end of September, we have settled upon,' Ruth replied. It sounded blessedly far off, and yet the uttering of any date at all made it seem grossly real. She looked at Matthew, where he was deep in talk with her brother. 'I never thought I would marry,' she said.

I thought, She thinks of marriage like a promotion overdue, like a clerk who has hankered after a higher stool, a larger pen. I felt my baby move, the almost-pain of it, and tried to refrain from rubbing my back.

Ruth Edwards was telling me how she would simply wear her best tawny gown for the wedding. That she had decided against any flowers in her hair. 'I don't want to seem girlish,' she explained. I tried to imagine Ruth Edwards looking girlish. I tried to imagine them lying together, but it was like thinking of two wooden boards, two playing cards. I knew I must make an effort with her, for I would soon depend on her goodwill as surely as on Matthew's, and my child would, too. I watched her talk, wondering what had led Matthew to match with her. For certain he would profit from having the Edwards family as kin. It was hard to think he wanted Ruth for love, or even lust. As she talked on about her wedding plans, I thought how at her age she would have had little choice, when Matthew proposed himself: and for a moment, I pitied her.

Richard Edwards joined us, took his sister's arm and tucked it into his own. 'I do not know how we will manage,' he said, smiling. For his Ruth had always made sure, he told me, that all the lights were out last thing. She rotated the linen and taught his little girls their lessons. She was even up first in the morning, making their butter and cheese in the cold room they had at the back of the house. I wondered if he was in some fashion saying what would be expected of me, the unwed sister; I thought of myself, churning in the before-dawn light, my hands as chilled as milk, waiting patiently for the butter to come.

Ruth smiled, then lowered her head in compulsory modesty. 'But, brother, Alice is quite as useful as I am. She is trained as a midwife, and Matthew tells me she quite took care of herself and her husband when they lived in London.'

I felt my face grow hot: I had forgotten my lie. Richard was nodding, and not fully listening: he had been hailed from the entry by his wife's brother, and excused himself to make his farewells. I wished that Ruth would go away as well, but I made myself turn to her, and smile. 'Shall we?' I said, gesturing after him. Together, Ruth Edwards and I wandered out into the fresh air. The day was mild, and it was pleasant to stand in the breeze beside the great holly tree. I said, 'I confess I was surprised, when I heard of it. I was not aware that you and my brother knew each other so well.'

'It is true, we have not been much together,' she said. She seemed glad at my softening.

'Well,' I said, 'you will be able to remedy it, this summer.'

I felt her look at me. 'Perhaps I will see more of him,' she said, 'though I do think he will be well enough occupied, and I must encourage him, must I not, to do his duty? For you know there have been more accusations, at Thorpe-le-Soken, and all thereabouts.' This I had heard the night before, and I knew Matthew's warrant included that place. But then she added, 'I did ask him whether he wanted to be married sooner, so that I could go with him and see after his comfort. But he said we would never get the banns read in time. He seemed to think you would not be able to accompany him. But he said there is a girl in your household who will do well enough to go and help. Grace, is it?'

I tried to keep my face even. 'Yes,' I said: thinking, But help with what?

Just then Matthew came out of the church porch and towards us. He stopped beside Ruth Edwards and took her arm, holding it awkwardly, as you would a stick. His eye had been caught by something at the lych gate. I turned my head and saw what he was looking at. It was Bridget.

I asked Ruth to excuse me, felt Matthew's eyes upon me

as I hurried down the path. As I got nearer, it was clear that Bridget had slept in her clothes. When I was close enough, I said, 'What are you doing? Why did you not come in to the service?'

For a moment, Bridget searched my face. Then she said, 'What I think is, you are still jealous. After all this time. You were his wife, Alice. You've got his child in your belly. What has Rebecca got?'

'Quiet,' I said, and thought, Surely she is drunk. Glancing back, I saw Matthew watching us, smiled at him and raised one finger. 'Get here,' I said, between my teeth, hauling Bridget with me through the gate and around the corner. She pulled away from me. I was stronger, but only just. Finally, out of sight behind the hedge, she slipped my grasp, and we stood, regarding each other, panting.

'I have been waiting for you to do something,' she said. 'But now I hear he is going all through Essex, and still you've done nothing.'

Folk were starting to drift out through the gate. I had to make her hush, come away. I tried to speak calmly. 'And you think this will help, do you?' I said. I governed myself. 'It is a bigger matter than we first thought, I grant you. But they will be held for a time and let go. I am certain nothing has been done that is unseemly.'

'Not unseemly? What – apart from bruises like that on Rebecca West's thigh?' She showed three inches with finger and thumb.

I stopped. 'You didn't go and see them?'

She smiled. 'I took a quantity of beer for Stephen Hoy, who keeps the gaol at Colchester. I said that Matthew sent me to check on the women.'

I watched her, disbelieving. 'Have you been knocked simple?' I whispered, but her face stayed mutinous, cold.

'Have you even tried to talk to him?' she said.

'Of course I tried,' I said.

Folk emerging from the gate turned curiously towards us: I tilted my head, and Bridget followed me a few yards up the road. Then I turned to her again. Her eyes were swollen from weeping or lack of sleep. I had to find a way to calm her, but at the same time, I wanted to tell her how confused I was.

I said, 'Bridget, Grace told me a thing. She said that the day before Mother died, before you came to see her, she saw something in her bed. Some manner of poppet or doll. But when she went back in later, she could not find it.'

Instantly I saw something pass over Bridget's face; I saw her breath pause, and then she looked back towards the gate. 'What is that to do with anything? I cannot think your mother would have been bothered with any such frippery. It will have been nothing. It might have been a bundle of herbs – she did sometimes tie up rosemary in little parcels, about the size of your hand –'

'Bridget,' I said. 'What is it?'

'What is what? Whatever she had, it was nothing I gave her.'

'I can't help you if you do not tell me the truth.'

Her face turned hard again. 'I'm not asking you to help me. I'm asking you to help the Wests. I'm asking you to help Elizabeth Gooding.'

My eyes flicked over her shoulder to Matthew standing by the lych gate, watching us. His face was a pale smudge, and I could not tell what was written there, whether rage or fear, or something else. He was too far away, just, for her to need to greet him, for him to hear what was being said. Bridget followed my gaze, and for a moment I was afraid she would go to him, and I thought that if she did, I could not prevent her.

But Bridget only hunched her cloak more tightly about her, and she met my eyes again. 'Call him off, Alice,' she said. 'You call him off.'

And with that she turned, and began to walk away slowly up the hill. I settled my face, and tucked my hands into my sleeves, weak with relief. But by the time I looked back towards the church gate, the road was empty, and Matthew had gone.

18

When I got back to the Thorn my brother was out, as I had expected he would be. Later that afternoon, I happened to hear Mary Phillips go in for his chamber pot, and I readied myself to slip back in and replace the daily book. But when she came out onto the landing, I heard her put the pot down and lock the door behind her before she went down the stairs to empty it.

I scarcely knew what to think. I could not forget Bridget's manner when I had asked her about the item Grace had described. She had seemed pale, jumpy; she had seemed guilty, but I did not wish to think of that. Of what it might mean, for one woman to have given another a strange trinket, and the recipient then to die.

But there were a few plain things of which I was certain. Though they were not saints, I did not think any of the women taken were guilty as they had been charged. And Elizabeth Gooding, Bridget was right about her: I knew that while Elizabeth Gooding breathed she had never done any harm to anyone.

That evening, when Grace brought me my dinner, I nearly asked her there and then about what Ruth Edwards had said, about the Tendring Hundred and helping my brother. But then I heard Mary calling for her, and I decided to speak of it another time. The meal was lamb, and though during the dark days of Lent I had craved meat, now I could not accustom myself to it. The lamb tasted sickening, like metal. As I put my plate aside, I wished Grace might be spared what Ruth Edwards seemed to think my brother had in store for her.

I got up to check my reflection in the darkened window, and thought how, with my brother sated and sleepy, it must be as good a time as any to plead for leniency. I knew that to do it I would have to be brazen, would have to forget my own interests and those of the child I was carrying, and risk making Matthew angry. I tried to remember how we had sparred and argued as children that I might face him with the same confidence. But much had changed since then: the sight of the legal books in his chamber had not been lost on me, and I felt at a disadvantage for not having read them, not having absorbed the latest thinking as I knew Matthew would have done.

I went to him in the parlour. I averted my eyes from the surprise on his face, and closed the door behind me: then, without invitation, I crossed to the other chair beside the hearth and stood behind it.

'There was a man I used to see,' I said, 'near our rooms, near where we lived in London. He would sit on the mounting block by the inn over the road, and if they turned him off it he would sit on the boot-scraper by the door. He used to make a sound like a fire spitting. He did it when ladies walked by him, to give them a start. And he could not only make sounds but he could speak, too, clear words without ever moving his lips. He said he was inhabited by an angel, and he would use its voice to tell people when they were going to die, any person who walked past.'

Matthew's face opened with interest. 'And? Did he reckon it truly?'

'Who knows? The date he gave was never too soon.'

Matthew cleared his throat. 'Angels never speak thus. It was a devil that was in him.'

'So I always thought. And in letting the devil come into the world in such ways, God seeks to make us a lesson.' I came around the chair, and sat down.

He sat up straighter. 'You have the sense of it.'

'Then – if you could set me right on this, brother – if God may do that, send the devil to us direct, if you will, what need has He of witches?'

Matthew bent to throw another log onto the fire. 'But why would God make laws against witches, if there were none? Scripture tells us how to deal with them, and the laws of the land, like any other nuisance.'

I cleared my throat. 'I seem to recall Simon Magus, in Acts, was he not a great wizard? Yet he did repent of his sins, and was baptized.'

Matthew stayed standing, leaning by the hearth. 'The text is silent on how he ended his days. Not so vague on what became of Babylon. If you look for the redemption of witches, Alice, the Bible is a poor place to start. Exodus is clear enough.' His tone was almost pitying, almost kind.

Thou shalt not suffer a witch to live: that was the verse he meant.

Perhaps I made a mistake in trying to talk to him in this fashion, for I never could best my brother in citing scripture. His grasp of it was against me, and not only his grasp of it but the certainty he derived from it. Father had always liked Matthew's interest in scripture: it allowed him to treat

Matthew as he did his other sons. He did not see, perhaps, that when Matthew believed a piece of scripture, he believed it wholly, without any gloss of pity, without any breathing room for others' imperfections.

So when he quoted Exodus, I was helpless to argue: I saw how in the years I had been gone, washing shirts and sheets and making dinners, my brother had spent that time in reading, in thinking, and the gap between my learning and his had widened still further. I saw that I would have to narrow my target, and take a different tack. I saw that I would have to plead. When I spoke, it was in a low voice. 'I am sorry, brother, if Bridget and I made a spectacle this morning.' I kept my eyes on the floor. 'I am sorry about your dinner – if I said too much, or out of turn . . .'

'What do you want, sister?'

'Your – Ruth Edwards, that is, she said that you are planning to take Grace with you, when you go into the hundred. She said that you are planning to go.'

'Yes?'

'But for what purpose? Why do you need Grace?'

'To assist me while I take confessions, while I make any necessary examinations.'

'Examinations?'

He moved in his chair. 'She is my servant, sister, and she will do as I tell her. Unless you wish to come instead? But it will be a fortnight of hard riding. I did not think that would be to your present taste.' I felt my breath stop in my chest, as he leaned forward. 'Likewise I can lend you a horse and you may take yourself back to London, if you have friends there still. Perhaps only two days' hard riding will suit you better.' Then he stretched out his hand, and I flinched: but it was with one finger, just one, that he touched my belly, encased in my gown. He knew. Mary Phillips had told him.

I got up, and moved away to the table. 'Bridget told me the truth of how your accident came to pass,' I said desperately. 'It was Mother alone, the sickness in her brain –'

But he cut across me. 'You have no business speaking to her of that. I know what it was. I can make up my own mind, Alice.'

Softly, I said, 'Grace is young to go, that is all.'

'She may be young but she knows her duty. It gives me to wonder, sister, whether you do not need a lesson in yours. Perhaps you might manage some gratitude that you are allowed to keep yourself here in quietness, and do only the small tasks I have set you.' He pulled his case of papers towards him. 'On which note, sister – Elizabeth Gooding, you know her house? She was obliged to leave suddenly, and I need someone to look in and be sure that all is well.' He gave me a distant smile. 'Go tomorrow,' he said. 'Mary Phillips will give you the key.'

19

It was Robert Taylor's horse they had got Elizabeth Gooding for; that whining pinch-mouthed man's dead horse, and knowing that sharpened the waste of it, when the next morning I let myself into her cottage with the key Mary had given me. It was quiet. Her dog was gone, taken in by a neighbour perhaps, a small vain show of support. There was her Bible where it had been laid aside, and her husband's cap on its peg by the door, though he was dead and gone. Trying to be brisk, I began by taking out the ashes, along with some crusts, a hardened heel of cheese, a jug of milk that had turned. I rinsed the jug, and set it upside down to dry. I rested a minute before I crouched to check the chamber pot and then went to empty it, breathing through my mouth. Thinking myself finished, I put my head into the scullery.

They had come for Elizabeth Gooding on a wash day, then, for there were her wet sheets in a tub, ready to be hung outside. I lifted the corner of one, and the feel of the soaked linen in my grasp took me backwards, to London, to getting the last load wrung out before Joseph came home. But the smell that rose up was stale, and the cold, damp sheet was already spotted black with mould. The smell's taste stayed in my mouth the whole of my slow walk back to the Thorn.

When I got in, I wanted nothing more than to go to

my chamber and sit, recover myself. But once I was upstairs, I heard a sound coming from down the passage, the room Grace and the other servants shared. When I drew near the open door, I saw Grace sitting on her bed, weeping.

She showed me a grey swathe of cloth draped over her arm. 'Mary Phillips has got me a new cloak for riding,' she said. Her face was grey, too.

I checked the landing, then closed the door behind me. 'Are you unwell?' I said.

She bit her lip. Tears escaped down her cheeks. 'I don't want to go,' she said.

I sat on the bed beside her, and put a hand on her back. More tears spotted the pale grey cloak, where she had bundled it in her lap. She took a great shuddering breath.

I spoke to her soothingly for a while, then made her change and get into bed. I said I would tell Mary she had a poorly stomach. Grace was fretful, wanted to leave the candle lit till the scullery maids came up, but it was burned down to a stub, so I told her I would slip downstairs to get her a fresh one. But in the cold passage I heard my brother's voice in the kitchen and I hesitated, just behind the door. It was partly open, and I could see him standing by the sink with Mary Phillips, still in his riding boots. I heard Mary say, 'I wasn't sure what you wanted doing with her.'

'Put her in a chamber, of course,' Matthew murmured. 'The one next to my sister's will serve.'

'And, pardon, master, but Grace is too short to lend her anything. Shall I give her something of mine, for now?'

My first thought was that my brother had arranged some kindness for a beggar, for then Mary Phillips disappeared into the scullery and led a person out. Her hair was filthy, almost matted, and her face, too, making her pale eyes larger as they fixed upon my brother; as they fixed upon, and then recognized, me.

It was Rebecca West.

As her face changed, I was forced to step into the room, that Matthew and Mary Phillips might not guess I had been lurking, and as I came forward into the firelight, I could see Rebecca properly. She was slighter in her frame than I, more delicate in her bones – Joseph had once said that a strong wind would blow her away – and she had grown still slighter, I was certain. Most likely that was the gaol food. Her filthy face made me notice that she had the same blue eyes as Grace.

Mary Phillips took hold of her then, and steered her out of the kitchen, and I heard her leading the girl away upstairs.

In my shock, I forgot to watch my tongue. 'What is she doing here?'

'She will be here until the trials,' Matthew said. 'She is to testify against the others, so she cannot stay at the gaol. And I won't let her go home. I can't have her absconding.' I met his eyes. 'She will be under your charge, sister,' he said evenly. 'Keep her occupied. Make her useful.'

My heart was beating hard, and perhaps that was why the child twisted inside me. I looked at the stone flags at his feet, and governed myself; dug in the pocket of my apron for the key. 'Elizabeth Gooding's house,' I said, and put it into his hand. 'I have seen to it.'

†

In bed, I lay flat on my back with my hands on my stomach, listening to Mary Phillips settle Rebecca West into the chamber next to my own, thinking about my child. About the week in December when I had missed my bleeding, and how sorely I had wanted to tell Joseph, but hesitated, since I could not yet be sure. I had almost told him the night before he died, that Saturday night as he was climbing into bed and about to blow out his candle.

But then he had said, 'Oh, listen, love – I shall be out tomorrow, after church. We've built a new kind of flintlock, to try if we cannot make the workings any cheaper. We shall be going up to test it on the heath.'

'I never see you any more, on a Sunday,' I replied. I tried to speak lightly, but I know it came out plaintive.

Joseph frowned. 'Well, I have to go to church, Alice. You go to church.' He touched my arm. 'But if you do not like it, I need not go to the heath after.'

I wanted to say, 'Yes, I go to church. Where you go, that is not a church.' But I did not say anything. I only turned over to face the wall. I could feel Joseph looking sadly at my back. After a moment, he said, 'You must not be jealous, my love.'

I did not answer him: I was too proud to say, 'Do not go.' I still resented Rebecca West, his old fondness for her, and how gently baffled my resentment made him. It was easier, in my pride, to pretend I did not care. Before he blew out his candle, he kissed my cheek, but I did not say anything. I did not reach out for him, or return his kiss.

The next day when they brought back his body I only knew him by his shoes, his clothes, his familiar arms, which they had folded strangely over his chest. I never kissed his cheek again, for they implored me not to lift the sheet: not to look on what remained where my husband's face had been.

The next morning, when I came warily down to breakfast, Rebecca West and Matthew were sitting opposite each other, eating, almost like a long-married couple. Rebecca West looked a different creature. I had dressed myself, after waiting in vain for hot water, for I had heard Grace's low voice in Rebecca's chamber that morning, and now Rebecca's face was scrubbed to a blush, her washed hair shining pale and hanging in a rope over her shoulder. Mary Phillips must have been trimming greens, for a pair of scissors lay close by on the table; at the sight of them, my fingers itched.

Rebecca was wearing one of Mary's gowns, which, though it was plain and loose, was somehow still becoming. The girl was seated in my usual place, so I went to Matthew's left; he did not look at me, as I pulled out my chair. Rebecca was helping herself as though she had not eaten for a month. When Grace put down another platter of bread, my brother said, 'Will you have more, Mistress West?' and she nodded, her mouth too full to speak. He proceeded to choose the two thickest slices and load them onto her plate, carefully keeping his eyes from her face, or where her dress was loose at the neck. Before Grace turned away I marked again the similarity between her appearance and Rebecca's, except that Rebecca knew of her beauty and used it. Matthew watched her tuck her hair behind an ear, then pushed his plate aside, and got to his feet. Rebecca made to get up with him, but he said, 'No, Mistress West. You must eat your fill.' Then, to me: 'Find her a cap, will you, sister?'

I wondered whether to forgo my breakfast and follow him, simply to avoid being alone with her, but the moment passed, so I tried to continue calmly eating. Rebecca West likewise applied herself again to her meal, taking great bites that she could hardly fasten her lips over.

'My brother's table seems to suit you,' I said, as she finished what was on her plate and reached for more.

'As it does you, Mistress Alice,' Rebecca said. 'You want to be careful. It tends to stay on the arms, on the jowls, as a woman gets older.'

I kept my eyes on my plate and ignored the remark, as though I had not heard it.

†

Rebecca was in the house three days, before Matthew and Grace went into the hundred. I half expected Bridget to come beating down the door, demanding afresh that Matthew stop, that I stop him. But she didn't. She didn't come, and Matthew didn't speak of her.

Though Rebecca made herself hard to bear – whistling when I set her to polish a chair, talking to the stable-men instead of feeding the hens, and eyeing me in her amused, leering way when I went out to chide her – I was almost grateful for her presence. For Grace didn't like her either, and Rebecca gave us a subject to talk of that was not Grace's impending journey. And there was plenty to talk of: it had emerged from among the scullery maids that

Rebecca's testimony would include evidence against her own mother.

On the last night, before they were due to go into the hundred, I heard Grace take Rebecca her dinner in her room. Through the wall, I heard Rebecca give some pert answer, then, on the landing, Grace's sigh. I went to the door, and beckoned her in.

'I'm sorry you have to wait on her.' I smiled. 'Though not as sorry as I will be, to be alone with her, until you are back.'

Grace smiled, and raised her shoulders. 'I don't know. I pity her, in truth, mistress. Though for certain I am sure she is better off here, away from those she will speak against.' She saw my questioning look, and turned her eyes to the floor. 'I heard your brother say this morning to John Stearne that he scarcely even needs her evidence, apart from the shock it will give the public benches.' I noticed that she had not called him 'master' but, rather, 'your brother'. She went on. 'He has enough other testimony, he says, that he could hang them all easily enough without her.' Grace dipped her head. 'It seems cruel, to have her speak against her mother, if it is not needful.'

It was sobering to hear her relate how coldly and practically Matthew had spoken of it all. But I could not believe he was so certain of gaining convictions. Surely that was just boasting among men.

We heard a cough through the wall, the creak of a bedframe. Grace said, 'I think, mistress, you will be doing her a kindness if you keep trying to find her some occupation. For I heard your brother say the trials will not be until July. Better she does not have the chance to think too much while she waits.'

I touched her arm. 'And so you are going in the morning. Are you ready?'

She tilted her head. 'I think I can do what is required. Mary Phillips has explained it to me. There will not be much. In truth, she says I am to be there in case the accused woman needs to go to the privy or she faints or somesuch.' She looked at me. 'Your brother has given me a dried orange with cloves in it for when we have to go into low places.'

From the way she spoke, I could tell that whatever liking she might have had for Matthew was dissolved and gone. 'Remember, Grace. You did not elect this. You must just obey him and come back safe.'

'He bade me tell you, while we are gone, to find something for Rebecca to wear at the trial that will fit her better. Something respectable,' she said.

'Right,' I said. She had turned towards the door. 'Take courage, Grace,' I added.

When she had gone back to her room, I sat on my bed. It suited Matthew, I could see, to have one of the accused women speak against her own kin. He would convince a court of their guilt much more easily if he could make the women seem unnatural, like beasts in the eyes of their watching neighbours. The thought turned me cold.

I had been so certain, my first days at the Thorn, that whoever was accused, whatever fuss was made, they would surely be acquitted.

†

The next morning, I wished I could feel a quarter so certain when I stood on the yard steps as Matthew helped Grace up onto my old horse, then mounted his own. In her new riding cloak, Grace seemed very small, her face pale under the hood. Matthew glanced down at the three of us, Mary Phillips, Rebecca West and myself. Then he was moving off through the gate, and they were gone, to see about finding company for the five Manningtree women waiting in Colchester gaol.

21

It was as though the sniping on Rebecca West's first day at the Thorn set us in a pattern of scrapping children, though I think it almost helped me to have a thing of such small consequence to worry over. We took our meals together in the parlour, and not two days had passed after the departure of my brother and Grace into the hundred before I could not stand to watch Rebecca chewing any longer. I put down my knife crossly and said, 'Will you close your mouth?' But her only reply was to take another large mouthful of meat, so that I had to look away from the mess between her lips.

For lack of other work to do, Mary Phillips had found Rebecca some bags of wool that wanted carding, and it was my task to sit with her and sew, to be sure she did not shirk. It was awkward, being thrown together for long hours in that way, for the natural dullness of the task would have led most women to talk. But we did not, only sat either side of the fireplace, hands busy, the pale spring sunshine flooding in from outside.

Though I was there to watch Rebecca, I could not shake the feeling that Mary Phillips had been ordered to watch me. She would go through the mime of asking me what was wanted for meals, and when I spoke of going back to finish the work at Mother's house, she gave me the keys to my old chamber and my brother's without comment. But it was Mary who woke us in the morning, and Mary who locked up at night.

Yet though Mary Phillips kept her eye on me, still it would have been easy then for me to leave. I thought about it every day. Only the baby, the stubborn aliveness of its tapping, kept me rooted at the Thorn. For I knew that if I risked the journey and lost it, my last remaining link with Joseph, I would never forgive myself.

Gradually, my sitting with Rebecca daily seemed to exhaust our mutual dislike. When I took her with me to collect my new gowns, she even ventured to remark on the fine weather. I agreed that it was very fine.

'God, I can't take a breath or move my foot but Mary watches me,' she added, a moment later.

'Take it lightly,' I said. 'She is the same with me.' Rebecca slowed. We were out beyond the houses now, and the warm sun pleasant. 'I know you do not like it with us,' I said, 'but it is better, is it not, than where you could be?'

She kicked a twig. 'At least I'd be with my mother.'

'But that is why you are here – to keep you separate from her, and the others you will betray. To keep you safe from them.'

'You think so?' she said. She seemed interested in the thought.

'That, or to make sure you do not go wandering.'

'Perhaps,' she said. 'Though your brother knows I have little enough money to wander anywhere.' She stopped, to gaze out over the estuary. 'I think in truth I am here so that the good folk of Manningtree cannot come where I live and torch me in my bed.'

She turned, and at the shock on my face her own drew

inwards again, and she walked on, kicking things on the ground now and then, sticks and pebbles, and I followed a few feet behind her, governing myself to bear patiently with what I thought of as her dramatics, and not to point out that she would ruin her boots.

†

But I started to think that Rebecca might not have been wrong about the pure hatred that was abroad for any woman with a whisper against her name. For rumours, fragments of rumours of what my brother was about, began to come back from throughout the hundred, and I gleaned them where I could: from the overheard talk of the scullery maids, or where I stood with Mary and Rebecca at the back of the church.

That was where I heard of Susan Cocke from St Osyth, to whom the devil had come out of a hedgerow and promised that he would provide for her, promised her vengeance on her enemies, and that he would share her bed. I heard of others who confessed that they had only lain with the devil in reluctance, when their own beds had grown lonely.

I heard of Sarah Sparrow and Mary Greenliefe, who at one time had shared a house and a bed with their daughters, each fourteen, and more than once something had bitten the girls and bothered them around their legs under the blankets, and Sarah said it was Mary's doing, that she had brought something upon them, that she never would have lived with such a woman, would never have been forced to it, if she had been fortunate enough to have a son.

Bridget still did not show her face at service. But though

I had thought my brother's business prompted by his suspicions of Bridget, certainly now it seemed to be little to do with her. What he was doing seemed larger and less discriminate.

As April turned to May, Mary Phillips began to go out some days to the nearer villages of the hundred. My brother needed more assistance, it seemed; I heard the scullery maids talking of it. But Mary never told me when she was going – and she was never gone overnight, always back to lock up at the usual time. I thought plenty about Father's daily book, which I had still had no chance to replace. I wished I could return it, and search for the missing pages, for I could not shake the feeling that it was among them I would find the root of what my brother was doing. But Mary kept the key to Matthew's chamber always with her, and there was no other.

As the days passed, I knew I could leave the work at Mother's house no longer, and I felt in any case that being there, where I had lived with Matthew, might take me nearer the heart somehow of what he wanted: nearer the heart of how to stop him. So I went, taking Rebecca with me, carrying a crate between us for the clothes that needed packing. It bumped my leg as we walked, though I took care not to hurt my belly. When we reached Mother's house, I set Rebecca to scrubbing the kitchen floor while I took the crate upstairs.

First I unlocked my own chamber, but there was little there. Mother must have given away the few outgrown things I had left behind. Next I went into Matthew's chamber. But if I had thought to find any clue there, I was disappointed. I did as he had directed, packing most of the contents of the room for giving away or burning. His old books I saved from their shelves, but I threw into a sack the row of a dozen conkers, prized once, now turned wizened beyond hardness. Old shirts, small shoes: I sifted it all carefully but found none of the hints I had been hoping for of what lay in my brother's adult heart; what the secret was, to influencing him.

Giving up, I went into Mother's room, where I brought out her gowns from the cupboard one by one, and folded them into the crate. Most could not be altered for me: I had a good five inches of height on Mother, and few contained so much at the hem. Mother had been more Rebecca West's size, I thought. I took out her sewing box, and set it on the bed, thinking of when last she must have used it, the day before she died. A new mattress had been brought, since my last visit: as I set the sewing box down a feather escaped from it, and lofted upwards in the draught.

Downstairs, I called Rebecca from her scrubbing, and made her wash her hands properly. 'I've found something that might fit you,' I said. I opened the crate and pulled out a green gown, holding it up between finger and thumb. She didn't thank me, only looked at the smooth cloth. 'Well. We should try it on you,' I said. 'Grace said you'll need something better for when you give your testimony.'

Obediently she followed me into the parlour, and I turned away while she got out of Mary Phillips's gown and into the green one. I turned back. The fit was good. 'If you stand still,' I said, 'I'll pin the hem.' I plumped a cushion on the floor and knelt. 'Stand straight, on both feet.'

I began the work of pinning up the hem, leaning back on my heels to judge the effect. It felt odd, to be crouching at her feet. Once, I would have feared she would step on my fingers, but now there was a peaceable quiet between us, until she said, 'Bridget, when she came to see us in the gaol in Colchester, she told me your husband died.'

'Yes.' I had jabbed the pin I was holding through the fabric and into my finger. Narrowly, I kept from cursing.

'She was always kind to me, Bridget,' Rebecca said. A spot of blood had got on her hem. I stuck the finger into my mouth. Then she said, 'Your brother told me the trials will be in Chelmsford.'

'They would be, being assizes.'

'That's where they had my little son taken, to Chelmsford. That's where the couple live, who have him.'

I stopped pinning. 'I never knew you had a child.'

Her voice was trying for steadiness, failing. 'I had left Bridget's house by then. We needed money, and there were easier ways to get it than Bridget preferred me to use while I was under her roof. I didn't even keep him till he was weaned. She found the people to take him.'

I stood up, dusting my hands. 'I'm sure he is loved there.'

'I know. I know,' she said. 'But if I could only have a sight of him. Last night I dreamed that the couple who had him brought him to the courtroom, and held him up over the heads of the crowd for me to see. In the dream he was a baby, whereas in truth he would be rising three years old now.'

'Whose was he,' I said, 'your child?'

She laughed bitterly. 'Thomas Hart's. Who else? He was just like him, too. I always thought that was nonsense, until I had one of my own, but then it was like looking into Thomas Hart's own eyes. Except that I loved them.'

Her eyes were full. 'He'll be better off, my little lad, not knowing his father.' She met my gaze. 'Your husband and I, we talked of our fathers, sometimes, when I lived in Bridget's house. Since neither of us knew them.' She placed her hands on the back of one of the draped chairs, smoothing the dust-cloth. 'It was daft, but we used to say, "Imagine if they came back, their fortunes made." They were both seamen. We used to say, "Imagine if they came back spice-traders." ' She laughed again. 'Mine didn't look like one, though. I saw him, I think, just once, when I was small. I never told Joseph this. He had hair just the colour of mine, but thinning. I remember him kissing my mother. Next day, when he went, she had a fat lip, and she could only drink her morning cup by tilting it careful, to one side of her mouth. For years after, I thought the fat lip came from kissing,' she finished, her voice dry. 'Which in a way, it does.'

We stayed quiet for a minute. 'Bridget told me when she came to see you, you had bruises. Here.' I circled my finger over my lap.

She smiled a crooked smile. 'They were the gaoler's doing,' she said. 'Bridget saw them, for I was washing when she came. No doubt she dreamed up her own cause for them. But your brother, he never laid a hand on me. No, he and his friends, they never touched me. Though for certain I could feel them wanting to.' Her smile faded. 'But it will be worth dealing with them, to see my mother spared.'

I turned away as she began to unfasten the green gown. 'That is what you have arranged?'

'She thinks I have bargained for my own freedom only. She thinks that one of us might as well escape. But she'll get off, too. I need only say trifles about her, Master Hopkins says.' Her face turned hard. 'And as for the others, I know what I must say. To make them seem guilty.'

I was appalled by how easily she seemed to speak of giving evidence against her neighbours, and appalled, too, by how Matthew had taken her in. She said, 'Your brother has told me the kinds of things the court would want to hear. You could make anyone seem guilty if you wanted.' Her face went softer again. 'My mother was no witch, but she used to tell my fortune, you know. Looking into our well with a mirror. Just to amuse me, when I was little. She would always see a rich husband from London, a white pony to ride.'

The tenderness in her voice touched me, and I saw that it was love for her mother – only that, and a fierce will to survive – that was making her do as she did. The fault was not with her, I thought. It was with Matthew, for using her so. For I doubted he intended to honour his promise. I thought of what Grace had said: that they would all hang anyway. I could only hope that she was wrong, and that somehow this summer's madness would run its course.

Something perturbed me, though, in what Rebecca had said, and as she got back into Mary Phillips's gown, it came to me: the woman I had met at the Chelmsford inn, who had slept uneasily after studying my palm. I folded the green gown and returned it to the crate, trying to put the memory away. But then I saw the gown under the green one, a mourning gown that had belonged to my true mother. She had been tall, I knew, like my elder brothers and like me. I took the hem, and saw how it had been altered; that rather than trimming the spare fabric Mother had folded it in on itself so that perhaps the hem could be let down again, the skirt made long enough for me. I shook the gown out, and held it up against myself.

'My mother left off telling my fortune, when I got older,' Rebecca said, and I looked up, startled, for it was as though she had guessed something of my thoughts. But she only smiled sadly. 'Mother knew that it would not please me any more to hear about the pony, the rich man.' She stopped. She did not need to say why: there had been only one husband who would have pleased her after she came to Manningtree, and he had not been wealthy.

I closed the lid of the crate. 'You love her a great deal, don't you?' I said.

'Of course,' she replied. And then: 'You cannot think what it is like, to see them go after her as they did. Even though not one used his fists. What they do to you, him and the others, it's mostly done with words. They make you doubt yourself, you see. You are hungry, you haven't slept. They ask you questions, and they write your answers down, and then later they ask the same ones again. Did it happen that way, you think, or didn't it?' She shook her head. 'They ask you whether you were at such a person's house on a certain date, and they tell you they will be checking with others whether you were there, and you can't see what they are writing. And my mother, you know, she gets such pain in her back, she hardly sits down if she can help it, and they made her sit for hours.' Rebecca was angry, now, weeping. 'I know you think I should not speak in the court but, truly, I think if you were in my place, you would do the same,' she said.

I reached out and took her hand, felt the small thin bones of it. 'At least,' I said, 'you did not have to see her harmed.'

191

She swallowed. 'They were almost better to have beaten her,' she said bleakly. 'For my mother, she could have kept her spirit through a few minutes' whipping. But how she was in the gaol, I have never seen her thus. She would not eat. She would only stare at the wet stone wall. As if she could see something there that I could not. As if she had a bad feeling, but did not dare speak it out loud.'

From that late pamphlet objecting to the searching for a witch's mark; response to be written and circulated.

Every old woman with a wrinkled face, a furred brow, a hairy lip, a gobber tooth, a squint eye, a squeaking voice, or a scolding tongue, having a rugged coat upon her back, a skull-cap on her head, a spindle in her hand, and a dog or cat by her side; is not only suspected, but pronounced for a witch. For if you will not admit a big, or a boil; a wart, or a wen; a push, or a pile; a sear, or a scab; an issue, or an ulcer; for a palpable witch's mark: yet then shall it certainly be determined to be in such a place, as for shame, and in very truth, is not to be named.

22

Rebecca and I hoarded away any scrap about the taken women, overheard from the scullery maids or in the town somewhere, as the stories continued to multiply. One evening, Rebecca had finished carding her third lot of wool, and was sitting, picking her hands. We had been talking of Mary Johnson from Great Clacton, who had had a child once, the kind of boy that is blond and wins at running races. But he had long grown up and gone to be a sailor, and Mary Johnson had fallen to asking too many questions about other people's children, and occasionally giving them an unsolicited apple and a kiss.

I was taking up the green dress, which Rebecca would wear at the trials, and thinking it did not feel real that any-one should be convicted of witchcraft, that they should be hanged. Why did it not feel real? For the danger surely was present enough: Mary Johnson had confessed to brushing one of her apples with poison and been taken away.

I halted between stitches. 'Why would a person confess such things?' I said.

Rebecca shook her head. From her face I could see that she knew what I meant; that she had been thinking, like me, of what was unfolding across the hundred. 'I suppose a person will confess to anything,' she said, 'if they have not slept.'

She looked up then, as a knocking came from out in the passage. Someone at the back door. Mary Phillips had gone out for an hour and was not back yet; we waited for one of the scullery maids to go. But then the knocking came again, so Rebecca got up to answer it. A minute passed, and she did not come back. I pushed my needle into a seam, and got to my feet, but then Rebecca came in.

'Bridget is here,' she said.

I stopped still. Then I went out past her, shutting the parlour door behind me. Though my doubts surrounding Bridget had persisted since Grace had told me about the item she had seen in Mother's bed, still I was glad she had come. But in the passage I hesitated. I was keenly aware that what Matthew was embarked upon, I had failed to halt or even slow, so I was hesitant as I pulled open the back door, and saw Bridget standing on the steps. But she did not seem angry. Rather, she pulled me into a rough hug, and as we broke apart she laid a hand on my cheek.

'Thank God you're all right,' she said. 'And the child?'

'Well. Moving a lot.' I glanced around, but could see no stablehands. 'Come out here,' I said, taking Bridget by the arm, and I hurried with her across the yard, out through the gate and over the road, drawing her into the shadows by the warehouses. It was growing dark, and there was no one about, except one whistling man coiling ropes down by the quay, who paid us no attention.

Bridget looked strained, twitchy, as she drew her shawl closer about her. 'I was fearful when I did not hear from you. It's turning into a bad business, this.'

'I live in hope that it could still amount to nothing. Though Grace, before he took her with him, she thought

195

otherwise.' I stopped. 'He has said nothing of you, though, Bridget.'

She pressed her lips together. 'Perhaps his regard for you is strong enough to keep me safe.' She kept her voice low. 'But I am minded to agree with Grace. The wind is behind him, now, and he is running with it. You have heard, I take it, what Grace is there to do?' She studied my face. 'You have heard about the searching?'

'What do you mean?'

'You know it is imps they look for, the signs of them having visited a woman.'

I bit my lip. 'I have heard they sit still hours together, and watch for them coming.'

'But that is not all. They are looking for marks, from them sucking.' She made a small gesture. 'Under the clothes.'

'What do you mean?' I said, amazed. 'Matthew is searching them?'

'No, no,' Bridget replied. 'He has women in his pay, and Grace there to see all goes ahead smoothly.' She dropped her voice further. 'He knows how it could be disputed, were they to settle on a mole or a birthmark as proof of sin. In court, a woman might expose a wart or somesuch on her arm, and ask the jury if they had not a half-dozen themselves the same. So they are inspecting elsewhere. Where a woman may not expose, or scarce even speak of.'

I stared at her, disgusted. How could anyone let such a filthy proceeding go forward? How could it ever be made to stand in court? But I saw at once how it could be done, how my brother might make it stand: using delicate hints, using sad, reluctant shakings of the head.

Bridget put a hand on my arm. 'I did not come here to

frighten you, only to see you were well,' she said. 'And to give you this.'

My mind was still churning with the horrors I had just heard. I took the note, thinking it was from Bridget herself. 'What is it?'

But she answered, 'I don't know.'

I tore it open. It was from my landlady in London, Ellen: she did not have my brother's address but must have remembered Bridget's old one from seeing Joseph's post. The note was to say that Ellen hoped I was well settled in Manningtree, but also that her knees had been plaguing her so there was work now and a position in her household, if I wanted it. I read it aloud to Bridget, then looked up. She seemed relieved. But how could I risk a journey now, so near the sixth month? And then, when the child was born . . . My old landlady was kind, but even she would not want a servant with a baby on the breast.

I refolded the note. 'I will think on it,' I said, and Bridget smiled, but I could not smile back. I knew I must press her about what Grace had told me; about the talk she had heard between Bridget and Mother the night before Mother died. About the thing she had found in her bed. The man coiling his ropes had gone, and the only sound was the gulls calling in the estuary as they picked and fought over what the ebbing tide had exposed.

'Bridget, listen . . .' I said, but then I heard the sound of hoofs in the road: a moment later, I saw Mary Phillips walking her horse towards the gate of the Thorn. I grabbed Bridget out of sight, further into the shadows. 'I must go,' I said.

'I'll wait here till you're in,' she said, and caught my hand. 'Take care.'

A stablehand had come out to take Mary Phillips's horse; I waited until she had gone inside before I slipped into the yard. The man saw me but said nothing as I let myself in at the back door.

Mary was still in the passage, taking off her cloak. She did not greet me. 'I was in the privy,' I said.

Mary only said, 'I have been with your brother. He will be home in three days.'

I went back into the parlour. It was unsettling to think of seeing Matthew again. He had been to every large village in the hundred, and I had heard rumours of his doings as if he was some great and distant figure, but now he was coming home. I wished I could be as certain as Bridget of his regard for me.

Later I whispered to Rebecca the contents of my old landlady's note. 'If you wish, I could arrange for you to go,' I said.

'No,' she replied. 'But why don't you?'

'I can't,' I said.

'I don't see why,' she replied. I saw her plain, enquiring expression. I had wondered if she had not guessed about my condition, but I saw now that she had not. I thought of speaking out, about the coming baby, but then I remembered what she had confided to me at Mother's house. About her own lost child. I took up my sewing again. 'I just can't,' I said.

†

The next day we went back for the last time to Mother's house. The work there was near complete: when I let us in, the rooms were swept and echoing, smelling of new whitewash and beeswax, ready for my brother and his bride. The last items were in crates, ready for men to carry to the Thorn. I sent Rebecca back outside to pick weedlings from the gravel, while I had a last check round.

I glanced over the parlour and the kitchen, then upstairs I checked Mother's old chamber, which would now be Matthew's. Last I went into my own old room. It felt sad and small, airless, so I opened the shutters and stood at the window to catch my breath. Soon, I knew, I would have to let out my gowns, and for certain stop lacing so tight. The house across the field, I remembered, was Bess Clarke's. Her shutters were open, and there was a bedsheet hung out in the yard; even at this distance, though, I could tell that it was streaked with bird shit. It must have been out for weeks.

When I closed the shutters again, the darkness was complete. I thought of when my father and I would go out walking after dinner, in the winter's early dark. I had always been reluctant to turn down a certain sunken lane; I confessed to him, in the end, that I was afraid there would be monsters. 'There are no monsters down there, Alice,' he had said, nodding towards the lane's darkness. 'The worst thing that could be down there is a person, like you or I.' He had meant it as a comfort.

I went more quickly down the stairs, calling to Rebecca outside, and I was thankful to hear her answer me, her small and ordinary voice echoing up through the dark, panelled spaces of the house.

23

Mary Phillips had me take Rebecca into town again the next day, to get the dinner things to welcome my brother home, and though I felt far from glad at his coming, I obeyed her, and we went. It was the first properly hot day of the year so at last I laced myself a little more loosely, and left off my cloak. Mary Phillips did not look twice at me as we left the Thorn, but I caught Rebecca glancing at me now and then as we walked.

'What will happen?' Rebecca said, as she caught my gaze. 'Now his warrant's run out?'

'I suppose it will proceed to trial. I can hardly credit how, these days, but I suppose it will.' After a minute I added, 'This may be your last chance, if you wish to leave.'

Rebecca met my eye. 'It will go bad with my mother, if I do.'

'You know,' I said, after a moment, lowering my voice, 'I have been praying that he meets with some accident on the road.'

Rebecca spread her hands, as if to say, 'Of course you have.' But my thoughts had been weighing on me, for I knew they were a sin. More than once those weeks I had imagined Matthew lost in the hundred, beyond the main roads, the fields lying soft in the dark; I had summoned up that land, how it is confusing, how you might hurry towards home but a track you think leads out on the Harwich road gets smaller, narrower, and ends in a wall and a silent thicket. The world turned against you, flat and silver, under the moon.

I knew it was a sin, my ill-wishing: I knew that there was not even a hair's breadth between that and what some called witchcraft.

Upon reaching town, Rebecca and I divided the errand between us: I would buy the fish, while she went to the victualler's. When I had what I needed, I waited for her at the appointed corner near the assembly rooms, but she did not come. I waited longer. I might have been mistaken, but I thought folk were casting glances in my direction. Some I knew by sight, but I had no way of telling whether they were staring because of my slight yet evident belly, or because of my brother's business. My face burned. A few minutes passed, and still Rebecca did not appear, so I began to walk in the direction of the victualler's.

But as I approached I saw a commotion outside the shop. I quickened my pace. It was a woman, Robert Taylor's wife, grappling with someone – she had her by the hair. It was Rebecca. As I broke into a run, the woman threw her out into the street. By the time I got near, Rebecca had picked herself up and lurched towards me, weeping furiously, smearing the tears away with the back of her hand. I saw Robert Taylor's wife's fat, frowning face as she stepped back from the doorway into the dimness of the shop, and I thought to ask her what on God's earth she had thought she was doing, but Rebecca was already away up the road, so I turned and hurried to catch her. Breathing hard, I fell into step beside her, and put a hand on her back.

'Are you all right?' I said. 'Christ help us. What happened?'

'They wouldn't serve me,' she said, her face hard.

'But why?' I said, and her mutinous look dissolved into fresh tears.

It took me half the walk home to make her tell me how she had gone in for the things Mary Phillips had ordered, but Robert Taylor's wife had ignored her. Knowing the things were paid for and seeing them in a tidy pile on the far side of the counter, Rebecca had reached across to claim them. But one of the other women in there had grabbed her wrist, hissing that she was not welcome. Rebecca had pulled away, and the woman had caught her smartly across the face, as if by accident. Then Rebecca had called her a name, and Robert Taylor's wife had come round the counter.

'I've had worse,' Rebecca said, after I made her sit on a wall, a few minutes away from the Thorn, so I could brush her down. She was rubbing her scalp. 'She didn't pull any out.' But I could see her shock. Suddenly, I could see her fear.

She was still upset that evening, so I was trying to chatter more than usual, as we sat over our simple supper: and that was why I dismissed it, when I first felt the ache. I tried to ignore it, but before long I pushed my plate away.

24

It was that night I lost my child. Strange, that we say 'lost', as if it were an act of carelessness. Rebecca told Mary Phillips I had a headache, and helped me upstairs; when I stepped out of my gown, the skirts of my shift were red. Rebecca grasped straight away what was happening, and she wanted to go for a doctor.

'A little blood might not matter,' I said. 'It could be I will hold onto it, if I can just lie down.'

But I did not hold onto it. Pains came upon me, through the evening and into the night. Rebecca was scared, and I had to lie to her, say how I had helped many women do this before, and it would be just like a birth but easier. In truth, I was frightened: I had lost them before, but never so late. Around midnight, I nearly sent Rebecca for Bridget, but I knew enough from listening to Ellen that there would be little she could do to help me, until we knew whether it had all come out. We had to be quiet, so as not to bring Mary Phillips down the passage from her chamber. Rebecca, thinking clearly through her fright, gave me a twist of cloth to bite on. I remember the pains, and having to push properly. I know that I must have made noises. I remember getting up from the bed, and something hanging down, and telling Rebecca not to pull on it, and hearing a sound and realizing it was my own chattering teeth. When the rest came away, Rebecca caught it in a cloth, and I asked her if it looked whole but she sounded doubtful, so I got up to check. From other times I had expected something botched-looking, the colour of what a butcher will spare for his dogs. But this was not like that: granted, there was the mess that came after, but in the midst of it lay something tiny, and recognizable, grey and asleep. I had to cover my mouth with my hand.

I remember groping my shift over my head and pulling on another, hauling myself into bed, as Rebecca turned away to build up the fire.

I drifted miserably into sleep, thinking, So, then, that's the last of Joseph, gone. I could not stop telling myself how we had rushed, I had rushed us, into marriage; how I had lied about being with child to have our banns read quickly. It was easier to be fierce with myself than to think of the small grey tight face I had seen that night, now burned all to nothing.

In the morning, while Rebecca was fetching my bath, I crouched by the fireplace. It had been swept, but I pushed my fingertip through the film of white ash on the stone. I cried, for a few minutes, with my fist in my mouth. I thought of how I had kept myself laced so tight those last months. I thought of the day I had come to Manningtree, and the woman in the inn at Chelmsford who had not been able to see me holding my child; how I had fallen in the cart, and made the bruise on my belly. I thought I could feel my heart, just like when, at seventeen, I had fallen from my horse. The fall put my shoulder out of its socket, and Bridget had wrenched it back in; afterwards, I could feel in detail the gritty surfaces of the injury, the scoured hurt inside.

It is still raw with me, my last lost child, but the grief has turned cold now, and become more akin to anger. For though it may be I would have lost it anyway, I think of those months at the Thorn – the daily shock and strain of what was happening – and it is hard not to think that my brother's doings had some hand in my loss. When I think of my child, I think now of vengeance.

25

After my early bath, I crawled back into bed and slept again. When I woke, Rebecca was still in my chamber. She had a cloth and bowl and set to cleaning my face: I had sweated in my sleep. It made me guilty, how good it felt. When she had done, she set aside the bowl and regarded me. 'How do you feel?' she said. 'When you can stand I'll strip your bed.'

'How long have I been sleeping?'

'It is noon now. Your brother is due back soon.' She avoided my eyes. 'Mary Phillips must have heard something. I told her you had a bad stomach as well as the headache. I think she guessed the truth, but I didn't know if you would want me to speak of it.'

'No,' I said. Those last weeks I had kept the child to myself, crushed into me. Now, not having announced my condition, I had no one to condole with me. No one except Rebecca.

'Shall you get up?' she said.

'I must.'

She moved to help me, but I put out my hand. 'Rebecca, I wish to thank you,' I said.

She looked down. 'I feel badly, mistress. If I had not frightened you yesterday —'

'Oh, hush,' I said. 'This was no fault of yours.'

She said, 'I tried to look for you, what it was, but I could

206

not tell.' I saw tears spill down her cheeks, and she withdrew her hand to swipe them away. I thought, How many ways there are to lose your children.

'It just . . .' I began, and stopped. I studied my hand. 'It only grieves me that I never told him.'

She nodded, her face wet. 'But think. If he had known, he would have been so delighted,' she said. Then, more quietly, 'We never did, you know,' she said. 'Joseph and I. For what it is worth. We lived in the same house. That was all. We were young.'

I glanced up at her, and smiled sadly. How, I thought, had I carried that fear so long with me? Some small flickering between a boy and a girl that flared and then was snuffed out. For even if he had been weak for a moment, and she was soft, what was that now? Compared to five years of dressing and undressing, embracing, skin and dampness, the shortness of breath, the finishing, the washing and the small discomforts of afterwards. Compared to hope of children. I saw in that moment that, for my five years of marriage, I had been afraid of a shadow. But as Rebecca helped me to dress, my thoughts grew muted, for as soon as I moved all I felt was raw, creaking pain.

†

When my brother rode into the yard I scarcely looked at him. I was dull with discomfort; my breasts were leaking inside my bodice. Even through my grief I was anxious about that, for I did not know whether it was supposed to happen, with a five-month loss. But despite my worry, Grace caught my eye. She was slumped forward in her saddle as she halted her horse, her face drawn. She got down gingerly, like a woman of seventy years, and when she met my eyes, she did not even smile. I heard Rebecca greet Matthew politely, as one of the men caught Grace's bridle and led her horse away; but Grace paused in the yard, as if unsure of which way to go or of her welcome, and Rebecca was there before me, taking her arm, lifting her bag and walking with her into the house. As they passed me, I murmured to Rebecca to take her to my room, where there was a fire. I felt dazed, my tongue clumsy in my mouth.

I stayed in the yard long enough to be sure that Matthew was occupied with Mary: he stood talking to her in a low voice, his leather case tucked under his arm. I turned away indoors.

Rebecca was coming out of my chamber just as I went in. She bit her lip, smiled at me thinly, and went into her own room. Grace was sitting by my fire, in my chair, and when she saw me she made to get up, but I waved her down. Carefully, I sat opposite her. I wanted to tell her about the child. But she seemed so weary.

'I didn't think to receive any kindness from her,' she said, gesturing at the wall.

'She's been good to me. I – I think we judged her harshly.'

'Four of the women in the gaol are dead. I told her, just now. Perhaps I shouldn't have – but she asked after them.'

I sat still. 'Dead? Not her mother?'

'No. Although she's in a bad way.'

'And how did they . . . ?'

'Some fever. But they were starving.' Grace folded her hands. 'Rebecca was paying the gaoler for their food before your brother brought her here.' She grimaced, to show how Rebecca had been paying the man, and I looked away.

The fire shuffled itself, and we let it subside. Grace was clearly too weary to build it up; for my part, I feared that crouching might bring on my bleeding again. I wanted to tell her about the offer that had come from my old landlady, for it struck me that there was nothing to stop me going now. Nothing to stop us going. But she was too frail to think about the future.

After a time, I said, 'Do you want to tell me about it? The hundred?' I spoke slowly, hesitantly. In truth, after what Bridget had said about the searching, I did not know if I had the strength to hear of it.

I saw Grace was weeping, not the hiccuping childish crying of when she had been afraid to go, but silent, contained tears. 'Sometimes I would sit in the room,' she said. 'But other times they would put a stool outside the door and say, "Grace, don't come in, whatever you hear."' She hugged herself. 'There were folk in each place, taking matters into their own hands. And they had women there, the ones who wash the dead, who would do anything for a coin, and they –' She broke off.

'No need,' I said, and touched her knee. 'No need, Grace, if it's too hard.'

'The thing is,' she said, determined, 'that some of them seemed to enjoy it.' She pulled a hand across her eyes. 'Mary Phillips rode out to join us, and I tell you, mistress, I have never seen her thrive better.' I saw, then, how suddenly she had been forced to grow up. It made me sad.

'Why is she thus?' I said. 'Mary? So hard like that?'

Grace frowned. 'I knew a girl from Ramsey, where she was born, and I heard her hint once that Mary's mother was not married. That they were despised, and Mary taunted.

I know she grew up poor. I know she hates the barest thought of anything not respectable. But I do not see – Would that not make her keener in her sympathy?' She shook her head. 'Whatever the truth, it is no excuse.'

'As long as you did not fail in your charity,' I said, and touched her knee again. 'Which I know you will not have, whatever you were made to do.'

After a moment, Grace said, 'I think – when I told you of what thing I saw, the day before your mother died, I am worried that I gave you to suspect . . . I think now I was wrong to say it.' Her face was troubled.

I leaned nearer. 'You were mistaken?'

'No. I saw the thing I described. But I think now I put a construction on it, I made Bridget out guilty when I did not know for sure. Though I did not know, I made up my mind.'

'It is only natural,' I said, wishing to soothe her, but slow to find the right words. 'You must have heard my brother speak ill of her, so then, of course, you would think her bad.'

But Grace replied, 'It was not that. I never heard him speak of her at all,' she said. 'But it was I who took that gold ring to her, and your mother's Bible, when she died.' She rubbed at her hands. 'Your brother had turned the pages down in Exodus, Deuteronomy, Leviticus, Samuel. Twenty pages turned down, or thirty, all of them with verses about witches and whores.' She began to weep again. 'I'm sorry I didn't tell you sooner. But when I saw he had done that, I thought she must be bad . . .'

I struggled almost to understand her, was lost for what to say. I reached out to her. 'It's all right, Grace.' I squeezed her hand. 'You only did as you thought best. It's done with, now.'

But I knew it was not done with. After she left me, I tried to forget the low, ticking aches in my belly and force my mind to work. Perhaps Matthew's hatred of Bridget was not only to do with the item Grace had found in Mother's bed. Perhaps it was also to do with Father's daily book, the nameless remorse it contained. How Bridget always seemed to feel guilty, responsible for Mother, her bad state. How Bridget had given in so easily, and left our house in Wenham that night long ago, on foot and through the snow. The ghost of a suspicion suggested itself, though I tried to dismiss it swiftly from my mind. But I was worried. Matthew's business through the hundred had led my eye away from Bridget. Now I was not so certain he had forgotten her.

As for Matthew, when I came down to dine with him that night, his eyes rested only for a moment on my belly, and then he was talking pleasantly of the hospitality they had received in the different villages. He wore a larger hat, I noticed, and higher boots. But though his talk was varied, animated, he did not seem content, more like a rope, stretched too tight. It had chilled me, the way his eyes rested on me so briefly as I sat down, before he confirmed his suspicion and moved on; that my scoured numbness could be of such little consequence to him, could be only one more inconvenience removed from his path.

After dinner, he talked for a time of Ruth Edwards, about the arrangements he had in hand for his wedding. I struggled to follow his talk, for my pain had expanded till it was all I could think of. Then he said to me, 'When you were a midwife . . .'

I stopped still, thinking I had at last been caught in my lie. 'What of it?'

'Well, how many women did you deliver, would you say?'

'Not many,' I said, shifting in my chair. 'Perhaps ten.'

He nodded, frowning. 'Still. That should be sufficient.'

'Brother, I don't . . .' I said. 'I think Ruth would want someone else. Surely she would not want me.' But at my reply he only looked confused, and began to talk of other things.

26

I saw over the next days how Matthew's eyes rested briefly but often on Rebecca. She had put on flesh, and grown golden, sleek. She took to wearing Mother's green gown, the one I had altered for the trial. I was almost grateful for how she drew his attention away from me: I did not need to trouble to hide my dull face, my slow movements.

I heard him coaching her sometimes, in the middle of the day, his murmur coming from the parlour. *What they might do is put it to you in this way. Then you must say this. And if they press you, you must shrink as though afraid, and then I will ask permission to question you instead.*

Rebecca began to avoid my eye at mealtimes. But one morning, when we were coming out of our chambers at the same time, she glanced at me and said, 'I must think of my mother, her being spared.' When I looked her in the eye, she added quietly, 'He asked me whether, while he was gone, you went to Bridget's house. And I said you didn't. Because you didn't.'

I smiled. 'I thank you for that,' I said.

Then she said, 'And he asked me whether you had been ill, while he was away.'

I saw that she had confirmed for him what had happened. And though I had grown to care for her, I saw, too, that when I was strong enough I must go to London without her, for she had made her choice. I was sorry, but I did not blame her for it. She loved her mother, and you cannot always help love, what it brings you to do.

'I must thank you also,' I said, 'for how you took care of me.'

She met my eyes. 'You have thanked me already,' she replied. I thought she would go on down the stairs but she remained standing close to me, as though she did not want the moment to pass. 'At least now your brother's business will be finished with.'

Matthew had travelled the length and breadth of his warrant. To go further, he would have needed to take the great roads north or south or west, and to do so would be fraught with risk. For, since he had been gone, armies had been on the move. While Rebecca and I had been packing crates and washing floors at Mother's house, there had been alarm through Cambridgeshire, Suffolk and Essex; rumours that the King was ready to move on the eastern counties. Odd reports had been heard, of large groups of men seen from a long way off, but nobody could say whose men they were, or what their business was. It was too dangerous to travel far, and so now Matthew would be occupied in collating his evidence against the women accused.

But over the next days I noticed dully that Matthew did not seem like a man tying up loose ends. Travel had taken its toll on him: he was thinner, his hair sparser. But he did in no way slacken his pace. John Stearne, whom I had met at the dinner, visited a good deal. From my chamber window I would see his foreshortened face with its unmistakable brow as he ducked in at the back door. More than once, I heard their voices raised in disagreement or excitement, but I could not catch the substance of their discussion.

When he was not with John Stearne or coaching Rebecca,

Matthew was at his desk. I glimpsed him through the open doorway, writing and writing, his shirtsleeves rolled up to show his thin forearms, skin over muscle over bone, and browner after his travelling.

Though the sun still shone, I could not get warm. Grace crept about the house, meeting no one's eye. I vowed that as soon as I was strong enough to travel, I would ask her to come with me to London. I thought the day had nearly arrived; at each meal, I was managing to eat a little more. I did not know that I was about to run out of time.

†

I remember the news of it, passed quickly, half gleeful, half reverent, and not just among the men. For Naseby was not some manoeuvre, with merits to be argued over this way or that, but a piece of delicious fact. It was Grace who told me of it, when I came down to breakfast: how our side had swept downhill upon the King's men, stomachs light and psalms in their mouths, how we had flattened them. She showed a flicker of pleasure as she spoke of it, the first I had seen from her since her return. We did not yet know, of course, what the victory would mean.

That Sunday, a service was to be held in honour of it, a thanksgiving service, and a special sermon to be preached. On the Sunday morning we waited in the yard for my brother to be ready: myself, Rebecca, Grace and Mary Phillips. Matthew came out and down the steps, putting on his hat.

Walking to the church, I noticed how Grace struggled to keep pace with me, how her walk had turned inward, shuffling. I had thought, when she had come back from the hundred, that it had been only sore legs from riding. But now I thought it was not her legs that were damaged. It was her spirit.

The minister was pale and agitated as he gave his sermon. I kept waiting for him to speak out, as I had waited all those weeks for him to declare himself against what my brother had done. But he spoke only of Naseby, what a great battle it had been. He took as his text something bland from the psalms, about the wonderful works of the Lord.

Afterwards, I stood near Matthew, where he was talking to Richard Edwards and some others in the church entry. Hands folded patiently, I allowed my thoughts to wander, until I heard Robert Taylor say, 'For myself I would burn such women, as they do on the continent.'

I saw Matthew make a dismissive gesture. 'It is foolish to speak of burning. Everything must be done in the proper fashion. And you know, Robert, that under our own law, for *maleficium* it is hanging that is the penalty.'

'Quite so,' said Richard Edwards. 'And how do your plans go forward for your journey into Suffolk, Hopkins? For that is where you are bound next, is it not?'

I looked at my brother, and saw it was true. Suddenly I could not stand to listen more, and I made to step past them, but then Matthew said, 'It is indeed. My plans go forward nicely. And my sister, Alice, will go with me, this time.'

I stopped, and put a hand on the cool stone arch of the entry. Richard Edwards must have made some reply, for Matthew said, 'No, it would be too much riding for Mary.'

I felt myself sweating as they began to drift outside, while I stood rooted. At last I followed them, and watched as a crowd gathered and Grimston presented to my brother a letter of safe conduct, written on fancy paper, handing it over in front of the assembled townspeople. He slapped my brother on the shoulder and eyed him with what seemed to be respect, touched slightly with fear. Matthew even made a little speech, said he hoped to remain in the prayers of every man and woman there. Then Grimston stepped back, and Ruth Edwards came forward. She took my brother's arm.

As I watched, I saw the minister was at my elbow. 'Are you well, Mistress Hopkins?' he said.

I turned to him, but kept my gaze down. 'I thought this business finished with. I thought by now someone would have prevented it. Someone with the influence to do so.'

I glanced at him. But his face was carefully blank. 'I'm sure we all wish for peace,' he said.

I felt frustrated, but when I saw his eyes I had to lower my own away from their tenderness. Quietly, I said, 'I have seen enough. I think I must leave here.'

The minister turned back to watch my brother, where he stood beside Ruth Edwards. 'There is more than one way out at your disposal,' he said, and I knew he was speaking of marriage. I thought of the life I could have with a man like him: his gentleness, his hopefulness, so unsuited to the times. I thought of the children he would want to have, to fill the rooms of his pleasant vicarage. Long moments passed. But no, I thought. That way out is not the one for me, not any more.

I faced him. 'I wish my brother joy,' I said frankly, 'and that I could summon the courage to marry again myself. But I lost five children, sir, with my last husband. And now, you see . . .'

He smiled sadly. 'Well, then, my best wishes to you,' he said. 'Whatever path you choose.'

27

While folk were still approaching Matthew to wish him well, asking him to remember them to some cousin at Hadleigh or St Edmundsbury, I turned to Grace, and spoke under my breath: 'Will you tell them I felt ill? I must go to Bridget . . .'

Grace looked queasy, but she nodded, and I slipped away in the shadow of the yews and out of the church gate. I felt light and hollow as I walked, almost jittery. In a few minutes, I was at Bridget's. The row of cottages seemed different in the early-summer heat: dust rather than mud in the road, and white washing hanging out to dry.

Bridget did not seem surprised to see me when she let me in. Her eyes were so busy looking into my face as she greeted me that, at first, they did not travel downward. The back door stood open; someone's cat peered in at the entry. 'I was wondering where you were,' she said. She flicked her dishcloth at the cat, then turned back towards me: saw what was missing.

'Oh, love,' she said, and came towards me. 'When did it happen?'

'A few days ago,' I said. I had worried she would weep and that I would have to calm her, when I was only just preventing myself from melting into tears.

But she did not weep: instead she pressed my belly gently with her fingers, checked the colour of my tongue.

'He has a safe-conduct letter, now, from Grimston,' I said, once she was satisfied. 'He says he is taking me with him, into Suffolk.' Bridget's eyes widened. 'So I have decided I shall go south, to London. I think he will not follow me.'

'It's right you should go,' she said.

'But if Grace needs help,' I said, 'if she comes here, will you give her my mother's ring?'

'Of course I will.' Bridget smiled. It felt like a long time, suddenly, since I had seen anyone smile. 'So you are truly going,' she said.

I pulled out a chair and sat at the table. It was clear of papers and food; looked as though it had been recently cleaned. I was aware that I had not asked her to go with me but I knew that she would not, for, if only because she had loved Mother so well, she would not leave Manningtree until matters with Matthew were resolved.

'I am sorry to leave you, Bridget,' I said. 'You have been a friend to me.'

'You know, Alice,' she said, 'that the only reason I was wary about you and my Joseph marrying – you think that I preferred Rebecca, or that I wished him to stay with me, but it was not that. It was just, for all I loved him, my Joseph, he was a man like any other. And Rebecca, she was brought up to that, she knew what to expect.' She averted her eyes. 'I knew that he could never have disappointed Rebecca. Could never have been too rough for her.'

I paused, speechless. Then, 'Bridget, look at me,' I said. 'Joseph loved me. He was the gentlest man I ever met.'

'Well,' she said, and peered down at her hands. 'I am glad of that.'

I knew that I should go, that I would be missed, but somehow I could not. For there were things still unsaid between us. All at once I felt I might never see her again, and there were a thousand questions I wanted to ask her, about herself, about Mother. I would have asked for one last sight of Mother's ring, too, but I did not want Bridget to think I craved it. Then I remembered what Grace had said about Mother's Bible.

'Before I go,' I said, 'will you show me my mother's Bible?'

She hesitated. But then, 'Of course,' she said, pushing herself up with her palms. She went to her shelf, and reached it down. It was an old one, which had been my grandmother's. Bridget placed it on the table, then slid it across to me.

Sure enough, the page was turned down that contained the verse, *A man also or woman that hath a familiar spirit, or that is a wizard, shall surely be put to death: they shall stone them with stones: their blood shall be upon them.* Then another turned down in Proverbs: *For the lips of a strange woman drop as an honeycomb, and her mouth is smoother than oil; but her end is bitter as wormwood, sharp as a two-edged sword.* Ten or fifteen more like it were all turned down, each treating of witches and whores. I looked up at Bridget. 'Why would Matthew do this?'

She avoided my eyes. 'I cannot say.'

'Bridget. Were you and my father – Did you and my father have some . . . dalliance?' The word sounded offensive as I spoke it. I half expected Bridget to get angry, but she did not.

'No,' she said quietly.

'Forgive me. It's only that – I found Father's daily books that he wrote his confessions in. There were pages missing from one of them. I think that Matthew . . . I think he cut them out. But the pages that remained – my father seemed to feel some great remorse.'

'I don't know what was in your father's heart, Alice,' she said briskly, 'though I cannot think it was much different from what is in the hearts of other men.'

I could feel her closing off against me. I sat back, shut the Bible. 'My brother knows,' I said. 'He knows, for Grace told him, about the item she saw in my mother's bed. Will you not tell me what you can of it?'

She sat up straighter. 'It isn't mine to tell. It won't help, Alice. Let him think, if he wishes to, that I was seeking to harm your mother.' She sounded almost angry, but then she quietened. 'Do you know? When I came into your mother's service, I was eighteen years old. She was thirteen. They were short of a maid, and I was knocking door to door for work, and your mother answered my knock. She wrote my character with her own hand, and showed it to her father, and after that I never needed to worry again about the roof over my head, or having enough to eat.' She leaned forward. 'Alice, believe me, if I ever loved anyone, I loved your mother.' She sighed. 'Though I don't expect Matthew to believe that. But I did think he was fond enough of you. Forgive me, but I thought you would be able to check him.' Suddenly, she stood up. 'What I don't understand is, if he thinks me guilty, why does he not arrest me? Does he want me to leave? To confess? Or what? Why does he go after these others, and not me?' She shook her head. 'But you believe me, do you not, Alice? That I had only your mother's good in my heart?'

I moved in my chair, frustrated. 'I wish – I wish only that you would tell me all you know.'

'I can't. It would not help. Your brother knows no more than you, and as for your mother and what truly happened with his burns, you must not speak of it to him. It won't help you to know what I know, if you are going. And I truly believe it would not have helped you to fight him.'

I felt a flicker of anger that she would not be frank, not even now that lives were at risk, the lives she claimed to care so much about. But Bridget seemed not to see my anger. Her face was firm, but troubled. 'You should go. None of this is your doing, and somehow it will find its end. He is not invincible, Alice. It can't go on for ever. He is flesh and blood,' she said.

Even at the time I thought, I never suggested he was anything else.

28

I did not sleep that night, or if I did, I dreamed of lying awake, of hearing something in the dark. I had decided to go at first light. I knew there was still some deeper part to the business that I could not see, some blacker shade of black. But I thought, I shall not stay to see how it ends. My old landlady, Ellen, has made me an offer: I shall take it.

Getting back from Bridget's, I had found the Thorn quiet and my brother out still. I had burned Father's daily book for, though I was loath to destroy it, any chance to replace it seemed gone, and I could not safely hide it or carry it with me. I knew I would need my sleep, but I was kept wakeful by a sense of danger, as nameless and certain as a horse must feel when it flicks back its head and shows the whites of its eyes; when it will not be coaxed or led across a bridge, and later the bridge gives way.

I put back my bedclothes when I could just discern my hand in front of my face. The Thorn was dark still, and silent: I had not heard Mary Phillips yet, or any of the scullery maids. I dressed myself, wearing as much as I could, for I judged it to be too risky to be seen with a bag, and tucked Joseph's letter to Bridget into my sleeve. I would be on the road before it was fully light. I took the stairs slowly, leaning my weight before I placed it, and keeping my feet near the edge where they would not creak.

When I reached the bottom, I saw that the back door was

open, and someone sitting on the topmost step, looking out into the pale morning. I thought it was one of the stable-men, that I would have to ask him to move to get by, and then wait in the privy until he was gone. But then the figure stood up, and I recognized Matthew's travelling coat before he turned.

'You're up early,' he said. 'You are packed, then?'

I was aware of him taking in the bulk of my clothing. When I did not immediately answer, Matthew turned away. There was the cold, clean smell from outside, and the sky was shifting from grey to the palest blue. 'I would change,' he said. 'You'll boil like that. It's going to be another hot day.'

'I won't,' I said. 'I won't do it. I won't go.'

Matthew kept his back to me, as though he had not heard. 'I have been puzzling over what to do with Rebecca,' he said. 'After the trials. For there will be bills returned against her, I cannot prevent that, not after Prudence Hart's testimony. They will need to be thrown out so that she might stand witness. But it strikes me that other bills may be brought – stronger ones.' He turned to me. 'If they are, there may be little I can do to save her.' He examined his palm, licked his finger and rubbed at an imaginary mark. 'What happens to her, Alice, it is nothing to me. What happens to her honestly does depend.' He sounded almost bored. It was that which made me shake.

Without reply I turned, and went quietly back up the stairs to my chamber. I opened the shutters, then stood at the window, I do not know for how long. Down in the yard two stablemen stirred, stretched. They greeted each other, and one spat. On the landing I heard Grace's soft footsteps and Mary Phillips's firm ones, and soon the creak and sigh in the next chamber as Rebecca West swung her legs over the edge of her bed. I saw I had no choice but to go. Dimly, I thought that I should never have expected to outwit him.

I took off all the clothing I was wearing, beyond a light gown and a shift under it, and folded the other items, laying them on the bed. I looked at the large box I had brought from London, but instead I picked up a small, soft travelling bag, and put some things into it, leaving out the thicker cloak. Without thinking, I made the bag light enough that I could have carried it a distance myself, though Matthew's steady countenance had cowed something in me, and it was hard to think of disobeying him.

When I got downstairs, my brother was directing the loading of the horses. There was no talk of breakfast. Grace stood in the kitchen entry, her eyes brimming, and though I suspected she might have given me away to Matthew the night before, still I tried to give her an encouraging smile. Rebecca stood just behind her, biting her bottom lip, her face in open dismay.

Matthew came in. 'Ready?' he said.

Out in the yard, I mounted my horse. It had been years since I had ridden her, and I felt heavy and still weak since losing the baby. But the mare stood quietly while Matthew and Mary Phillips mounted their own beasts, Matthew speaking last-minute instructions to the stablemen and to Grace. I remember my last sight of them in the doorway, Grace's fair head and Rebecca's, as I followed my brother and turned my horse out of the yard.

As we started towards Ipswich, the motion of the animal

under me made me think of my youth. But I did not want to be comforted. The roads were quiet, so soon after Naseby, and familiar as far as the Wenham turn. Matthew and Mary Phillips rode ahead together, his dog running at their heels, leaving me to come up behind them. We had brought no stablehand. The morning grew warm, as we rode between hedges flush with unripe hazelnuts, the sun speaking to trees laden with green apples and quinces. It tempted you to close your eyes. It felt ill-fitting to be riding out on such dark business on such a fair day. But for all the warm sunshine, I did not tilt my head back to enjoy it. Instead, I squinted at the dark figure of Matthew, riding ahead of me.

We put up at the Lion in Ipswich, a decent house that was full of the calling and singing, the feet on the stairs and the slamming of doors that I had missed at the Thorn. The next day we rode out the short distance to Copdock, Mary Phillips with us. When we got there several women were waiting, lining up to tell tales on each other, and my brother took notes, leaning on a board on the church steps. I listened to one woman speaking to my brother of Mother Skipper, whom she said was no Christian. When Matthew asked what evidence she had: did Mother Skipper stay away from church? The woman said that, on the contrary, the devil had told Mother Skipper to attend church and make a great show, but that if she attended diligently he would nip her.

Before long, Matthew turned to me and said I might go and rest. The fierce joy he had shown in Manningtree seemed gone; he was serious now. Intent. I wandered away, and sat under a tree. I felt dazed, as though I had taken a hard blow to the head. The stained glass of leaves above me made a queer green light where I sat in the shade.

After a time, some men brought the woman called Mother Skipper; Matthew and Mary Phillips took her into the minister's house. Their small figures a distance away were like figures in a dream. I thought they must be taking further testimony, or perhaps doing the searching that Bridget had described. I did not trust my brother's seeming leniency, how nothing seemed to be required of me. Why would he have brought me with him only to have me sitting idle?

I see now that my brother was letting me grow used to my new circumstances, letting me lower myself into the scalding bath of them, inch by quarter-inch. He stayed with Mother Skipper two hours or three, and when he and Mary Phillips came out, he let me overhear the arrangements being made for Mother Skipper to be taken to the gaol at Bury St Edmunds. Then we went on our way. As we rode, it got dark, the country quite still except for the small pale owls that had come down to warm themselves on the baked road. Our approach set them winging upwards, and they looked as souls might look, parted from their bodies. Seeing them, I could not help thinking freshly of my baby, but I held back my tears. I did not wish Matthew to see me cry.

†

It was the next day, towards evening in the village of Chattisham, that I first took part in a watching. Matthew opened the back door of the house, and beckoned me in. He pointed to a low chair by the fireplace, and bade me sit in it and keep my eyes open.

'Watch for anything coming near her,' he said briskly, 'whether it be a fly or whatever else, however small.'

Anne Alderman sat on her stool, and glared. She was an old woman, and thin in the manner that makes a person seem dried-out. At first I thought she was holding that position herself, knees up to her chest and grasping her ankles, but then I saw the bindings that secured her wrists discreetly to her feet. Someone had done them with scarves rather than rope, someone kind, I thought. Not Mary Phillips.

At the foot of the stool, I saw a small puddle on the stone-flagged floor. Another woman was watching, sitting on a bench by the front door. 'There was an ant's nest there,' she said, her chin rising, 'but your master said they could not be imps, for while Mistress Phillips was searching her he had me boil a kettle of water and pour it on, and they floated up dead.'

Matthew turned to Anne Alderman. 'The imp you suckled. For what did you employ it?'

She looked at him coldly, for long moments, then said, 'I'm sure you ask your own imp daily to help you grow a beard. And to inflate your head that it might look less like a dried pea.'

I took a sharp breath: I wished there was a silent way to tell her to keep civil with him.

Matthew turned to the other watching woman. 'Do not walk her at eight after all,' he said. 'Leave her as she is, till I come back. Alice, you are to stay and keep up the watching.'

He went out then, and Mary Phillips with him. We sat in silence. After a time, the clock struck seven. The quiet grew on me, the almost-held breath.

Then the clock struck eight, and soon Anne Alderman

began to let out occasional gasps, as she shifted about to ease her joints. I wanted to get up to ease her bonds, but I could not. At each gasp the other watching woman looked to me, as if it were my decision whether to spare her. I wished Anne Alderman would ask to piss, for if she had I would certainly have let her get down: but I was wary of the other watcher, that she might report to my brother any offered kindness, and he might punish me for it, and the woman on the stool be made to suffer the more.

Once I got up and went towards the fire to stoke it, thinking as I went to whisper to Anne Alderman that she must ask me to be let down, but as I got near she glared at me, as if she would rather have her hands cut off than ask me for anything.

It must have been near an hour later when Matthew came in with Mary Phillips. He seemed in good spirits; I think they had been dining with the minister.

'Well, Anne?' he said. 'Anything to tell me yet?' He looked at me. 'Anything to report? Nothing seen?' I shook my head. 'Not a fly? Nothing?' He turned back to the woman on the stool. 'Well, Anne, we will leave you with this woman here, and soon more folk will come, that she might sleep. But you will not sleep. Do you hear me? Not until you have told us what employment your imps were given.'

He spoke almost regretfully, as he gathered his things. Mary Phillips signed to me to get up and I put on my shawl. The woman on the stool was rocking – you could hardly see it but she was. They did that, to ease their joints; on other occasions, I saw them rock so much as to upset the stool and go crashing to the floor, only to have relief from that one position.

While I was putting on my shawl, the clock struck nine, and as Matthew was about to open the door for Mary Phillips, at last Anne Alderman spoke. Her voice had that hoarse sound, for she had not used it for many hours together.

'Sir,' she said. 'Sir, it is true. I employed my imps to make away with my grandson.' She hung her head. 'I wished my son's child cold in the mouth, and it died soon after.'

Matthew halted in the entry. 'Get her down,' he said, and the other woman got up to untie the scarves that held Anne Alderman in place, then put out an arm to steady her as she painfully extended each limb.

'Walk her up and down,' Matthew said. His voice was even, calm. For a moment, I thought he meant it as a kindness. But then he went on, 'Do that until eleven or so, and then back on the stool. I think she has not yet told us all. We shall be back in the morning. You can tell the others.'

Then he let me and Mary Phillips out ahead of him, into the cool evening.

†

That night, Matthew went out into Ipswich, to the house of someone he knew from the years he had lived there; he took his dog and his leather case with him. I sat by the fire in one of the Lion's back rooms. My brother's new maps were spread out on the tables, maps such as I had never seen. I studied the place names up through Suffolk, tracing with my finger the shape of the coast, tracing my way into the unknown territory for which we were making, through places I had heard Matthew speak of. My heart stilled at the thought of the folk in those towns and villages, how they did not even know what was coming.

At least, I thought bleakly, I would be removed from seeing harm done to anyone I knew. At least I had not had to watch Elizabeth Gooding be confined to a stool, watch time do twice the work of any beating, watch her climb down as though her legs were broken. I thought, If I was ever blameless, now my blamelessness has ended.

Soon, I knew, we would be moving beyond Ipswich, beyond anywhere I had ever been, and taking the road north. I knew that I must somehow find the means to fight my brother. But I could not put from my mind what Bridget had said about that piece of truth; the one she claimed would have been no use to me against him.

29

Matthew knew what he was about when he went softly with me as we began our journey through Suffolk. He waited to show me the full extent of what he would make me do, until we had gone beyond anywhere I might have found a friendly face, beyond anywhere I could have got by alone without a horse and without money.

He waited until the next day, when we rode out from the Lion, with our saddle bags this time, making for a place called Playford, from where we would go on north. We reached it in the baking heat of mid-morning: a few houses, a church and a water mill, where Matthew signalled that we would stop. There were no women waiting, and the place looked half asleep. I tied my horse to the hitching post and turned away – thinking to go down to the river, find somewhere shady to sit, for the riding had worsened the pinching feeling in the left side of my belly, where my baby had been.

But Matthew called me back. 'No, Alice, you stay with me,' he said. 'I think you shall be needed today.'

I see now that there were certain conditions that made places ripest for my brother's success. To begin with, fear of Catholics helped him, not new fear but old fear, fear in the marrow; fear that has had time to translate the *hoc est corpus* of the Latin mass into the *hocus pocus* from which meaning has been entirely lost. At Playford, the minister was a godly man, but some of the landowners round about were from old Catholic families.

My brother also did best wherever there were scattered dwellings, where a woman might keep one or two cows and be almost independent, where she might live alone in her cottage at the edge of the woods, as Margaret Legat did. I found out later that at one time Margaret Legat's family had been gamekeepers to the old landowners, and that Margaret was not as strict with her churchgoing as some others might be. Her son had gone to war, a vigorous boy who had once climbed up on the miller's roof in gauntlets and thrown a wasps' nest down his chimney. Margaret Legat had refused to let the miller beat her son. After that, the man had waited his chance, and the chance was Matthew.

When we arrived, Margaret was sitting by the window in the one large room of her cottage as though she was waiting for us, a Bible in her lap. She looked up as we went in through the low entry: myself, Matthew, Mary Phillips, the minister of Playford and the miller. Glancing around, I thought, She must have borrowed that Bible. It's too clean. There was a dead leaf smell, like soil, and a smell of the two chickens that scratched and pecked at a few torn cabbage leaves under the rough table. When she saw the three of us and the minister, Margaret stood, with difficulty. She held herself low, like a wounded animal, and somehow, though I had not yet been present at a searching, though I did not yet know more than the vague shape of what it entailed, still I knew in that moment, I knew exactly what it was Margaret Legat had done.

'Searching first, I think,' Matthew said to Mary, and Mary

stepped forward. The woman did not move, as if she was slow to understand what was happening. Mary took her arm, a little roughly. 'What's through there?' Mary said, pointing.

'That's where I sleep.'

'Right,' Mary said to me. 'Time for me to show you the method.'

I took a breath. 'I am not feeling well,' I said, looking at Matthew. 'I feel faint.'

The miller cleared his throat. Tactfully, the minister turned his gaze.

'Come now, Alice,' Matthew said. 'You'll help Mary.'

'I can't, forgive me,' I said, and went for the door, but Matthew was quicker than I thought and he reached me before I had it all the way open, and I remembered how strong he is, though he does not look it. He seized the door in his hands and blocked my progress, all the while making it look gentle, making it look like nothing. The men turned politely aside, as Matthew placed his own foot over my own, softly at first, but then leaning his weight forward until I felt something in the top of my foot give, and it took my breath. Eyes watering, I stood still. I could not have moved an inch.

'Do not shame me, Alice, in front of these others,' he said, and he made the murmur low and the tone of it caring. 'Now. You'll help Mary, won't you? You have the knowledge, do you not?' Through my pain and confusion I could not think.

I cleared my throat. 'Leave her, then,' I said to Mary, crossing the chamber, trying to disguise my limp. I took the woman's elbow, more gently than Mary had done, to lead her into the alcove where she had her bed.

Behind a curtain there was a filthy mattress. I thought I saw something move under the blankets. Mary said, 'Take off your things,' and I averted my gaze. Despite my own pain, despite the woman's humiliation as she pulled her smock and her shift over her head, I was holding my own skirt away from the walls, to keep it from touching anything, for though some attempt at tidying had been made in the larger room, the smaller one was the filthiest I had ever seen.

But then Margaret Legat dropped her smock onto the mattress, and I saw the crusted streak of blood that ran down the inside of her leg, hip to knee, then smeared away. It could not have been mistaken what had happened. No chance of the bleeding being the monthly kind: Margaret Legat was past sixty. I had to prevent myself turning away. 'She's interfered with herself.'

'What did you have there?' Mary said. 'A wart? You foolish woman. We do not regard them.'

Margaret Legat stood, slightly bent. Though it was warm she was shivering. I had never seen another woman so naked. Her face and hands were brown and her body yellow-white, like a root. She did not look mutinous, as Anne Alderman had, but rather fearful; I could tell she was not of the full understanding. Mary made her squat that she might proceed with the searching. I saw the place where she had cut off part of herself, the blood crusting now.

The air in the room grew thick; the woman had not, I think, washed that week. She began to weep while Mary examined her, and I crouched to hold her hands, to keep her upright, though her palms were slippery with sweat. As if she sensed my sympathy, she would not leave off insisting that she had never had any imp, as if my believing her would make her free to go.

Mary soon found what she was looking for, but before she would let Margaret stand up and get dressed, Mary made me look and see how to apply the tip of a long, blunt needle to any likely tag of flesh, to find the patch of numbness which was proof. She talked me through it, pointing and jabbing without ceremony, heedless of the woman's weeping and the blood that was starting from the places she had pricked, adding to the damage that time and childbirth had done. Seeing my grey face, Mary snorted. 'I'd have thought you'd be accustomed. You were a midwife, weren't you? What did you think you were here for, child?'

We left Margaret Legat to settle her clothing, went through to the other room, and Mary reported to my brother what we had found. He made notes, and I used his distraction to step outside to wash my hands. My heart was beating too fast. I could see no pump, so I made do with the horse trough by the church. I remember the water was clear and good, and I saw a tadpole move in the deeps of it, but then I had scarcely time to grasp the cold stone rim before I dropped to my knees, and threw up into the water.

I threw up once and then again, until what came was bitter and thin, and then I sat down on the edge of the horse trough and wept, as if I would never stop, the folk of the village going about their business as though they did not see me, and only little children turning to stare. I had sat there half an hour when I began to feel the throbbing pain in my foot.

I was excused Margaret Legat's watching, though in the parlour of the inn that night I overheard Mary Phillips telling someone the woman had confessed: she had never know-ingly kept an imp, she had said, but there had been a thing that did live beside her, like a child, though she never saw it or heard it speak. That was enough, and before we turned in for bed I heard Matthew making arrangements among the men to have her taken to the gaol at Bury St Edmunds.

The next morning I got up early to see Margaret Legat being taken: though it meant nothing, I felt it was the only thing I could do for her. It was a cold morning, with a heavy dew. Several women from the village had also come out of their houses to see. I remember Margaret Legat had packed a small cloth bag of things, and it touched me that she thought she would be able to keep them. There was some delay with the cart, and while the men conferred among themselves, the woman saw her neighbour come out onto her front step, pulling a shawl around herself.

'Nance,' Margaret Legat said, pulling a Bible out from her bag. 'Nance, I must give this back to you.'

But the neighbour lowered her eyes; she turned away inside, and shut her door. I felt my brother draw level with me, where I stood near the cart, though he did not speak. I still remember the sight of Margaret Legat's stooped back as she stood, just looking at that closed door, before she went to lay the Bible on the step. The men let her do it, before they pushed her up into the cart.

As it pulled away, I could not help but turn to Matthew. 'Brother, why must you go on with this?' I said. 'What have you to prove? You're getting married, Matthew. Why not go home, and give that your attention?'

He did not answer immediately, but stayed watching the cart as it drew away down the lane.

'You do not think, do you,' I tried, 'that this is what our mother would have wanted for you?'

At that, his head snapped round. 'Mother's dead,' he said. 'So it little matters what she would have wanted.'

He marched away indoors, and after a moment I, too, turned back towards the inn, my left foot dragging behind me.

That same morning was the one Mary Phillips left to return to Manningtree. It is odd to think of now but, not wishing to be left alone with Matthew, I was almost sorry to see her go. Before she mounted her horse, she pressed something into my palm. 'You will have need of this,' she said. I opened my hand, and looked at the blunt needle, the length of my thumb, its dull silver sheen.

When we dined later, Matthew was civil with me, as if nothing had passed between us; he enquired how I had slept, and passed me the bread. It was dry, and stuck in my throat, and I felt my brother watch me chewing. I tried to keep my face blank, but I could not tell whether I was successful. Though on the surface everything was the same, underneath everything was different. He had crossed a line, the way he had hurt me, the way he had spoken of Mother: suddenly, I felt as if I had never known my brother at all.

30

The next weeks were like one of those nightmares, the ones from which you cannot wake. I searched women gently, and reported as little as I could to Matthew. But those women who drew a discontented crowd, hungry for what proofs had been found against them, there was little I could do for those ones. Each had a different tale, fit to break your heart, but what they had in common was loneliness, and too many nights spent listening; loose flesh where they had given birth or gained weight in other, better summers. What they had in common was fear.

We moved up through Suffolk from village to village, Matthew writing ahead to seek information and a welcome in each new place. The back of my neck burned and peeled and burned again. Often I thought of leaving, of sitting in the road and refusing to move. But in the end I thought it better to stay, and attempt to work against my brother for, as I tried to gather my courage back, I saw I was well placed to do it, without him even realizing that it was being done. Though my foot pained me so that I had to bite my lips together as I rode, I could not bear the thought of what would happen if Matthew were to replace me with some other woman, who had less gentle hands than my own; someone with less compunction, who would make liberal use of the blunt needle.

Those women Matthew made me search, I used our time

alone to counsel them on what to say to him, on what questions they might expect him to ask, and how to keep a respectful and frightened countenance. I let them freshen themselves with water, and when my rare chances came to steal them I slipped the women small coins, that they might persuade a gaoler to fetch them a clean shift to keep for their trial, and look decent when they came to the dock. Some of them I catechized, and made them repeat their prayers, correcting them gently on how bread came before forgiveness.

But it took its toll on me. Quickly the mornings and evenings of travel became my only respite. More than once we turned down the wrong lane and found ourselves where the way ended at some low farm, where dogs would come out but no people. I was grateful for the time it took to retrace our steps, for the further minutes it would spare the women where we were going, and the further minutes it would spare me. For I began to see, as the days passed, that with whatever small good I was attempting, I was doing twice as much evil. So it was that each day I rode miserably behind Matthew, watching flies land on my horse's hot ears, trying to ignore the unpleasant slush of blood in my foot. I stopped looking about me, so that much of what I remember now of our route is reduced to the head of my horse nodding in front of me. Sunlight, and loose white seeds in the still air.

✝

It felt peculiar to come to Framlingham, for Father had spoken of the place sometimes, having inherited a plot of land there at the back of the castle, and long leased it to a man who kept ducks and geese. As the innkeeper showed us our rooms, I noted how coldly he looked on my brother: it gave me a plan. Turning matters over in my mind, I walked out from the inn, saw the ditch of the castle filled with rubbish, churned to mud where folk were keeping pigs, and the weeds waist-high within the castle walls. I remember thinking, I wish Father were here to counsel me now. For whatever the mysterious remorse in his daily book was for, I knew it would be only some minor sin, compared to what my brother was embarked upon.

The first woman the constable set us to watch at Framlingham was Margaret Wyard, who told us that the devil himself had come to her, first like a calf and later like a man with yellow hair. Her face took on an unpleasant interior expression as she told us how the devil had sent her seven imps for her five teats, so when they came to suck they had to fight, like piglets with a sow. She was a heavy woman, Margaret Wyard, of middle years. No one could recall that she had ever been married, and she breathed through her mouth.

The twelfth woman we examined at Framlingham was Ellen Driver, who lived in one room with her six hens, and confessed that she had married the devil, the year the Queen Elizabeth had died.

'What's that, then, forty years?' said the constable, when we went back to his house to make our report. He laughed at his own joke. 'You'd think matters would have grown stale by now.'

But Matthew did not smile back: he only gave a curt nod, and presented his bill. He was just the same with the women: impassive. Whether they were broken or spirited, he treated them the same. The hard days on the road, and the long watchings, they seemed scarcely to touch him.

He kept his shirts and collars clean, his questions sparse and to the point, and he noted all answers carefully. I saw how he used the pause as he made his notes to create a silence into which apprehension would pour, and many women would say more than they meant to, and so unmake themselves.

But I did have some success in thwarting Matthew, and as we went on through Suffolk I tried to remember our last afternoon at Framlingham, when I had taken the stern inn-keeper aside to mention the villages I had heard from Matthew we were making for: Great Glemham and Swef-fling; Stradbroke, Wingfield, Fressingfield. And sure enough, when we reached those places, many of the women we had been called to examine had mysteriously gone to visit their relatives in other parts – even those who were known to have no relatives living.

As we tracked our way north, never resting, I kept working against my brother in small ways, scarcely detect-able, and I do not think he guessed it, for I remained biddable and asked no questions, was no different from any woman servant he might have hired, except that I read his moods, knew his small wants before he knew them himself, and smoothed the way with arrivals and departures that he might not grow discontented, that he might stay in his thoughts and notice me the less. If he was suspicious of my sudden tractability, he did not show it. At all times, he kept his brown leather case at his elbow, but my curiosity had dulled as to what might be inside it, about the mystery of the missing pages of Father's daily book. The further we travelled, the duller my senses had become; even the pain in my foot sank to a low, sickening ache that kept me awake in the night, and all I could think about, all that seemed to matter, was finding small ways to thwart my brother.

At Rushmere, we were called to examine one Susanna Smith. The verger met us by the church, and took us to the house where they were keeping her. She was of middle age, with a husband living, but he had not been to see her in weeks. They had cut her hair short, to prevent her working it into knots. 'She has been like this six months or more. What I mean is, it would be expedient,' the verger said, 'it might ease matters somewhat, if she could be removed to the gaol.'

The nurse sitting with Susanna Smith in a low upper room told us that the woman had been a good mother, until the fit that needed four grown men to restrain her. She had been tied after that, and the nurse set to watch her. I suppose it was an expense on the parish, paying for the nurse, and then they had heard of Matthew.

'She told me the devil came to her as a red-coated dog, and spoke to her of killing her children,' the nurse said doubtfully. 'Then the day after, though I had asked the minister to come and talk with her, her throat had swelled so she could not speak – from the finger-marks, I did judge that she had been plucking at it herself.'

The nurse showed us the knife they had found in her clothes, rusty and blunt; somehow it was worse to think of a person doing themselves harm with it than it was to think of them using one that was clean and sharp.

It made me think of the fellow in London, the one who had told fortunes, made that noise like logs spitting. Folk would give him coins sometimes; at others he would disappear for a day or two, labouring. But even the worst work for women – even scrubbing floors, washing corpses – you must trust the one who does it. Women's work is done in homes, in private, where men keep their children and their wives. How much harder, then, I saw, for a woman to find work, if she was not right in her mind.

After speaking to the nurse who watched Susanna Smith in the daytime, Matthew came back later to talk to the one who watched her at nights.

'We called a physician out, once. He said it was a brain-sickness,' the night nurse told him. 'But I do not believe in brain sickness. She is entirely the devil's creature.'

The next morning, Matthew asked Susanna Smith his questions, ignoring her wary, hateful look. Some of her speech displayed a confusion about what was real and what was dreamed, a confusion which made me think of Mother. But Matthew seemed untroubled as he noted her answers down. I had to shift my weight onto my good foot to be able to stand for so long, and I winced as I did so. There was a powerful smell from Susanna Smith's hair, and I noticed the thick yellow skin on the soles of her feet, as she sat with her back against the wall and stared at us, stared at Matthew, and myself standing behind him. Suddenly I saw that, to her, we were exactly the same.

31

When I had almost grown used to my strained, careful days alone with him, a letter pursued Matthew on our course up-country, telling him that the date was set for the Essex trials. And so it was at Rushmere that Matthew decided we would turn our horses and head back towards Manningtree. I was riding with my left foot hanging free of the stirrup. It had swollen badly. In mounting, as I had put my weight on it, it would almost give under me, but by then I scarcely felt the pain in it or in my hands, which were covered in blisters that swam with water from gripping the reins.

Though the Thorn was no home to me, I confess I was relieved to be returning, that an end was in sight. But it turned out that Matthew had promised to look in at one or two places as we made the journey back.

We came off the road south at the turn for Halesworth. I knew, for he had left it open on the breakfast table, that Matthew had received a note from that place about a woman sending imps to spoil a cornfield. Matthew took us to Halesworth the long way round, that he might pass by the field and see the damage for himself. Compared to other accusations I had heard, the cornfield sounded almost a dull business: so I was hardly paying attention, as we began to catch sight of the field in snatches, between the trees.

It had been a long time since the night of Bess Clarke's

watching, since I had seen the marks in the soil of the straw-berry bed. I had forgotten how suddenly the hairs on your neck can rise.

Matthew pulled up his horse, and I got down, too. It was not like anything I had ever seen. The whole field was flattened perfectly, as if a giant hand had pressed it down gently in the night. I knew at a glance there was no point in crouching to search for footmarks. I would still swear it, even now: that field had not been trampled by men or beasts. I looked at Matthew. His face was impassive, and I tried to keep my own as blank as it had been while listening to old women talking about the devil speaking to them from hedgerows. But this was not the same. To gaze out over that field, the half-fattened heads of corn rotting on the ground, was to be touched by strangeness, by some-thing beyond understanding. I knew I was in the presence of something evil.

We rode back towards Halesworth, to the house of Mary Everard, who was accused of sending the imps that had done the damage we had seen. I sat by while Matthew ques-tioned her, trying not to be fearful. I had to speak to myself sternly: I could not know how that field had been flattened, but for certain if there was evil in that room, it would be my chair it crouched behind, if I chose to believe that the poor, shaken woman before me could have brought about that wrong.

But I think Matthew guessed I had been afraid, for that evening, when I sat watching him eat the supper he had ordered for himself, carefully chewing his crusts of bread, he said, 'I should think, sister, that what you have seen today was proof enough even for you. You, who seem to think all these wretches so innocent.' He locked his eyes with mine; I forced myself to look away.

'I saw a thing I cannot explain,' I said, 'though no proof it had aught to do with any human hand.'

Matthew was silent for a moment. Then he said, 'I know you saw something the night I came to Mother's house, the night you let me in. You won't say what, but I know you did.' I did not answer, but saw him swallow, his pale throat bobbing up and down, and at once I realized he was not angry but that he, too, was afraid.

That night he spent longer than usual writing in his ledger. I had caught glimpses of it before, over his shoulder, and I knew that against a woman's name he would sometimes write 'old', sometimes 'young'; sometimes he would write 'poor' or 'widowed', 'children' or 'no children', before the details of a woman's confession. I know now that he would also write how many imps she had and what their names were, the dates on which they came to her and in what circumstances, what harms she employed them to do. But he did not mention in his ledger how young a young woman was or how old an old, the state of her health or her wits. My brother was afraid, and to manage his fear, just as he had once declared a grave to be no more than a hole in the ground, he classified each woman: rubbed out her individual features that she might no longer be a threat.

I did not see his ledger up close that evening, but I glimpsed scraps of what he wrote, those neat rows, and I remembered the frenzied mood in Manningtree that had marked our departure. How much easier it would be, I thought, for Matthew to convince others of the guilt of the women whose trials he had arranged, having reduced them already to columns, to entries in a log. How much more vulnerable they would be, with their own particular tragedies stripped from them. I understood most fully now, the horror of what my brother was doing; the horror that Grace had been unable to describe. How mundane it was, and so how terrible. And doubt crept in that reason would win, that the women would be acquitted. Suddenly I feared I had been part of something that could have nothing but the reddest of ends.

†

That night, at about two in the morning, I gathered my things, and crept downstairs to the front door of the inn. As I drew back the bolts, a dog growled in its sleep from beside the big hearth. I took one step out of the door, my bag on my shoulder, and stood in the night air, listening. From a short distance away came low, harsh laughter; after a minute, a woman's shriek swiftly cut off, though impossible to tell whether it was in play or earnest. My stomach made a sound, loud in the night air. I was hungry. I had grown to fear my brother enough, to hate what we were engaged in enough that I had thought to creep out. But I found now that I was afraid of that, too, of being without food and help, of being without a horse, and my foot as it was.

I stood on the threshold for minutes together, feeling Suffolk spread out like a web all around me, a web of small lanes and smaller villages, and in all of them by now they knew my brother's name, and few would have wished to make an enemy of him by helping me. I stood there until my foot began to ache with cold. Then I went inside, and shot home the bolts, and climbed back upstairs to my bed. I was not brave enough to take the step of leaving.

I lay awake the rest of the night, shivering. I tried to pray, but the proper words deserted me. I thought of Papists, the idolatrous beads they have, and how comforting it must be to be able to pray with only a movement of the hand. I thought of my brother, the fear I had glimpsed in him. Suddenly I sensed that, all this time, while he had seemed so implacable and so certain, he had also been running from something.

32

The feeling when we rode into Brandeston the next day was different from how it had been in any other place. When we halted by the church, none came out to greet us: I saw a woman watching from the upper window of a house, but when she saw my eyes on her, she turned away. Soon some two or three men appeared, one a fellow who had a servant with him. He took Matthew into the minister's house, leaving me to wait outside, near the horses where they stood in the heat, twitching their tails at flies.

I had heard Matthew speaking to someone about the minister at Brandeston. I had assumed that the minister did suspect some woman, but I was wrong. For it was the minister himself that my brother had been called to examine. An old woman stopped in the road and regaled me with the whole business; she had seen me arrive with Matthew, and took me for his servant. Leaning on her stick, she told me that the minister was an old fellow, numbering the last of his years. He had been thick with the family who had the hall, she said, though they had long since gone to join the King at Oxford. Since then, the minister had been eaten up with lawsuits, and quarrelling with the godly portion of the town. The old woman called good riddance on him, before she shuffled away. But it was not all the town that hated him: that would become clear soon enough.

The minister, being a man, his body was not examined. Rather he was walked, for longer and faster, more brutally, than any woman had been. I did not see but I heard it spoken of, for my chamber at the Brandeston inn was above the kitchens, and by lying flat on the boards I could hear the talk of the women working below. I heard one say that it was a sin and a shame, the state of the gaol at Bury, where there were women crouching in their own muck, the over-crowding was so bad, and no doubt there would be sickness and it would spread out into the town and beyond. I heard another say that she did not like Matthew's face: his scars made her sick.

Matthew came in late that night, and summoned me down to eat with him, though for once I had no appetite. He looked weary and frayed. It was roast meat the woman brought us, and I knew her voice: she was the one who had said she did not like Matthew's face. The meat was dry, and I could not have said what kind it was. Matthew took some in his fingers and held it out to his dog. She ate a little, but when he held out to her another slice, she whined, turned away her nose and went under the table.

It made me fearful, the woman's expression when she had served us. The faces of most folk in Brandeston made me fearful, and I wished we could leave that night. I did not know what Matthew's plan was for me, once we were back in Manningtree; after all that had been said and done, it was hard to think of living peaceably in his household, help-ing his wife. But even with that prospect, still I found myself eager to be gone from Brandeston. The town seemed equally weighted for and against the man my brother had come to examine.

'I think you reach too far to go against a minister,' I said.

'They are but flesh and blood,' Matthew said, frowning at his dog, and pushing his dish away. 'They are not immune to error.' I remembered how Bridget had said the same of Matthew, insisting that surely he could be stopped. But Matthew saying it, and of a minister, made me also think of Father, who, when we were children, had seemed barely made of flesh and blood – almost infallible in his holiness.

Even when we were small, it had been clear how badly Matthew wanted to become a minister: the expression on his face gave it away, as Father stood at the door of his church in his simple surplice – marked out as different, perhaps, but in a manner that commanded respect. You could see Matthew hankering after Father's position when he would listen patiently after the service to some woman, distracting the child at her skirts that she might finish her story and receive Father's advice. It often did seem to me that Father's principal job was the discovering and keeping of secrets, and perhaps that was what Matthew envied: to know the thoughts of others' hearts. But he had been kept from a life as a minister, and set upon another path.

'He may only be flesh and blood,' I said, at last, 'but I know our mother would have wished to see that office respected.'

Matthew's face changed, and roughly he stood up. His chair fell behind him, but he did not bend to retrieve it. It was as if he had not even heard it fall. 'For God's sake, Alice. What is that to me?' he said. He spoke a word to his dog, but when she did not move he roused her roughly with his foot, and she followed him out of the door. I heard his feet on the stairs.

'They are but flesh and blood,' Matthew had said; I thought of those words that night, and of Father's daily book, the remorse that soaked between its lines. I thought of the minister at Manningtree, how gently he had spoken of there being more than one way out. Lying there in the inn at Brandeston, I almost wished I had turned to him, said, 'Very well, then. Save me.'

33

The next morning I woke to shouting and slamming of doors. I got up quickly and dressed myself. I paused a moment, listening, then pushed my things into my bag, just to be ready. I half thought there must have been some further news of the war, some alarm or rumour of men approaching. I went out onto the landing in time to see Matthew disappearing out of the front door. He left it to swing open in the breeze, and a woman appeared to close and fasten it; the woman from the night before, the one who had said she did not like his face. As if she felt my eyes on her from the top of the stairs, she turned.

'What's the matter?' I said, still stupid from sleep.

It was the first time, to my knowledge, that she had looked straight at me in the hours we had been at the inn. She stared up at me from the bottom of the stairs, and her face was twisted with dislike.

'His dog's dead,' she said. And then, 'I'd get down if I were you. He's bringing your horses round.' She tucked her hands into her sleeves. 'I wish you speed,' she said, and went away.

Outside, I found Matthew handling the tack himself. There was no sign of a boy to do it.

'Brother?' I said. 'What –?'

But all he said was, 'Here, hold this,' and he yanked the girth strap under my horse and pushed it into my hand.

While I held the strap in place, I saw some men outside the inn. They did not look friendly. As Matthew led my horse to the mounting block and I pulled myself up, they stood clustered around the inn door. None of them spoke, but when we turned our horses out of the yard, I saw something strike Matthew, and a small stone skittered away. Matthew flinched, but he did not turn back, only spoke a word to his horse and we picked up speed. When we were almost out of earshot, though, I heard one shout, 'Fucking stay gone!'

We rode in silence, my brother keeping up a pace. I wondered whether they would bury Matthew's dog. I thought of the dry, grey meat the woman had brought the night before. I thought of asking Matthew about it, telling him I was sorry, but he rode so fast that I knew it would be easy to anger him. I doubt he even saw the villages and fields we were passing. Usually he would turn occasionally to see that I was following and, I think, to check the road behind. But today he did not. I wondered if he was weeping.

We did not see the soldiers until we were almost upon them. It was a mile or so south of Wickham Market, and they were just off the road, sitting at the mouth of one of the clay pits that were common thereabouts. Some clay-cutters were further off, stacking their cut bricks with a wary eye, and several stood still to watch as one of the officers stepped into the road and hailed us, some of his companions getting to their feet, brushing themselves down and straightening their coats.

Four of the soldiers had guns, and they were all I could look at, the smoothness and weight of them as the men let them hang carelessly by their sides.

'Your papers?' the officer said, and Matthew passed him the safe-conduct letter he had from Harbottle Grimston.

'You are out of this gentleman's jurisdiction,' the officer remarked.

'We have only been where we were sent for,' Matthew replied.

'And where is that now?' said the officer, looking at me.

'We are going back to Manningtree,' Matthew said, his voice sharp.

I thought, Brother, be pleasant to him. But surely they would not harm us, not with the clay men there to see. The soldiers were all peering to get a look at my face. I shrank back into my raised hood.

The officer was staring at my brother with dislike, and I wondered if he had heard our name, knew of our business. He folded the letter crisply and handed it back to Matthew. Then he made a movement with his hand, and one of the other men took hold of my bridle and Matthew's.

'Come down,' the officer said.

'What for?' said Matthew. But I saw the man's face, and climbed painfully out of my saddle.

'This is your servant?' said the officer.

'No. This lady is my sister.'

I saw that while one man held the bridles, another was unfastening the saddle bags from our horses.

'What do you mean by this?' said Matthew. 'Who is your commander?'

The soldier who had unfastened the bags dropped them in the dirt of the road, and I scrabbled to gather them. 'Let me help you, sweetheart,' another said, and as he passed me the bag, he took the chance to put his hand on me.

'Leave off that,' his officer told him, and the man backed away. I turned, shouldering the bags, and began to walk on down the road. 'All surplus horses are forfeit to the army,' I heard the officer say.

'But these are not surplus.'

I glanced back to see Matthew trying to take hold of one of the bridles. The officer gave a word in the ear of one of his men: while Matthew was arguing further with the man holding the horse, another crept near with a bucket of something, and threw it over him. For a moment Matthew stood stock-still.

I turned away again, and walked on, biting my lip with pain, moving slowly with my injured foot, though I knew, if matters turned sour, they would catch me quick enough. But in another minute Matthew overtook me, soaked to the skin. I wondered whether it had been only water in the bucket.

When I looked back and saw no one following, I began to shake, and the trembling persisted as we walked the miles on to Ipswich. Matthew kept ahead, not waiting for me, not taking any of the bags. He carried no gun, and I thought how it could have gone otherwise, and for a moment I almost wished that it had, that they had taken him into the woods and made him cry out. I almost wished it, but not quite, for the similar fate it would have meant for me.

As we drew further from the soldiers, I dreaded what we were going back to. When my brother's work had confined itself to Manningtree and then to the Tendring Hundred, I had thought it was the good opinion of our neighbours that he craved. But those weeks we had ranged far from Manningtree, I had come to see how it was not their approval driving him, or not only. What was driving him lay deeper.

I thought of the missing pages from Father's daily book, and the remorse in what had remained: how Bridget's voice had tightened when I mentioned a dalliance. I thought of the night of Matthew's birth, what he had suffered. Likely enough, I would never know the truth. Likely enough the missing pages were burned long ago. But whatever was the case, something had lit a fire under Matthew, and though I had hampered his course, in truth my success had been small. Now the trials were coming, the reckoning and measure of all his carefully laid effort, and they were drawing Matthew back, and me with him.

34

That night in the Lion at Ipswich, for the first time since our childhood Matthew shared my room. I think he guessed that the further south we went, the greater the chance of me slipping away from him. Before we retired he locked the door, with a great noisy bolt that rasped and scraped, so all I could do that night was lie on my pallet staring into the rafters, aware of him in the bed on the other side of the room, muttering in his sleep as he had when we were children.

I had heard him earlier arranging borrowed horses for us, and so the next day, I thought, we would be back in Manningtree, and sooner than we had reckoned to be. But the following morning I had to pull up short when Matthew turned his horse off the great road south and towards Wenham. He had business there, he called over his shoulder. Only a paper that wanted signing, for the sale of the last portion of Father's land: it could not have been urgent, but I think he was ashamed to arrive home so early, and to need to say why. And so I came, that day in July, to ride into the place I was born.

It was as I remembered it, the way the road swung round left at the corner farm, the bad pothole that always washed itself out at that place. The same chickens scratched in the dust, and faces I knew, or almost knew, looked out from their doorways as we passed. The same two hollies stood guard at the churchyard gate; I can still recall the gloss of them, and the dark mass of yews behind. We halted our horses in the road outside our old home. The years rolled back, and it was almost as if at any moment Mother would come out of the house, or Father, and be perplexed by our great limbs, our lined faces.

But Matthew swung his feet to the ground, handed me his bridle and strode straight to the front door. He knocked, and a woman came, a servant, and behind her a little fair-haired boy still in his smocks, who stood watching us and chewing his fist. I did not hear what was said, but the servant seemed uncertain. She went away, leaving the door a few inches open, and a minute later a man appeared from the side of the house. He carried a trowel and a stout bucket, and these he set down to dust his hands, before he held one out to my brother. The man was wearing only a coarse shirt and breeches, a handkerchief tied to keep the sun off his neck, but I knew from his bearing, from the way that he put a hand on the little boy's head when the child ran back outside to lean on his leg, that this was the man who had taken up my father's position as minister at Wenham.

The minister shook hands solemnly with Matthew, and after a few more moments' exchange, my brother came back towards the gate. 'He says his wife has gone to visit her sister,' Matthew said. 'But you may sit in his parlour and wait for me, and he will give you something to drink. I shall be half an hour,' he said, gesturing with the slim roll of papers he held in his left hand. Then he left me, trudging away up the road towards Little Wenham, determined and brisk. I had to accept the minister's help in steadying the horses while I got down.

'I am William Cardinal,' he said, with a correct little bow, and I introduced myself in return. 'Let us water your horses,' he said, then allowed me first around the side of the house to where the old trough still stood, and an iron ring for hitching. When the horses were tied, he suggested that, it being a fine day, I might like to wait for my brother in the garden. As I followed him round, I saw that the roses were mostly gone, and the great elm that Matthew had used to climb was now only a stump by the back wall.

The minister showed me to the old bench in the herb garden, where Mother had liked to sit when she wished to recover her spirits. He talked with me for a few minutes, pleasantly, blandly enough, but from the way he asked about the progress of our journey, and whether it had met with success, I guessed he knew very well what we had been about. As I answered him, it came to me with a cold jolt that, though our pressing on had meant a reprieve for Shottisham, Alderton, Ramsholt, those places thereabouts, it might mean something else for Wenham. There was no reason to imagine our old home would be exempt from Matthew's attention: rather, I thought, he is more likely, having a day or two in hand, to wish to purge the place and leave it, as he would think, clean.

'I dare say you have heard,' I said, when there was an opening, 'what my brother's business has been.'

William Cardinal had picked a long sprig of rosemary and was crushing the tip between finger and thumb. 'It has reached my ears,' he said shortly.

I cleared my throat. I saw the old apple tree had a heavy crop coming that year, the small hard apples hanging in fists. I pointed to them. 'We could never decide whether that tree was cooking or eating or cider,' I said. 'The fruit turns out so red, but so sour.'

He glanced up into the branches. 'Aye. My boys won't eat them.'

I took a breath, and said, 'He might ask you for names. When he comes back.'

The minister's eyes widened. 'What – here?'

'If he does, my advice is that you give them – one or two, at the least.'

He shook his head. 'He will get no names from me.'

'You know what passed at Brandeston?' I said, for even as I spoke the minister of that place was sitting in the gaol at Bury, awaiting his fate.

But William Cardinal stood up, and put his hands in his pockets. His smile was gentle. 'Even still.' As he said it, his face clouded; over my shoulder, he must have seen my brother coming. Then Matthew was beside us, and the minister said, 'Ah, sir, how did your business go forward? Is there anything I can do, before I set you on your way?'

Matthew frowned. 'The man I needed was gone into Ipswich.'

There was a quiet, while Matthew watched the minister's face, waiting. Then the minister said, 'Perhaps you would like to stay the night.'

†

William Cardinal told us he had better wait for his wife to show us our chambers. Matthew said it was no matter, for in fact he had a letter to write. Might he have use of a desk? The man seemed uneasy as he showed us into his study, though I was glad that he made no move to tidy away any particular papers.

While Matthew wrote his letter, I perched in the window

seat. I had sat there often before, on wet days mostly, watching drops of rain make their journey down the thick and serviceable glass. There were still books in their cases all around, books bound in brown and black and green, which from a distance might have been the same ones I had known as a child, and on a closer look, there were even titles I recognized. I sat, my brother's pen scratching behind me, watching the minister, who had gone back to his digging. It was almost like being surrounded by Father; his echoes, his doubled ghost.

When the minister's wife returned from her sister's house, she showed us up to her guest chambers. Matthew had his old room, but I had the one where Mother had put our few guests; the little boys had mine, and I was thankful for it.

Dinner that night was stilted. I asked whether the minister had ever met our parents, and the minister said he had been at the same college as my father, though a year or two below; beyond that, he offered no further comment. The minister's wife, in turn, asked which part of London our mother hailed from; Matthew, seeming to dislike the question, answered only briefly. The minister asked whether Matthew had a family himself; when my brother stayed quiet, I said he would soon be married, and then of course the minister's wife asked about the wedding, but my brother did not seem to wish to speak of that either.

The minister's wife seemed on edge, and hid it less well than her husband; she kept exhorting her boys to sit up straight, and chew their food. I asked after our old servant Sarah, for I knew she still lived in those parts, and I was told that she was well, and still at the same farm. Her brother had it now. At that the minister's wife tilted her head; from an upstairs room her youngest was wailing. Then the floorboards creaked as the servant went to him, and he hushed. The easy things to speak of seemed exhausted, and I allowed the table to fall into silence.

After dinner I thought to step outside for a moment, but in the passage by the back door, I paused. The kitchen door stood half open, and I saw a good fire blazing, and a kettle set upon it. A rocking chair was placed beside the hearth, just like our old one. I thought of Mother, sitting there, Matthew laid in her lap. Just then the servant crossed to the kettle and, catching sight of me, she turned. 'Can I fetch you anything, mistress?'

'No – I beg your pardon, there is no need,' I said, and hurriedly let myself out into the darkening garden. I closed the door behind me and stood still beside the herb beds as they breathed out their scent.

Someone said, 'Your father also had three sons, did he not?'

I turned. It was the minister.

'My apologies for disturbing you,' he said. He put his hands into his pockets. 'I like to take the air before bed.'

'He had four,' I replied. 'Three with my mother, but she died, and he married my brother Matthew's mother after.'

'My wife sometimes jokes that this place is lucky. We have three ourselves, so.' Craning his neck, he made a shooing motion, and I turned in time to see two round pale faces disappear from an upper window. He looked at me, rueful. 'My older ones, in the summer they perhaps do not attend to their bedtimes as they should.'

'It must be a pleasant thing, to be in a house where there

are children,' I said. 'Myself, I am a widow.' Then, after a breath: 'I sometimes think I would accept any position in a household that had children in it. If you were to hear of any such place . . .'

The minister was quiet. From the bottom of the garden, a blackbird called, that low, pure sound. Then he said, 'It saddens me, mistress, but I do not know that I can help you. For my wife, she, too, has heard what passed at Brandeston.'

'Ah,' I said.

He lowered his voice. 'May I be frank?'

'Of course.'

'All we want,' he said, 'is your brother gone. How can we speed it?'

I met his eyes. 'Put him on another scent,' I said. 'Somewhere else between here and Manningtree.'

The minister's eyes widened. 'I cannot,' he said.

Behind us, I heard a window open. 'William!'

It was the minister's wife. She nodded to me, and closed the shutters.

'I should go in,' he said.

I lingered in the garden after he had gone. I could hear from inside the house my brother bidding someone a brief goodnight. I took one more breath of night air, then went in, shutting the door on the silent and unyielding garden. From long habit I put home the bolts, top and bottom, though when I turned, the minister's wife was there with a lamp. 'I was just coming to do that,' she said. She did not smile.

'Forgive me,' I replied.

35

My father's grave was so far under the shade of the churchyard hollies that only moss would persist there; a lush, springy carpet, which was almost tempting enough for me to kneel and lay my cheek on as I stood beside the grave with Matthew, waiting for the service to begin.

I regarded the gravestone, for which Mother had left money, with the name spelled correctly in handsome large letters and the dates all as they should be, but still it was hard to believe that Father was truly there, in the earth. I had never seen him put under for, of course, only men go for the burying. To me, it was as though my father's flat body had been vanished from his bed, like a card trick when your eyes are not fast enough to see how it was done. While Matthew was still standing over Father's plot, I wandered among the other stones. It came to me that I did not even know which grave it was that Matthew had fallen into, all those years ago.

In church, the minister preached stiffly; I wondered whether he was always thus, or whether it was because my brother was there. His text was from Corinthians. He said the verse about speaking, understanding and thinking as a child; about how a man must leave off childish things. It made me think of something Bridget had said once, about how when you hear a man spoken of in the Bible, whatever is said, that goes for a woman, too.

It was impossible to sit in that pew and not think of Father preaching. Out of the tail of my eye, I caught sight of Matthew listening intently and felt a flash of sorrow for our old closeness: for how sad, how lonely he must be now, as well as angry. For I was sure he knew what Mother had done. And if he did, it must have been weighing on him.

It was not until we were filing out after the final prayers that I caught sight of Sarah. At first I thought I was mistaken, but then she turned to take the arm of a young man who was with her, and I knew it was her. She had stayed longer than some of our later servants, had only moved on when I was six. Only Father had called her by name: Mother had called her 'you'.

I turned to see Matthew talking with the minister, the minister's wife standing by, and without thinking further I followed Sarah and her companions down the church path and along the lane. Soon I saw them turn in at the gate of their farm. When I reached it I hesitated. The place was still cleanly kept, and two of the barns had new roofs. I had taken a risk in coming there, but if anyone knew more about what had passed in our household at the time of Matthew's birth, it would surely be Sarah. For she had been born in Wenham, lived all her days there, before and since her time serving my family. If there was anyone who could say why Matthew would think Bridget a witch and a whore, perhaps it was Sarah.

I went to the door and knocked, and when a girl answered, I said who I was. Sarah must have heard my voice, for she came out at once, and welcomed me in. At her insistence the children were cleared out of the kitchen. The girl fetched us something to drink, then left us, shutting the door behind her.

For a moment or two, neither of us spoke, though Sarah studied me closely. She had always used few words. I was foolishly surprised to see the touch of grey in her hair: I still thought of her as the quiet, brisk girl she had been when she had worked in our household.

'I dare say you had forgot my face,' she said.

I smiled. 'How could I?' I said. 'Your face is my first memory, near enough.'

There was another quiet, and then she said, 'Can I ask what your business is here? For I know you didn't only come to visit me. My Lucy said she saw you sitting beside Mistress Cardinal in service.'

'I am here with Matthew. He is selling land. That piece by the churchyard, with the apple trees.'

'We did not know if he was here to drag us out and hang us,' she said evenly.

'I do not think your minister would countenance it,' I said.

'I am surprised any can. Of course I know none of this is your doing, Alice.' She leaned back in her chair. 'I always wondered how your brother would turn out. God knows, he was a strange child. The bed-wetting, and the listening at doors – but your mother, she wouldn't be strict with him. She used to cry herself when he would have his tantrums, and that was all that would halt him. My lot, they've always had a slap to correct them, and a kiss to soothe it later, but that never worked with Matthew . . .' She hesitated. 'Even when he was a little lad he seemed – low, like a grown man will get. It must have been the shock, I suppose, from that lazy wet nurse dropping him in the hearth . . . He was later to walk than any child I have known. He did it in the end, but I had to take his little stockings off, hold his two hands in mine and drag him all the way across the kitchen floor, his toes stubbing on the flags. It nearly did my back in, but he was walking in a week.' I remembered what Matthew had told me the wet nurse had said about his late walking.

'We were always told he had crawled into the fire himself, at the wet nurse's house,' I said.

But Sarah gave her head a little shake. 'Must have been a white lie. Perhaps they said it so he would not grow up blaming her. For certain your brother was never one to forgive a slight.' She sighed. 'I used to wonder they didn't keep him at home, or at least bring him back sooner, but then the mistress was always so poorly in her health.' She stopped. 'How is the mistress now?'

'She died. This winter gone. I was widowed the same month.'

'Oh, my dear,' she said. 'I am sorry for it.'

'The woman who was my mother's servant, before you – Bridget. I married her son. Well, her adopted son.'

'Adopted?'

'Yes. She had none of her own.'

'Did she not?' Sarah looked interested.

I was nearing the reason I had followed her home from church. 'Do you know much of her?' I said.

Sarah tilted her head. 'I spoke to her once or twice.'

I lowered my voice. 'Do you know why she left my family's service?' I went on. 'I have heard that she left not long after my brother was burned. I have heard that he was not burned at the wet nurse's, but before he ever went there.'

'I never heard that,' Sarah said.

'I have heard that she might have had a hand in it. Even

that she and my father might have had some manner of flirtation.'

'Flirtation?' Sarah's face was a careful blank.

'Did you not wonder? About why she left when she did?'

Sarah looked at me, for long moments. 'I never heard she had anything to do with your brother's misfortune,' she said. 'That was the wet nurse's doing, that's what I was told. As for Bridget, her going –' She broke off. 'In truth, I did think she was with child. Nothing showed, but with how quick she went . . .'

'You think it could be true, then?' I sat back. 'That she and my father, they were in love?'

Her eyes came back to my face. 'Love?' she repeated. Then she pushed back her chair, and stood up to mend the fire. She did it slowly, and when she came back to her seat, she sank into it. 'I was twelve when I came to your family's house,' she said. 'Sixteen when I left it. When it started, I thought I was mistaken.' She glanced away. 'Rather than standing back, your father might come through a doorway at the same time as me, so that the front of him would brush against me. I tripped, once, on the back step, over a pair of his boots, and he came out of his study, and in helping me up, he put his hands otherwise than he should have.' She looked uncomfortable. 'I am sorry to say it. I know you were fond of him. But men, you know – and I wouldn't have you think Bridget went looking for anything she might have got from him.'

'I cannot credit this, Sarah,' I said. 'Might you not have imagined it?'

'He never did that when my chest was flat,' she said. And then, more softly, 'Though, mistress, I know plenty who've had worse from their masters.'

I stood up. I did not know what to say. 'I had better be going,' I said. 'I shouldn't be away too long.'

Before she let me out, Sarah raised her eyes to mine. 'You think, then, that your brother will soon be on his way?' she said. 'It's only that he may not need the minister to give names. If folk hear he is near, they may come themselves, without any bidding. Any who have reason to think they might be accused. For everyone knows how it is in the gaol. They hear of those who have died in there already. And so they think, better to be arrested now, than next month and have to wait for the spring assizes. They think, like as not it would kill you. A whole winter in there, before your case is even heard.'

†

I walked back to the minister's house, unseeing and unhearing. I could not believe it, about my father; did not want to believe it. Arriving back, I found no one in the parlour. From the kitchen I could hear the clank of dishes, and the servant whistling softly through her teeth. Seeing the minister's study door open, I thought to look out of the window, to see if they were in the garden. I could hear voices, and leaning close to the glass I could see Matthew talking to someone near the back door. The glass bent the shapes of them, but the fellow seemed earnest, and was clutching a hat in his hands: the man buying Father's land, perhaps. I turned. There on the desk lay my brother's brown leather case, open.

I ducked into the passage, and crept to the back door, which was open a crack. I heard the fellow running on in talk, and Matthew saying yes or no at intervals. I retreated into the study, and pulled the door to behind me. I thought,

271

If Father's missing pages are not burned, they are in that case. If I could find them I would know: whether he had forced Bridget, whether she had left our house in shame, whether they had been in love. So I opened the case. Some of the contents fell out onto the desk, and I began to sort through the documents. But Father's missing pages were not what I found.

At the top of the pile were unsent bills for some of the towns we had visited, then two or three letters from my brother Thomas. But I did not read them. For what had also fallen from the case was Matthew's ledger, and this I opened, turning back through the pages, my horror growing. The lists of women, the bland and terrible words written next to their names. I turned all the way back to Bess Clarke's name, and read the notes of her case. I turned further, to an entry dated long before I had come to Manningtree, before the witch business had even begun. And there, from December, was a list of the five Manningtree women, the first accused. A list dated before some of their alleged crimes were even said to have been committed. There they were in black and white:

Elizabeth Clarke
Anne West
Rebecca West?
Nan Leech
Helen Leech?

I turned cold, thinking of what Grace had said, my first day at the Thorn: about Matthew having a great book with witches' names in. He had selected them, then. Quite coldly he had chosen them, those he had known would be vulnerable, and before any rumours had even started. Perhaps what had begun as anger, as grief towards Mother, towards Bridget, perhaps that had taken root and spread into something disciplined, some poisoned way of seeing. My hands shaking, I fumbled the book and half dropped it, and as I did so, some further sheets fell out where they had been folded inside the back cover. As soon as I saw the foremost of them, I knew at one glance what it was.

It was the sketch Matthew had made Grace produce of the item she had seen in Mother's bed. The drawing was carefully worked, and showed a figure about the length of a palm, and round, but as though it had its knees tucked up, head lowered and hands folded close against the body. She had drawn tiny dense lines all over, to show the texture of it, for I remember she said that it had been rough-looking, and, as she thought, made of hair.

On the next sheet I found a series of questions, and below each, several answers, and beside every answer a name. I recognized the names, from stories Rebecca and I had gleaned and pieced together from the gossip of my brother's business in the Tendring Hundred.

What is this thing drawn here?
Margery Grew: *I have no knowledge of such things.*
Margaret Landish: *I believe it is a charm or poppet.*
Margaret Moone: *It is a spell or charm.*

What is it for?
Margaret Landish: *It is for the conceiving of a child.*
Margaret Moone: *It is for conception.*

Do you not think it is intended to hurt or harm?

Margaret Landish: *If it had no thorns in it then it is not meant for harm.*

Margery Grew: *I have no knowledge.*

They were accused women, all of them. Yet Matthew had taken it upon himself to ask them, to consult with them, about the thing that Grace had seen. It made sense: to his mind, who would know the nature of that item, if they did not? But he had not taken any one of them at their word. My eyes scanned the responses. He had asked his questions, but he had kept on asking. Perhaps because he did not like the answers he was getting. For it made no sense: why would our aging mother have slept with a conception charm clasped in her hand?

I turned the page.

Margaret Moone: *It could not harm the mother. But any child conceived using such a proceeding, I have heard it said – by others, you understand, for I have not come across such a thing myself – I have heard it said that any child resulting would take a fever if you burn the charm that brought it, would breathe too tight if you buried the thing. The charm rules the child's fate. That is what I have heard. That is all I know – except that such a thing is no use by itself. It is no use without a man's seed. And the gypsies and wise-men that sell them, often as not, it's not only the charm they're selling.*

'What are you doing?' Matthew said, behind me. I jerked before I managed to flip the ledger open to a different page; calmly, Matthew took it out of my hands. 'If you wanted to read it, Alice,' he said, 'you had only to ask.'

My voice shook, as I reached for something to say. 'Your handwriting,' I said. 'It's nothing like our father's any more.' It was true: it had once been rushed and slanted. Now, it was like the writing of a different man.

Matthew opened the ledger, and touched the page, losing himself as I had at first, absorbed in the neat list of names. 'I have spent many hours improving it,' he murmured. 'What I think is, I owe it to God. To do His work with as much thoroughness as I can.' He looked at me. 'You have helped me, Alice. You know that, don't you? I could not have applied myself so diligently without you.' Matthew closed the ledger then, and pushed it back into his case, with the other papers behind. 'You had better change,' he said, with a cold smile. 'It will be time for dinner, soon.'

†

Each time I closed my eyes in bed that night, I saw the sketch I had found in the back of Matthew's ledger. I had almost ceased to think of it, the item, the doll made of hair. But it was clear that Matthew thought his safety was in some way bound up with it. I wondered where it could have gone, whether Bridget had it after all. I thought of how quickly she had deflected me when I had asked her about it, how swiftly she had told me that Grace must have been mistaken in what she saw. I felt a fool for having begun to believe that the secret Bridget spoke of concerned something else entirely, and that what Grace had seen had been nothing more than a bundle of herbs that Mother had taken to bed to scent the sheets.

Yet I struggled to accept that the women Matthew had questioned had it right: what would Mother have wanted with a conception charm? My brother had been born hardly more than a year after her marriage to Father. I knew from my landlady that Papists had special prayers for a woman who remained barren, but even they did not resort to them quickly: most women trusted to God's providence, for the first year or two at least. So why then would Mother have meddled in such a foolish proceeding? But I saw that, whatever the truth, the women's answers must have changed what Matthew felt about her. For it came to me that he had not spoken of Mother with affection, not once, since coming back from the hundred. Rather he had snapped or grown silent at any mention of her.

For certain, though, it was Bridget whom Matthew hated, Bridget he feared. I remembered what Sarah had said about the threat of the long winter in prison prompting more confessions among the women round about. That there were those who would rather put themselves to trial this year than risk being arrested later and face rotting in the dark till the spring.

What if, I thought, what if, knowing the friendship and support she enjoyed in Manningtree, he had never intended to arrest Bridget too quickly but, rather, had planned to establish a precedent, to test his powers by gathering that ledger full of women? If the coming trials went his way, then who might he not accuse? What if, I thought, he was always planning to arrest Bridget in the autumn, then have her die forgotten in the dark months, or face a foregone trial in the spring? I wished I could get a message ahead to her, one that somehow did not endanger her or me or whoever I trusted it to. But there was no safe way to do it.

I tried not to think of the other thing Sarah had said. I

could not conceive of my father overstepping the bounds in that way. I decided that she must have had it wrong, must have read into some clumsy friendliness what had not been there. I thought of how, when he talked to the women of his congregation, Father would always stand further back than he did from the men, with his hands folded behind him. Always proper. The memory was a league apart from the kinds of men who had plagued me in London, called out after me words I could not catch. Yet I could not dismiss the nagging recollection of the remorse I had found in Father's daily book. And still I had found none of the missing pages that might name the cause.

Matthew had treated me no differently that evening, since catching me with his ledger. At dinner he had told the minister he had concluded his business, and that we would be leaving in the morning. The minister's wife had set down her cup and begun to chide her eldest son for kicking his brother under the table, the better to conceal, I think, her relief at our departure.

36

Before noon the next day we were mounted, having thanked the Cardinals for their hospitality. But when Matthew turned his horse, it was not towards the road for Manningtree but in the other direction. 'Where are we going?' I called. 'This road takes us out of our way.'

He smiled a thin smile. 'We have one more piece of business at Little Wenham,' he said. 'Don't fear. We'll be back in Manningtree tonight.'

Little Wenham was scarcely a mile's ride, but I had not often been there as a child: for anything we needed, it was to Capel St Mary or Ipswich that Father would ride. The path to Little Wenham was narrow, and on either side the hedges were thick with summer: rough grasses and the drooping heads of late cow parsley brushed my legs as my horse followed my brother's. The crops in the fields stood high, tangling at the edges with rampant flowering weeds. The pleasant greenness all around served only to increase my fear for, though it was a summer day even more perfect than any that had come before, I knew we could not be going to Little Wenham for any good purpose.

As we crossed the stream near the great barn, I saw the church and the hall over the millpond. Its surface was still as glass, a pale, untroubled blue. But beside it a knot of folk awaited us, and in their midst stood a young woman.

Matthew collected his horse and got down, and the crowd moved towards us, but as someone thrust the young woman to the front, it was she who spoke. 'Sir,' she said, 'I have come for swimming.' She was simply dressed, perhaps seventeen but no older, and still with that round child's face. I thought she was speaking of some summer lark, before I saw what she meant.

'You are mistaken,' I said. 'We do no such thing.'

'You are Master Hopkins, are you not?' another woman asked.

Matthew became wary. 'I am. But I was not told that these were your wishes. I understood I was coming to question someone. Where is the fellow who came to see me yesterday?'

'No point questioning this one. You'll get no sense out of her,' the woman said. 'Swimming, that's the only thing for her.'

'It is not permitted under the law,' I said, looking at Matthew. I turned to the girl. 'You must understand, that was never my brother's method.'

'Please,' the girl said, looking only at Matthew. She leaned closer, her face intent. She spoke confidingly, but loudly enough for the crowd around to hear. 'Please, sir. I am afraid that the devil has got into me somehow. I have been afraid of it these four months. Sir, I need to know if I am saved.'

'You should pray to God, then,' I said, my voice unsteady.

'That will not benefit her,' said the other woman.

I touched the girl's arm. 'What would make you think such a thing?'

She did not lower her gaze. 'I try to pray for folk,' she said. 'I try to remember them in my prayers, but then I find myself thinking about how I would hurt them. If I could.' She spoke simply and sadly. 'I love God, and so it grieves me. But I have been told that if I am swum and I sink, I will know for certain that I am beloved of God in return, how-ever the devil might try to plague me.'

'Who said this to you?' I asked.

'Go on, master,' one of the women said. 'Will you not try her? There's something not right with her. She has often been unchaste, but in broad daylight, and without shame.'

'Swimming cannot be taken as evidence,' Matthew said thoughtfully, 'if the matter should come to court.'

'That is of little account,' said one of the men. 'If she does float, you can go on and do your usual proceedings.'

'We've got up a collection,' said someone else, 'and the necessary rope.'

'Will you come, sir?'

I looked over the crowd, searching for any face familiar from my youth. But I knew none of them. 'Matthew, you cannot,' I said. I was almost laughing with nerves. 'Surely? It is folly.'

Matthew stood, and turned to the waiting crowd. 'I will observe it,' he said. 'If you wish. For that, there is no charge.'

'Brother,' I said, grasping his arm. 'Brother, do not do this.' But he pulled away, as the crowd moved towards the millpond, Matthew and the girl among them. It looked mad, like a May outing, like a pageant.

I stood on the spot watching them go, torn, then hurried as well as I could back to the nearest house. I did not knock but opened the door and shouted.

'Give me a minute!' a woman called. I could hear her upstairs, her feet on the boards. She was moving about, singing to herself, and I yelled again. At length, I heard her coming down the stairs. When she appeared, she was middle-aged, brisk. She seemed disposed to be annoyed, but then she saw my good clothes. 'What's your pleasure?' she said.

'Would you know of a girl, about my height, about sixteen years? Somewhat natural? They're talking about swimming her, and I need to know where her family is. Someone must speak up for her.'

'She's nineteen,' the woman said. 'She's different, that one, for certain. She isn't allowed to church now, for she kept making a scene, convinced herself that the steward's son had fallen in love with her.' She gestured with her head. 'They live up the road in Capel St Mary, only a quarter-hour if you run.'

'My foot, I cannot,' I replied. I fumbled for money in the pocket of my gown, the few small coins I had. I put them on the table. They did not come to much. 'Have you someone you can send?'

'Of course,' she said. She patted my arm. 'You keep your money.'

But I did not wait to pick up my coins. Outside I saw the crowd milling, halted where the water looked deep. One of the men had gone round by the other bank, and was trying to throw a thick rope across. On each attempt the knotted end fell short and hit the water, but as I spotted Matthew and the girl, another man caught the knot and held it, and the crowd gave a stifled cheer.

Matthew saw me, and beckoned me across. 'You'll get her ready, now, Alice,' he said. 'Behind there.' He waved at a small clump of trees.

'I'll have no part in it.'

'Is that your servant, master?' a man said, the one who had caught the rope. 'I'd have my servant whipped if she spoke like that to me.'

Matthew stepped close to me. 'Do it or not as you choose,' he said evenly. 'But if she goes in as she is, that gown alone could sink her, or the cap strangle her. Don't you want her to have a chance?'

I took her behind the trees he had indicated. You could hear the folk from the village milling about. As I turned away to let her unlace herself, I saw the path winding out into the fields. No houses that way for miles. I turned back to her, about to take her arm, tell her to come quickly, stay quiet and low to the ground. 'I could get you away . . .' I began, keeping my voice low.

'Away from who?' she replied.

My next words died in my throat when I saw how mildly she was waiting. She had blue eyes – like Grace's, like Rebecca West's – the kind that bespeak innocence, the kind that make a man think a woman sees less than she does. I was struck by how white her shift was, how very white in the sun, as if she had thought about this moment for a long time, and dreamed of how it would look. She made me think of the folk at Joseph's church – it was the bright eyes, I think, and the thinness, and the difficulty with standing still. From her elation it was as if to be submerged in the pond in the sight of so many, as if that moment would prove some essential quality in her that was more than dispelling the grubby hearsay of witchcraft. A proof of faith, perhaps; a proof of redemption. There was something of Mother in the way her hands moved ceaselessly.

I saw that it was useless to try to prevent her. The girl

followed me out from behind the trees to the edge of the pond, where Matthew was waiting, the crowd looking on. I cast about desperately for someone to put a stop to it, for her family to come. But those gathered only looked expectant. Someone had left ready a coil of narrow rope; Matthew held out his knife, for cutting the spare ends when the knots were done. I shook my head, and he turned to the man beside him. 'You, then,' he said. The man reached for the knife with his thick red hands and began to tie the girl, her arms pulled behind her. The rope rasped across her skin, leaving its red marks.

'You go thumb to toe,' my brother said to the man, demonstrating. The man began to adjust the bonds as Matthew had told him, but though he did it clumsily, he was working too fast, I thought. For surely soon the girl's father would come, surely someone would come. The man was showing no care for how the rope was pinching her and hurting.

I stepped forward, and took the knife from the man. Before I crouched, I caught the satisfaction on Matthew's face. I began to adjust the rope at the girl's hands and feet, as slowly as I dared. Then I looped another length several times about her waist. I thought about bringing loops up over her shoulders, to make it stronger, but though she had worn two shifts for modesty I did not want to cross the rope over her chest. So I merely tied the waist loops tight, then took the end of a thicker piece that one of the men held out to me and knotted it strongly to the harness. Those knots were what would haul her out. Innocent or guilty, they were all that would keep her from drowning.

I worked carefully, trying to slow down, the girl watching me with interest. I strained my ears for any voice or disturbance at the back of the crowd. But the minutes passed, and Matthew grew impatient with my tying and retying. 'Very well,' he said crossly.

Last I took the end of the second life-rope that the man on the far bank had flung across the pond. It was already wet from the several missed throws, and as I tucked it among the loops at the girl's waist and tied some good big double knots, its wetness must have reached her skin, for then I felt her shiver, and when I looked into her face I saw the first hint of fear in her eyes, swiftly smothered. 'I am ready,' she said.

Matthew pushed me out of the way, and stepped forward then, to check the knots I had made. The girl's eyes did not leave his face, as he tugged at the ropes where they joined the loop at her waist. Through the linen, as I had, he would have felt her warm skin. You might have thought, observing him, that he had placed his hands on a woman any number of times, if you did not know him as I knew him, if you did not know that the sweat on his upper lip was nothing to do with the heat of the day. Disgusted, I turned away, and stood on tiptoe, my eyes moving over the back of the crowd.

Those holding the life-ropes on their opposite banks made them slack, and one of the taller men lifted the girl into his arms, just as she was, and began to wade into the shallows. The water deepened quickly and he lost his footing, stumbled, then recovered himself, amid much shouting of instructions from the other men on the bank. If you had shut your eyes, they might have been loading a cart, or bathing a flock of animals, but there was a waiting tension to the group that you could taste. They all looked to Matthew to give the word for when to drop her, and I saw

284

how he understood it, what the crowd had come for. That what they wanted was not the same as the dates and instances the courts needed: what those people craved was something holier, something older. Something that my brother wanted just as much to provide.

I turned to Matthew. 'If you let her die, I'll not speak for you in court.'

He shrugged. 'I'll find some other woman to give evidence, then,' he said. 'I'll find one with hair like yours, no one will know the difference. It is enough that you searched them, they were seen to be searched. It does not matter to me, what expertise you do or do not have.' His face was satisfied, as he watched mine fill with fear. He had long guessed I was no midwife. And he barely even cared how I had lied to him.

'Brother,' I said. 'Please. You must stop this. She's done nothing wrong. You can see that. Her mind is not right.' I took hold of his arm. 'Please, brother. You can see for yourself she's mad.'

At that I felt him twitch under me. The sun was in my eyes. He stepped forward, shook off my grip. 'She is not mad, Alice. She is a devious whore. Jesus help me. Under your gowns and your false piety, show me one of you who is not.' He turned to the man who was waiting for his signal, raised his hand.

I heard the splash as the girl entered the water, but Matthew was not looking. He was turned towards me, his face ablaze with bitter triumph as though he could see only me, as though he cared only that I was watching while he showed me what he could make these people do.

I think now of how he lamed me at the start of our journey, and how he kept me always beside him, and what I think is that for the work he was doing, my brother wanted an audience: and from the very start, the audience he wanted was me.

†

That day of the swimming was hot, as hot as the day upon which Matthew caught Joseph and me together. My brother had left in the morning for Ipswich, and later Joseph had come to mend the outhouse door. I had watched him work, hugging my knees, sitting on the scullery step amid the fresh smell of drying washing. I knew I should go in and see if Mother needed anything – she had kept to her bed that day – but instead I had brought Joseph a bucket of water, in which he had washed his hands, then met my eyes, lifted the bucket and tipped it over his head. I screamed and jumped backwards, and he chased me into the entry, laughing, and that was how I ended up with my back to the doorframe, the stone through my dress as hot as blood and the white sheets like a steaming tent around us. Joseph was hesitant, at first, until I pulled him into me.

I cannot think what Matthew would have seen, from his chamber window above, but he must have seen enough: it was pure chance that he had come back for some forgotten papers, and pure chance that I looked up at last to see him turning away. I got rid of Joseph quickly, made some excuse about hearing Mother call me, but I did not stop to tidy my hair or fasten the top of my dress where it had come loose. I ran into the house and up the stairs, and was brought up short by his chamber door, closed against me.

'*Matthew*,' I hissed through the wood, fearful of waking Mother. He opened the door straight away and I stepped back: I thought he was going to strike me. But he did not touch me. He stood, clutching the doorframe, as though it were keeping him from falling.

'I am going to marry him,' I said. 'So there is no blame.'

'You will not,' he said. His knuckles showed white where he gripped the wood.

'Why?' I said.

He kept his voice even. 'You are mistaken if you think I will let you marry him.'

'Why shouldn't I?' I said. Suddenly his calm angered me. 'He's got his arms and legs, hasn't he? He's learning a trade. You're apprenticed to a merchant. What are you going to do? Clerk us up to a great fortune? You'll be lucky to marry yourself, let alone support our mother and me. Besides,' I said, and even now I could not swear that I did not wish to taunt him as I said it, 'we'll have to be married now, for we have gone too far to go back on it.'

His face darkened, and he seemed almost to sway. Then he leaned nearer me. 'You ought to be shut away till you learn to keep your skirts down,' he said, in a screaming whisper. I felt flecks of spittle hit my face. 'I have long suspected you, though I wished to think better. But now you whore yourself –' At that word he stopped, almost panting.

'*Whore* myself?' I was near speechless. 'You might not be so fastidious,' I said, 'if any girl looked twice at you.'

I was beyond caring how I spoke: I was furious, humiliated, as he answered that he could have found me a husband, if I was in so much of a rush to let a man – to let a man –

In anger, I laughed at him. '*Let a man – let a man*,' I mimicked. 'Maybe Jane Witham might have let *you*, if you weren't such a jealous peeping child.'

I saw something break a little in his face before he slammed the door. And he did not open it again, however many times I whispered that I was sorry through the wood. For I was frightened, suddenly, though why, I could not have said.

That afternoon Matthew rode off to Ipswich, not speaking a word to me before he left, and I went to Joseph. By that evening we were promised, and married in weeks. Matthew had not come to the wedding, and I had not seen him again. Returning to Manningtree, I had hoped to find myself forgiven. But that day, the day of the swimming, I saw that I was not. That I would never be.

†

The man had shoved the girl out into the deepest part of the pond. He shed bright beads of water as he splashed onto the bank again, taking an offered hand. When the girl came up, she was face down. Through her wet shift you could see the separate bones of her spine. The men on the banks hung onto the life-ropes as the weight of the water in her clothing tried to pull her down; the ropes went taut. I could see the girl struggling, struggling to get under, to where innocence was, as her dark hair spread out in the water.

'Let her sink,' a woman shouted. 'Jog the ropes – you're not giving her a chance.'

The crowd cheered, and I turned to see whether the girl's family were there yet, whether they would not come even now, and I did not see what happened next, but there was a shout. In the effort of jerking the ropes to try to sink the girl, the man on the further bank had dropped his end. He scrambled down the bank to retrieve it, but the rope slipped and rolled into the water; as it did, the girl went under. 'She's sunk!' someone shouted. 'That's it, get her up!'

But the combined weight of girl and rope and the heaviness of the water was too much for the man on the near bank, and he could not get purchase. There was confusion as others went to help him, and another perhaps half-minute passed before they managed to get her out. There was quiet, suddenly, in the crowd. 'Does she live?' someone shouted.

A man knelt to cut her ties, but the girl's limbs did not slacken out of how they were curled like a sleeping child's. The heavy wet linen of her shifts was stained with silt and weed, and the others averted their eyes from where it clung to her body.

A woman had come pushing through the crowd and dimly I heard her screaming. In the scramble she knelt and pushed the sodden hair off the girl's face. Folk were turning away and walking, running, back towards Capel St Mary. The girl looked in a deeper sleep than sleep, as if she had been in the water for days and dreaming. I found myself going closer, horrified, to where the mother knelt in the muddy grass. Wildly she turned about, said to me, 'Can't you fetch someone? Can't somebody do something?'

I turned to my brother, but Matthew's face showed no distress, only consternation, as though some minor plan had gone awry, and now he was inconvenienced. He took hold of my arm, and as he led me away, faintly I heard the woman screaming his name, and telling him he would pay, she would make certain, he would be paid out for this.

But Matthew kept his calm. We rode from Little Wenham to Capel St Mary, and I watched him eat a long meal at the inn there. One of the town constables came in before he had finished, but my brother dismissed him with mention of Grimston, showing his safe conduct; doubtful, the constable went away.

I watched him chew and swallow, trying to make my plans. As he ate, Matthew mentioned evenly that it would fall to me to come to Chelmsford for the trials, to mind Rebecca West; he took a draught of ale, and reminded me that only if she conducted herself perfectly could he vouch for her safety. I kept my eyes down, but I felt a surge of excitement and fear. For Chelmsford would be the perfect place for me to escape my brother, if only I could find the chance. From there, I could walk south, to some large place, like Romford; Rebecca, too, if she would come. Two nights there, in case Matthew came after us, then into London. We would stop a night or so at Ellen's, and move on. Though I did not know how I could get a message to Bridget, or how I would arrange for Grace to come. For certain I did not know how we would pay our way. But I knew that I must manage it all, somehow.

I still think now of the girl we swam. It is strange, but I think of her most when I get a rare chance to wash my hair. As I lower the mass of it into the basin, feel it grow heavy and dark with water, I think of her, and the guilt is enough to choke me. As we rode back to the Thorn that day, I prayed for her, and those I feared would follow her; I prayed for Bridget and Grace and Rebecca West. Along the lanes the hedges were laden with fruit. Hired men leaned idle on gates, watching us along the road to Manningtree. In the fields the harvest stood high and still, ready to be cut down.

37

itchcraft begins in Exodus, a cold shock in a chapter of bland rules. If your cow strays to another's field, Exodus says, you must give that man the best of your own crop; if you hire an ox and it dies in your keeping, pay the owner, but if it was ox and man you hired, there is no blame on you if the beast should fail in the task. Bland rules, and even-handed; and then it comes, like a cup of water to the face – *Thou shalt not suffer a witch to live*. Harvests, and oxen, and the small arbitrations of a quiet farming life. But in the midst of it, bad knowledge. Death.

I have had many hours to read the Bible, here where I am kept. I have read in Deuteronomy how idolaters must be stoned: even if your wife, even if your sister, reverence anything but God, she must be stoned to death. A witch is supposed to be a kind of idolator, though my brother, to my knowledge, has never proposed stoning. For who could have the appetite for that? Pitted head wounds, crushing, the spreading of black blood trapped under the skin. But perhaps folk had stronger stomachs then. The ones who wrote the Bible down. Perhaps their land was dusty and poor, and trees too rare for the building of scaffolds. Perhaps all they had were stones, and the light work that many hands make.

I think of that night, the night of the swimming, and I think of other parts of the Bible. I think of the Book of

Matthew, and Jesus in his dying calling out to God, *Why hast thou forsaken me?* For that night, riding back to the Thorn as the dark drew down, for the first time I felt that God was not there. Or if He was there, then He was vengeful and cruel, and I wanted none of Him.

I think of that night, riding through the lanes with their blind folds and corners, watching my brother ahead of me, running over and over all that I had seen him do. All that I had done at his behest. Remembering how Father had said to me once that the most fearful thing you could meet down a dark lane was another person. But it is not so, I thought, as we rode towards the Thorn: what you meet in the dark is yourself. And that is truly a thing to be feared.

Transcript of the assize court at Chelmsford, convened by Robert Rich, the Earl of Warwick, on the seventeenth day of July in this year of our Lord 1645.

M.H. Now, Rebecca West, do you mark how you have been enjoined to give us the truth. Now tell the court how you are acquainted with these women. [He points to the dock, where stand Anne West, Elizabeth Clarke, Elizabeth Gooding, Nan Leech and Helen Leech.]

R.W. Sir, Anne West is my mother. The others I did meet at Bess Clarke's house, where my mother took me in the evening sometimes, and where I did hear their talk.

M.H. And what was the nature of their talk, Rebecca? Was it open talk, or was it secret?

R.W. Sir, they told me that I was to keep close and secret about any thing said or done there.

M.H. So on these evenings, they would not only talk.

R.W. No, sir. They would read from a great book. They made me kiss it. They brought imps to them, and they made me kiss those, too.

M.H. How did the imps appear?

R.W. Like dogs. Sometimes like kittlings.

M.H. Very well. So, then: you did go more than once with your mother to Elizabeth Clarke's house, and you saw these other women there.

H.L. This is folly! This is folly, masters. I never went to Bess Clarke's house in my life.

R.R. Hush, woman. I will not have interruptions in this court.

M.H. No, Your Honour, but – if you will permit me? I would wish to put the jury out of doubt.

R.R. As you will, then.

M.H. [to H.L.] You say, Helen Leech, that you were never at Bess Clarke's house.

H.L. I never went there. And if Elizabeth Gooding did, then it will have been to do Bess Clarke some charity, nothing more.

M.H. And your mother?

H.L. Pardon?

M.H. And did your mother ever go to Bess Clarke's house?

H.L. I cannot say, sir.

M.H. Why cannot you say?

H.L. [Here H.L. does hesitate.] My mother and I, we have not spoken these three years.

M.H. Very well, then. My thanks, for settling this matter. Your turn will come to give some further evidence. Now, [to R.W.] you say that your mother did bid you go with her to Bess Clarke's house one night in February of this year, and there you saw these women.

R.W. Aye.

M.H. And that on that night they did read from a book, and after the imps came, as they had done before.

R.W. Aye.

M.H. And you do say that each of these women did ask her imp that same night to do her some particular service.

R.W. Aye, sir.

H.L. Your Honour, a parrot set upon its perch could give fuller testimony than this be.

R.R. You will get your turn, madam. Till then you do yourself no favour.

M.H. Mistress West, can you tell the court now to your own recollection, what evils each of these women did ask her imp to perform?

R.W. That one there, Nan Leech, she did ask for a cow to be lamed, I do not remember whose. Then Liz Gooding she did ask the same, for Robert Taylor's horse. Then Bess Clarke, she desired her imp to make Richard Edwards's horse to throw him, on the middle bridge when he should next be coming home from East Bergholt –

M.H. Your honour has heard from the gentleman himself how that did come to pass.

R.W. Then that one there, Helen Leech, she did desire that two hogs might die, the Parsleys' hogs, but that they might die some weeks apart, to avoid drawing notice. [Here R.W. does hesitate.]

R.R. And your mother, Anne West. What did she ask of her imp?

R.W. I do not remember, sir. But I myself, I did ask mine for vengeance on Thomas Hart's wife. I wished heartily for Prudence Hart to be lamed down her right side.
[There are gasps from the courtroom.]

M.H. Now, Rebecca. We will come to that presently. But first you must say what your mother did desire of her imp.

R.W. She did desire . . . She did only desire that she might be freed of all her enemies, and have no more trouble or sorrow in this life.

M.H. Remember, child, how you have sworn yourself to tell the whole truth here.

R.W. I do, sir, I do only speak the truth now, I promise you. I'll have no more of Satan.

38

It was Mary Phillips who was up to let us in that evening when we reached the Thorn, the rest of the house having gone to bed, but the next morning it was Rebecca West who brought me up my hot water. She looked unlike herself: paler, fatter.

'Rebecca,' I said, and went behind her to shut the door. 'How do you?'

She looked at the floor. 'Mary Phillips went to see my mother,' she said. 'She took her a pie.' She glanced up. 'Mary says she has not enough to eat there. And the damp has got on her chest.'

I touched her arm. 'Where is Grace?'

Rebecca turned to pick up my empty cup and plate from the night before. 'She is dismissed,' she said. 'And two of the scullery maids with her. Mary Phillips said we had no need of them, that your brother has changed his mind and will not keep this place beyond his marriage. I do not know where Grace has gone.'

I felt a pang. But though I had grown fond of her, I thought, for certain, Grace would be better off away.

I saw Rebecca watching me. 'Take heart,' I said. 'I am to come with you to Chelmsford. So you may sit with me, before you testify.' I stopped. 'I hope Mary Phillips has not been harsh with you.'

Rebecca turned her eyes up to me. They were dull. 'She

has not,' she said. 'She has not been cruel. Mostly, she does not say two words to me together.'

I watched for an opportunity, that afternoon, to send a message to Bridget somehow. But Mary Phillips, all day she was up and down the stairs. Night came, and I heard her lock up early. I would have to find a way to get a note to Bridget when I reached Chelmsford instead.

We set off the next day in the white, chilly dawn, Rebecca West in her green dress and a travelling cape I recognized as the one that had been bought for Grace. It gave me a pang, and made me wonder again where Grace was: what cape she was wearing. We rode unseen out of Manningtree, Matthew in front, and I following next beside Rebecca, Mary Phillips after. My brother looked back at us so seldom that it felt almost as if we happened to be riding behind a stranger.

We went in silence, back along the roads that had brought me that way not four months before. It all looked different, with the hedges in their fullest weight of leaf. As we rode on, the day warmed: soon, the sun was finding the spaces where the necks of our gowns did not meet our caps, where our cuffs did not meet our gloves. We went through Colchester, past the empty gaol where Rebecca's mother had spent these last months; where, on the steps, Bridget had found Joseph. His letter to her, though it was soft and ragged by then, I was still keeping in my sleeve.

Though I had plenty of opportunity to whisper to Rebecca, she seemed too dull and stunned for me to mention leaving. I thought perhaps our ways must part, but I decided to watch my chance and stay with her as long as I could, before asking her to make her choice. Since the girl, since the swimming, it seemed impossible to leave and save no one but myself.

†

It was noon before we passed the accused women on the road. The only warning of it was Matthew calling out a greeting, and then I saw the laden cart pull to the side to let us pass. There were thirty of them, in the cart, and only room to stand. Their hands had been tied together, so that they could not save themselves when the cart laboured in the ruts. Most were crowding away from one among them who had soiled herself. I will not forget their eyes, as we pulled up our horses behind Matthew while he spoke with the gaoler.

I recognized Helen Leech, who looked darkly back at us. Then I saw Anne West. Her face had got so thin, I almost did not know her. Someone had blacked her eye. She was near the back of the crowd of tightly packed women, but as soon as we stopped a murmur passed among them, almost a shiver, and they seemed to part away from Anne as she met her daughter's gaze. I saw Rebecca's hands falter as she gathered her reins. She said, 'What happened to your eye?' Her voice trembled.

Helen Leech spat, richly, over the side of the cart.

'It's nothing, love,' Anne said. 'I fell in the dark.'

Matthew twisted in his saddle. 'Quiet,' he called back, before turning again to the gaoler. 'Ask at the Market Cross where to take them,' I heard him say. 'My money's that it won't be big enough. Anyway, wherever they bed down, I will owe you for three bales of straw. It will not help us if they are too stiff to walk.' The man nodded.

Matthew moved off, and Mary Phillips followed. I had to take hold of Rebecca's bridle and turn her horse myself. Her eyes stayed locked with her mother's as the slow cart receded.

Rebecca said, 'Do you think any will be spared? Apart from my mother?'

'I hope so.' My chest felt tight. 'We must pray so.'

Rebecca was quiet for a moment. 'And my mother,' she said. 'He will do it, won't he? If I do what he says? He will let her go?'

Silently I asked for forgiveness. 'I am certain of it,' I said. For I did not want to think of what my brother would do to Rebecca, if she backed out now.

The eyes of the women in the cart followed us silently away up the lane. When I think of them now, they look so strange and quiet that I could almost believe they were already dead.

†

We sat up late that night while Matthew went to find us other lodgings: so many folk had packed into Chelmsford for the trials that the keepers of the inn had put the board up to five shillings for each of us for only the two nights. Rebecca and I sat together in the inn's back room. We could hear Mary Phillips out at the front, arguing still with the landlady. Rebecca looked drained.

'Did you see my mother?' she said. 'Do you think the others are being cruel to her, knowing she will be freed?' She stopped. 'You do not think she has changed her mind about me speaking?'

'No,' I said. Because, I thought, what else can she do?

After a time Matthew came back, and we moved our horses to a different inn, where Rebecca and I had to share a bed with Mary Phillips, who lay all night between us, silent and large, like a listening stone.

The next day, I walked beside Rebecca through the crowds towards the court, Matthew several paces in front, and I thought of how easy it would be to slip away alone. But it was as if Rebecca read my thoughts: as we drew near the building, she took my hand. 'Alice,' she said, 'you won't leave me, will you?'

I smiled, and squeezed her hand. 'Of course I will not,' I said, and as I said it I knew that it was true. I could not leave her. I felt the weight of what I had done in Suffolk, what I had not prevented, and I knew that I must stay with Rebecca now, for as long as there was a shred of a chance to help her.

We sat on a bench reserved at the left of the courtroom. It was hot, the damp, fierce heat that prickles, and it grew hotter as the correct papers were given out among the twelve jurors, the six justices and their clerks. It was hard to be calm, for though I had pretended for Rebecca, I feared what the outcome of the business would be. Sitting on the hard bench, my hands sweating as the room around us continued to fill, I felt as though anything could happen. I saw Rebecca craning behind her to survey the public benches, and I remembered her dream, that her son would be brought there. But when the town crier began to call matters to order I felt her stiffen.

It was the Earl of Warwick presiding. We had seen him riding into town from the window of the inn that morning. They had rung the bells to try to clear a way, but it had only made folk pack nearer. He was one of those blood-red men, like a plum about to burst, with moustaches and hair down his back like the pictures of men in the King's train you see

on news sheets. That morning he had stood up in his stir-
rups and raised a hand to the crowd. Now, he seemed
harassed as he made a short speech about how much business there was to get through.

First the bills were sorted, the *vera* from the *ignoramus*:
the latter would be dismissed, if it was judged there was not
enough known about the cases to hear them. Rebecca's was
read out *ignoramus*, as she said Matthew had told her it
would be. But when it was announced, someone cried out,
'Shame!' from the public benches. I turned to see Prudence,
the wronged wife of Thomas Hart, her face marred with
rage. Though my heart lifted for Rebecca, after my own
misfortune, my own lost child, I felt a flash of understanding for Prudence Hart. In any case, it was as if the woman
had not called out at all: the court officials did not bother to
hush her, accustomed as they were to disruption.

They brought up the accused women in batches, like cattle at a market: Nan Leech and Bess Clarke were in the first
lot, as well as Anne West. At least, I thought, it will be over
quickly for Rebecca. Matthew took the stand, testifying
against two of them, followed by the other witnesses, each
trooping up in their turn. A smell grew in the room, of foul
sweat and the trodden flowers near the justices' bench, the
blown roses, which did not serve to freshen the air but,
rather, to make it fuller, heavier.

Soon it was Rebecca's turn. First, as Matthew had instructed
her, she had to pretend to be afraid of Warwick, and she did
well with that, seeming to try her utmost, calling him 'Your
Highness' and stuttering, so that when Matthew stood up
to suggest that since he knew the girl he himself did question her, it could seem to the justices to be a service rather

than a liberty. Once Matthew began, though, Rebecca went on fidgeting, leaving long gaps of silence as Matthew put questions to her – and she became more and more upset, when Helen Leech began to interrupt, calling her a liar at every turn, and protesting at how Matthew put the questions so that Rebecca need only say yes or no.

But Helen Leech was made to hold her tongue, and Rebecca confirmed that her mother had met with the other accused from Manningtree, that they had read from a certain book, that they had summoned imps. Haltingly she described for the court what service each woman had asked of her familiar, including what her mother had requested. A discontented hum grew up. Whatever they thought of Anne West, folk didn't like seeing a girl send, as they saw it, her own mother to hang.

It was Matthew who settled the mood of the room, with his exact and tireless questions, his equanimity and his pleasant drone. By the end of Rebecca's evidence you could see the attention of the justices wandering, for his questions were phrased dully, though framed carefully to be precise about times, about happenings, about dates, and Matthew did not once falter in his manner or his memory. Questioning the midwives later on what they had discovered during the searchings, he was perfect in his respectful demeanour: for of course, he said, of course he would not make them say exactly where they had found the marks.

Watching him was not like watching my brother. It had been so long since the closeness of when I had first arrived; months now since the night of Bess Clarke's watching, when I had helped him to change his shirt. It was like observing a stranger, despite my knowledge of the fear that drove him. Matthew had achieved a near-unthinking proficiency, just as, even now, when I see a stain on a bedsheet, I still wonder, without wishing to, how best to get it out. And so the courtroom that day felt nothing like the swimming at Little Wenham: there was no sense of rawness, of triumph. Rather, it seemed that in his high boots and spotless collar, my brother had found his vestments; in the court, his pulpit. He was as effortless as a minister giving his hundredth sermon.

At last Rebecca finished her testimony; Matthew had to remind her to sit down. When she came back to me, she looked flat and shocked, as if she had been cut out of paper. After that, there were so many batches of women that the jury weren't let to retire, but had to give a verdict on the spot. Two of the women had their cases postponed; another few were dismissed, those of the most evidently witless fantasists. But nineteen were not postponed: nineteen were not dismissed. The coughing in the room came and went, and the heat only increased, as one by one the verdicts came in.

Matthew was up at the justices' bench, whispering, as the sentences were considered. When the Earl of Warwick at last stood up to confirm that all the convicted witches were to hang, he added that it had been brought to his attention that Chelmsford was a long way from the Tendring Hundred, the origin of this ugly business. He said how it was important that justice, as well as being done, was seen to be done; and so, while for convenience most of the convicted would hang in Chelmsford the next day, some few would be sent instead back to Manningtree, to be executed there before the month was out.

303

A clerk read out the short list of women to be taken back north to meet their deaths, and I felt sure it had been arranged by Matthew, for Anne West was among them. When she heard her mother's name, Rebecca went slack on the bench beside me, as if all the air had been knocked out of her body.

39

I slept ill that night, and I knew Rebecca, too, was wakeful, on the other side of Mary Phillips. In the morning, we followed Matthew through the crowded streets to where, overnight, the scaffold had been built. There was a press of people, but an expectant quiet among them, as they waited to watch what they had helped to occasion, as if they would not believe it until it happened in front of their own eyes.

We were allowed to stand near the back, and I was glad that we did not have to move in closer, for Bess Clarke, Nan Leech, Elizabeth Gooding, all of them were to be hanged that day. I would have wished myself a hundred miles away from that evil business, but it felt a mercy at least that Rebecca and I would be able to close our eyes at the moment of it.

For Matthew had pushed forward with Mary Phillips to join the court officials near the front; he had left one of the manservants from the inn with us and, I am certain, put a word in his ear to watch us, prevent us slipping away. The servant stood a few feet off, but every time I turned, his eye was on me. I was on edge: I had still not spoken to Rebecca of escaping with me, and I was starting to wonder whether I could even accomplish it. I had not expected to be so closely guarded.

I was thinking of this when, close to my ear, someone

said, 'Alice.' I turned, to see a small, older woman next to me in a dark shawl. She put back her hood a little. It was Bridget. 'Make no sign,' she murmured, and flicked her eyes towards the manservant. Rebecca saw at once what was happening, and slowly she stepped to block his view of us. My heart was in my mouth. In her shabby cloak, to the man, Bridget was just one more face in the crowd. But if Matthew should turn?

I kept facing the scaffold, found her hand; it was warm, and dry as paper. 'You shouldn't be here,' I said. 'It isn't safe.'

'I knew I wouldn't be able to see you at the Thorn.'

'I have matters to acquaint you with. The thing that Grace saw in my mother's bed, I know now it was a charm for conception. I know it because Matthew knows it. He asked the accused women when he went through the Tendring Hundred. So he knows it, and I think you know it, too.' Bridget said nothing, and I could not help turning to look at her. 'I spoke with our old servant Sarah.'

She paled. 'You were in Wenham?'

'She said that my father – she said that my father –' I had to fight to keep near Bridget, as the crowd moved around me. Rebecca stepped nearer the manservant, said something to him. Desperately, I said, 'Sarah said my father was free with his hands.'

Bridget gripped my elbow, and spoke in my ear, low and fast. 'It is true, about the charm, Alice. I didn't want her to do it.' She stopped. 'But you must understand it is nonsense. It has no bearing on Matthew as he is now, it cannot have. That is why I did not wish to tell you. I did not want you to be afraid.' I turned to her, uncertain what she meant, and she cast a glance at the manservant, and then kept her eyes on the ground. 'When your father first married your mother, even then she was not like other women. She had dreams and fancies – but soon after the wedding, she was cast down more than usual, and when I asked her why, she said she did not like it with your father. That he was rough, and he hurt her.' Bridget paused. 'She said that, and I dismissed her. I could weep to think of it now. I told her she must bide with it, and that she would grow accustomed, that soon a baby would follow and after that he would leave her alone. For your father seemed a cheerful soul. I said to her, "Marriage, this is what it is." But she said she wished she could only get with child, so she would be free of it for a while.'

I watched the hangman, who had climbed up onto the scaffold to check his knots. It would be fifteen, that day, across the three scaffolds: they would not have had room for more.

Bridget let go of my elbow and spoke still more softly, as the crowd jostled around us. 'And so they had not been a year married but there was an Easter fair in Manningtree, and we went, and I even took you, though you were in arms. And we saw the entertainments, but soon your mother said she was tired so we started for home ahead of your father.' She took a breath. 'There were some folk camped by the side of the road, not far out of Manningtree. They were grazing their horses there, and they had a tent up. And there was a man among them, a bearded man, and he stood up and said, "Something to fetch your suitors, ladies? Something to make your bellies big?" And I was going to jog the horse on, but your mother said, "Stop."'

I looked at Bridget. 'I did not like it,' she said, 'for I had you to reckon with. I did not like to stop the cart among such folk, but your mother was set upon it, and time was, I thought a foolish charm a harmless thing. I mean, I still think that.' She shifted her feet. 'So we went into the tent, your mother, and I following with you in my arms, and she told the man she wanted a baby. And he brought out a hank of hair – God knows where he got it, but he looked severe at your mother and said, "This I grew specially on my own head." And he began to twist and wrap it into a certain shape. And he said, "What this child will have is a father above and a father below." He said, "The child will be strong. It's only fire or water that will kill this one." I said to him, "Stop it, you're scaring her." And when he had done I told her to pay him, that we might be gone. But he looked at your mother, and he said that to make the spell complete, the two of them must be alone. And I did not like that. I told her, "Don't be foolish." I tried to pull her out, but I had you with me, and I was her servant, remember, and she said, "Go," and so I went.' She was struggling to find her words. 'It must have been ten minutes, before she parted the tent and came out again. I don't need to tell you, Alice. She was settling her clothing, and she was white as a sheet. What I think is, when that fellow saw us, he thought he saw some easy coin, but he also thought he saw some easy flesh . . .'

The crowd stirred. They were bringing the women out, each of them no bigger than a thumb at that distance.

I averted my eyes. 'And that was why, that night he was born, why she thought Matthew was no good. Why she –' I stopped in horror. 'But, then, why did she throw you out? If it was she who –?'

'She did it that I might be free,' Bridget said. 'Your father had never laid a hand on me before. To my knowledge, I never made eyes at him. But once your mother's condition showed –' When she spoke again, her voice was dry. 'I believed your mother, after that, though it was too late. But I think when she saw what he was doing to me, she blamed herself. And though she was not settled in her mind, she found a way, even in her trouble, to help me. For the night your brother was born, the night she dropped him and I saved him, when your father came home and sent me out, there in the kitchen she showed your father the charm, said she had found it under her pillow, that I had put it there. And so he put me out into the snow. What else could I do? I walked as far as East Bergholt. The water was frozen three inches thick in the horse trough. I could not bide on the doorstep. I would not have left her, but I could not tell him the truth.'

The crowd moved, and a great roar went up as the women finished clambering onto the scaffold. There had been some delay: one had fainted. Bridget said, 'I was not carrying any child when I left. I had made sure of that. It almost felt as though I had got clean away, left her caught, and I always felt it,' she said, 'how I abandoned her. For after that, in the years I was gone, she was with him so long and I think she began to think that she herself was at fault. That was why I came only rarely to your house, for her sorrow, day by day it would grip her close, or spin her away – and you could not always tell which it would be. When you have been a prisoner as long as she, you grow to love your gaoler.'

'But when you came the day before she died,' I said, 'she gave you the charm? That was why Grace could not find it?'

When she replied, there was nothing in Bridget's eyes but honesty. 'Until then, I thought it was long gone. I could scarce believe she had kept it all those years. She hadn't wanted to destroy it, in case it – It is nonsense. But that day, she tried to make me take it. I tried to persuade her how it was foolishness.'

I looked up at the hangman, carefully draping the necks of the women. Numbly I saw the back of my brother's head, as he watched, motionless. I thought, I do not even know who you are.

'And is that what you still think?' I said. 'That it is nonsense?' I turned to her. 'Bridget, I saw things, in Suffolk –' I stopped. 'But what do you think – that my brother is that fellow's son? The one from the side of the road?'

'Perhaps,' Bridget said. 'He is so much darker than the rest of you.' She followed my gaze. 'God help us, but I could not say whose son he is.' She turned to me. 'The charm, I did not think he would find it, much less learn what it was. These things are what women most usually keep among themselves.'

A roar went up as the first of the women dropped. She went cleanly, and then I saw the small figure of the hangman move to the next. He dropped them steadily, one by one. After the sixth the great din of the crowd faded somewhat, but still as each woman fell there was a sharp noise, like a swiftly taken breath. The twelfth woman kept moving, after the drop, her legs twisting in the air. I was thankful that at this distance, I could not recognize any of them; could not tell which of them Elizabeth Gooding might be.

Trying to keep calm, I said, 'I do not think he found the charm, Bridget.'

'What do you mean? Who has it, then? Where is it?'

'I do not know.'

The suspended women had all grown still, some of them turning slowly with the light breeze. There were cheers and whoops for the hangman from the front of the crowd. I was aware of the eyes of the manservant, and folk dispersing around us. Matthew stood talking to John Stearne: either of them could turn at any moment and see Bridget.

I reached into my sleeve, and brought out Joseph's letter. 'I am only sorry I kept it so long,' I said, 'but you must go now.'

'I know,' she said. 'You take this.' She opened my hand, and I felt Mother's gold ring in my palm. 'For her.' She gestured to Rebecca.

The crowd was thinning around us, and Rebecca had managed to lead the manservant a few paces away.

'Sometimes,' Bridget said, 'I think what would have been, if I had never saved him.'

There was so much left to say, but there was no time. I felt Bridget stepping away from me; I wanted to reach out for her, but I could not. 'Take care of yourself,' I said, and watched her dark covered head move through the press of eating, drinking, talking people. By the time I lost sight of her, Matthew had come back, and I heard him telling the manservant to escort Rebecca and me to the inn. When I turned, for the first time I could see the gallows properly. What hung on it looked from a distance like fifteen cloaks on their pegs, discarded only for a short time, until their owners should need them again.

40

I could scarcely keep Rebecca West from hurting her own cause, through the strained days of waiting that followed before the Manningtree executions. At the inn at Chelmsford I had given her the gold ring, and advised her to be gone; that her mother could follow her, when she was freed. But she said she would not go, that she must wait, so I waited with her. I half hoped that, with her testimony done, Matthew would send Rebecca back to her own house and forget about her, but he did not. And if he did intend to get Anne West pardoned, he was waiting for the last possible moment.

Matthew kept mostly to his chamber, writing, or a few doors away at John Stearne's house, so it should have been easy for Rebecca to do as I had advised her, and keep out of his way. But Rebecca did not take my advice, did not keep to her room and out of his sight: she seemed not to be able to leave it alone, to refrain from seeking the constant assurance that all was well, even though evidently all was not well, the not-wellness loud enough, that fortnight, to deafen you. The Thorn was like a bell-tower with a bell that is ringing and flinging itself to pieces, and you can feel it in your teeth, but all you can do is wait for it to cease.

Though I feared for Rebecca, I found myself thinking often of Joseph: it felt almost selfish to notice it, but the date was almost upon us that would have been my time to give birth. I found myself remembering Joseph's hesitation in putting his hands on me. I thought of what Bridget had endured from my father, and wondered what advice she would have given Joseph, as a boy, as a young man, about how to approach a woman. The uncertainty that had distanced me from my husband, I saw it now in a new light, and I wept over it more than once in those days of waiting, and wept, too, at how helpless I felt, to halt what was happening.

For Rebecca had begun to take on a carefully pious look whenever my brother was even mentioned, and she began to refer to him, around Mary Phillips and the remaining scullery maid, not as 'Master Hopkins' but as 'the master', as if she, too, were a servant at the Thorn. She was frightened, that was clear, though perhaps in a way she did not dare admit to herself. Frightened of what would happen to her, if Matthew did not spare her mother.

Rebecca was sitting in the kitchen, three days before the executions, when the scullery maid expressed the mildest inclination to learn to read. Rebecca pounced on it. 'I'll teach you,' she said. Matthew was just outside in the passage, talking to Mary Phillips. 'I'll teach you in the evenings,' Rebecca said loudly, and sat the girl down there and then. 'No, look, that's a *b*,' Rebecca said, as Matthew followed Mary Phillips into the room. 'Do you see the difference, from a *d*?' She dusted smooth the flour she had sprinkled on the table, and drew the two letters next to each other with a shaking finger.

That evening, the firelight moved over Rebecca's hair, over the frown on her face as she bent to correct the girl again, as Matthew stood watching her for just a minute too long. She was acting in those few days, acting the virtuous servant to save her own life and her mother's, as if by playing her part well enough she could stretch their time out further than it wanted to go, like a piece of cloth you convince yourself is enough to make a shift, an apron, enough to make a cap: but, in truth, it is not enough for anything. For I feared she would win no mercy from Matthew.

It made me think of Thomas Witham's daughter, how badly that had ended: how, soon after the day I had seen Jane's grazed palms in church, she had admitted to me that she had taken Matthew's arm as they walked together, but when they had reached a secluded part of the path she had stopped, and tilted her face, for she knew that was what other young men most wished you to do. But then my brother had clutched at her, and his hands were colder than she had been expecting, and she had made a sudden movement, or else Matthew had, and she had pushed him away, but as she did so, slipped and fallen. And before she could even pick herself up, she told me, half ashamed, half derisive, he was running away. I had seen for myself his face when he came home that day: had glimpsed his frozen rage.

†

In the daytimes, as before, Mary Phillips delegated me to give Rebecca tasks. But since she would not let Rebecca near hot things or knives, I had to invent work that did not truly need doing, such as polishing the banisters until they shone, and when she reached the bottom beginning at the top afresh. Rebecca set to with a will at whatever I gave her, but with no guests, it was clear that if Mary Phillips would not trust her in the kitchen, there was no need for another servant at the Thorn. Once, I heard Matthew and Mary Phillips talking about the almshouse at Colchester, and I was sure they were discussing whether a bed could be found for Rebecca there, where she would ruin her health with ropemaking.

The day before the date appointed for the hangings, I went uninvited to Matthew's chamber, where I knew he was sitting. I knocked firmly, and I think he mistook me for Mary Phillips, for carelessly he shouted, 'Come.' I went in. He was sitting at his desk in his shirtsleeves and stood up when he saw that it was me. It was odd to be in that room: it was the first time I had seen it since I had crept in secretly. I noticed again Father's daily books on the shelf, the sparse emptiness of the rest of the chamber. I did not look Matthew in the eye.

'I have come to speak to you about Rebecca,' I said, trying to keep my voice steady.

'What about her?' he said evenly.

'I have been thinking. Whether or not you mean to spare her mother –' I stopped, took a breath. 'I wanted to say that, if I were you, I would let her go. Not back to her mother's house, perhaps, but I could find her a place in London, I am sure of it.' I tried to slow my breath.

'I will think on it,' he said, turning away, almost as if it bored him, as if it were only one of a list of things he had to do.

'But do think, Matthew. What do you lose by letting her go? You lose nothing. But you may gain a reputation for mercy. For keeping your word. For everyone knows how she has served you. No one can doubt what you must have promised her.' He had turned back towards me. His eyes were dark as always, their meaning veiled. I thought perhaps I had won him round.

'I will think on it,' he said again. And I had to restrain myself almost from dipping him a curtsy, before I turned and went quietly out of the room.

That night, I told Rebecca that she need not come down for dinner, that surely my brother would excuse her, but still she appeared, and took her seat opposite me, as the three of us ate in silence. Rebecca kept her eyes on her food. Matthew watched her ever more closely now: watched her chew and swallow, watched the hand that held her knife tremble.

After dinner, Rebecca went upstairs. I sat in the parlour for a time, trying to guess my brother's mood from how he frowned over his papers. Soon Mary Phillips came in, to see whether anything was wanted. Matthew asked her to bring him another bottle of wine. I excused myself and went up to my chamber. I sat in my chair by the fire, and perhaps for a few minutes I dozed; I heard feet on the stairs, which I took for Rebecca going to bed.

But I was soon wakeful again, and took up my sewing, in order not to think. Somehow it did not seem right to go to bed, knowing the women appointed to die the next day would be awake and watching. My task was easy enough: picking out Mother's initials from my brother's linen, and sewing back an RH, ahead of his wedding, which, though he had not spoken of it, would soon be approaching. Before long, though, I needed my thimble. Remembering that I had left it in the parlour, I opened my chamber door. Hearing nothing, I went carefully down the stairs, but when I was halfway, I caught the note of Rebecca's voice. Clearly she had not gone to bed.

The parlour door was slightly ajar. I crept nearer, and saw a glimpse of Rebecca by the fireplace, standing beside my brother's chair, her hand close to where his own rested on the wooden arm of the seat. He was looking at it, his face pale and set. I saw him breathe out, slowly.

'What I mean is, we could make terms, master,' I heard Rebecca say softly, and then I could not believe what I saw, for she lowered herself into his lap. Matthew's hand did not shift from the arm of the chair, but his fingers twitched. Her hair was loose, and obscured his face. I thought, Rebecca, you foolish girl.

She had taken his other hand, and seemed to be rubbing it between her own. 'You're chilled, master,' she said. Then she placed his hand flat on her chest, below the collarbone, above the breast. Over her heart.

I could not think what else to do. I stepped away from the door. 'Mary!' I called loudly. 'Mary, have you seen my thimble? I must have put it down somewhere.'

Mary Phillips came out from the kitchen. As she did so, Rebecca slipped out of the parlour door, her face flushed.

'Here it is, mistress,' Rebecca said. She held out her hand, and tipped the thimble into my palm. 'I borrowed it, and forgot to give it you back.' Then she was gone, clattering up the stairs, Mary Phillips watching her retreat.

'Thank you, Mary,' I said. I wanted to look in on Matthew: I could not believe that he had not taken Rebecca by the throat and thrown her out into the yard. But, thank God, he had not; and with Mary Phillips regarding me suspiciously, I had to wish her goodnight, and go slowly upstairs myself.

41

The next morning, I watched Rebecca eat a good breakfast, watched her try to be confident of the reprieve that she hoped was coming. I myself could not stomach any food. Matthew seemed preoccupied, and scarcely broke off eating to assent, when I said that I would take Rebecca to the square. Perhaps he meant, after all, I thought, to give her a position at the Thorn. He had not punished her for her behaviour the night before and, for certain, he looked at her a good deal.

'You go on ahead,' Mary Phillips said. 'Get a good place, before the press grows too great.' She waved a hand towards Rebecca. 'It will be a good lesson for her, to see it.'

Rebecca was quiet as we walked into town. Wisely, she had worn a cap that, when she ducked her head, mostly hid her face. I thought again of asking her whether she would not just come away with me, there and then, but I knew what her answer would be. The streets grew thick with people, all going our way, so that all I could see were the backs of heads, hunched shoulders. As we drew near the square it was the stink of roast hog you caught first, and then, as you rounded the corner, the noise of the crowd.

By the steps of the assembly rooms they had built the scaffold. The crossbeam looked strong, smooth and unflawed, as if it had been the mast of a ship, or was on its way to being; suspended from it, the four nooses waited. Off to the left side, on the further edge of the square from where we were standing, a low platform had been built, from which the great men of the town might stand and watch.

I tried taking Rebecca's arm, but it was too awkward: instead I took her hand, and began to thread us through the already tight-packed crowd. Some were folk up from Harwich or Colchester for the day, and these I had to push between. Others, though, were Manningtree or Lawford people, mostly sober and plain-dressed, not passing meats among themselves but rather only a clipped word or two, there to see it done. They did us the service of shrinking back as we came near, twitching their children out of our path. When we reached the crude step that led onto the low platform, I pulled Rebecca past it to a place at the edge of the crowd.

After a time, I saw my brother arrive, and climb up to the platform beside Richard Edwards, deep in talk. Without meaning to, I caught Matthew's attention, before I turned back to Rebecca. As I moved, though, another face snagged my gaze, small in the crowd on the other side of the square, and I shaded my eyes to see Bridget. What is she doing? I thought. Close by her I saw the minister, his face grim and contained.

'Alice,' Rebecca said, suddenly, as the crowd moved and murmured.

They were bringing the women out from the assembly rooms, rather than risk disorder by walking them through the press of people. The four were led out in a row, wearing identical smocks that someone must have troubled themselves to sew. First came the woman from Ramsey, and the woman from Great Clacton after her: those two were there

319

to show the reach of Grimston's influence, hailing as they did from the eastern and southern limits of the hundred. Next down the steps came Helen Leech. Her mother had hanged in Chelmsford, and Helen, at any rate, expected no reprieve. Near the bottom she tripped and fell hard, forwards: a man hauled her up, but the front of her smock was black with mud. Anne West came last, her face withdrawn.

'Now it will come,' Rebecca said, turning to gaze up at Matthew on the platform. 'He will call out now, or make some sign.'

I watched the executioner point and speak. I watched each of the women climb up onto the four stools set there for the purpose, four stools that would afterwards return to their accustomed use, for the merchants striking their deals at the assembly rooms, or breaking their midday bread. Anne West seemed eager, almost sprightly, as she climbed up onto hers.

The executioner was tall enough, once he had tied the women's arms, to reach up unaided to place the loops about their necks, and as he did so, the crowd filled with whispers that made a rushing sound in the air. It has sometimes been the practice for folk on the scaffold to be permitted to speak, that their contrition might make an example for those come to look on. This time, though, it seemed not.

I felt Rebecca gripping my hand, twisting to watch not what was unfolding in front of us, but Matthew. She was still waiting for a sign, while I watched the executioner knock the stool from under the Ramsey woman's feet, like a little boy playing a nasty trick, a painful trick, and the crowd gave a great angry cheer.

The woman must have dropped right, because she fell

like a stone and was still: likewise did her neighbour. Rebecca turned, her face slack with shock and dismay. My eyes moved to Anne West, where she perched on her stool, gazing out over the crowd, face by face. The executioner kicked out the stool of Helen Leech, and then it was Anne's turn.

For what happened next, I do not remember any sounds. It cannot be true, but what I remember is perfect silence. The executioner kicked Anne West's stool, and it fell soundlessly on the platform. But he had placed the nooses too close together, and Helen Leech's arms had come untied. As Anne West bucked and writhed, her face a red dot, Helen Leech swung too near and began to climb her for air, and the executioner had to beat her arms away.

Beside me, Rebecca gasped. 'No – no . . .' she said, softly at first and then louder. 'Help her! Someone help her!' I took hold of her arms, as I saw some folk in the crowd turn to look, in curiosity or disgust.

The feeling went from my hands. I felt the prickle of it going as Rebecca gripped me tight. Perhaps Anne West knew only a blur of light and darkness, a roar of sound, in her last thrashing. But I have heard some say that in those final moments all things are sharpened, and if that is so, perhaps she might have seen her living daughter leaning on me, and taken comfort.

Rebecca was weeping, keening loud in my ear, turned into my shoulder as the executioner took Helen Leech's feet and added his weight to finish her. Then it was over, the four still shapes hanging in a row.

Behind me, I heard Matthew's voice, furious, saying he would see about docking the man's fee. Minutes must have passed; I remember part of the crowd drifting away, but all the time Rebecca weeping as I stood with my arms around her. I felt as if she was trying to burrow inside me.

When I saw my brother coming down from the platform, he looked pale, as though he was about to be sick. As he reached the foot of the steps a woman moved into his path, and he made an irritated gesture. But then she put back her hood.

Matthew stopped still on the last step, as he recognized Bridget. 'Get out of my way,' he said. He spoke quietly, but everyone heard. She did not move.

'No,' she said. And then, more loudly, 'You do not own Manningtree, whatever you may think, sir.' She spoke out clearly, and some in the crowd turned to look. 'And I'll tell you something else,' she said, as the men on the platform broke off their talk to watch, 'which is that if you think Grimston is your friend, you are mistaken, and if you think Edwards here is your friend, you are mistaken there, too. And if you think his sister will marry you, well, then, you are triply mistaken, for all they do, all this town does, is think on how to be quit of you, sir.'

I do not know what she was hoping for: if it was a cheer from the back of the crowd, it did not come. For a moment, everyone watching stood large-eyed, in silence.

Matthew had turned red. When he spoke, his voice shook with rage. 'I will visit you tomorrow, madam. Depend upon it. I will be visiting you tomorrow, and I will bring some others, too.'

'Oh, fie!' Bridget said. 'You have help enough here, if you want to arrest me.'

I thought then that Matthew would ask some of the men

standing about to lay hands on her, but they looked uncomfortable. If he had asked them, I do not know whether they would have done it. If they had not, then perhaps the tide would have turned on him that day. But I saw my brother master himself, turn again from red to pale.

'Why should I want to arrest you?' he said clearly and calmly. 'You are nothing more than a scold, madam. I would not deal, these days, in such a small indictment.'

There was a moment where no one moved, and then the crowd began again to disperse, to talk among themselves. Already the executioner's men were climbing up to cut the bodies down. Matthew's friends were lining up behind him; he made me a curt signal. Gently I helped Rebecca stand straight on her feet, and led her after him. Desperate, I met Bridget's eye. She looked stunned. Then she was lost in the departing crush, as I led Rebecca behind my brother's friends, Richard Edwards, John Stearne and the others, all in their best Sunday clothes, back towards the Thorn.

Weeping, Rebecca gripped my arm. She was talking, talking, I could not stop her, but she was hardly making sense. 'I told him where you were. The night before he took you into Suffolk,' she said. 'It was I who told him, not Grace.' I pressed Rebecca's hand, said to her that it was all right, that it would all be all right. I was distracted with the thought of Bridget, of how to get her to safety. I told Rebecca how sorry I was, over and over in a low voice, as the men walked ahead of us, Mary Phillips among them. That was all I could think to say: how sorry I was. I was planning to get Rebecca straight upstairs, to make her bathe her face, and be calm again, so that I could persuade Matthew to let me try to find her a servant's place somewhere, now that all was done.

We had reached the yard of the Thorn, and I made to lead Rebecca up the steps to the door. But Matthew said, 'No, Alice. That whore won't be coming back in my house.' I saw Richard Edwards raise his brows, but the other men cleared their throats, and looked away.

I dropped Rebecca's arm, and went closer to him. 'Please, brother,' I said. 'I know she is not yet all she ought to be. But I can teach her, she can still learn. Let me take her indoors, and tomorrow we can discuss –'

'It is you, Alice, who is not all you ought to be,' Matthew said. The men gaped. 'For I know you are under this girl's thrall. You have given her our mother's ring to help her go and live her life of vice.' He produced it. 'I found this under her pillow.'

'Madam, you did not?' one of them said. It was John Cutler: I remembered his face from when he had come at Easter to the Thorn to dine.

'And she connived with her late husband's mother to do it,' Matthew said. He sounded almost sad, now; almost regretful. He turned to Richard Edwards. 'You know her? The one who gave me those low words in the square just now.' Edwards shook his head.

I turned on the men where they stood around Matthew. I saw where he was aiming, and I was desperate. 'Bridget has done nothing wrong,' I said to them all. I spread my hands. 'You must not – you cannot let her be hounded as those others have been. For you know why my brother has done all this? Well, I say my brother, but in truth he may be none of mine.' I pushed my hair out of my face, and looked at Matthew, and at the men around him, and I saw that they did not care about my fate or Rebecca's. I saw that they wanted their dinner, nothing more. I saw that I was not troubling them. I was merely making them awkward. And Matthew's face was the calmest of all.

Inside me, I felt something give. 'Shall I tell them? It is for shame he is doing it. For his mother disgraced herself to get him. Lay with some travelling labourer, so do not let him deceive you that he is a gentleman. For God knows whose son he is, whether he is our father's son, or that low tricking fellow's, or the devil's bastard for what I know.'

At last I stopped. As my voice rang into silence, I heard the high, tight note of it. I felt how my hands were clenched at my sides, how my cap had slid backwards off my head. I was breathing hard. All the men's eyes were on Matthew, and I was ready for his rage, wanted it even, wanted him to strike me so I could strike him back.

We all waited, for one moment, two. At last my brother sighed, then turned to Richard Edwards, with a face full of sadness.

'You see how it is, gentlemen,' he said. 'You see how delicacy can turn so soon to madness?' Some were nodding.

'What are you talking about?' I said. I turned to Richard Edwards. 'I mean it. It's true.' But none of them would look at me.

John Stearne said, 'It is as we spoke of, Hopkins. She spent so many years in your mother's company, and we know how that poor lady suffered. A weak mind like that, in a woman, it can be bent so easily to vice.'

I looked about me wildly. Rebecca had backed away a few paces, but now she stood still, transfixed. Beside the steps, Mary Phillips watched impassively.

'Gentlemen,' Matthew said, 'I fear I cannot entertain you

as I had hoped to. I must see my sister settled.' And they all replied, 'Oh, of course, Hopkins. Please take our best prayers for her health.' Disapproving, uncomfortable, they wanted only to be gone.

'Mary?' Matthew said, and Mary Phillips stepped towards me, took hold of my upper arm, digging her fingers into the flesh.

'What are you doing?' I said. 'I am quite well.' She started to haul me into the house, and I shouted, tried to wrench my arm away from her, but stumbled, was dragged up one step before I got on my feet. I saw the retreating backs of the men as they left the yard, and Rebecca's shocked white stare where she stood by herself at the gate. Mary Phillips pushed me over the threshold, shut the door on her and shot the bolt.

'Brother!' I said.

But Matthew turned to Mary Phillips. 'Give me your keys.' With steady hands, she extracted them from her belt.

I remember her satisfied face, and then Matthew had me by the arm, and I said, 'Brother, you're hurting me,' but he was pulling me up the stairs so that I tripped more than once, and then I kicked against him, tried to make myself heavy, and almost got loose. But then Mary Phillips was there, blocking the way down, and I felt her firm hands on my back pushing me upwards, and Matthew got my arm again so that I tripped and staggered beside him. 'Brother,' I said, 'please, listen –'

But then we were at the attic door, and he opened it and thrust me in. I heard the key turn in the lock, and then I heard no more.

42

Christmastide, this year of our Lord 1646

As I told you in the beginning, I have been notching a floorboard to reckon the days since I have been locked up here. I have watched the moon as it has tracked across the slit window, waxing and waning. I believe now that it is Christmastide again, though I could not say the precise date: when I am hungry I sleep more, and I cannot vouch that I have not lately upon occasion slept a day and a night and another night through.

This that I have written has been another way of marking time. When I was first imprisoned, the words rushed out headlong; now there are days when I manage to set down a few only before I am weary and have to lay aside my pen. I fear now that these words that have cost me so much, they will never be read. For if anyone meant to come for me, then surely they would have come by now.

In the first days, Matthew came up to see me from time to time. He never brought food, or took away my chamber pot – that is always Mary – but he would talk to me. He would tell me that I must not worry, for he did not think me bad, only weak; in my mind, I knew he meant. And I would say that he was right, that I was weak, but I was resolved to do better. He would say that I could come out when I had mended my behaviour, and I would say that I believed I had mended it, and he would tell me not to interrupt. But then, the next time, I would keep quiet, and he would chide me for my sullenness; though when he did so, he would wear a little smile.

I think the smile was for how perfect it is, his plan. I think that though by the end he did not believe Mother sick, but rather eaten up with vice, still he took her reputed sickness – the weakness of mind I had insisted upon – and turned it on me. And though I think his plan will be the death of me – though I am certain I will die in this attic, for one more winter will surely accomplish that – still I came to look forward to his visits. I think of what Bridget said of Mother, how a person can grow to love their gaoler.

When he stopped coming, I thought it might have been the smell. For though the attic is not short of fresh air, the weather was warmer then, and I do not deceive myself, I know it must have been unpleasant. But I was aware, too, that I was hearing less and less from below: there were no visitors, and the noise of the stablemen disappeared from the yard. September passed, and I did not hear Ruth Edwards's voice. Some days now I hear barely the creak of a stair, so I know that Matthew must be gone from the Thorn. I hate to think what business draws him so often away.

Once, early on, I set up shouting and yelling through the slit window, yelling for help to anyone who would hear me. It was when you would still hear the whistling and laughter of the stablemen, and I heard them fall silent at my calling. Before long, Mary Phillips came up. On that occasion, she told me scornfully to hush my noise. She said, 'Do you think anyone will come? We have told them you are mad, like your mother was mad. We have told them you are a danger to yourself.' Then she smiled.

The next day, instead of shouting for help through the slit window, I called out, 'Fire! Fire!' That brought Mary Phillips up running, and she hit me more than once. When she had gone, I touched my fingers to my ear, and they came away red.

After that I never put my back to her. I think it was only a few days later that I waited until she was standing with the door open, balancing my used chamber pot, and I pushed her. But she did not fall. She dropped the pot, which rolled and splashed its contents across the floor, but with her two hands she caught herself in the doorframe. She went out, stepping round the bad part of floor, and she did not come back then for four days. By the end of the fourth, when she brought a pail of hot water and a scrubbing brush, a change of clothes and a clean chamber pot, a jug of fresh water and a round of bread, I had been lying on my back, catching stray drops of rain on my tongue where the wind drives them through the slit window.

Since then, Mary has been almost civil to me. She brought me fruit when it was the season; though I suppose it would be inconvenient for her, were my teeth to fall entirely out of my head. She brings me news from the outside, though I know it is only the news she wishes me to hear. Of the woman burned at Ipswich, say: Mary Lakeland, burned awake, for no one would touch her to throttle her first. She had killed her husband by witchcraft; my brother convinced her jury of that. To kill your husband is counted not a murder but a treason, and the penalty for a woman is fire. When Mary Phillips told me of it, I remember thinking, Robert Taylor will be contented. She told me that the day was blustery, and that the woman was slow to burn.

There had been eighteen got at the Bury assizes, she told me that, too. I think of the tall, pale woman Matthew must have paid to give my evidence. I think of those hanged, and of Mary Lakeland, and the scores of others from the trials that have followed: in King's Lynn, in Huntingdon and Northampton. A hundred women, more: Mary Phillips never fails to bring news of my brother's accumulating successes. But she has told me nothing of Rebecca West's fate, or Bridget's. I have asked after them, more than once, but when I ask, Mary turns away, pretends she does not hear. I fear that Matthew did as he had promised, and that he paid Bridget a visit, the morning after he had locked me away.

At times I have feared also that my mind is growing weaker. I do not see the devil, but I see shapes in the shadows, and strange fancies plague me. Some weeks ago, a small bird found its way in through the window, and frightened me with its scuttering, panicked flap. When it had exhausted itself, I found that I was too afraid to help it to freedom for I had convinced myself that the bird was no natural creature. That it was waiting for me to come near. You might understand it, could you read his ledger, as I have, with all its listed imps. Try to dream up a thing that is like a rabbit, like a greyhound. A thing that is like a dog, like a fox, but is not wholesome. Creatures that take a simple shape, but you know they are not simple. The greyhound might drop down on you from the ceiling. The rabbit might open its mouth wide to speak, or to reveal a hollowness that is vast and beyond knowing.

To fight these fancies, which I know are not real, I know I must think of things that are solid and true. I must occupy myself: pace up and down, look through the items that are stored in the crates up here, or when it is dark, feel through them. Lately Mary Phillips brought up the trunk of Mother's clothes, and also boxes containing Matthew's books from his old chamber at Mother's house. Mother's Bible was among them, that Bridget had. I do not like to think of how it found its way back into Matthew's hands. At first I could not bear to read it, with the pages turned down to those verses pertaining to whoremongers, sorcerers and idolaters. But it is the only Bible I have, and so before too long I opened it, and when I did, I saw something.

That the bent corners were not of one page, but four or five pages clumsily turned down together. I saw that, and suddenly I knew that it was not Matthew who had marked those pages, in some rage against Bridget. It was Mother, with her swollen intractable fingers, who had turned them down. As some sad reminder to herself, perhaps, of what she deserved for her mistakes, she had done it. I see now that Mother was a prisoner of more than one kind. And I wish now more than anything that I had not joined Father in telling her so often that she was tired. Perhaps she might have found the means, somehow, to get better. But we told her she was tired so many times that, at last, I think that was all she knew how to be.

Sometimes I wish that I could follow Mother into death. For it is I, not she, who is tired now. But my chest has kept rising and falling, steady and stubborn. I have kept pushing my pen across the page, choosing words, trying to put down the truth about Matthew. But I have done, now: I have said what I can say. I have set forth the facts of the case, and I have not strength to do more. It will be up to someone else, now, to judge them.

43

The twenty-ninth day of September, this year of our Lord 1647

I did not think I would have cause to pick up this book again, this pen. But something has happened: three days ago I did something, and I scarcely believe I have done it. It is a sin. And though I know I should not justify it, here is my justification.

Think of being in the dark, day on day. Your arms and legs, despite your best efforts, they waste. Your hands grow pale and thin. You read and write, walk up and down, but it is hardly enough to occupy you between the appearances of the woman servant who brings you food and water, though never enough of either. A day comes when she does not arrive, and you cannot hear any sound in the house. That is not unusual; it has happened before. You are calm, because yesterday she brought you a rare bowl of water to wash in. It is cold, and the surface grimed, but if need be you will drink it.

Another day passes, and there is no sound of her on the stair, though you have done nothing to displease her. When she brought the water she took away your gown for washing, leaving you in a worn shift, and you are cold. These months, you have lost flesh, and a thought strikes you. You open the crate that contains the gowns your stepmother willed you. On top is the mourning gown, the one that belonged to your true mother once, altered to fit your stepmother. A little short, then, but no need to let the hem down any more, for who is there to see, in here, if you show your ankles and shins?

You try on the gown, but as you attempt to lace it up, there is something bulky, something scratchy in the bodice, something there that you had not noticed in shaking out the gown and folding it. You reach in to feel what it is, and what you touch makes you wrench off the gown and tread it away from you till it lies puddled at your feet. A minute passes. Tentative, you lift the fabric. To free what has been sewn into the bodice, you risk cutting into your fingers, for you have no scissors and you will not put your face near it to use your teeth.

When you have freed the item, you place it on the floor in front of you. It is a child made of dark hair. You do not touch it much, but crouch there for a long time, looking.

You have no fire or pins, but close by stands the bowl of water you were brought for washing. Knowing everything you know, you must decide what to do.

You examine the mourning gown again, how delicately the item was sewn in. Cleverer by far than putting it in one of the pockets. You think of your stepmother's will, the precise wording: *I do most particularly will her all my clothing.* At the time, you took it as a slight, thinking she meant some insult by it, to leave you a heap of gowns that she knew would never fit. You see now that, far from slighting you, she was directing your attention. That it was not the clothes them-selves that were the legacy: it was what they concealed.

At last you pick up the item, and handle it. It feels rough

and light. You run a thumb over the child's blind features, its nubs of arms and curled legs. Feeling almost foolish, you put it into the bowl of water, where it floats: with one finger, you push it under. Small bubbles emerge from where they must have been trapped in the weave.

†

An hour passed, two, after I put the charm into the bowl of water. Then I heard broad accents, rough voices and shouting down below. My breathing came faster, and I hesitated only a moment before I began to yell, ran to the attic door and put my lips to the keyhole, shouting, 'Up here!'

It took some time before someone called through the wood, 'Who's there?'

'I am the mistress of the house,' I said. 'I've been waiting – The door is stiff, you must force it.'

There was more than one: I heard them having some conference among themselves. 'Stand back, then, mistress,' one called.

I retreated a few steps, and the door burst open. One of the lads stepped forward, ran his hand over the shattered wood around the lock. The other two were looking at me, and their doubt was clear. I do not wonder, for though I was decently enough dressed, having put on Mother's mourning gown, I had seen the reflection of my face in the bowl of water, my chapped lips and whiteness. But I did my best to smile, govern myself. 'My thanks,' I said, stepping forward, 'but now, what is this commotion?'

They were young men, in rough clothing, shoes that were all holes. They were clearly fresh off some boat. 'They said to bring him back here,' one said, gesturing back down the stairs. 'We haven't touched his purse.'

I followed them down, and onto the landing, then saw what two of the lads behind held, slung in a piece of sail-cloth. 'Is he dead?' I said.

'No,' said another. 'He breathes.'

'Well, then,' I said. 'Bring him in here.'

I tried the door of Matthew's chamber, and it was not locked. They laid him on the bed and rolled him off the cloth they had used to carry him, which was soaked through: his clothes and hair left dark patches where they touched the quilt. I removed my brother's purse. Matthew twisted and, without opening his eyes, he coughed out some water, which surely came out redder than it had gone in.

I went back into the passage, and half closed the door. The first of the lads was saying that he would not have seen anything, had he not cast a glance back over his shoulder. He and his friend had been going from Manningtree back to their ship where it was docked, having won a sum of money at cards, fair and square, from a hard-faced fellow at the Bell. The fellow, though, had not liked his loss, and the lad who spoke to me said he had been glancing behind them since leaving the tavern, to be sure they were not followed. They had passed the pond and were almost at the Thorn, but nevertheless he had taken one more look over his shoulder. There was only the same thin, ill-looking fellow behind them on the path, and he and his friend had laughed between themselves, at the thought of so puny a man being any threat to them.

But before they could go on their way, my brother had come to the pond at the hopping bridge, and the shape of him did seem to shift and flicker, which made the lad squint, and tap his friend's shoulder. For suddenly then he saw that there were not one but two by the pond, and the second figure had laid hold of the thin man and cast him down on the ground. Then the attacker did crouch, quick and spry, to where Matthew's head was lying in the water, and appeared to the first lad's sight to thrust downwards with all its might. And so both lads had shouted, run back along the path, at which the attacker left off and went away quick, back towards the town. 'And for certain,' the second lad said, 'we would have given chase, except that this man was still lying with his head in the water. So we had to stop, and do what we could for him.'

'For which I thank you,' I replied.

'We asked one of the women who mends the nets where to bring him,' he went on.

'Is this your husband, mistress?' another asked doubtfully.

'No,' I replied. I opened the purse, but it contained only one or two of the smallest coins. 'But can you tell me, sirs, what manner of man it was did this? Did you see him clear?'

'I saw them clear enough,' the first lad said. 'As I see you now. But, mistress, it was no man that set upon him. I believe it was a woman. An old woman, but with a strength unnatural.'

'A woman?' I said.

'Aye. And older than fifty, but –'

'No,' said the other, nudging the first. 'No, she was young. She had yellow hair.'

The first lad looked at his friend. 'Are you blind?' he said. 'Her hair was grey.'

In the end I cut them off in their dispute: it was clear that each feared I would not pay them, did their accounts not agree.

'Come down with me,' I said, and I took them into the parlour, and gave them two silver plates. The first lad reached for them eagerly.

'Though for certain, mistress,' he said, as he turned them over, 'I would know the woman again, were I to see her. Which I hope I never do.' He restrained himself, just, from crossing himself, you could tell. He was close enough for me to smell the beer on his breath, but as I judged, he was not gone in drink. And they were both of them young, keen of sight.

'You can divide these between you?' I asked, and eagerly they agreed. As I let them out, I said, 'Forgive me, one thing more – what is the date?' When they told me, I had to make them repeat themselves.

Once they were gone, I went up to Matthew. His eyes were open, and wandered the room: his hands were pale and shaking. He kept trying to speak between his snatched, bubbling breaths. He seemed to think I was Mary Phillips.

'Peace,' I said. 'Do not try to talk.'

I felt no pity for him. I was almost surprised to find it gone, to find the gap where it had been, from which I could watch him struggle for air, and feel nothing. I almost enjoyed it, for a minute or two, watching him shiver, though then he set up coughing, and that made me think of Father and his last months, watching him fight with his lungs each day, and lose, and lose.

I thought of lighting a fire, but I did not. I thought of going for a doctor; though there was nothing to pay him with, I knew he would come on the strength of Matthew's reputation and his standing in the town. But he would not come, if I did not call him. I think in some close part of myself, I had already decided.

I saw my brother's case of papers on the floor beside the bed. So I did not have to look at him, I opened it, and out fell a pile of household accounts, tradesmen's bills. Among them I saw a letter from my brother Thomas. My breath caught, in the hope that he had written to admonish Matthew. I let myself read.

My dear brother,

You do tell me of your business in Suffolk as if it were unknown to me, but there are many here with family still in those parts, and I have heard from more than one quarter of your success with the finding and prosecution of witches in that county. I would be grateful if you could answer me further on some points in your last letter, and put me out of doubt over how long the witch should be watched at a time, and also write again explicitly about what the marks be and where they are located, and I promise you I will be close with the knowledge. I would be indebted if you did send me in addition more details of your own cases and whatever works on the subject you do recommend, I myself wishing to be instructed in every aspect of magistracy.

With all my prayers for your own health, I sign myself

Your loving brother,
Thomas Hopkins

Impossible to know whether Matthew had answered the letter. When I looked up from it, he seemed to be asleep.

I sifted further into the case, and there they were. I had thought them lost, but I knew them instantly: the missing pages from Father's daily book.

Unwilling, my eyes passed over them. *I can hardly believe I did desire such an unnatural woman,* Father had written, *for though she certainly enticed me, with glances and looks, when at last she drew me to approach her I thought her shy, for how she would turn her face away, how she would stiffen. But I see now that Bridget was never shy. It was all feigned. She was brazen.*

I turned the page. *It is my fault,* I read, *my own fault that lust led me to keep her so long in my house, where she could menace my wife with charms and spells, and lead her to try to destroy our little son.* And: *I see now I have grievously wronged my wife, and how delicate she is left since I sent that woman away. So it is my duty now to have patience with her, and to see there is never anything to trouble her again. I am fearful, for the physician has tried bleeding, has tried as many powders as there are powders. But I think now that her sickness is not in the body, but rather it is in the mind.*

I thrust the pages back into the case, and put it aside. Suddenly I had no appetite to read further, even after those months of curiosity. Suddenly I had no desire to know more of Father's thoughts: what Matthew had known and suppressed all those long months.

But the rustle of paper had roused Matthew, and his gaze was clearer than before. 'What are you doing down here?' he said. He twisted in the bed. 'Where's Mary?'

Calmly, I said, 'I'll tell you. If you tell me where Bridget is.'

But he would say only, 'She's gone,' and when I pressed him further – said, 'Then where is Rebecca?' – he would only repeat himself: 'She's gone.' Then he set up coughing, and water came out, pink water that ran down and stained the front of his shirt, and he said, 'Alice,' and I could not help but take his hand where it was groping as he fought for breath. But as I took his hand, the cough subsided, and his grip tightened, then tightened again. I knew there would never be another chance.

I took hold of a pillow. He thrashed, and we rolled, and I was pressing, pressing, and he was kicking. Then he went slack.

For minutes, I kept the pillow pressed over his face. I felt everything very far away, like a pale light under a glass. When I took the pillow off, I brought my hand to my mouth, for his eyes were open, and it took me a moment to breathe again. When I could, I covered my brother's face, and went away, into a different room.

It was a sin, the worst sin. But to say the truth, I would do the same again.

44

Summer, this year of our Lord 1648

We cannot help but give weight to last words, to endings, as though they carry some greater truth than all the other words a person has spoken and written since they learned to write, learned to speak. And now that I am getting to the last of this account, indeed running out of time to write it, therefore I will try, I will do my best to come to some pith of truth in this last of what I say.

The number of women my brother Matthew killed, as far as I can reckon it, is one hundred and six. He accomplished it in two of our short English summers, and the months between. One hundred and six women, through Essex, Suffolk and beyond: that much is certain.

But though I know that much, and much else of Matthew, still I cannot quite capture him, just as how when we were children and learning to draw, he would move before you were finished; he would turn his face away. In the end, he was not one thing but many, and though I want to tell the truth about him now I want to make him more than a shadow on the wall used to scare children. I want to make him more than that and also less: I want to show him as a man who chose to call himself a witchfinder, who deserved every inch of pain that found him, and also the sad wreck of a small boy. For he was both those things, and none could know it better than the sister who watched him grow.

What you would like to hear, I think now, is that Matthew was evil, that he was a monster: but it is not as simple as that; it cannot be. For certain he contained evil, as I do, as you do. In many respects we were similar, my brother and I, with our shared facility for taking words and changing their order to get the effect we want. Believe me, I think on our similarities; but I think, too, on how differently we chose. For it is a choice, I think, to close the heart, just as it is a choice to open it. It is a choice to look at what distresses you, and a choice to shut your eyes. It is a choice to hold tight your pain, or else to let it slip your grasp, set it free to make its mark upon the world. But I cannot, despite everything, I cannot wish that Bridget had left my brother to burn, on that winter's night, so many years ago. With Matthew, for certain it all goes back to birth, but not, I pray not, to a baby born of the devil. Not to a baby born with bad deeds sealed already in his heart.

Whatever my prayers, I can never be certain, and there is much about my months with my brother that I cannot explain. Even still I think of the strange marks in the strawberry bed, and of the flattened field of corn. For certain, evil does touch our mortal lives from time to time, but not, I am given now to think, in such a way as can be explained. Not, perhaps, in such a way as it is possible to know who to blame.

I sit here, in the upper room of my old landlady's house, and find I have much to thank God for. I am whole in body, and, I trust, in mind. I have my freedom. And yet despite these blessings I have been finding it hard to pray. I try with the simplest prayer, the Lord's Prayer, the one we are supposed not to neglect. Which asks only a little food, a little forgiveness. Things that should be simple, although they do not feel simple now. Still, I pray to God to forgive me my trespasses, as I forgive those that have trespassed against me. And perhaps those nameless trespasses have been yet another reason to set my story down: in order to forgive, I have to know what has been done to me. Surely, in order to be forgiven, I have to know exactly what it is that I have done.

My old landlady's nephew and his wife keep this house now, and they have given me the rooms I had with Joseph, and they have let me stay on for nothing. He is a printer, the nephew, and though the press where he works is not a sober one, though it does print all sorts of ruffian marvels, still it is to him that I intend to leave these pages in payment of what I owe, and that this tale might be printed, and known.

Before I left Manningtree, I made a good fire in the hearth of Matthew's chamber. But I rescued some few things; a few statements and a few lists. I have slipped them between the pages of this book to keep them flat, and that they might be printed along with my own words. I would have kept more, but I feared that to publish all his notes would only preserve my brother's methods, encourage those who would repeat his horrors. So I kept only a few scraps, to show the truth of what I have told, and the rest I burned. I watched the fire consume Father's daily books, the covers charring and shrinking. White choking ash almost smothered the blaze, as I added more paper in fistfuls.

I remember one crumpled sheet escaping the flames. I picked it up, saw that it was an inventory of Bess Clarke's goods: every pot and kettle, every spoon and sad blanket. It had been made so that her belongings could be packed and taken for selling in another place. Perhaps they wouldn't have fetched as much in Manningtree because of who had owned them. Perhaps they would have fetched more. A kettle that the devil might have drunk from; a pillow on which he might have laid his cold and heavy hand.

Despite my caution with my brother's papers, still I am in some respects reluctant to allow this account to be printed. I fear that it will be read only by those who live to peer at a scandal, who would pay a penny to look behind a curtain at a fair. I must hope not, for what would that make me? I do not wish to be a pedlar of thrills and murders, a displayer of freaks. I wrote this to be a history, and though it is not so learned as the great histories men write, I hope it sheds as much light on what has passed. I hope it sheds more.

†

I stayed in Manningtree only long enough to see Matthew buried, quietly and without ceremony. The minister and the gravediggers were the only ones who saw him lowered, for I kept away, and Mary Phillips did not show her face; the minister told me that she had gone back to her kin, once my brother could not afford to pay her. It turned me cold to think that, had I not been freed, Matthew might have left me in the dark to starve.

I was keen to be gone from Manningtree; though I went, of course, to Bridget's house to look for any sign of her, only to be met by the new tenant there, clutching a letter for me. As she put it into my hand I thought of my first day back from London, going to Bridget's old place, and for a moment it was as though time had stood still.

But time had not stood still. While I had been locked away, the minister had married Ruth Edwards; he informed me of it himself, in a careful, hesitant voice. But that was a small blow, in comparison with how I failed to discover any news of Bridget, or of Rebecca West. They had not been seen, after the Manningtree hangings, two years since. And since they were no one's mother, no one's sister or daughter or wife, no great enquiry had been made after them. No ditches had been searched, no ponds dragged. It was as though they had been allowed simply to melt away, into the air. I like to think that Bridget found Rebecca, after that day in the yard, and that they escaped together; though I know if they had, I would be like to have heard from them by now. What I cling to, with my last bit of hope, is the state of the post, how it is thrown into disorder still with the war dragging on. I cling to the chance that I might have missed a letter from them, full of good news.

The letter waiting for me at Bridget's house was from Grace. It tells me she is safe and well in Massachusetts. When Mary Phillips put her out on the road she had got back safe to Cambridge, and been put in the way of a friend of her mother's brother, who had six children, of ages between four and fourteen. Their mother was dead, and he had it in his mind to go to America. *It is a difficult voyage,* she writes, *but if you take it, then on the other side there is the chance to step cleanly from the boat. That is what this place offers,* she writes. *A new beginning, and your way to make.*

Grace herself – I could feel her reluctance to mention it – she herself is looking for a servant. She is not settled too near my brother Thomas in the city of Boston. Rather, Grace has gone to a small, simple, hard-working place; and even if in the end I change my mind and move on, I think I could do worse than begin in her household, as my old servant's servant. Though I do not deny that it will pain me to leave this last familiar place. The memories it holds. For every morning since coming back here, before I open my eyes, I feel Joseph lean down to kiss their lids, as he did that last morning, even after our quarrel the night before. And again I allow him into my arms, sleepy, too stubborn to quite forgive him just yet, too stubborn to admit I am awake.

But it is Joseph's name that I am taking with me, when the boat leaves in a few short days – the name he gave me, which for safety I have left out of this account. I will take my husband's name, and not much more: a bag of coins, some hard biscuits, several limes, a clean cap and apron for when I arrive. I will leave behind the name of Hopkins, along with this that I have written: both are heavy, and I have carried them far enough now. It is time for a new beginning, for new work in an honest place. I like the sound of it, where I am headed. It is a quiet village, a place of little consequence. But they have named it Salem, which, as you know, means peace.

From John Stearne's book, A confirmation and discovery of witchcraft, the part that touches on my brother's methods; on his death, and his afterlife.

And in truth, concerning him who is dead, who likewise was an agent in the business, for my part, I never knew that he either unjustly favoured any, or received bribes or used such extremity as was reported of him; only at first, before he or I ever went, many towns used extremity of themselves, which after was laid on us. And I do not deny but at first he might watch some; but to my knowledge, he soon left it, or at least in such a way as to not make them uncapable: but if he ever did at first, evidence was not taken till after they rested.

But to my knowledge, we have both been much injured in words, and he since his death: but I am certain (notwithstanding whatsoever hath been said of him) he died peaceably at Manningtree, after a long sickness of a consumption, as many of his generation had done before him, without any trouble of conscience for what he had done, as was falsely reported of him. And though many of these things may seem very strange, and hardly to be believed, yet this is the very truth; and that he was the son of a godly minister, and therefore without doubt within the covenant.

Author's Note

Matthew Hopkins left only a sparse trail of paper behind him. This book is necessarily a work of fiction, woven between the fragments of record that remain. Although little evidence remains of Matthew as a private individual, we know more about his activities as a self-styled witchfinder. I am particularly indebted to Malcolm Gaskill for his brilliant and accessible work in compiling and assessing Matthew Hopkins's life.

Bridget and her son, Joseph, are invented. It seems probable that Matthew's father married only once, but for the purposes of this story, I have given him a second wife. Yet while the Alice I've written about is fictional, Matthew Hopkins may well have had a sister. His father, James, was ordained in 1609 and presented to the living of Great Wenham in 1612. We know that, within four years, three sons had arrived – James the younger, Thomas and John – but by the time the elder James died, there were six children, including Matthew. One of the other siblings may well have been a daughter, and this would explain her slight presence in the record.

Little is known about Matthew's schooling and early life. There was enough money in his family for him to have followed his father and brother to Cambridge for training as a minister, yet he did not. I have suggested a reason why.

The places Hopkins visited and the names of his victims have been pieced together from assize records and pamphlets of the time – not all of which agree. In order to tell Matthew's story, I have played down the role of John Stearne; but his book, *A confirmation and discovery of witchcraft*, quoted at the end of this novel, has been a key resource in corroborating the shocking facts of what happened to women like Rebecca West – who really did testify against her mother at the Chelmsford trial, presumably after intimidation and suffering that can barely be imagined.

Rumours of Matthew having been swum as a witch and drowned are now dismissed as myth; likewise the theory that he escaped to America. It is likely that he simply died of consumption, though I've given him a different end.

The documents that open some of the chapters are compiled from historical sources relating to the witch trials Matthew Hopkins instigated between 1645 and 1647. The extracts on the detection of witches are in fact by a minister who was protesting against Matthew's methods; the minister deliberately kept his descriptions vague, fearing that if given more detail, people might mimic what they read.

In the 1640s England had not yet adopted the Gregorian calendar, meaning that the New Year began on 25 March. Following the pattern of most histories, this book dates years from 1 January.

Glossary

Assizes – Courts that sat at intervals in each county of England in the seventeenth century. They were less frequent than quarter sessions, and were used to try more serious crimes.

Daily book – A journal or record kept by many godly men and women in the seventeenth century. The books often blended discussion of personal or political events with spiritual reflection.

Godly – The term adopted by Puritan Christians in the seventeenth century to describe themselves. The godly were opposed to Catholicism, and favoured further reform of the Church in England.

Imp – A familiar spirit, often disguised as an animal, supposed in the seventeenth century to be sent to a witch by Satan, to seal their pact by sucking blood from a 'teat' on the witch's body.

Lady Day – Falling on 25 March, this was one of the quarter days of the year, when rents were collected. In the seventeenth century, Lady Day was also officially the first day of the new year.

Natural – A term used colloquially in the seventeenth century to refer to any person seen as neurodivergent. The term may have been used to describe those with conditions as varied as autism, Down's syndrome or learning difficulties.

Searching – A method of identifying witches, during which the suspected woman would be physically searched for 'teats'. Often found in the genital region, these would be used as evidence of an imp having visited the woman to suckle.

Swimming – An ordeal by water, used to identify witches. The hands and feet of the suspected woman would be tied, and she would be lowered into a pond or river. It was supposed that an innocent woman would sink, as was natural, while a guilty woman would float – the water having rejected her. Matthew Hopkins and his accomplices were rebuked for allowing swimming to be used as a method of detection at the Suffolk assizes in August 1645.

Tendring Hundred – An ancient administrative division of Essex, named for the village of Tendring, which is at the centre of the area. Manningtree lies at the northern edge of the Tendring Hundred.

Watching – A method of identifying witches, during which the suspected woman would be placed on a stool in the middle of a room and observed for hours. The purpose was ostensibly to wait for her imps to come to her to suckle.

Witch bottle – A charm, often containing hair, nail clippings, pins, stones, thorns, knotted threads and similar objects, which were placed in a bottle and concealed within a dwelling, with the aim of repelling witchcraft.

Acknowledgements

I'd like to offer the following people my heartfelt thanks:

My agent, Nelle Andrew, for her astonishing energy and belief, and the fabulous rights team at PFD.

My UK editor, Katy Loftus, for her boundless patience and cheerfulness, and for loving this book from the start.

My US editor, Kate Miciak, for her unwavering enthusiasm and dedication.

Emma Brown, Isabel Wall and all at Viking for their hard work and creativity; Julia Maguire and everyone at Ballantine Bantam Dell, for just the same.

Hazel Orme, for a sensitive and rigorous copyedit.

Justine Stoddart, for making a photoshoot feel suspiciously relaxing.

All from the Centre for New Writing at the University of Manchester – and particularly John McAuliffe, for telling me to go away and write this book.

Susan D. Amussen, for sharing her intuitive and detailed understanding of the period, and her excellent reading recommendations.

Sarah Batten and Hester Pode, for lending extra pairs of eyes and thoughtful suggestions.

All my friends and family who have given me advice, space and support of every kind; who remained polite when I said that I was writing a book, and refrained from asking me (too often) when I was going to finish it. You know who you are.

My parents, for the years of financing and forbearance, and constant, unstinting love.

My little brother, for allotment times when I needed them the most, and for being as unlike Matthew Hopkins as it's possible to be. Cheers, Pod.

Anne Alderman, Mary Bacon, Anne
Barker, Sarah Barton, Bridget Bigsb
Joyce Boanes, Helen Bretton, Anne Cad
Margery Chinery, Elizabeth Clarke
Susan Cocke, Mary Cooke, Anne Coope
Joan Cooper, Joan Cooper, Ellen Crispe
Alice Dixon, Ellen Driver, Mary
Edwards, Mary Everard, Elizabeth
Gibson, Elizabeth Gooding, Mary Green
liefe, Margery Grew, Rose Hallybread
Elizabeth Hare, Elizabeth Harvey, Sarah
Hatyn, Marian Hockett, Mary Johnson
Rebecca Jones, Mary Lakeland, Marga
ret Landish, Helen Leech, Nan Leech
Margaret Legat, John Lowes, Elizabeth
Man, Susan Marchant, Bridget Mayers
Judith Moone, Margaret Moone, Rebecca
Morris, Mother Neville, Mother Pal-
mer, Joan Potter, Mary Scrutton, Mar-
Sexton, Anne Sherwood, Mary Skipper
Mary Smith, Susanna Smith, Susan
Sparrow, Mary Starling, Susan Stegold
Anne Thurston, Elizabeth Warne, Alice
Warner, Sarah Warner, Susan Wente
Mary Wiles, Margaret Wyard.